The Girl With The Tiger Tattoo And The Magnificent Six

Written By

Elina Salajeva

Created By

Elinadeivid

Touchladybirdlucky Studios
A David Gomadza Production.
Elina Salajeva, Elinadeivid have asserted their rights
under Copyright, Designs and Patents Act 1988 to be
identified as the author of this work.
ISBN 978-1-9164397-0-2
[Touchladybirdlucky Studios]
ISBN 9781539917250   [Createspace]

DEDICATION

To my sister Ewa and my family who have been very supportive and to Deivid who has been a source of great inspiration and support over the years. Lots of Love.

DISCLAIMER

This is a work of fiction. Names, characters, businesses, places, events, and incidents are either the products of the author's imagination or used in a fictitious manner. Any resemblance to actual persons, living or dead, or actual events is purely coincidental.

ACKNOWLEDGMENTS

Many thanks to the Elinadeivid brand and a big thanks to Touchladybirdlucky Studios.

Sometime in the future few days before 25th of
November.

CHAPTER ONE

Ewalinka had shown real excitement about the meeting with her uncle the following day. She was so excited that she could hardly control herself. She had not seen her uncle for some days. Her uncle had been gone for a few days now with work and she was excited and eagerly looked forward to seeing him. This could only mean one thing she thought to herself. Every girl's dream, which is shopping. She wanted to feel and look like a princess. All her friends looked like fashion models. She had almost forgotten how fun it is to go shopping; she was excited. They had regularly gone shopping together on several occasions since the death of Ewalinka's parents. She had looked forward to meeting her uncle the following afternoon. Normally he would take her to the city for shopping. After shopping on some occasions, they had gone to watch a movie. Last time they had gone for a picnic in the park to relax and sunbathe. The following afternoon they had agreed to go for shopping first and then after that Ewalinka had insisted that her uncle take her to the ice-skating arena just outside the city. She loved to spend some time ice-skating. She knew it would be perfectly magical to spend sometime in the ice-skating rink. Last time she had been to the ice- skating area, it was the atmosphere and the families that were there that made everything magical. The nerves of ice-skating in front of so many people had guaranteed her bruising yet she absolutely loved it. The idea of spending quality time with her uncle and watching other families in the ice-skating arena made it worthwhile. The ice-skating arena was always filled with families the most important thing she wished she had just like everyone's else. These are enough time to prepare and get ready for going to the city for shopping. Her friend Doris had paid her a visit and woken her up just after twelve in the afternoon. Doris had insisted that they go together to the city that afternoon. Ewalinka had vehemently insisted on waiting for her uncle to come back first.

"Ewalinka! Ewalinka! Let's go to the city!" shouted Doris as she enters Ewalinka's bedroom.

"Wish I can but I have an appointment with my uncle later in the afternoon. Sorry," Ewalinka replied innocently getting out of the bed.

"I heard stories that something happened in the city," said Doris as she tried to convince her friend to go with her to the city.

"It seems everyone is heading to the city right now," added Doris as she sat down on Ewalinka's bed. She looked worried and mystified.

"Look outside your window. A lot of people are

going to the city center right now. There are reports that….," she did not finish talking before Ewalinka interrupted.

"Oh, my God! You are right," said Ewalinka as she peeped outside through the window to see what was going on.

"Why are all these people marching to the city?" she asked looking at her friend Doris.

"I am not sure to be honest but I heard something big has happened there. That is why I came here so we can go together and find out." Said Doris standing up and walking toward Ewalinka who was still peeping outside through the window.

"So, are we going now or what?" asked Doris holding her friends' shoulder.

"Honestly, I wish I can go with you Doris, but I am afraid that my uncle might come back and not find me home. Surely, he will not be pleased," replied Ewalinka. Ewalinka went to sit down on her bed and her friend Doris followed.

"I am curious I want to find out what has happened in the city today. Come on Ewalinka! Let's go we will be back soon before you know it I promise." Doris tried to convince her friend. Ewalinka looked unmoved, she had waited for this appointment for a long time. All she wanted to do was to get ready for the appointment before her uncle arrived. He was always there for her since the death of her parents. He had been of much help to Ewalinka as far as she can remember. The last thing she wanted to do was to let him down. She was curious though. At one-point, she wanted to go and see for herself what had happened in the city but she changed her mind at the last minute. There were chances that her uncle might come home early and not find her, so she decided to stay. Doris left her friend's house and headed to the city no center. Ewalinka had insisted that she waited for her uncle at home. She picked up her phone to ring her uncle but there was no answer. The phone kept diverting to voicemail. Probably he was busy she thought to herself. Meanwhile in the city center people were gathering from all over the city. Doris passed through the crowds going toward the center where it seems the incident whatever it was had occurred. There were a lot of people holding weapons as she advanced forward. She zigzagged her way to the front, but she kept being pushed backward. It seemed that someone was captured and was being attacked by people with weapons. She heard people shouting.

"Kill him, kill him now". People were rushing forward to strike the captured man with whatever they had. Some of them stamping on him as he lay on the ground.

"He is a traitor, kill him now. Show no mercy." Shouted one man as he kicked the captured man in the ribs. The captured man had his face covered in blood. He had blood oozing out of his nostrils and mouth. He could not be easily recognized as his face had blood all over it. Doris approached this captured man to have a quick look at him, but people kept pushing forward and obstructing her. People took turns to punch and kick this man. He stood up and as soon as he was up someone else would come and either kick him or punch him that he ended up laying on the floor again in pain. Doris managed to advance forward and came very close to the captured man. She crawled forward to see his face as he lay on the ground. His face was beyond recognition as he was covered in blood. He tried to open his eyes but there was blood flowing from the head down. He lifted his left hand to wipe the blood from his eyes. He opened one of his eyes and looked at Doris. Doris got scared and stood up as fast as she can and started retreating backward. The captured man stood up from the floor and sat upright. He wiped both his eyes to remove blood covering his eyes. As soon as he had cleared the blood from his face, another man came forward and floored him back to the ground with a fist. The other man stamped on his ribs as he lay on the ground. That he growled screaming in pain and he rolled over to one side. This time he struggled to get up as the fist he received had knocked some of his teeth that blood started gushing out of his mouth. For a spell, he lay on the floor. Somehow, he later found his strength, energy and the courage to get up. He sat upright with his legs stretched and looked down for a while. He put his hand in one of the pockets of his jacket. He tried to get something out of his pocket but before he even took out his hand, another man who was next to him crushed his hand with his boots. He growled in pain as he took out his hand from his pocket.

"What do you have in your pocket?" shouted the man who had broken his arm.

"Do you have a gun, in there?" He went further on to ask the captured man as he searched his pockets. After searching his pockets, he kicked him very hard in the ribs. Five minutes or so passed as he lay on the ground. Doris moved forward again to have a look at the captured man who was still laying on the floor. He opened his eyes slightly and tried to sit up straight.

He looked at Doris and wiped his eyes with the back of his hands. He looked at Doris with a staring look. Doris looked at him but could not recognize him. Soon after that she started moving away from the captured man. The captured man looked up and wiped blood from his eyes as fast as he can. He tried to say something but only managed to mumble a few words. He tried to speak to Doris as she was leaving but on second thoughts and from fear of being attacked again he kept his silence and watched Doris going away from him. As he looked at Doris walking away from him, he was knocked to the ground. Some people in the crowd kept shouting that he was a traitor and therefore deserved to die. The city had paraded this man as a traitor and their enemy. They wanted to set him as an example so that no one else will follow him. The leader of the group had ordered everyone not to help him or to inform the authorities. They wanted him to die in the city center. Ewalinka had lived with her uncle since her parents died. They were both killed in a car accident. Uncle Luke had raised her as his own. He took it hard when his girlfriend walked out on him. His girlfriend had left him after he adopted his sister's child Ewalinka. The last few days he had been working away from home that they rarely spent more time together like they used to. They had spoken about this and uncle Luke had promised to take Ewalinka for shopping in the city. He had promised to take her to the museum and the ice- skating as she wished. This was like making up for the lost time when he worked away from home.

"Uncle so definitely you are taking me for shopping. Yes? We will also go to the museum and then to the ice-skating as you promised. Right?" asked Ewalinka seeking confirmation from her uncle.

"Yes. Ewalinka my niece," said uncle Luke with a warm face nodding his head as well.

"Get ready the following weekend so that when I come back from work, then we go to the city for shopping together," said Luke. After working away from home, the time finally came for him to go home. The week had flown past. It seemed like the shortest week he had ever had. He had looked forward to this weekend. The feelings of guilty and the fear of losing his niece to the social services thereby letting his sister down had tormented him the whole week. He had seen it fitting to take his niece for shopping. Life had been tough for both. Losing both parents at such a tender age is hard enough for anyone. He was also worried about her safety. Ewalinka had told him that he had seen some man sat in front of their house several times. Some of them seemed to have taken pictures of her from a distance. She had told all this to him. He was scared that he would lose his niece to the social services. That day he had asked his manager to finish work early. After work he headed home. It was like any other day, everyone minding their own business. It was a good afternoon. He had just got paid as well, and it seemed they were going to have a great time with his niece. He had just finished work and wanted to go to the city first to have a haircut and after that buy some food before going home. He stopped for a while thinking whether to go home first to his niece and have the haircut later. Or to go to the barber first and then do shopping for food first before heading to the city later with Ewalinka. That is when he noticed that someone was following him. When he stopped walking the man stopped walking too and stood at a distance away from him. He looked at him closely and remembered that he had seen the man near his place of work. He started walking again and turned into a side street. The man followed him in the side street. There was no doubt the man was following him. It was payday he realized that this man might be after his money. He turned into another side street and this man followed him again. He kept walking and ignored the man. He went into a shop and waited to see the man's next move. The man walked past first and then came back and stood outside the shop. He took out a phone and dialed someone. He put back the phone in his pocket and waited. Luke walked outside and went to where the man stood.

"Who are you? Are you following me? What do you want?" asked Luke with a raised worried voice.

"Who is the girl you are hiding at your place?" asked the man in a challenging way poking Luke in the chest.

"We know all about her. It is all over the news. You filthy Moran," shouted the man.

"None of your business. Are you with the social services? Who are you to ask me these questions?" asked Luke.

"We know that that's not your daughter," shouted the man.

"I did not say she is my daughter. After all what does that have to do with you?" Screamed uncle Luke. "Leave me alone. What do you want? Do you want money? Stop following me! Ok?" Shouted uncle Luke who seemed confused as to what this conversation was all about.

"I don't want your money or anything from you. I want you to pay for that girl." Said the man raising his hands. Uncle Luke looked in the direction the man was pointing and saw another man running toward him. He remembered many years ago when he was in a situation like that. He had quickly resolved the issue by remaining calm and walking away from trouble. His initial thoughts were that they worked for the social services. He had been busy lately. Since the day Ewalinka's parents died. He had not left Ewalinka alone. He was always there for her. Recently he had been spending time at work away from Ewalinka and home. The other man arrived, and they started pushing him from one side to another. It was a matter of time before things got out of hand. Soon he found himself being kicked and punched. He felt a hand reaching for his wallet. He felt a punch in the ribs. He felt a blow in the head. He opened his eyes and saw himself on the ground. There were so many people surrounding him. He saw different leg shapes and shoes. He remembered when he was a kid. His father had taken him to the football match. After the match ended he had stayed behind for a while and got separated from his father. He crawled on the ground. He saw a lot of legs and shoes going in all directions. He remembered screaming and shouting for his dad. It took him ten minutes to find him but it seemed like forever. This time his father was not there to rescue him. He got up and started running for his life. He felt warm blood running down his face nearly blinding his left eye. He wiped the blood off with the back of his palm. He staggered ahead but the mob soon surrounded him. Everyone started kicking and hitting him. He had never felt so helpless. He saw

Ewalinka's face and somehow, he jumped up and started running away from his attackers.

"Kill him. He does not deserve to live. Kill him today!" shouted one person within the crowd. He looked backward to see if his attackers were following him. They were a few feet away. He knew he had to run for it or die. He turned around to look ahead, and he felt the most severe pain on his forehead and nose. He felt like his head had split from forehead downwards. Fresh warm blood gushed out from his forehead and nostrils. He slumped to the floor. He just realized that that could be his end. He remembered raising his niece Ewalinka. He remembered holding her in his arms. He remembered the smile on her face. He remembered the first time she talked. Everything was a wonderful life experience. He also remembered the day his girlfriend walked out on him. He knew he had made a great choice in adopting his niece and raising her as his own. He only felt sorry that he was never going to keep his promise. Today was meant to be the happiest day in their lives. He had the money and time to make her niece happy. But somehow these cowards had taken that away from him. He felt a kick in his ribs and growled in pain. He looked to see if he can recognize anyone in the crowd. He wanted to see his niece one more time. He had a lot to tell her. He never thought he could be robbed like that. This was daylight robbery. Why was this happening to him? Surely was this the punishment he deserved for leaving his niece home alone? He had so many questions but without any answers. He knew that he had taken too many blows. His head was very heavy. Blood from the head covered his face and neck. He constantly had to wipe the blood from his eyes to see clearly. He wiped his eyes with the back of his palm but that did not work. He stood up from the ground and sat down. He remembered his niece putting a handkerchief in his pocket. Without any much thought he put his hand in his jacket pocket before feeling the most excruciating pain he had ever had. He heard a cracking sound as if his arm was crashed. The man standing near him had stamped on his hand. "Do you have a weapon in that pocket?" shouted the man. Luke lay on the floor in agony. Someone came and kicked him in the head as he lay on the floor. He blacked out for some seconds. He opened his eyes but could not see. He then wiped his face with his other hand. His heartbeat raced very fast. Somehow, he found a lot of energy. He wiped again his eyes and looked careful in front of him. He recognized the girl who was kneeling in front of him. He tried to shout at her but for some reason he stopped. He looked around all over before looking down. A punch knocked him down again to the ground. He quickly wiped the blood from his eyes and looked around. There was no sign of his niece. He saw the other girl getting up and walking away from him.

"Doris. Doris. It is uncle Luke. Doris," whispered uncle Luke in a small low voice as he lay on the ground. He smiled as he lay on the ground, he saw Ewalinka and Doris waiting for him outside his house. He felt very happy. He opened his hands and run toward them. He promised himself to never leave her alone again. Uncle Luke ran as fast as he can but somehow, he never got to where they were standing. He felt his legs very heavy and slowly he drifted away. Doris arrived back at Ewalinka's house. She knocked at the door and Ewalinka opened the door. She looked very sad. Her eyes looked puffy and swollen. She was crying. For the first time her uncle had let her down. It hurts. She had found courage and the will to live after her parents died in uncle Luke. She just could not believe that her uncle had let her down. He had disappointed her by not turning up. They were supposed to go for shopping. Doris comforted her friend and told her about the thief that was killed in the city that afternoon.

"I was shocked today! You will not believe what I saw!" Said Doris in a high voice with her eyes wide open.

"I went to the city today. I saw that man people were talking about. He was badly beaten up. He could not see. His face was covered in blood. I knelt down as he lay on the floor," paused Doris as she leaned her face in front of Ewalinka's.

"This man looked at me and he suddenly got up and sat down. He raised his right hand and pointed at me. He touched his nose with his left hand and jiggled down shaking his body as if going under water." Before she even finished talking Ewalinka interrupted her.

"What did you say!?" asked Ewalinka in a high-pitched voice.

"Did he raise his left hand afterwards and showed you the OK thump sign?" asked Ewalinka jumping from the bed where she was seated.

"Answer me Doris, did he?" Shouted Ewalinka.

"I guess so. It happened so fast?" replied Doris. On hearing this Ewalinka ran toward the door screaming. "No! No! No! That is my uncle. Uncle Luke!!" screamed Ewalinka running out of the house as fast as she can to the city center. She ran as fast as she can. She did not care if her legs broke off. She wanted to see her uncle. She blamed herself. If she had gone to the city with Doris, she could have saved her uncle. He could still be alive today, but how could she had known? She thought she was doing the right thing. She had waited for him at the house. She had looked forward to this day. This was going to be the best day in their lives. But these people had robbed her of the only person she loved. The only person who cared about her. The water diving dance was his trademark. He had danced for her every time she felt sad. Every time she cried he had danced for her. So, he had recognized Doris and was sending the message to her, she thought to herself. She arrived where her uncle lay dead. She looked at him. It was him no doubt. No words can explain the pain and hurt she felt. She just wanted to die too. She lay beside him and fell into a trance. It is winter in Moscow Russia. The temperature is - 17'C. It is very cold outside normally the temperature at this time of the year is around -11'C. This morning is an unusual morning with temperatures down to -17'C. The river Moskva is frozen and there is no major activity on the river apart from a boat that can be seen breaking ice making its way toward the other end of the river. On the other side of the frozen Moscow river a big beautiful, Cathedral of Christ the Savior can be seen partly covered in snow. Religion plays an important role in the lives of the people in Russia and all over the world especially in recent years. The Cathedral is one of the largest church in Moscow. It is enormous and most expensive Cathedral with its copper domes dominating the Moscow skyline. In winter this

Cathedral is beautifully covered in snow with its copper domes partly covered in snow as well. The denomination is the Russian Orthodox also known as the Moscow Patriarchate. The main belief is that God revealed himself in Jesus Christ. The Holy Spirit guides and directs the holy church. The fathers of the church are nominated and their wisdom is central to the church as they are there to guide the church members. Belief and worship is key to the church's faith. Baptism of infants is by immersion in water three times in the name of the father, the Son and the Holy Spirit. It is both the initiation into the church and the sign of forgiveness of sins. After baptism chrismation follows and is by anointing with the holy oil called charism. After chrismation then the holy communion commences. This act is meant to acknowledge that babies and children are fully communicant members of the church. Consecration of the charism can only be performed by the Patriarch or the Chief Bishop of the church. The priest during charism says the words; 'The seal of the gift of the Holy Spirit', as he makes the sign of the cross. In a village in Kalachi, in Kazakhstan a young couple have just escaped the rebels who had surrounded their village. No one seemed to have known exactly what had happened. But one thing that was for sure was that the locals had been sleeping for days without waking up. The locals had complained that they have been sleeping for days without waking up. No one had believed them. The doctors had ruled out diseases from contaminated water. Still this mystery sleeping sickness had baffled the doctors. The residents had raised concerns that they feared that they might not wake up from this sleeping disorder. Despite efforts by scientists and doctors to find the cause. This sleeping sickness has remained a mystery. Although the likely cause was radiation from the abandoned former Soviet-era uranium mine. Radiation tests have been shown to be normal. Nevertheless, radiation remained the likely culprit. All major tests carried out in the city's hospital had not pointed out the main cause of this sleeping sickness. All the subjects were seen to have more than normal brain fluid which has baffled the doctors. Scientists have tried to find any chemicals in the soil to identify the cause but with little success. Some believed that the abandoned mine still produced some toxic gasses. These were blown by the wind toward the village depending on the wind velocity and intensity. This could explain why at times when the wind is relatively calm the gasses cannot be detected in the nearby village. Some locals have accused the local rebels of gas poisoning them while they were sleeping which was received with bad contempt by the rebels. This had upset the rebels and the night in question the rebels had surrounded the village. Most of the people were asleep apart from a few and the young couple were among the few. Vladimir and Mia had been childhood sweethearts, and they were together as far as they can remember. At the age of twenty-one they married each other in a customary private ceremony per their tradition. They were in the Russian Orthodox church in Kazakhstan. Kazakhstan is one of the largest countries in the world and it shares borders with Russia and China. Vladimir and Mia were members of the Russian Orthodox church having been married in the church and being baptized there they had strong beliefs about Jesus and God.

The rebels had surrounded their village, and they had killed some people who were not asleep the time they arrived. Luckily Vladimir and Mia were wide awake when the rebels arrived, but they had escaped together. Without any chance of saying goodbyes to their parents and relatives they left their village heading for Russia. Mia was pregnant with their first baby. They had looked forward to starting a family together. The previous months before this incident, Vladimir and Mia had traveled to Russia Moscow to see the doctors there. Vladimir's main concern was with Mia's pregnancy. Mia like the other villagers had fallen asleep for days and Vladimir was very worried that he decided to contact the Orthodox church to help with traveling arrangements to Moscow for check-ups. Unfortunately, they had not told the practitioners at the European Medical Center (EMC) in Moscow about the mystery sleeping sickness. The doctors at the EMC had acknowledged that pregnancy can make a person sleep longer than normal. Deep down Vladimir was worried especially about the baby. The day the rebels invaded their village Vladimir did not want to take any chances. For him his pregnant girlfriend and his baby's safety came first. On the first opportunity, they had left Kalachi in the middle of the night escaping and heading for Russia. The Orthodox church had made all the necessary arrangements for traveling. In the morning, Vladimir and Mia arrived at Domodedovo airport in Moscow. The day was very cold and there was snow everywhere, with rivers frozen. The temperature was -7 degrees less than average temperature. The temperature was a -17'C, and it was bitter cold and windy. The two were greeted with some icy-wind that threatens to slice their faces. Vladimir was worried about his wife and his baby. The first thing that came to his mind was to run for shelter and avoid the cold and to wait for transport already arranged by the Orthodox church. Fifteen minutes later a woman appeared in the waiting room with a big card written their names on. The pair stood up and approached that woman. The woman spoke in Russian language and they both followed her to her car which was parked outside Domodedovo airport. They arrived at an Audi A6 Quattro white car outside and they all got inside. The woman spoke in Russian language and Vladimir replied in Russian language as well. Mia was shivering with the cold. The woman looked in the rear- view mirror and said something to both before opening the glove compartment and taking out fur hats. She looked forward as the car swerved a little as she passed the fur hats to Vladimir who in turn gave the other one to his wife Mia. The car drove for some minutes and Vladimir looked outside the window and wiped the window with his left hand. There was snow everywhere, for some time he had forgotten about what he had left behind. The snow reminded him about the ordeal back home. He felt very afraid and guilty too. He had left his family and escaped with his wife. What had befallen his family, were they still alive? Or had the rebels murdered them. The only hope was that they could have been spared slaughter as they were all fallen asleep which meant less resistance. The rebels were known to kill on the spot those who put any form of resistance. Surely, they would not slaughter the old and innocent, sleeping villagers, so he thought to himself. He promised himself to go back as soon as possible once his wife

was safe and sound. The lady driver who had picked them up asked him a question in Russian language, and for some time he seemed lost in his thoughts. It was Mia who poked him in the ribs drawing his attention to the lady's question.

"It's a long story I hope they are all OK but things were not good the time we left." Replied Vladimir in Russian language. They both looked at each other and hugged and kissed each other, it was such a tough time for both. Only God knows what had happened to his family which he had left behind. Mia noticed the tenseness of his husband and tried to comfort him.

"Darling there is nothing you could have done we could all have been killed." She said holding back her tears. There were so many issues at hand for them to stomach. Every time they thought about this, they felt sick to the bone, there were so many questions to be answered yet there was little or no answers at all. What was the reason for the mystery sleeping sickness? Vladimir remembered the first time Mia fell victim to this mystery sickness. It was such a traumatic experience. He had cried himself to sleep thinking that Mia had died. She had slept for days without any major activity. She was breathing but so faintly that at first, he did not dictate the pulse. This was the first time he had witnessed this mystery. He came home early one sunny day to find Mia still asleep, although at first, he had assumed that she had woken up and went back to sleep. This was not the case. Mia had not woken up since the last time he last saw her. He had initially checked her breathing and everything was OK. He just assumed that her being pregnant probably that meant that she was just tired.

She slept through the next day and despite efforts to wake her up it was all in vain. The second day her breathing had stopped or so he thought after checking her pulse. He had assumed that the worse had happened. He had summoned his parents to see if there was something they can do. They were all astonished but his parents did not seem to be concerned very much as he had expected them to be. It was them who advised him to wait a bit longer in case she comes around again. He knew his parents knew something but were not willing to share the information with him. After the incident, it was there and then he had learned that this had become a common thing in their village. He remembered some time ago when his wife had visited her mum leaving him alone for the weekend. He had woken up on a Sunday afternoon feeling dizzy, unable to stand and with memory loss. He was convinced that the last day he remembered was the last Friday before the incident. He had no memory of the Saturday let alone of that Sunday. He had felt like he slept on a Friday only to wake up on a Sunday but had found it very unlikely. It was later that he considered the possibility but with no other further explanations. This had remained his own secret, for the first time he found it difficult to tell his wife about this event. He looked outside the window and saw a very tall building with copper domes on top half covered in snow. An automated voice system coming from the dashboard can be heard saying; 'You are now arriving at Ulitsa Volkhonka Moscow. Please turn left.' The Audi A6 Quattro turned into the Cathedral grounds and moved very slowly at around five miles per hour. "You have arrived at your intended destination."

Confirmed the lady driver looking backward at the couple. She switched off the car engine and continued talking to the couple.

"Now someone else will look after you. If you go to the front door someone will be with you after a few minutes." Said the lady in a soft respectful voice.

"Thank you very much." Replied Vladimir looking at Mia who seemed to be worried more about the cold than with anything else. The couple came out of the car hugging each other and strolled toward the big Cathedral doors. The couple looked backward as the Audi car was leaving the Cathedral grounds. The big brown Cathedral door opened as soon as they arrived in front. A man in his late thirties opened the door and greeted them in Russian language. He invited them in and as soon as they entered the building he started talking about the Cathedral. Vladimir looked above, surely the Cathedral was gigantic probably the tallest he had ever seen. It was beautifully decorated inside and very big. As they walked inside, they could see the pictures of the apostles on the decorated ceiling. As they approached the central room which was well lit, they saw a big picture which represented God and his son and the angles. It was the most beautiful Cathedral in the whole world, he thought to himself. They were taken to another room in the church where they were asked to sit down and wait for a safe house to be arranged. They hugged each other and Mia laid her head on Vladimir's chest and her arms around his waist. A man came to them after twenty minutes or so and introduced himself as the Chief Bishop Anton. He explained what was going to happen and what he was going to do. He apologized for the delay and what had happened and wished the best for the couple. He handed a paper with an address written on it; Vima Rublevka Village Laikovo Odinstovo Moscow city. See Mr. Boris.

"I wish you the best Mr. Vladimir and your wife, you will be safe there anything you want just ask." He said in Russian language as he handed the paper with the address to Vladimir who stood up and took the paper. They both looked at the paper with Mia hugging her husband in the waist.

"There is a car waiting for you outside, that's your address and any problems please don't hesitate to contact us or Mr. Boris." He stretched his hand and shook hands with both. He led them out of the Cathedral. A car was waiting outside, it was a black BMW X5 with tinted windows, they went inside through the back doors. A lady driver was inside the car, she looked very young probably in her mid-twenties, of slim built, with very dark black hair. She was wearing glasses, she had a white shirt, a black tie and a pink jacket with black pants. She greeted the two as they entered the car first in Russian language, when they did not respond, then in Latvian language. Still there was no reply from the couple that she decided to speak in English language.

"How are you? I am your driver today, I am Elinkasha," she said as she prepares to set off. They both replied and hugged each other in the back seats. She waited for them, looked in the rear-view mirror and asked if they were ready. They signaled OK, and she checked her view mirrors and put the wipers on. "Seat belts please!"

She said looking at the couple through the rear-view mirror. They both fastened their seat belts, and the car headed to Vima in the village of Laikovo Moscow.

After twenty minutes of traveling they arrived at Vima complex on Rublevka, Moscow. This house was in the village of Laikovo, Sainthood in Moscow, from outside this was a beautiful modern house with an oval front and a three- story house. It was on an estate, and had snow surrounding it, there were spaces for four cars outside with a huge veranda.

"We have arrived; this is the place you will be staying in. When you ring the bell, ask for Mr. Boris. Best Wishes," said Elinkasha as she turned off the car engine of the BMW X5. They unfastened the seat belts and braved the weather going outside of the warm comfortable car to the front door of this beautiful house. They were both shivering, Kalachi was cold too in winter but not as much as Moscow. Vladimir remembered looking at the dashboard and noticing a minus 17'C displayed. Vladimir rung the doorbell and waited for an answer. A woman in her late 40s wearing a black and white apron opened the door and waited for Vladimir and his wife to come in.

"Hallo! Welcome I am Oliviya, please come in," she said to the couple still holding the door for them to enter. As soon as they have entered the house, a man came downstairs and greeted them, he introduced himself as Mr. Boris.

"Oliviya, first take them to the guest room. They must be exhausted then we can talk afterwards," said Mr. Boris.

"Follow me please," asked Oliviya heading toward the guest room. They both followed her cuddling each other, they were both exhausted. Oliviya opened the door to the big guest room, and she stood at the door and waited for them to enter.

"After you have rested, I will come back and let you

know when you can come to the lounge to spend some time with Mr. Boris," said Oliviya as she closed the door. The two sat on the bed side by side recalling what has happened and contemplating what the future holds for them. It is a Sunday morning in Kurgan, part of the Kurgan Oblast region in Russia. It has been a cold morning and most people are still in bed. At the church of Alexander Nevsky in Kurgan it is business as usual. This is the busiest day of the week as they are preparing for the Sunday church service. The church is covered in snow as it has been snowing the previous night. Inside the church the Bishops are preparing for the service. Sunday services is normally packed as they are usually a high turnout of people. Recently there has been more people coming to the church, it seemed the town needed God more than ever before. There have been some strange occurrences in Kurgan and the whole Kurgan Oblast region. More and more people have been to the church to seek for answers. The doctors and the scientist had no clues as to what had befallen the residents. The recent occurrences had left even doctors with no words to say. It seems when things like that start happening humankind turns to God for answers. Only the divine intervention would be appropriate.

CHAPTER TWO

Somewhere in the Limousines area, in South Central France. Operator: "State your emergency."
Caller: "I need help! My wife is going into labor. She is having a baby! I need an ambulance fast!"
Operator: "Where are you?"
Caller: "Bellac, 30 Bellissimo, Limousin area
Operator: Where is your wife?"
Caller: "I am with her in the house at number 30
Operator: Ambulance is on the way. Please stay on the line until they have arrived."
Caller: "Okay. Please. Hurry!"
Benjamin remained on the line waiting for the ambulance to arrive. His wife Bridgette was in labor, about to have a baby. The contractions had started so fast and unexpectedly. Although they were expecting the baby in a few days' time, it seems she was going to give birth to their baby girl so sooner than they had expected. They were all seated in the lounge when

Bridgette suddenly yelled at her husband Benjamin who was seated next to her.

"Darling my water has just broke!"

"What! Are you sure! What is today's date? That can't be right!"

"Hurry. Get some blankets! Call the midwife for help! Call the maternity ward. Call the ambulance Darling! OMG! Hurry."

"Okay, I will get the blanket first!" said Benjamin rushing to the bedroom. Within seconds he was back with the blankets and was already dialing the maternity wards emergency line. They had rehearsed repeatedly for this day and prepared well enough but did not expect the water to break out this soon. The couple were expecting a baby girl in two days' time. This was the happiest times of their lives. This was their first child. They had patiently waited and prepared for this day. Benjamin stayed on the line until he started hearing the siren of the approaching ambulance. He then left the line on hold and ran to open the front gates. The ambulance arrived at their gate and entered the yard at number 30 in reverse. Soon afterwards, two ambulance crew men jumped outside from the back of the ambulance preparing drips and the push bed. They ran inside the house. Benjamin had thought of taking his wife in his car to the hospital himself. But she had insisted that he called the ambulance because she was having continuous contractions. She did not want to spoil the car in case all the water broke. There was no way she was going to the hospital in a car driving for more than thirty minutes or so. She knew that the midwife had discouraged them calling an ambulance unless it was unavoidable. The midwife had advised the couple to call the midwives at the hospital. Bridgette knew that ambulances were very fast and there was enough room for her too. The ambulance crew would administer drips and give medicine if necessary. Bridgette was rushed to the hospital as the contractions became increasingly stronger and they arrived at the hospital after twenty minutes. But surprisingly as soon as she arrived at the hospital her contractions slowed down. They hooked her up to the belly monitor to take a continuous reading. They strapped the monitors on her and watched them for about thirty minutes. The midwives indicated that she was dehydrated and asked her to drink water but that made Bridgette feel nauseous. To re-hydrate her they started a saline IV since water was making her feel nauseous. The midwives had insisted that this was needed to stabilize her blood pressure. After two days, her contractions were getting very intense and very painful to bear. As the contractions became intense, she started to feel back pain. The midwives had insisted that she stayed laying on her left side but the back pain was unbearable that she decided to take some painkillers. The midwives gave her a shot of Nubain in her IV, which turned out to have helped as the pain subsided after some minutes. After an hour or so then the contractions became so intense that she knew labor had begun. Benjamin all this time was by her side encouraging her to push and reassuring her that everything was going to be fine. After some pushing and contractions the baby finally came out, the midwife helped by picking her up. As the baby was born the midwives took the baby and put her on Bridgette's chest as she was so exhausted. The baby weighed 7.2 pounds. As soon as Bridgette saw the baby she began to cry, this was a special time for her and the baby. The midwife waited for the cord to stop pulsating and then cut the cord. The midwife showed her the placenta and which side was attached to her uterus. Bridgette was still bleeding, and the midwife asked if she can be given Pitocin to reduce the bleeding which she accepted to help her uterus contract down a bit. Mother and baby had a special bond as she lay on Bridgette's chest naked in a state of pure love, calm and bliss. The midwife and Benjamin looked at the pair as they lay on the hospital bed. After a few minutes, Benjamin and the midwives witnessed something strange. They both screamed in surprise and shock. They stared at each other and Benjamin opened his eyes looking at the midwife with a look that seemed to ask her if she had seen what he saw. Quickly Benjamin took a blanket and covered the baby and mother. They stayed in the hospital for another day as Bridgette had a high blood pressure. The doctors had insisted that they stayed a bit longer for observations. After two days both mother and baby daughter were discharged from the hospital and headed home with Benjamin. The couple were very happy and felt very lucky to have a beautiful baby. Six days after birth Benjamin and Bridgette are in the bedroom and their beautiful baby is lying on the bed flicking her legs up looking at the ceiling.

"Darling, we have to have our beautiful baby baptized very soon."

"Yes Yes, that's great. You have just reminded me. I need to let the church know that we were blessed with a beautiful baby daughter. I will also tell them that we want to have our daughter baptized as soon as possible."

"So, when you are going to book an appointment?"
"The sooner the better sweetie, I was thinking of phoning the Bishop today."
"I spoke to the priest a few weeks ago, we can just book the baptism straight away as they already know us. At least that is what the priest said."
"If that's the case then, I have to call the church now." Benjamin took out his phone and dialed the church. The phone rang for some time before someone answered.
"Hello, hello, how can I help you?" asked the man on the other end.
"Myself and my wife we have just been blessed with a beautiful baby daughter and we would like to…."
Before Benjamin even finished talking, the other person on the other end interrupted.
"Congratulations, congratulations!" Said the man on the other side of the line.
"Thank you. We would like to have our daughter baptized soon."
"What about this Sunday? Say 10am in the morning? But you must see the priest first."
"That won't be necessary, we know the priest very well. In fact, my wife spoke to the priest…,"
Benjamin did not even finish talking before the other man interrupted.
"Okay, 10am Sunday, name?"
"Benjamin and Bridgette, of 30 Bellissimos, Bellac,"
"30…… Bellisssi…. mos, Benjamin…and Bridgette."
"Ok see you Sunday then." The phone line was dead soon after that as they all put their receivers down.
"Ok that's sorted out." Said Benjamin.
"Thank you, Darling."
"Last night, you said you wanted to talk to me about

something, what is it Benjie?"
"I have to wait until we have enough time Darling," said Benjamin.
"What more time do you need, Darling?" Benjamin stood there for some time not knowing what to say. He did not know how he was going to start this conversation. Since the day their daughter was born, he had wanted to talk to his wife about what he saw in the hospital moments after their baby was born. This was a difficult subject. Was his wife prepared to talk about this? He knew by now she had noticed what he saw that day soon after their daughter's birth. He had not found the energy to talk about this to his wife. He had confided to his best friend whom he thought might shed light to what this could and what this meant. He had wished he had not seen what he saw that day. To make things worse, the midwife had witnessed this too. So, it was not a secret. Was the midwife ever going to keep this as a secret? I bet she might be frightened too to keep this to herself. What did all this mean? Especially to their daughter's future. Fear of losing his daughter had at one-point made him want to take things in his own hands. But surely his hands were tied. He felt sick every time he thought about this, especially the fact that he hides this from his wife. Off course by now she had noticed this too, but why for the past six days she didn't mention anything about this? He thought to himself. Silence broke between them and after some time Benjamin went to the kitchen to fetch a glass of water. Mid-way he heard his daughter crying. He put the glass of water down and went back to their bedroom and saw Bridgette, with their daughter about to breastfeed. He sat next to them and placed

his arm around his wife. He kissed her on the forehead and rubbed his lips on the baby's forehead murmuring something. Mother and baby had a one-to-one moment before Benjamin put both his hands on his face and breathed heavily.

"Darling……. have you noticed the marks at the baby's back?" asked Benjamin looking at his wife who was breastfeeding their daughter. She looked at the baby and then at Benjamin but did not answer straight away but instead kissed the baby.

"Not the first day, as I was really exhausted. It was only after I was discharged from the hospital that I noticed that there was something," she paused and looked at her husband who seemed very worried by the look on his face.

"I lifted the baby one day and felt like there were some kind of…. you know!", she did not properly finish the sentence.

"At first I thought she might have slept on something that engraved her on her back, but then again, few days ago, it looked like a…. you know?"

"Woman learn to finish your sentences." Said Benjamin as he was expecting his wife to say tattoo.

"Look like what?" He asked his wife.

"I just don't understand how this is possible," Bridgette now looked lost, she felt to find words. She looked at her husband who just stared at her with a look that seemed to say, say it.

"She is only six days old. How on earth did that happen? Are you sure this is our baby? They might have switched our baby? Even considering that possibility, still that does not explain why an infant has a tattoo so perfect to be real?"

"The first day I saw this, when I was bathing her, I

am sure, the tattoo was not like it is now?" Bridgette, finished breast feeding her daughter and put her on her legs. She pulled up the baby top to expose the tattoo. This was a real tattoo no doubt about that. You could feel the ridges of the tattoo protruding at the back as you touch the baby's back. The tattoo was not inked and from a distance you would not notice it as it was the same color as the skin with no ink as modern day tattoos. Benjamin knelt to look closely at the tattoo. This was real strange, what did this mean? Sunday arrived, and they were all prepared to take their daughter to the church for baptism.

"Darling, do you think we should tell the priest about our baby?"

"What are we going to say?"

"Honestly, I thought about this but, will the others accept her and us in the future? I am just saying; we must be careful who we trust. I don't know what this is."

Benjamin looked at his wife and continued.

"I have heard some stories about this area especially the whole of Limousin," he paused for a while. "Rumors has it that, strange things had been happening here a long time ago."

"Darling, I think let's do one thing at a time. Today let's concentrate on the christening of our daughter," his wife agreed, and they continued with preparations for the baptism. At the church the priest welcomed everyone especially the child who was to be baptized and Benjamin and Bridgette and the rest of the congregation. The parents of the baby, had called her Eva as they saw the name fitting for their daughter. The priest addressed everyone first and went on to explain the meaning and importance of baptizing the baby, Eva. 'Faith, is the gift of God to his people,' he paused before continuing.

"In baptism, the Lord is adding to our number, those whom he is calling. People of God, please welcome baby Eva, Benjamin and Bridgette to God?"

"Benjamin and Bridgette, do you promise to love and support your daughter, Eva, from this moment?" asked the priest.

"Yes, we do." They both answered at the same time with one voice. The priest turned and looked at the people in the church.

"People of God, in the name of the Father, the Son and the Holy Spirit, will you welcome the baby Eva, and her parents, Benjamin and Bridgette, and uphold them in their new life of Christ?" asked the priest.

"Yes, we do," answered the congregation. The priest spoke for some time with Eva's parents and the whole congregation. He kept reciting some words and prayers until that time he invited the parents and their baby to the front of the church. The priests made the sign of the cross on the forehead of the baby saying.

"Christ claims you for his own," he paused and continued talking.

"Receive the sign of the cross," after that they moved to the baptizing water Font. The priest stood before the water of baptism and said; 'Praise God who made the heaven and earth. Let us give thanks to the Lord. Amen.' The parents Benjamin and Bridgette hold the baby, over the water and the priest, took the water and poured it onto the baby's forehead saying, 'I baptize you in the name of the Father, the Son and the Holy Spirit. Amen.' As soon as the water was put on the baby's head, the baby screamed in pain. The baby's clothes turned red at the back where the tattoo was engraved. Blood made an imprint of the tattoo and the baby's white clothes were left with an imprint of the tattoo. Drops of blood fell in the water. There was a big splash as if something jumped into the water. There was a whirlpool in the water which suddenly disappeared. The priest jumped backward as water was splashed on his face. Bridgette screamed as soon as she had seen what had happened. The baby's eyes rolled backward as if in a trance. Soon afterwards the baby seemed to have fallen asleep. It all happened very fast that no one seemed to have noticed what had happened. The priest moved toward the water Font, which was now slightly red. He looked inside the water but there was nothing inside it. Eva's parents rushed back to their seats carrying her. Bridgette quickly put Eva down on her knees and turned her facing down. The imprint of the tattoo was seen drawn on the baby's clothes.

"Bri, check if she is breathing." said Benjamin.

"Oh, my God! What happened to my daughter?" screamed Bridgette. After sometime Eva woke up, it seemed she had fallen asleep. This baffled those who had seen what had happened. The priest and the parents spoke together about what had happened. The Chief priest advised the couple to take the baby home. The couple soon afterwards left the church. The parents after the incident at the church tried to find answers to all this but with no luck. Soon after this incident at the church, the baby's tattoo at the back became blackened as the blood dries within it. After that the tattoo at the back of the baby looked like a real tattoo as the blood dried giving it a dark color. One night, weeks after that incident the baby, Eva fell asleep in her room. The parents were fast asleep in their bedroom. The night was very cold. It was after midnight when the parents were woken up by a large smashing of glass sound coming from their living room. Benjamin and his wife woke up and rushed first to their daughter's room. The baby was safe as she lay in her bed comfortably. Benjamin realized that someone had broken into their home. He rushed to the spare room upstairs grabbed a baseball bat and started going downstairs. He checked everywhere. There was no one in the living room but the bottom panel window was broken. There was a big hole. It seemed something or someone had entered the house through the big hole. Quickly he started searching the whole house, room by room. All downstairs was clear, no sign of anyone. He went back upstairs to check again. All rooms, all clear. He went to talk to his wife in their daughter's bedroom. "What is it, is it a break-in?"

"More likely, but I think whoever it was he is gone now."

"Did you check all the rooms?"

"Double checked all, no sign of anyone but the French door glass is broken. I think someone tried to come in through there."

"Bennie, maybe you should call for help."

"Lock this door stay in here, I will check outside around the yard." Said Benjamin. He closed the door behind him asking his wife to lock herself and their daughter inside their daughter's room. He strolled downstairs with a baseball bat in his hand. He opened the front door from inside and looked around the yard first. There was no one. He went around the yard and back but there was no one. He was about to enter the house when he heard a sound as if someone was hiding in the nearby bushes. He felt a cold shiver of fear running down his spine.

"Who is there? Come out now!"

"Who is there? Show yourself now," shouted Benjamin. He stood there for some time before going back inside the house. He made sure that all the doors were locked properly. He went upstairs after sliding a box to close the hole in the broken French door. Upstairs Bridgette was waiting with her daughter for the return of her husband before opening the door. "Darling, it's me open the door," shouted Benjamin as he knocked the door. Bridgette, opened the door, and asked Benjamin.

"Did you find out who it was who smashed our window?"

"Whoever it is I think he ran away Darling. Is Eva OK?"

"She is in a deep sleep but she is breathing fine."

"Body temperature high though. Maybe we should call the doctor or the police."

"Personally, I think it's too late now, probably do this first thing tomorrow as nothing had been stolen." Bridgette stayed with their daughter for some time before joining her husband in the bedroom. They went back to sleep soon afterwards. In the morning, their housemaid arrived normal time as usual to carry out her duties. Since having a baby, Bridgette and Benjamin had employed a housemaid by the name of Lianka, to help Bridgette with house chores and looking after their daughter. Just after 6am she had arrived at 30 Bellissimo, Limousin. She had her own spare keys, so she let herself in. Once inside she noticed that the French door glass had been broken, and a box had been used to cover the hole left. There were broken glasses everywhere. She went in the kitchen to make a cuppa as usual before starting work. five minutes later she thought she heard a growling sound and a banging sound coming from the lounge area. She quickly left the kitchen and rushed to the lounge area. She stood there for some time unsure of what to make about what she was seeing. The box had been moved as if something had entered through the hole in the French door. She had at least spent five minutes in the kitchen making her cuppa. The box covering the hole in the French door was a heavy box, and it required a lot of effort to move it. Soon afterwards the baby started crying upstairs. She rushed upstairs to Eva's room only to find Benjamin inside holding Eva in his hands. "Good morning Sir, I heard the baby crying I thought she was alone," said Lianka.

"Morning, Lianka, I heard the baby crying too," said Benjamin rubbing his lips on the baby's forehead. Lianka, realized that it was Benjamin who was downstairs. Probably he moved the box covering the hole in the French door before hearing the baby crying then rushed upstairs. Lianka went back straight to the kitchen. Benjamin had also heard the noise but knew that it was Lianka. Lianka went back downstairs to have her cuppa and to start her chores. As she was going downstairs, she saw what looked like a foot or paw prints of an animal going upstairs. She had missed these earlier on as she rushed upstairs. The paw prints were made from water. She followed the prints to see where the animal or whatever it was had gone. Tracking the prints, they took her upstairs, past the spare room and past the guest room.

"No Way! Holy Sugar!" exclaimed Lianka stopping in

the upstairs' corridor. The prints looked as if they were recently made, she had not yet dusted the floors, they could not have been left on the floor last night, she thought to herself. She followed the trail and stopped again, this time her heart started beating very fast. She knelt and observed the pattern of the water prints on the floor. They look like prints made by a four-legged animal. She stood up and looking downwards trailed the prints again. The prints led Lianka toward Eva's room where they seemed to have just disappeared outside her door. As she was kneeling outside Eva's room, the door to her room suddenly opened wide. And as she was still looking downwards, she saw Benjamin's legs. She looked further down and saw his feet. She noticed that he was not wearing any shoes, slippers or even socks. "What seems to be the problem, are you OK?" asked Benjamin.

"Sorry Sir, no problem at all, I was just looking for something, I must have lost my…" Lianka couldn't finish her sentence and in embarrassment she headed back downstairs. For a moment that made a little sense, she thought to herself. Benjamin must have made the prints himself. But wait a minute, how come they are so close together and they seem to be two pairs of paws or feet. Could he have been tip toeing? As soon as she had tried and finished tip toeing herself matching the prints, she slapped herself on the forehead.

"Stupid," she said to herself and headed downstairs to start her chores. Benjamin had noticed that the baby had been sleeping since yesterday without crying or waking up. This was the first time the baby had cried. They both were in her room on several occasions checking up on her, but she seemed to have been in a deep sleep. It seemed a bit out of character.

"Darling, are you sure the baby is fine? She has been asleep since yesterday. This morning she just cried a bit, I just picked her up, and she slept back again." Said Benjamin entering into the bed. Bridgette was still in bed. It was Benjamin's turn to check on the baby.

"Yes, Darling. I have noticed that too. Honestly, I am not sure why. But babies sometimes they sleep for long hours. It is part of growing up. I checked her last night everything seemed fine apart from the elevated temperature reading. Perhaps we should call the doctor," said Bridgette turning to face her husband who had just got back into the bed.

"Good idea, perhaps I should do that right now."

"Ok sweetie." Benjamin picked up the phone and dialed the doctors number. The phone on the other end rung for some time without being answered. Benjamin kept on the line. After ringing for some time the call was diverted and Benjamin could hear a new ringing tone. It only rung for a few seconds before it was answered.

"Allo, doctor speaking," the doctor answered the phone.

"Oh yes, doctor, my daughter is not feeling well, she has been sleeping since yesterday." Benjamin paused for a while before continuing.

"She has an elevated temperature and seem not be interested in breastfeeding."

"Ok, what's the name again," asked the doctor.

"Benjamin, of 30 Bellissimo, Bellac,Limousin."

"Oh Mr. Petit. Mr. Benjamin."

"That's right, so what time?"

"Ah. Let's say after half an hour. I am half an hour away. I will set off now. OK?"

"Ok, thank you doctor." "Ok, see you soon. Bye." The call ended and Benjamin relayed the message to his wife. Dmitri and his wife Enya had just left their house heading to Volodarskogo Street in Kurgan city. They had been making this journey every Sunday for the past ten months now. Since the previous month things had been very difficult for the couple. They had found comfort in the hands of the Bishops of the church. Only God had the answers, they had been everywhere but nothing had provided them with the answers they needed. Dimitri and Enya had met a year ago. They had clicked from the start and things got serious soon afterwards. They felt they were meant to be together and decided to move in together. Family and friends were quick to support them, it seemed Dimitri and Enya had a lot in common. They were inseparable and two months down the line they announced to their friends the great news of a baby coming their way. Although Enya's pregnancy was not planned, they were happy and willing to have the baby. This was a blessing to both. They had married in the church in the months following the pregnancy news. Dimitri and Enya arrived at the Cathedral of St. Alexander Nevsky in Volodarskogo Street. This was a Russian Orthodox church; the importance of the church had been heightened recently because of the mysteries that had struck the local inhabitants of Kurgan city. It seemed everyone needed God and the church's support through these tough times. The Bishops have been busy comforting people and doing the will of God. They have seen a rise in the number of people coming to the church in recent months. Dimitri and Enya have been happy since the day they met. News of a baby have had brought them together and made their relationship stronger. They had been to the EMC in Moscow two or three times a month since they found out that they were expecting a baby. More often they had been to the local hospital in Kurgan for maternal care. Things were going on normal until the time when Enya was seven months pregnant. One night they said good night to each other, and they slept together like always. In the morning, Dimitri woke up and went to work. He woke up very early and did not want to wake up his wife. He went to work in the morning and came back just after sunset around 7pm and found his wife Enya still in bed fast asleep. The time he came back from work at first, he thought that Enya had woken up and went back to bed so he did not worry too much about this. She normally made a meal for him and herself, she had always insisted on cooking and eating at home. She loved cooking, and it kept her busy whenever Dimitri was at work. This day there was nothing prepared, but still Dimitri did not worry much about this. He went in their bedroom to wake his wife up. She did not respond to his surprise but everything seemed okay. She was breathing normally but fast asleep. She was snoring, so he thought of letting her sleep a little longer. It was after one or two more hours of sleep that she woke up but not remembering much. She had insisted that she slept the previous night and had not woke until that time. Dimitri wanted to believe his wife but found it very impossible to believe. If it was possible, then it might be because she was pregnant. He called in his wife's doctor that night and explained what had happened. The doctor rested his fears as he explained to them that it could have been because of the pregnancy but insisted that they visited the local hospital just to make sure that there was nothing wrong with the baby. Dimitri believed his wife and that same night decided to take her to the local hospital for a check-up to make sure that the baby was OK. Everything was ok with the baby and the mother. The doctors had reiterated that it was common for pregnant women to sleep more often than usual. The couple were expecting a healthy baby girl two months from the date of the incident. She had stayed in the hospital for more tests. The time coincided also with their appointment at the EMC in Moscow. After leaving the local hospital in Kurgan, they made the long journey to the capital city Moscow. At the EMC, a variety of tests were carried out which included blood tests and ultrasound baby scans. These tests were carried out to check and assess the development of the pregnancy and Enya's well-being and to screen for any conditions that can be of concern. After this, they explained what had happened, they had a urine test done to check for any proteins and albumin but they were all clear which meant no infection. They had blood pressure tests which all came back as normal. All other blood tests came back as normal as well. That very same day they had an ultrasound scan carried out, to see the condition of the baby in the womb. The sonographer careful examined the baby's body in the womb. Dimitri was present, and he saw the baby moving her legs and hands. As far as the sonographer could see there was nothing wrong with the baby. It was a healthy baby girl. The only small problem they came

across during the ultrasound was that the baby was lying in a difficult position for the sonographer to be able to see clearly. She had requested Enya to turn sides and back to correct the baby's position after that everything seemed normal. After thirty minutes the ultrasound was completed, and the sonographer made no concerns about the baby's healthy. The sonographer had estimated also the baby's delivery date and time. The following day at the EMC Enya had an MRI scan after the doctors there had a long conversation with the couples of the dangers of the MRI scan but they also stressed that over the past thirty years' pregnant women had MRI scans without any harm to the baby. After nearly forty minutes of lying still the MRI scan was completed. It was after reviewing the images that the doctors noticed that Enya's scans showed excess accumulation of fluid in her brain. There was no clear reason for this condition and the only likely possible cause per the doctor was a poisoning of some kind or chronic fatigue syndrome. Dangerous gas was leaking at their home maybe because their home was not properly ventilated. The couples had a gas stove which might have contributed to the release of carbon monoxide which is the likely cause per the doctor at the EMC. This was a more convincing explanation since Enya liked to cook all the time although the doctor was skeptical about this because the carbon monoxide released from a gas stove would not be so much to likely cause the condition. Nevertheless, the doctors advised that Enya eased up the cooking and to get enough rest. After a few days in the EMC Enya was discharged, and they were all ready to go back home. Ever since this incident Enya did not have any major issues with the pregnancy. The only big concerned they had was when the baby's' due date arrived. Like any expecting couples, they had planned and made appointments with the hospital for the baby's delivery. The doctors at the EMC had referred them to the Perinatal Medical Center (PNC) in Moscow. The facilities there were very modern, and this hospital was extremely well equipped and clean. They had more experienced doctors, and they were patient focused. They had a gynecologist assigned to them. Dimitri's medical insurance had paid 385 000 rubles for the natural birth of their daughter. They had checked-in early and had more blood tests and scans carried out. The last few days just before delivery were the best the two had shared together. They were optimistic, expected a lot, and were looking forward to start a new life with the added member of their family. The due date arrived and the hospital staff prepared for the delivery of Dimitri and Enya's baby. As one of the few rare situations the baby was not delivered as labor did not start. This waiting for labor to start was very stressful for Enya and Dimitri and all the medical staff concerned. The couple had been anxious because of this. After a long discussion with their assigned gynecologist, she had stressed out that not all women go into labor on their exact due date and they had emphasized that even though this was the case most women around ninety percent start to experience contractions within two weeks of their due date and because of this the doctors as they emphasized to be on the safe side they wanted to start doing more tests. The doctors had done their best to try to comfort the couple, they had emphasized and reiterated that the expected date of delivery was just an estimate and therefore not one hundred percent accurate. It was supposed to be a guide line for doctors to consider inducing labor artificially or not. The doctors had explained that some babies are born a week or two after the expected due date with the first week delivery risk free. The only concern was after the first weeks and into the second week, due to an increased risk of infection, malfunctioning of the placenta and unexpected complications during delivery. The couple were now worried especially considering the carbon monoxide incident some months ago. Dimitri was worried about Enya and the baby. So many questions kept running through his mind. What was the real cause of the sleeping sickness? Was the baby ok? Was Enya going to be ok after this. Dimitri had asked the medical staff for some privacy as he wanted to talk to his wife Enya in private. They hugged each other and Enya started crying. What was this now? What was happening? She had so many questions which needed answers. Surely it was not her fault, she would not jeopardize the baby's safety let alone her own. She apologized to her husband. He had done his best to console her, they had both done what any couple could have done. They had been to their local hospital, and straight after they had endured the long journey to the capital city. They had several tests done at the EMC. What did they miss? Was this not enough? After some time, together they explained this incident to their gynecologist Dr. Ewa Ayaveska who in turn acknowledged that she was aware of the incident from the medical records transferred from the EMC. The weeks that followed saw more appointments, checks-ups and test arranged and carried out on Enya.

The couples had been informed about a list of possible complications ranging from a stillborn baby to complicated labor and delivery as the baby will be oversize weeks after the due date. More and more tests were done on Enya, a non-stress cardiotocograph was done to measure the fetal's heart rate. This was the first major indication that there was something wrong with the baby. The heart rate was abnormal; the second test was even worse and the third test was worse than the first two. But overall, the doctors were not putting too much weight to the results obtained. First the heartbeat rate was high and literally further increased which can mean that, first that the baby is fine and it is receiving enough oxygen. Secondly that the baby is sound and well and that it is very active. The only concerned was raised by the third test. This meant that the baby was hyperactivity which the doctor suggested that it could be a sign that the baby is stressed up and could point to a future problem. Two weeks after the expected due date had passed the doctor had come up with a plan. They informed the couple that it was rare but possible for a baby to be delivered two weeks after the due date. So, the initial plan was to wait for the two weeks. If not, then they will try to artificially induce labor or to consider cesarean operation. So, it was now only a matter of time. They had advised the couple to remain in the hospital so that they can be monitored by the doctor in case the contractions started any time. They had agreed until the medical insurance adviser of the couple had informed them that, any more days stayed in the hospital were not covered by their insurance. They had no choice but for Enya to be discharged and to return to the

Perinatal Medical Center (PMC) after two weeks had passed. This Sunday was the last Sunday before Dimitri and Enya traveled back to the PMC in Moscow. They had taken this opportunity to go to church and ask God for help and to ask the Bishop to pray for them and their precious baby. They had been through a lot for the last two weeks. Only God can hear their prayers, divine intervention seemed to be the only answer. The Sunday in question was very cold and Enya was heavily pregnant. This was to be a very special Sunday for the church. Other Bishops from other surrounding churches had been summoned to attend this service. The Patriarch and the Chief Bishop were all present, they had gathered early in their chamber preparing for this service. Dimitri and Enya entered the church and were invited to sit in the front row in front of the Patriarch and the Bishops. As people entered the church, they made the sign of the cross in front of them, some went on to light up candles. After lighting the candles these people have moved to the front of the church and started kissing icons in front of the church. These icons were like statues of previous well known prophets and Christians. The kissing of icons, lighting of candles went on and on if more people kept coming into the church. The Chief Bishop then stood up and made the sign of the cross, firstly touching his head, his heart, the right shoulder and then the left shoulder at the same time saying the words;

"In the name of the Father, the Son and the Holy Spirit". He addressed the church, introduced the Patriarch and other stood up and cut the seal, and the rest of the loaf was cut into smaller pieces and placed into a large basket. The Patriarch then blessed the bread, he then went on to perform the Eucharistic prayer as the congregation stood up. After reciting some prayers, he then went to the couples who in turn stood up. They opened their mouths, then the Patriarch called them by their first names and put the bread in their mouths. They made the sign of the cross and sat down. The Patriarch then moved back to the front of the church. People then started filing up going to where the Patriarch was, singing hymns waiting for their turn to receive the bread. They open their mouths, eats the bread, and makes the sign of the cross and proceeded to their seats. After that, the Patriarch then approached the couples again but this time with a golden wine cup. In his left hand, he was holding a white cloth and in his right hand the golden wine cup. He gave the couple to drink wiping the cup after each one of them had sipped some. They made the sign of the cross and sat down again. He then returned to the front of the church and this time only the priests and the Bishops formed a line to receive the wine. The church was packed and some people could not find space inside that they stood and participated from outside near the entrance. After the service, they all gathered to offer and wish the couple of blessings. For Dimitri and Enya this was more than they had wished for, was God going to help them through these tough times, only time will tell. After that emotional church service Dimitri and Enya headed to the PMC in Moscow. On arrival, they had a long conversation with their gynecologist.

"I have conferred with the other doctors, and I think it's time to consider doing a C-section. If you would like I will make arrangements so that this can be performed in two hours' time," Dimitri and Enya looked at each other not knowing what to say to the doctor. Dimitri put his arms around Enya and kissed her on the forehead.

"What are the risks and or complications?" asked Dimitri clearly uneasy with the idea. There was too much weight being placed on his shoulder. There were all risks now. Waiting for the natural birth or going for the C-section, how would one know how to choose? If they wait any longer, the baby might die, Enya might die too. If they go for the Section, there could be complications too.

"Can we talk in private first, then we will get back to you as soon as possible?" requested Dimitri looking at the gynecologist.

"That is fine, just let me know when you are done, I will be in my office." The gynecologist stood up and left the two couples to decide.

"My love, I don't know what to do or say about this," Dimitri paused as he kissed Enya on the lips.

"It's your decision too. What do you think, what do you want, my love tell me?" Pleaded Dimitri. Enya looked more worried but seemed a little relieved by the idea of a C-section. In her thoughts, she knew nine months alone were hard enough let alone ten months. She loved the baby no doubt about that but the last 2-3 weeks were the most stressful of her life. Honestly, she wanted to give birth like yesterday. This was good news to her. She remembered when she was a little girl that a woman in their neighborhood died after refusing to give birth by C-section. She had preferred to give birth naturally and after ten months she was still pregnant. She later died of complications as she had a stillbirth. If she had accepted the C-section, there were chances that both mother and child could have made it or at least one of them could have survived. There was no doubt that this is what she would choose as the gynecologist had told them that this could be performed in two hours' time. After 2-3 hours, she could be carrying their baby in her hands and all this would behind them.

"I think we should do like the gynecologist had said." She paused and looked at Dimitri before continuing. "I do not want to take any more risks. I think this is the safe option. In fact, I just want my baby. I do not care anymore if they cut me or not. They can do anything they want if I have my beautiful baby safe and sound."

"It's true Darling Enya, but I was thinking that we should ask others for advice and opinions as well. It is a lot of weight on my shoulder. What if something goes wrong or…," Dimitri did not even finish his sentence as Enya put her hand over his mouth? "Shh… Dimitri, don't make it worse than it is. I know why you are concerned about this."

"Do you?!" asked Dimitri raising his eyebrows and staring at his wife.

"Yes. Of course, it's ok, my love."

"No, its. Not," Dimitri became very emotional and hugged his wife. They both started crying holding each other. Minutes passed by before they continued with their conversation. Dimitri took out a handkerchief and blow his nose. He pulled up the watery mucus running down his nose. He looked at Enya and snogged her.

"I have never been this scared, I am more scared now than that day, you know?"

"I know but everything is going to be okay," replied Enya in a soft voice. Dimitri was more scared than he had ever been. He recalled that time when Enya slept for days without waking up. He felt like he had died himself. He loved Enya very much. He would rather lose the baby just to save his true love. His main concern was that up to now even the doctors had no clue as to what had caused that sleeping mystery. What if that happens again? This procedure is well known also for complications. Surely Dimitri wanted a second opinion from someone he trusted, someone he had known well enough. But it seemed he was on his own on this one. He had wished that his father was by his side as he had always been. He needed his brother more than any time in the past. If something goes wrong, will he be able to forgive himself?

"Enya my Darling, I love you so much. Honestly if I must choose between you and the baby. I would choose you a million times, repeatedly," he paused and looked at Enya. He snogged her and continued. "We can have another baby. Honestly, I do not want to go with this C-section. Some babies can be born up to four weeks after the due date. This operation has risks. What if you do not wake up?" asked Dimitri squeezing Enya as he hugged her.

"Dimitri. Dimitri. I cannot breathe Darling," said Enya as she releases herself from Dimitri's grip.

"Oh sorry, my Darling. I am just really afraid I might lose you," said Dimitri apologetically.

"Don't say that. Be strong for us now. We both need you. Do not fight. Everything is going to be fine," said Enya touching Dimitri's head.

"You promise? Say I promise!" requested Dimitri emotionally kissing Enya's forehead.

"I promise," replied Enya with a strong high voice but with less much conviction. Only if Dimitri could see through Enya's eyes as to how she was feeling inside. Surely, he was never going to agree for her to go through this. Enya was exhausted, frightened, and tired. At this moment in time one thing was for sure. She just wanted to give birth to their beautiful daughter, just like anyone else. No matter what they do to her, cutting her or not was not important now. The only thing that mattered as far as she was concerned was to deliver her beautiful daughter. Of course, she was afraid, was this the best option around this? Honestly, she had no idea. She knew waiting could mean waiting for weeks. She had no contractions at all, she was not dilated at all despite all efforts to induce labor. This could mean weeks stuck in the hospital and who is going to pay the bill? Surely the insurance company had denied. This would mean weeks for Dimitri out of work and no money in the future. After a long one-to-one talk the couple called in the gynecologist.

"We have decided to go ahead with the C-section," said Dimitri hesitantly with a shaking voice and unsure about everything.

"That's great, we will do our best to make sure it goes smoothly. The nurse will show you to your waiting room. The surgery team will be ready after two hours. Any questions before or after let me know. I will be happy to help. Remember you can change your opinion anytime." She stood up and left after trying to comfort the couple. The couple waited there for a few more minutes before they were escorted to their room. In their room, they were introduced to their nursing staff who will be taking care of them for the next three or so days. They were introduced to their obstetrics (OB) who will be performing the C-section.

They met other doctors who helped with re-planning their birth and reviewing everything. Enya was hooked to the monitor. The time finally arrived for Enya to go to the surgery room. Enya was very nervous and understandably frightened. They both walked down the hall. At the other end, there were the nursing staff with a push bed. Enya was asked to lay down, and she was pushed to the operating room. She remembered the room being very cold. This was a temperature controlled room ideal for surgery. They arrived and Enya jumped on the operating table. "What kind of music would you like if the current selection is not okay for you?" Asked one of the nurses.

"Music is fine don't worry." Replied Enya politely. The nurse tried to comfort and reassure Enya. They asked Enya to wear an operating gown that can be opened from the back. The nurse asked Enya to lay down so that she can sterilize her back to administer the anesthetic. She remembers feeling very cold.

"Are you ok?" asked the nurse politely and concerned about Enya during sterilization.

"Honesty I can do with some form of warmth. I feel very cold," replied Enya sincerely and showing a bit of fear.

"Nurse, can you bring some blankets for Enya," shouted one nurse to another.

"Don't worry we are all here to make sure you and the baby will be okay," said the nurse trying to reassure Enya that everything was going to be okay. Soon afterwards they brought some blankets and covered Enya.

"I am going to be sick. I am going to be sick," shouted Enya holding her mouth. She looked at the nurse who was standing there already prepared with a bucket in her hand.

"It is okay take your time. It is common among pregnant women so do not you worry," said the nurse holding the bucket for Enya. Enya lifted her head and saw her husband Dimitri standing next to the operating table but a little distance further. He was wearing a spaceman suit or what looked like to be one. He raised his hand and moved toward Enya. The nurse stopped him. "Not now Sir. Sterilization in progress." After sterilization, a lot of staff came in and introduced themselves to Enya and Dimitri. Enya noticed that there was a midwife, an obstetrician, an assistant, a theater nurse and an assistant, an anesthetist and an assistant and a pediatrician. Fear crippled her for some time but the nurse re assured her that everything was going to be okay. Why all these people, it can only mean that the procedure is very risk, so she thought to herself. After a long discussion with the anesthetist she chose to have the localized anesthetic which meant that she will be awake. Dimitri was given a nurse to accompany him, who would answer any questions and clarify any issues as the operation was in progress. The obstetrician informed the couple that the baby will be delivered very quickly within the first 5 minutes of the C-section followed by the removal or delivery of the placenta. Once this has been done then there will be the closing of the wound which can take up to 30 minutes or more depending on other factors. The wound will be stitched very fast. The anesthetist administered the local anesthetic and made sure that it was working before the operation. Then came the time of the operation. The surgeon came and performed the operation. Enya could not see what was happening as her view was obstructed by a screen in front of her. Dimitri was watching every second as the procedure progressed. After five minutes the first cries of the baby were heard, and there were celebrations among the medical staff. All the nurses cheered and celebrated every moment with the couples. Dimitri was very happy and quickly as they had planned before the operation, he took the baby with the help of the nurse and started the cleaning up process. She weighed 8 pounds, 2 ounces and 6 inches. He went to Enya and showed her the baby. She was very happy. It was a beautiful girl. She was given the baby to nuzzle for a few seconds while the surgeons were carrying on with the stitching. Soon after the delivery of the placenta as the surgeons were stitching Enya. She suddenly opened wide her eyes before gasping for air.

"Something is wrong! Enya! Enya! Oh, please help! Something is wrong." Shouted Dimitri hysterically. Everyone rushed around yelling something to each other. One of the nurses started shouting to one another asking her to take Dimitri outside the operating room. Dimitri instead refused and went to where Enya was lying. He holds her hand with one hand while the other was carrying the baby. The other nurse came and took the baby from Dimitri while the other one tried to direct him outside the room. "Darling I am tired and I am very weak," she said slowly with a soft voice looking at the baby. She looked at Dimitri again and pointed to the baby. She forced a smile and closed her eyes. Dimitri begged the surgeons to do their best while he looked on helplessly. This was his worst fear. What on earth was happening? What did he do wrong to deserve this? He holds Enya's hand firmly and hugged her while she lay on the table. He kissed her emotionally. He started sobbing uncontrollably. The nurse who was directing him outside stood next to the operating table for some seconds holding back tears. Following the delivery of the placenta Enya suddenly became plethoric. She had suffered sudden unforeseen heavy bleeding. The surgeons rushed to try to stop the bleeding by administering sodium bicarbonate and oxytocin. Unfortunately attempts to revive her were unsuccessful. By this time, Dimitri was watching his wife from outside the operating room through the glass window. She had lost a lot of blood.

CHAPTER THREE

In Elliot Lake city, Ontario Canada, it is a very sunny day. Temperatures are above 27'C. It has been warm for the past days with frequent rain showers in between periods of sunshine. In one of the local neighborhoods, it seemed most people were minding their businesses. Everyone was busy trying to make ends meet. As the locals, would probably tell you, it seemed the city was bewitched. In the past years, the city has seen closures one after the other of all uranium mines in the nearby towns with the resultant loss of income and wages. This was due to lawsuits against uranium mines as miners ended up with a lot of health issues. The collapse of the mall killing people and injuring others has meant more lawsuits that seen the end of the mall and prosperity of the city. Nevertheless, there are still people living there despite fears of exposure to radiation. In one of the suburbs, Bob has been living in there since his father was a mine worker for one of the uranium mining companies. Bob is married to Sue, they had two kids a boy and a girl who have since died. Since their death, Bob and Sue rarely talked to anyone about their kids. They were taken away from them in mysterious ways. Their first born was a girl by the name of Tyra, by the time she died she was in grade six at school and had 12 years of age. Tyra had a baby brother called Amos, who died a month after Tyra died in a freaky accident. The two, Tyra and Amos had played together since they were kids. They got along very well. Tyra had a brighter future ahead of her, she was doing very well in school. She had been awarded certificates in English and mathematics and in science. Most of the time she spent reading books and doing homework with her brother. Whereas Amos, never liked school, but he was a clear boy. Bob had a perfect family he could not wish for anything else. He had a beautiful wife in Sue. They had met many years ago, dying few years after working for this company. Sue's father had died after a short illness followed by Bob's father after a short illness too. Their deaths brought Bob and Sue together. Months later they were blessed with a baby girl and named her after Bob's mother who had died as well. After birth of their son they had decided not to have any more kids. Bob had gone for the sniper. They had the perfect world until the arrival of what Bob has publicly called the little devil from hell and her family. They have had new neighbors in the form of Jeremiah and Nancy. Their new neighbors had a young daughter called Beverly. There was something about this family that made Bob curious and mistrust his neighbors. Their daughter it seems was never to school. She never left the house in the afternoon. Most afternoons she would stand on her bedroom window looking outside. Bob had seen her on several occasions outside, sometimes in the woods at night. This was very strange for a twelve-year-old. After moving in the neighborhood Beverly and Tyra had become very good friends. They spent most of the time together. Tyra started spending more time with Beverly away from her home. One day Bob came back home to find out that Tyra was not at home. He went across the street to his neighbor to look for Tyra.

"Good afternoon, Jeremy", said Bob approaching Jeremy who was outside his house smoking. "Afternoon Bob, how have you been? How is Sue and the kids?"

"Guess all right, they are all doing fine." They spoke for some time before Bob asked if his daughter was with Jeremy's daughter.

"They are both not inside I was looking for Beverly a couple of minutes ago, before you came."

"I guess they have gone to play somewhere nearby." Said Jeremy puffing his cigarette. Bob decided to go and look for his daughter but Jeremy thought that there was no point in searching for them. He insisted that they come back soon. Bob left Jeremy's house heading toward the nearby park.

"Tyra, Beverly, can you hear me? Tyra!" Shouted Bob searching for his daughter and her friend. There was no sign of them. Bob stood and listened for a while but he could only hear birds singing and the sound made by the light wind as it caressed the leaves on branches of the trees nearby. He called his daughter one last time before he started going back.

"Tyra, Beverly where are you!" He stopped and

listened but there was no reply. He started going back, he walked three steps heading home, then he heard a large sound like that made by an animal far away. He stopped and listened again. He heard that howling sound again. What is that? He asked himself before turning back and heading in the direction the sound was coming from. He was afraid but proceeded forward in case Tyra and Beverly were in that area. He walked in the woods trying not to make any noises in case the animal was nearby. He edged forward slowly and carefully looking everywhere. He saw a big tree ahead, he stopped and looked around before going forward toward that tree. As he was nearby, he saw his daughter Tyra kneeling. He ran toward her shouting her name.

"Tyra, Tyra, what are you doing here? Are you okay?" as he was close to his daughter, he saw Beverly lying on the ground. Fear gave him a shiver, and he ran even faster toward them fearing for the worst.

"What happened? Was she attacked? Why are you here? What did I tell you about wandering on your own?" Bob was really upset. He arrived under that big tree and Tyra seemed ok and as soon as she saw her father she started telling him what had happened so fast that he did not understand a thing.

"Catch your breath, is Beverly ok?"

He did not even wait for his daughter to reply. He knelt and picked Beverly up. She was unconscious as if in a deep sleep. He checked for any injuries or blood but there was nothing. He checked her pulse, and she was ok. She had a strong pulse. He tried waking her up, but she did not respond. Quickly he looked around and got up quickly carrying her. "Come let's go home now. Walk in front of me, walk fast. Come Tyra, let's go." Tyra quickly started walking forward constantly looking at her dad who was following her carrying Beverly.

"Daddy, daddy, I was very afraid, I saw I saw eh," she did not finish talking before her father interrupted. "Ok, you will tell me later, first let's go home. OK?" asked her father looking backward. He was now afraid because his daughter saw an animal. So, there is a real danger, he thought to himself. They walked very fast and Bob kept constantly looking forward and backward in case that animal was following them. When they were near Jeremy's house Beverly came around

"Daddy, daddy, Beverly woke up! Daddy," Bob quickly stopped and looked at Beverly.

"Are you ok Beverly? What happened?" Bob quickly asked Beverly expecting to get answers, but she seemed not to know what had happened.

"I can't remember." She said touching her head as if in pain.

"Ok, ok, don't worry we are near home." Bob knocked Jeremy's door and did not wait to be invited in. He entered the living room and went to lay down Beverly on the couch calling Jeremy and his wife. Jeremy and his wife came downstairs quickly and Bob tried to find out what had happened from his daughter.

"What happened, Oh my God Beverly! Are you ok." This was Beverly's mother who knelt beside the couch trying to find out what happened to her daughter.

"What happened, Beverly?" asked Nancy

"I don't know mama." Said Beverly touching her forehead.

"She fell down under a big tree and fell asleep." Said Tyra looking at Beverly's mum. Then, I saw an animal, I was very scared. I screamed very loud…" Tyra paused and looked at her dad before continuing. "I was really scared I screamed again." Tyra stopped to take her breath.

"Then that animal ran away, I tried waking her up, but she was fast asleep. That is when I saw my daddy".

"What kind of animal?" Asked Jeremy.

"I don't know but it was very big," said Tyra seating next to Beverly who was still laying down on the couch. Bob quickly took out his phone and dialed a number. He waited on the line for some time before he started talking to someone over the phone.

"I need help as soon as possible! There might be a dangerous animal lurking nearby. Who should I contact?" asked Bob.

"What's your location? Is the animal still there? Can you see the animal right now?" There was silence. "No I didn't see the animal, it's my daughter who saw the animal," explained Bob.

"I am in Elliot Lake city. Hello!" said Bob waiting for the other person to talk.

"What kind of animal was it? Where is your daughter now? How old is your daughter? Can I talk to her right now?" The operator waited.

"I don't know what kind of animal it was. My daughter saw the animal. I just heard the animal howling as I was a distance away. Tyra is twelve, and she is here with us." Said Bob.

"Ok I need to talk to her put her on the phone," said the operator.

"Hello Tyra, what kind of animal was it?" asked the

operator.

"I don't know but the animal was huge. I screamed very loud and the animal run away."

"Did you just say the animal run away?" asked the operator.

"Yes, the animal run away," replied Tyra.

"Ok thank you for your time, pass the phone to your father. Ok?" said the operator.

"Ok," replied Tyra.

"I will send someone to have a look as soon as possible. It will be wise to stay indoors for now until this is resolved." Bob acknowledged, and he put the phone down. Bob, left Jeremy's house and went to his own house. He took his wife Sue and brought her to Jeremy's house. The two man, Jeremy and Bob left in Bob's pick truck with guns to hunt the animal down. They had realized that it might take longer for the Sheriff department to send someone to hunt the animal down. The fact that the animal run away from the girls suggested that it might not be dangerous but there was still a danger. After discussing about this Bob and Jeremy concluded that it was highly likely the girls might have seen a fox or a jackal as these animals had been seen very often even in the city's woods. Half an hour later police from the Sheriff's department had gathered just outside the park leading to the woods where the animal was spotted. They held a brief conference which lasted around five minutes. People had gathered after Bob and Jeremy had gone around warning people to be vigilant after what their girls had seen.

"Don't panic. We urge you all to be vigilant and to stay indoors until such a time when we are sure that the area is safe." Said the commander of the group. A strong group of thirty officers with rifles had gathered outside waiting for the command to start searching for the beast.

"Listen people, we are going to hunt and kill that animal or we are going to search for the animal for the next ten hours whichever comes first. Do not be afraid and please stay in your houses. We are going to have another meeting five hours from now informing you of our progress. Please bear with us," said he commander. As soon as he had finished addressing the crowd, the people immediately started dispersing to their homes. Soon after that conference the search for the beast began. Operation flush and kill the beast as it was duped began. Bob and Jeremy also were asked to go home and wait for the briefing. There is something going on, I think the girls were very lucky today. I keep asking myself that, what if? I feel sick at the thought that a dangerous animal is on the loose somewhere there and our kids were out there," said Bob who seemed more worried even up to this stage. "I think the police will do their best. I was not aware myself. I thought this neighborhood was safe. That is the main reason we moved this side," said Jeremy as they were going home. Back in the park heading to the nearby woods officers began sweeping the park trying to flush out the animal. The officers had rifles, tranquilizer and sniffer dogs. The search went on for some time. They tried different methods to flush the animal from the woods. First, they used a method called bark out whereby dogs are used to make barking noises at one end while the other officers wait with guns to see if the animals come out on the other end, waiting to shoot it. Five hours later the second brief conference was called for. After five hours, the second briefing was called for as the commander of the police gathered to give the brief. There was good news.

"Listen, people. We have flushed out and killed a fox," he paused and raised his hand stopping the crowd from asking questions before continuing.

"I am not 100% sure that this is the animal the girls concerned saw. But I think with the way I was told. It is highly likely that this is the animal which the girls saw in the woods." The commander paused and cleared his throat before continuing.

"Operation flush out and kill the beast will continue for the next five hours as planned. I will answer questions later," as soon as he had finished saying this he left without giving anyone the chance to ask questions. The people soon after dispersed back to their homes. After searching for the animal for ten hours' operation flush out and kill the beast ended. The commander announced that they had only located the fox which they indeed killed. And it was highly probable that this was the animal the girls saw. They had search and researched the area for the beast but nothing was found. The commander urged the public to be vigilant and to call them if there were any further sightings of the beast. The police search and rescue team Elliot Lake, Ontario left after the operation. Six months after operation flush out and kill the beast Bob is in his garage. It seems he is looking for something in his garage. He staggered back to his car which is parked inside and opened the front left door of his car. He reached inside and then sat on the passenger seat with the door open. He murmured something to himself. He sat there for a while and looked under the car seat and reached for a bottle. He opened the bottle and poured half the contents in his throat. He squints his eyes and face and wiped his mouth. He went to the back of his van and looked for something. He then went at the back of the garage and started throwing tins and things in the air. He stops and then went to the car garage door and opened the door. He stood at the door and poured the contents of the bottle into his mouth again. He swore as he stood at the garage door. He looked across the street and covered his face, both his eyes with his palm. He holds his head with his hand in such a way that it looked like his head was very heavy and he was trying to support it to prevent it from falling. He stood there for some time. Across the street, a girl can be seen standing at the window looking outside. It seems she had been standing there for some time. She looks worried but unmoved. The world around her revolves around that place. This seemed like her special place. She had been seen there by Bob as far as he can remember. This looks like a special place for her. The only place that lets her understand the world around her. It seems this place gives her peace and comfort. One hour later, a pickup van is packed outside this girl's house. A man gets out of the van leaving the driver door open. He staggered out of the car and reached for something from the back of his pickup truck. He put it in the driver's front seat. He staggers back to the back of the van. He took out a big drum and rolled it to the ground. He kicked it with his right leg and the drum rolls toward the house stopping a few inches from the walls of the house. He kneels and unscrews the lid of the drum. Immediately, he gets up and walks back to his pickup truck. He jumps in and reversed his van further down. He rolls another drum from his van hitting the ground with a thump. He slides it toward the walls of the house, knelt and opened the lid of the second drum. A liquid can be heard gushing out fast from the drum. He gets back to his van and drove forward. He stopped the car a few meters from the house and unloaded some bottles before he started unscrewing the bottle tops. He approached the other corner of the van and took out pieces of cloths. He tears these into even smaller pieces. After sometime he goes to the front driver's seat and reaches for the rifle he had left on the driver's seat. He takes the rifle to the back of the van and put it down in the van. He took out a lighter and lit one of the bottles. As the cloth started burning, he then threw the bottle on top of the house. He does this for some time repeatedly and then goes back of his van and picks up his rifle. The house started burning on the roof first. For some strange reason, the girl standing at the window looking outside did not move or panic at all. She just stood there observing what the man was doing.

"Die, you little devil! You going to burn to death," said Bob as he jumped into his van placing his rifle on the passenger seat. As the house started burning, he drove off heading to the woods. He took some bottles of petrol and tore rugs making fire bombs. He took these into the woods. He staggered into the woods with the bottles in the other hand and rifle in one. He stood and rested a little. He put the bottles down and reached for a small bottle in his jacket pocket. He poured all the contents down his throat. He looked upwards to the sky and shouted with a raised voice.

"Why? Why them? You should have taken me."

He threw the empty bottle in the sky and staggered forward as if he was going to fall. He stopped, got his balance, and picked up his bottles and rifle and proceeded forward. After walking for some time, he reached the big tree and sat under it leaning on the tree trunk. He sat down and sobbed uncontrollably.

CHAPTER FOUR

Detective Inspector Smith is in the crime laboratory talking to the laboratory technician Lucas.

"I have something I need doing fast. I have been given a new case. It is driving me nuts. Everyone is pushing for answers. I wish I had ten hands like you, Lucas." Said the detective giving Lucas a plastic bag full of samples from the crime scene.

"Hey detective, how are you? Do not worry, you know you can always count on me." Lucas took the plastic bag and started taking the contents out carefully and systematically.

"Any particular order?" he asked the detective.

"Yes, DNA, blood group, bite marks, canine category, ballistic report and the rest. How soon."

"DNA 2; BG 2; BM 1; CC 1; BR 3, the rest within 5," said Lucas. The detective took out a small note pad and wrote the following down repeating everything loud. BM 1; CC 1; DNA 2; BG 2; BR 3; MISC 5. The detective left the crime lab and left Lucas sorting out the samples and evidence. After leaving the crime laboratory in the city detective Smith headed to the hospital. The coroner and the medical examiner's offices were adjacent to each other both located in the hospital. He entered the main building and waited for the lifts. The lifts arrived, and he entered the lifts. Level 5 a voice can be heard coming out from the speakers above. He left the lifts and straight in the corridor. He knew this corridor very well. He had been here more than a hundred times since he started working for the crime scene detectives branch of the police some 5 years ago. He arrived outside the coroner's door. He knocked and entered his office. "Come on in, I was actually expecting you," said the coroner. Detective Smith entered the coroner's office and stood in front of his table.

"Please sit down this is important," said the coroner pointing at the seat in front of him.

"You were expecting me, you must have something for me, right?" asked detective Smith as he was sitting down.

"Something about this recent case, is not right," said the coroner opening a file that was in front of him. He took a long look at the file and opened pages inside flicking them to one side.

"Oh yes, the report," said the coroner taking out the report and handing it to detective Smith.

"Look at the summary especially the highlighted part," said the coroner looking at the detective.

"There must be a mistake, don't you think so?" asked the detective.

"Oh, sure I thought the same myself, by I tell you this, this is correct."

The coroner removed his reading glasses and put them on the table. He sat comfortable in his chair and looked at the detective who was still reading his report. There was a moment of silence as the coroner waited for the detective to finish reading the report. "Are you sure this is correct? Has the results been verified?" asked the detective.

"I checked everything myself and collected new samples," said the coroner putting his hands together. "Ok, can you explain in layman terms?" asked the detective. The coroner pauses and edged forward looking at the detective before continuing.

"This is my version of events, are you ready?" asked the coroner waiting for the detective to take out his notepad as he always does.

"Yes, I am ready," the detective took out a pen and a notepad and waited to jot down something.

"Some kind of canine knock down the victim. Grabs his head in its mouth and drags him first, and that is consistent with the bite marks and the bruising on his body." The coroner paused and took out photos of the victim and gave them to the detective.

"Look at the picture see those two small holes on his head? They are the teeth marks of the animal as it drags him away from where it first attacked him."

He paused giving the detective time to look at the photos.

"Carry on Coroner," requested the detective impatiently.

"I think at one-point he woke up and tried to run away. That is when the animal mauled his left side piercing the heart and damaging major arteries which caused death in seconds."

Paused the coroner before continuing.

"A question for you, why do animals kill?" asked the coroner putting his hands together.

"Mostly for food or if threatened," said the detective. "In this case, even now I cannot find out why the animal knocked him to the ground, drags him and killed him when he tried to escape but not even have a single bite. All his hair is intact." They both looked at each other.

"Probably, and this being just my opinion, the animal was disturbed before it had its meal," said the detective.

"Oh, yes that brings me to the next aspect of this case," said the coroner reaching for some reports from the file.

"Time of death just after one in the morning and his body was found later in the morning. Normally even if disturbed animals will always come back to take their prize," said the coroner.

"Another thing." Said the coroner reaching for another report.

"A quick look at the blood group raises another mystery. The victim's blood group is A and the other blood type presumably of the animal is B as in B humans?" The coroner stopped and looked at the detective.

"What? Are you sure, there must be a mix up," said the detective reaching for the rest of the file. He read the file for some time and stood up. He paced forward and backward. He stood close to the window and looked outside. After a bit, he looked at the coroner.

"How is that possible?"

Asked the detective. The detective and the coroner spoke for some time and they agreed to let the coroner run the test again.

"Let me know when the results are ready," asked the detective leaving the coroner's office. After leaving the coroner's office the detective headed for the crime scene in case he has missed something else. On his way detective Smith was trying to piece together what had happened the night in question. He drove for around twenty minutes and looked in the groove compartment. He took out a CD and played it. He drove for another half an hour before reaching his destination. He got out of his car and rang someone on his phone. He lit his cigarette and started smoking. After five minutes, another car pulled up next to his. "Have you been to the crime lab? Any results?" asked detective Petrov.

"It's a waiting game, partner. But I have been to the coroner's office." Detective Smith paused for a while and puffed his cigarette before stamping on it. They started walking into the park going to the crime scene. Bob had been found dead in the woods by a woman walking her dog. The area was now cordoned off as the police were investigating his murder. No one seemed to know what had happened. His body was found mauled on the left side. He did bleed to death. A rifle that had been fired at least once had been discovered next to him. The detectives were waiting for the ballistic reports as well as DNA. They arrived at the crime scene.

"What do we have here?" asked detective Petrov. "Not sure mate! We have to try to put the pieces together," said detective Smith. They both squatted where the victim's body was found.

"It's tragic you know, the way all this ended," remarked detective Smith.

"How is that?" Asked detective Petrov looking at his partner.

"I remember the victim, some months ago, they had called for help after his daughter saw an animal in these woods," Detective Smith paused for a second before he stood up. He took off his sunglasses and wiped his forehead with the back of his hand. "Remember operation flush out and kill the beast?" asked the detective.

"Who doesn't? I took part remember?" Replied detective Petrov boastingly.

"Yes. He is one of the two man who requested our help. Is not it an irony that he ended up dead at the hands of the beast," said detective Smith looking at his partner.

"Life can be cruel, you know. We did our best ten plus hours." Detective Petrov sounded a little defensive. It was not their fault. They had done everything they could do. Even after killing the fox they stayed for another 5 hours trying to flush out the beast.

"It's not just him you know," said detective Smith.

"What do you mean?" Detective Petrov asked.

"His daughter, his son and his wife too."

Silence broke out. The only sound that could be heard was the sound of the birds in the woods.

"The whole family? Still the beast is still at large?" asked detective Petrov looking around. Detective Petrov had just recently moved to Elliot Lake, Ontario. He had been transferred from Poland as a joint exchange program between Canada and Poland. The former partner of detective Smith had resigned after the deaths of Bob's family. Detective Smith had vowed to find and kill the best. He had tried to reassure Bob that the police were behind him. Only for Bob himself to have been mauled to death by this beast. How tragic this was.

"So how did this happen?" asked detective Petrov. "One afternoon Bob's daughter Tyra, went to her friends' house to play. But for some unknown reason these two girls despite warnings not to go into the woods. Ended up in the woods." Detective Smith paused and touched his nose bridge before taking a long breath.

"Bob's daughter Tyra, was mauled and killed by the beast." He stopped and looked down as if trying to contain his tears.

"What about the other girl? What happened to her?" asked detective Petrov curiously.

"She escaped, went straight home to Tyra's house and told her mum what had happened." He looked at detective Petrov.

"So how did Tyra's mum and brother die? You lost me." asked detective Petrov.

"I coming to that part. That is the most shocking part of this story." Added detective Smith. They all started walking, going to where Tyra and her brother were found, a few feet away.

"As far as I know, this is what happened. After Tyra was mauled to death, Beverly ran home for help. Tyra's mum and son were home. His dad Bob was not home that afternoon. Tyra's mum, Tyra's brother and Beverly ran back into the woods to help Tyra. Beverly had gone there covered in blood. That must have shocked Tyra's mum that she and her son ran into the woods without asking anyone for help." He paused and looked at his partner.

"At this point I would have thought that Tyra's mum

could have called for help first. But for some strange reasons, she went straight into the woods. Her son followed them too. This is the confusing part. Beverly escaped the first time when she was with Tyra, right?" Asked detective Smith looking at his partner who replied.

"Right," he then continued.

"Beverly again escaped unharmed. Both mother and son mauled to death. The beast left Beverly twice. Now you understand why Bob set up Jeremy's house on fire?" Asked detective Smith. Detective Petrov did not answer straight away, he put his fingers in his mouth and started biting his nails.

"So, are you telling me that Bob thought Beverly had something to do with this? I thought you said she was only twelve years old?" asked detective Petrov confused at all this.

"Tyra is the one who was twelve years old. Beverly is only six years old. The night of their deaths, Beverly after witnessing the mauling of Tyra, went to ask for help. She brought Tyra's mum and Tyra's brother followed them. The mother and son got mauled too but Beverly still managed to escape. But this time did not go to look for help. She went straight into her room and stood at the window." Detective Smith paused and knelt at the area where Tyra's mum and son were discovered.

"But I think it makes sense. Beverly might have felt guilty for the deaths of Tyra's mum and son that she locked herself in her room. Would not you think so?" asked detective Petrov.

"It makes sense I agree with you. All this might have traumatized her. In fact, that is what the doctors said," he agreed with his partner.

"So, what was Bob's issue? You said he set Jeremy's house on fire. And as far as I know Jeremy is Beverly's dad. Right?" asked the detective. Detective Smith did not answer straight away, he stood up and cleared his throat.

"Bob was upset that Beverly led all his family to death and did not call for help but instead locked herself in her room." He looked down and continued.

"This is the disturbing part. Bob at one-point tried to break into Jeremy's house because he thought he had seen an animal in Beverly's room. This was way before all this happened. Now you understand. That is why he was so sure that Beverly was the little devil behind all this. At that time, Bob was safe and of sound mind. He was not drinking. He acted as a concerned parent. Jeremy had accused him of being crazy. He apologized as he thought that maybe he might have been mistaken."

"Only for some months down the road you lose all your family to the beast. If you were Bob how would you have reacted? Now you understand why he torched up Jeremy's house. The most saddening part is that in the end he himself is mauled to death by the beast that cleaned out his family." Detective Smith started walking back to where Bob was discovered. "Did Beverly ever said what happened that day?" asked detective Petrov.

"Honestly no. She insisted up to now that she cannot remember anything. She remembers telling Tyra's mum that Tyra was attacked by the beast in the woods. She said that she had no memory of what happened after. She woke up in the woods and went home. Ever since she had been quiet, she stood at the window most of the time before Bob set their house on fire," said detective Smith.

"What did Beverly's doctors say about all this? Was she evaluated?" asked detective Petrov.

"Beverly's doctor concluded that she had experienced traumatic events. She had experienced stressful events that did shutter her sense of security. Watching all three people, being mauled might have made her feel helpless. This situation has left her feeling overwhelmed," said the detective. They spoke for some time about Beverly and after that detective Smith took out a file they had brought with them. He took out a picture of the crime scene showing a rifle. "Let's try to picture out what happened here," Detective Smith gave a copy of the picture of the rifle gun. No one knew what had happened the night Bob died. He had fired at least one shot. The bullet had been found and sent to the crime lab. There were drops of blood found in the surrounding area. The samples were sent to the lab as well. The rifle had been fired and gunpowder was found on Bob's hands and clothes and the barrel of the rifle still smell gunpowder. So, Bob at one-pint tried to kill this beast which had devoured all his family.

"Can, you piece together what might have happened the night in question?" asked detective Petrov looking at his partner.

"Well, I will do my best partner," said detective Smith pausing for a while before continuing.

"Bob, comes into the woods with a loaded rifle, to revenge his family. He has three petrol bombs, a knife and a rifle. But he was drinking too. The beast might have made some noise first, or that he saw the beast first. I am saying this because he had a chance to take a shot at the beast. He shoots the beast before it mauls him. The beast after killing him, it seems is disturbed. Then runs away into hiding failing to have its meal. In the morning, a woman walking down her dog finds his body." He stopped and looked at the other detective waiting for his comments.

"It sounds more like it, your story takes everything into account, the ballistic, the DNA, motive etc. Did you get any reports from the lab yet?" asked detective Petrov.

"We will go there straight after here some reports are ready the lab paged me earlier on," said detective Smith. They talked about this case and the Elliot Lake. Detective Petrov was new in the area and it seemed he had a lot of catching up to do. The two detectives later left the woods and headed to the lab for results. Detective Smith led the way in his car followed by detective Petrov. The two drove to the city after spending some hours in the woods trying to solve Bob's family deaths. It was getting dark by now. They had so many questions unanswered and it only means a lot of work to do ahead of them. They arrived half an hour before the crime lab was about to close for the day. This was intentional as detective Smith knew that this was the best time to get answers and all the results. The lab this time of the day will be analyzing new samples and preparing for the next day. All the results should be in by now. All reports written and about to be handed in and given to the director of the crime investigation department. The crime lab was only a one-year-old. Before the lab was built all samples and evidence were sent to another big city for analysis. This used to make everything take days if not weeks. Detective Smith at times had to travel to another city just to get the results. Most of the results they deal with cannot be passed over the phone. It is sensitive material and any leak can have serious consequences. Cases had been dropped as soon as the crime lab evidence was leaked or corrupted. With the building of this crime lab here in Elliot Lake city this has meant reduced waiting times. The new lab technician sometimes would work over just to get the job done. Detective Smith and Petrov had too much pressure from the Mayor. Operation flush out and kill the beast had been broadcasted all over Ontario. An article appeared in the papers about this. The news crew were there. Detective Smith remembered one resident who was interviewed during the operation. This man was skeptical about the whole thing. He had suggested that the police force should have used the taxpayers resource in a better way. At one-point detective Smith had sympathized with the man. Now more than six months down the line at least four people were dead. The Mayor has been on this case too. How will people vote for him when he cannot protect them? How can four people of one family be killed without the force killing the beast? Even up to now there was no guarantee that the force will do anything about this. Now this explains why the Mayor requested help from Poland in the form of detective Petrov. Poland had had a similar situation, but the issue was instantly resolved as the beast was immediately cornered and killed. A lot was at stake as far as the Mayor was concerned. People vote for heroes, no matter how bad they perform economically, it is what they do in a crisis that they are judged by. They can be bad when it comes to dealing with the economy or finances but if they stand up to the challenge. If they address the peoples worries instantly, then they can be remembered forever. The Mayor knew this, and he was not taking any chances. He wanted the beast dead like yesterday. He had increased funding t o the crime lab and the whole police force. Officers had been patrolling in the park and woods ever since the incidents. Other operations had been carried out to flush and kill the beast but no beast was found. They arrived at the crime lab eagerly for good results as to round up the day.

"You got something for us?" asked detective Smith after entering the crime lab.

"Yes, check with the director all reports for today ready," said the lab technician pointing to the director's office. The crime lab was a big laboratory with state-of-the-art equipment and gadgets. There were different sections inside the lab denoting which field each section dealt with. There was the forensic fingerprints section, the forensic dentistry, the forensic pathology, forensic firearms and ballistic, and the forensic DNA and blood analysis section. All these sections had their own teams and their own lead role man but all answerable to the crime lab director. Thousands of dollars were being spent on research, investigations and analysis. The man in the lab was wearing a white overall coat with rubber gloves and glass protectors. He had a cap on and he always had what looked like a tablet where he kept keying in information. They knocked on the director's door and waited to be invited in. This was different from the coroner's office where you can enter straight away. The director handles sensitive information which should not end up in the hands of the wrong people. They could hear voices coming from inside the office.

It was after nearly five minutes that the director's door was opened and a woman came out. The director came outside and invited the detectives in. On his desk, there were a lot of files in a pile. For him this was the busiest time of the day. Everyone was directed to him. He had to be briefed by everyone. He gave updates on samples and evidence. He approved and signed reports. He was a busy man. He took out a file from his desk as detective Smith and Petrov sat in front of him.

"Yes detectives. I just had a special visit from the Mayor's office. I think you are all aware of the situation. My head is on the line so I guess yours too." The director said this picking up one of the reports from his desk.

"We are aware how important this case is. Yes."

"First the reports. Ballistic, DNA and bloods, whichever is ready," said detective Smith who looked at his partner who nodded in agreement.

"Ok we have the ballistic report, let's see," he paused for a little while scrolling down the report before continuing.

"Oh, yes, the bullet found, correct, fired from the gun. There is a match."

"What about DNA analysis?" asked detective Petrov.

"I was going to come to that, this is the most confusing part of the results," said the director.

"Just like the normal procedure the blood supposedly from the beast was sent for testing together with the victim's blood. At first, we thought we sent the wrong sample. So, the lab requested a saliva test to supplement the blood test. We sent this also from the bite wound." Paused the director sitting up straight in his chair.

"So, what is the issue?" asked detective Petrov. There was a moment of silence before the director continued.

"For some unknown reason both the sample are human. Honestly. I had my lab repeat these. 100% human." The director looked really astonished.

"The saliva from the bite wound?" asked detective Smith. "Yes. Like I said human." Replied the director reaching out for a file on a pile on his desk.

"Look, the blood type of the victim is A, and that of the beast is B which is in the human category. Further analysis of blood also supported that blood is human." They all looked surprised, and the detectives sunk their heads in the report at the same time trying to figure out the possible reason.

"So how to tell it's not animal blood?" asked the detective. The director cleared his throat and replied. "The analysis of the composition and percentages of cells in humans and animals are different." He paused and took a report which was in front of him before continuing.

"At the lab, they have a sample they used to check against. They have all the percentages of different cells found in animal blood and they use this to analyze the results. In this case both blood samples made human blood by 99.99%. If this was animal blood, the percentage of different cells would be far different. Per the lab both blood types are human." The director stood up and paced left to right in his office before asking for any questions.

"Yes. One other thing. What was the results of the saliva taken from the bite wound?" asked detective Petrov.

"Saliva test, the sample was human too. The lab

looked at things like the saliva PH, the compound, and ratios. Human saliva has more amylases which help in the breakdown of polysaccharides in our food directly in the mouth whereas animal saliva does not have these. A toxicology report also indicated that the saliva is human. It had no bacteria or virus that are often found in animal saliva. Therefore, the blood and saliva test indicates that the blood and saliva is human." The director sat in his chair and asked for more questions. The detectives were even more puzzled about this case.

"Another thing before you even asked, I asked for a second opinion and sent the samples to a private forensic laboratory. The lady who was in here the time you arrived confirmed the results as well. The blood and saliva are all human."

"What about the bite marks imprinted on the skull? What kind of animal was that?" asked detective Smith.

"Results now are inconclusive but the initial feeling is that the animal belongs to the feline, particularly the pantherinae. That is the big cats group, the tigers, lion, jaguar and the cheaters. A look at the jaw pattern and dimensions of the mouth and teeth points out to either a lion or a tiger," said the director. The two detectives looked at each other in shock. They could not believe that an animal like that was lurking around. They had spent the whole day in the woods. Surely another flush out operation was needed.

"Look detectives, this should not leave this room. I gave my word to the Mayor that this information is classified and should not end up in the public circles. Just imagine four known deaths and how many more we do not know about, all this make the situation look bad and the fact that the animal is still at large, is bad for anyone let alone the Mayor. This will not be good for the Mayor." The director seemed concerned and uncomfortable of keeping this secret. He continued.

"Today I have had a one-to-one talk with the Mayor. He told me that tonight there will be a major operation which is to be carried out in secrecy. As far as I know a stronghold of fifty police officers and soldiers is to be deployed tonight to flush out and kill the animal. The Mayor insisted that there was no need to frighten the already worried public. His aim is to kill the animal then inform the public after instead of the other way around." He looked at the two detectives. This made a lot of sense if there is immediate action taken. It seems they just must wait. Hopefully this will give them something to work on as all leads had dried up. The detectives left the director's office with more questions than answers and an even more disturbing twist to this case.

"Fire! Fire!" Shouted a passerby as Jeremy's house was burning. Jeremy was not home but was still at work. His wife was sleeping in the bedroom. Beverly was in her room as far as her mum was concerned. he terrified passerby was trembling as he saw the house on fire. He quickly ran to the door to see if there were people inside. He banged the front door but there was no answer. He decided to break-in and check if the house was empty. He broke the front door and checked all the ground-floor rooms. They were all empty. He went upstairs and smoke was everywhere making it hard to breathe and see. He shouted to make sure there was no one inside.

"Fire! Anyone home?" Shouted the passerby but

there was no reply. He went back downstairs and tried to call for help.

"What's, your emergency?" asked the operator.

"The house is on fire. I cannot breathe and I cannot see upstairs I am not sure if there is someone inside!" shouted the passerby.

"What is the address? Is it your house?" asked the operator.

"I don't know the address. It is not my house." He coughed for some time as smoke was building up before continuing.

"I was just passing by…."

He did not finish his sentence before the operator interrupted.

"Give us your location. Name of street. Anything!" Said the operator.

"It's in Elliot Lake. I am using the landline from the burning house to make this call."
Said the passerby.

"Okay. Just a moment."

There was a moment of silence before the operator was back on the line.

"Ok vacate the building as soon as possible and wait for the fire brigade outside."

The line went dead after that. The passerby was faced with a tough choice. Either to go outside for safety or to go and check if there was someone upstairs. This was a split-second decision to make. He then ran upstairs. The first door was not locked. He entered inside and shouted if anyone was in there. But after struggling to breathe and difficulties seeing clearly, he left knowing that there was no one inside. He rushed to the second room. This was locked. He skipped this room and to the next room. This was filled with smoke too but it was not locked. He quickly checked the room. There was no one inside too. Quickly he ran to the other room. By this time, he was struggling to breathe. The room was not locked, and it seemed as if someone was still in bed. He tried to wake her up, but she was unconscious. He carried her down the stairs staggering all the way. He took her outside and by this time a crowd had gathered outside and he could hear the sirens of the fire brigade approaching. The people who were outside helped him and the lady was put to safety but she was unconscious. They did what they can to help her. Quickly someone phoned for the ambulance. When the woman he brought out was safe, the passerby ran back into the house. This time the smoke was so heavy that he could not breathe or see clearly. He remembered that the door was locked, and he knew there was a chance that there could be someone inside. He went to that room to check if he can break the door. He staggered upstairs shouting. He approached the door and tried to push the door. Last time he had checked the door the door was locked. He was sure he had found the door locked earlier on when he tried to open it. The door opened, he stopped for a while outside the door, trying to breathe before he ventures inside. He was about to enter the room when he heard a large growling sound coming from inside the room. He immediately turned back and ran as fast as he could downstairs. Two fire engines immediately parked outside the house followed by an ambulance. The four fire crews ran upstairs wearing breathing masks to check if there was still anyone left in the house. They went upstairs and found Beverly who was unconscious. They brought her to safety. Both Nancy and Beverly were taken to the hospital by the ambulance. The fire crews fought a huge battle to try to put out the fire that had nearly engulfed the rooftop. The fire crews committed themselves to tackling the blaze, they were wearing breathing apparatus, and they used high-powered water jets to bring the huge fire under control. Jeremy wanted to die the time he came back from work to find his house in flames. He had tried to ran into the burning house but was told by the fire crew that his family were going to be fine. He was told that they had been taken to the hospital. He left as soon as he heard this heading to the hospital. The passerby had gone in the ambulance too which carried Nancy and her daughter Beverly. They were still unconscious and at the suggestion of the nurse he just hopped in. Everything happened so fast that he was assumed to be relative. They were both hospitalized as they were still unconscious. It was thought that smoke had made them fall unconscious. Jeremy on arrival went straight to see his wife and daughter. He spoke to the doctor responsible for her.

"What can you tell me doctor about my wife?" asked Jeremy.

"Your wife is unconscious, due to carbon monoxide poisoning. Now my priority is to stabilize her condition. We have provided oxygen and plenty of fluids. We are prepared for any seizures as well. As far as I know I think she will be around after a few minutes, an hour at most." Said the doctor trying to comfort and reassure Jeremy.

"What about my daughter, Beverly?" asked Jeremy.

"I guess you have to check with the pediatrician in the children's ward," replied the doctor. Jeremy left heading to the children's ward. On arrival, he was introduced to the pediatrician looking after his daughter.

"What can you tell me about my daughter, Beverly?" asked Jeremy.

"Your daughter is unconscious but in a stable condition. We have stabilized her," said the doctor.

"Is she going to be fine?" asked Jeremy.

"Yes. She is going to be okay. One other thing, is that she has suffered a wound, but she is going to be fine," replied the pediatrician.

"Wound. What kind of wound?" asked Jeremy. "Something might have injured her during the fire we don't know for sure but rest assured she is going to be fine." Soon afterwards the doctor left and Jeremy spent some time with his daughter. After receiving a phone call detective Smith and detective Petrov headed to the hospital. They discussed the case on their way to the hospital. They looked at the report from the fire brigade. This was possibly an attempted homicide. The fire brigade had indicated that the fire was started intentionally. They had discovered drums of petrol and possibly used petrol bombs. At the hospital, they met Jeremy and comforted him at these difficult times. They requested to speak to his wife and his daughter and the doctors concerned. Beverly had a wound, and the passerby was interviewed by the detectives because of this.

"Good evening Sir, we heard you helped with the rescue operation. We understand you were the first at the scene?" asked detective Smith.

"Yes, I was passing by when I saw the house on fire." He paused and looked at the detectives before continuing.

"I was terrified, so I ran inside to check if anyone was still inside," said the passerby.

"Who did you rescue and what happened?" asked detective Petrov.

"I found the woman upstairs unconscious. I carried her outside," he stopped talking.

"Yes, carry on. And what happened?" asked detective Smith.

"Has something gone wrong? I only tried to help." remarked the passerby.

"Yes, we know, you are not a suspect we just want to know what happened." Said the detective.

"Ok, I went back inside to check if someone was there. But there was no one. It was very dark and I could not breathe. So, I came out. That is what happened."

The passerby looked at the two detectives as one of them was writing notes.

"What about the young girl? Why you left her?" asked detective Petrov.

"Like I said earlier on. I did not see any girl. One door was locked and I could not open it." Said the passerby.

"Why did you leave the girl in there?" asked again detective.

"I didn't see any girl. The door was locked," replied the passerby.

"The report by the fire brigade indicated that the door was open in the room the girl was found. So, you mean to say that all these people are lying?" asked the detective.

"Closed or not closed. I do not care. I risked my life and now you worry me about whether the door was locked or not," shouted the passerby who was angry at the detectives.

"I don't like your tone and your line of questioning," added the passerby getting annoyed now. They looked at each other and tried a different line of questioning.

"We are asking you these questions because the girl was injured. We think the injury has nothing to do with the fire," remarked detective Smith.

"So, if the wound has nothing to do with the fire so what do you want from me," asked the passerby before continuing.

"I told you I went in there because of the fire. I was worried and frightened that someone might be trapped inside."

He stopped talking and looked at the detective. "Clarify this, you said you found out that the door was locked then you went on to rescue the other woman?" asked the detective.

"After rescuing the lady, you still went back in, is that correct?" asked the detective.

"That's correct," replied the passerby.

"When you went back inside was the door still locked?" asked the detective.

"Everything happened so fast. I could not breathe. It was very dark because of the fumes."

He told the detectives and waited for the next question.

"I repeat. When you went back inside the house was the door still locked?" Asked the detective.

"Does that really matter?" asked the passerby.

"Yes, the fire brigade's report indicates that the door was forced open. They are 100% sure it was not them who forced it open. There was no one else in the house apart from you. The girl was injured. We think she was stabbed by a sharp object as she lay in bed. This is how serious this is. So, start telling us the truth?" Said detective Smith changing his voice tone. The passerby realized why the fire brigade and the ambulance service had insisted that he come to the hospital with the family. Surely, he was equally confused by all this but he was harboring a secret, or was he?

"Ok. I will tell you what happened, but I did not harm anyone. I am telling you the truth the door was unlocked." He stopped talking and looked at the two detectives.

"Ok we are listening." Said detective Petrov.

The passerby took a long breath and continued with his story.

"I went inside, the first time the door was locked. I failed to open it. I tried to break it down but I could not. I thought that first I check the other rooms, which I did and found the woman in questioned unconscious. I took her outside. I went back in again to check the other rooms. All the other rooms were empty apart from that room that was locked. I could not breathe at one-point that I stopped walking. I picked up myself and went to the room with the locked door. I was prepared to knock the door open but this time to my surprise the door was open."

He paused and looked at the detectives who in turn all looked at each other waiting to hear what he was going to say next.

"I must say that I have never been so confused in my entire life than I am right now. At one-point, I thought that I was hallucinating. But I am sure that the door was locked at first. Otherwise I could not have proceeded to the room further down the corridor when this room was open and there was a person who needed help."

He paused and touched his face with both his hands. "After the first rescue when I went back inside, the door was open. I touched the door to judge how far I had to swing to break it down, but the door was open. I panicked and stopped. Was someone else in the house? I asked myself. I was about to rush inside the room when I heard the most frightening growling sound I have ever heard. I thought there was an animal inside. I panicked I was frightened and terrified, human instincts kicked-in. I ran downstairs as fast as I can. Pinching myself." He paused and showed the detectives the pinching marks on his arm. "They say smoke and fumes from the burning fire can make you hallucinate, so up to now I don't know what to believe. When the fire crew went inside, I was 1000% sure that they were going to come out running as well. But to my shock surprise they came out with this unconscious sweet little girl. So, I agreed to come here to the hospital, so that someone tells me that I am not hallucinating."

They both looked at each other. Detective Smith, decided to take the passer-by to the police station so that they can take a statement. He asked detective Petrov to stay at the hospital and keep an eye on Nancy and Beverly. Detective Petrov went to have a chart with Beverly's doctor.

"I am detective Petrov, how is the girl doing?" He asked the doctor.

"She is stable and she will be fine soon," said the doctor.

"Doc what can you tell me about this case?" asked the detective.

"Hard to say. At one-point, I thought she had a gun wound, but I later ruled that possibility. She could have been spiked by anything during the fire," said the doctor.

"Can I have a quick look at her?" asked the detective.

"Only if you don't wake her up. She need a lot of sleep".

"Ok thank you doctor."

Detective Petrov was afraid that anything can happen, he thought to himself. He gathered his courage and entered Beverly's hospital room. She looked like any other young girl. He went to check the wound. Definitely. A gun wound. He stood there beside her hospital bed trying to understand what was going on. He checked her body for any marks. She was clean, so he went back to sit down. Detective Smith and Eddie the passer-by were heading to the police station to get Eddie's statement. They drove for about half an hour, and detective Smith phoned his partner to check if Beverly was ok. She was in her bed and fast asleep. After some time, detective Petrov fell asleep in his chair. Half an hour later he was woken up by a huge sound of glass breaking. He ran into Beverly's room and found her peacefully sleeping in her bed. He touched her pulse to check if she was still breathing. Everything was ok. The only thing he noticed was different was the position she was now sleeping in. He went outside quickly to check what had made such a loud noise. As he was rushing out of the room, he remembered slipping and promptly managing to get his balance back. It seemed the floor was slippery, but he did not bother too much about that. The front entrance glass door bottom panel had been broken. There was a large hole. He circled the hospital grounds holding his gun in his hand. He shortly came back and checked inside the building. It seemed everything was ok. Drug addicts sometimes did that for them to enter the hospital and steal medicine to sell. He went to Beverly's room; she was there sleeping peacefully. He went back to sit in his chair. After 20 minutes his partner detective Smith rung him.

"Check Beverly. Is she in her room?" asked detective Smith.

"Why? Is everything ok?" asked detective Petrov.

He ran into Beverly's room. She was there.

"Yes, she is in her bed?" replied detective Petrov. Half an hour later, he had started to doze off, when he heard thumping on the ground. He heard what sounded like footsteps coming his way. He looked in the corridor but saw nothing suspicious. He was about to stand up when he saw watery footprints being printed on the floor. Fear struck him, he looked on as the footprints went into Beverly's room. He took out his gun and followed into Beverly's room. Only to find out that the girl was still asleep. Detective Smith and Eddie had a head-on collision with a lorry that night. No one survived the crash and their bodies were taken to the morgue. The next day detective Petrov was notified about detective Smith death. All this traumatized him. They had both thought that it was Beverly, but the poor girl slept all night. That explained why she had no memory about events surrounding Bob's family deaths. In the Mayor's office, the Mayor is very upset. He is addressing a meeting. There are so many people in the conference room. The head of the police, the director of national service, the director of the crime lab, the commander of the army. The detective and many others.

"I don't understand how an animal can cause such havoc and worry the people so much when we have the finest expertise in the world," paused the Mayor looking at everyone one by one.

"Can someone tell me what the major problem is? More than six months now, with seven officially recorded deaths caused by this animal yet no one seem to know why the animal is still at large. Detective what is the latest on this issue." asked the Mayor.

"My partner died a few weeks ago,"

Detective Petrov paused and looked at the Mayor who seemed not to care very much. To him this was the make it or break of politics. Just a few weeks ago, he seemed to have everything under control and now he was to lose everything just because the very best personnel have failed to contain this animal.

"We are sorry to hear that," said the Mayor. There was a moment of silence.

"I don't know for sure what to say. Is it an animal or not? No one knows. All the lab results suggested that the killer was human," said the detective. Dimitri is at the hospital with his daughter. She is two months old now. It had been two months since Dimitri laid his wife to rest. His daughter is growing very fast. In recent weeks, he had noticed some health issues that he arranged an appointment with the children's doctor.

"Doctor, I have noticed that my daughter sometimes sleeps for days without waking up. At first I thought it was part of growing up but I think there is something wrong with her," said Dimitri.

"If it's just sleeping then there is nothing wrong. Sleeping is a sign of a healthy growing up baby," replied the doctor.

"She literary slept for days without working up. She was breathing normally but unresponsive if I call her name. The day she woke up, she acted as if she had woken up from a trance. Looked disoriented and cried all the time." He said to the doctor.

"I have to run some test, bloods, etc. first then we can take it from there," paused the doctor before continuing. It could be nothing so don't you worry I know it's hard to raise a baby alone."

The doctor tried to comfort Dimitri.

"My main worry is that her mother had the same condition before she died. One day I came back from work and she had slept for more than twenty hours without waking up. Her pulse was faint that I thought she had died."

He paused for a while and looked at the doctor.

"The day she died I think she fell unconscious again and never woke up. I am afraid that my daughter might have the same condition as Enya." The doctor realized that there could be something wrong with the babe for sure.

"Ok, I will arrange for tests to be carried out as soon as possible and a check-up straight away." The doctor took his clipboard and started writing something down.

"So how often this has happened? When is the last time this has happened?" asked the doctor taking the baby's temperature.

"Not sure but I think two times with the last occurrence two days ago," said Dimitri.

"You told that her mother had the same condition,

had she been to the doctor regarding the condition and what did the doctors say?" asked the doctor looking at the baby.

"The doctor said this was due to some form of poisoning. She used to cook all the time," said Dimitri.

"Did she hallucinated, felt dizziness, headaches vomiting and memory loss?" asked the doctor.

"Yes, but we thought this was due to pregnancy. The doctor later said this was due to carbon monoxide and asked her not to cook often and to ensure proper ventilation," the doctor wrote down some notes. "Any other issues you want to add to this."

"There is something that's bothering me. The baby has a strange marking on her back since the day she was born. I have asked most people I know but I cannot seem to get any answers. I thought since you work with children you might have heard of similar issues," Dimitri did not know what to do or who to trust anymore. He showed the doctor the tattoo at the back of the baby.

"Is it a tattoo? How did you get that done on a two-month-old? I have never seen anything like this before. Who had this done? I do not know what to say. It is not the kind of things we see every day. The detail is astonishing. It looks like the tattoo has been drawn by a sophisticated computer," the doctor could not believe his eyes. In his entire life, he had never seen anything like this before. At one-point, he felt frightened. Did this had something to do with the mystery sleeping sickness or not? Surely this was beyond medicine.

"Have you asked at the church, I mean regarding the tattoo?" asked the doctor. "Not only you know about the tattoo. Even my wife died before she had the chance to see the tattoo," he paused and looked at his daughter.

"The first time I saw the tattoo was the moment after birth but the tattoo then had no ink, I mean the black markings". Dimitri looked at the doctor before continuing to talk to the doctor.

"The first time she had that sleeping sickness is the first time the tattoo was blackened. Every time she goes into that state, when she gets up the tattoo will be more pronounced and more black-inked." He looked at the doctor who now had removed his reading glasses.

"So, are you saying that the tattoo is growing up as well?" asked the doctor.

"I can't say for sure but it seems that way," said Dimitri.

"Ok first we have to look at this medically. Bloods, scans, etc. Then after that we look at the tattoo etc," said the doctor. After all the tests, had been down, Dimitri came back to hear the result.

"Yes, all results point to carbon monoxide poisoning but the levels in your daughter's blood are consistent with house fire cases. Which is disturbing I must say," he looked even more worried about Dimitri's daughter.

"I think I have to hospitalize your daughter to stabilize her. The carboxyhemoglobin is high in your daughter's blood. That means she has less oxygen in her blood," said the doctor.

"The scans also show an accumulation of brain fluids in the form of water." There was a moment of silence before the doctor continued explaining.

"Mainly this is due to carbon monoxide poisoning or

seriously due to exposure to radiation although this is highly unlikely," after two days of scans and tests and more treatment the baby was well and fine to go home so father and daughter were released from the hospital. Months after the hospital visit Dimitri had been to the Orthodox church for strength and courage following the death of his wife. He had confided to the Chief Bishop of the church about his daughter's issues. The Bishop had emphasized the power of prayer to overcome evil the tattoo was the mark of the devil. The beast was going to kill people, and the baby was a vessel of the devil.

CHAPTER FIVE

Six years later in Virginia state USA, Nick is a 9 years old boy born to Elinka and Tony. He is in the primary school kindergarten grade. His father Tony is a software engineer who got made redundant few years ago. Ever since he had been a self-employed software engineering consultant and life had been difficult as it had been hard getting lucrative contracts. At school Nick, had met a friend called Eva. She was two years younger than him but because she was very smart, she had skipped other grades and was in the same class as Nick. Her mum had insisted that she skips other grades. She passed the examinations of the lower grades with flying colors. When they first met up Nick thought that Eva was lost. It had nothing to do with the way she acted or reacted. It was simply by how young she looked to Nick. Nick offered to help.

"Hello. My name is Nick. I think you are in the wrong

class. Are you lost?" asked Nick really concerned and politely.

"No I am fine. This is my class, I am sure!" said Eva looking at Nick who seemed surprised.

"You look too young to be in here, six or seven years old? I am nine years old so surely one of us is mistaken here," said Nick so sure that Eva was in the wrong class.

"Listen. I think someone is too dumb to be in this class. How about that? I am not naming and shaming today, I am in good spirits today, people!" said Eva cunningly swinging from left to right. Eva was very upset that she fainted after trying to hit Teddy. Nick called an ambulance and went with Eva to the hospital after ringing his and Eva's parents to let them know about what happen.

"What happened?" asked the doctor at the hospital looking at Nick.

"She is my friend. She defended me today. She fainted after fighting off a bully at school. I still cannot believe it up to now. How can he do that? This bully knocked me to the ground. If it was not for her who knows what might have befallen me. But thanks to her. She has been my hero today; you know what I mean! Please make sure she will be fine. Okay doc?" replied Nick.

"Don't you worry young man, I will do my best to make sure that your friend is safe and sound in no time at all," replied the doctor with a big smile on his face winking his right eye.

"Has this happened before to Eva? Has Eva's parent's been informed?" asked the doctor more concerned for her well-being.

"This is the first time I have witnessed this doctor.

Yes, Eva's parents are on their way here," replied Nick. Ever since that incident Eva and Nick's friendship became much stronger. They had recently moved to the suburban area in the same street as Nick. Eva had spent most of the time with Nick and at times had slept at Nick's house. After three months of the incident Nick visited Eva's house. They had planned to meet that day. For unknown reasons Eva, did not turn up to Nick's surprise. Nick went to Eva's parents' home to find out why Eva did not turn up. It was like any other day warm with a cool breeze. Nick had eagerly looked forward to this day. He rang the doorbell but there was no answer so he knocked the door. Still no one answered. He leaned on the door waiting for someone to answer and the door suddenly opened. He pushed the door slowly and entered the house.

"Hello, it's Nick, anyone home?" shouted Nick as he enters the corridor area.

"Eva, where are you are you home?" shouted Nick looking forward to see Eva. He stopped at the bottom of the stairs and shouted again.

"Eva, it's Nick! Where are you?" he started climbing the stairs going upstairs. His heart beating very fast. He went to Eva's room and knocked the door.

"Eva it's Nick. Are you?" he leaned on the door listening with his ear against the door. The door was not locked he staggered inside.

"Eva, Eva! Are you okay? Can you hear me?" shouted Nick. He nearly got a heart attack when he saw Eva lying down on the floor. He checked if she was breathing and quickly and carefully lifted her to her bed.

"Wait, I'm coming back soon I am going to get help,"

said Nick as he rushed outside Eva's room. He felt like he had flown down from upstairs to where the phone was.

"Hello, Hello. I need an ambulance as soon as possible my friend is unconscious. Please hurry! Will you?" pleaded Nick. He gave the operator Eva's address.

"Remain on the line until the ambulance has arrived," ordered the operator. Nick left the handset on the table and decided to check upon Eva. Two three steps up the stairs he stopped and stood there speechless. He was totally flabbergasted he looked upstairs, Eva was just coming downstairs. He looked at her and he felt goosebumps. He did not know how he got to the top of the stairs he only remembered hugging Eva and lifting her up.

"Hey, I am glad you are okay! I was very worried about you. I have already called the ambulance. What happened to you?" Marveled Nick. Nick looked closer and noticed first that the girl had changed clothes. Hmm that was fast he thought to himself. There was something different about this Eva. She did not react to him as he had expected. Nevertheless, Nick hysterically jumped up and down happy to see her.

"Come downstairs I will phone again that we don't need the ambulance," said Nick grabbing the girl's hand and running downstairs with her.

"She tried to say something but Nick was concerned about canceling the request for an ambulance. Nick picked up the phone and before he dialed a number, the girl put her hand on his mouth. He looked at her. She tried to speak but murmured something. Nick looked at her and froze.

"Your eyes! Eva your eyes!" said Nick, gob smacked, holding the girl's hands looking straight into her eyes. Nick remembered Eva telling her that she was an only child. After, sometime, the girl spoke something in Russian language. Nick did not understand, so she holds Nick's hand and dragged him upstairs with her to Eva's room. Astonished Nick stood in Eva's bedroom speechless.

"Who are you? How did you get in here? Are you Eva's twin sister?" asked Nick looking deep into the girl's green shining eyes.

"Nyet," replied the girl.

"Can you speak English?" asked Nick.

"Nyet," replied the girl.

"What's your name?" asked Nick curiously.

"E-w-a, Ewalinka," said the girl as if drawing in the air her name. The ambulance crew arrived before he had a chance to ask her a lot of questions. They ambulance crew rushed upstairs to Eva's room and carried her to the ambulance outside. Nick went together as well. He insisted that the new girl Ewa go with them but she vehemently refused. He watched her as the ambulance left Eva parents' house. As soon as the ambulance set off, she ran toward them following the ambulance for a while but the ambulance sped off leaving her standing in the middle of the road. She stood there until the ambulance disappeared. Nick could not wait for Eva to wake up so he could tell her about Ewalinka. After hours of waiting impatiently in the hospital finally the doctors informed Nick that Eva was awake. Nick was very happy, and he rushed in Eva's room. Eva, Eva. You are two! There is another girl just like you. She is called….," Nick did not finish talking as Eva interrupted him.

"What! Another girl. What girl?" asked Eva.

"This one has green eyes, but she looks just like you," said Nick sitting on Eva's hospital bed. Eva looked at Nick baffled. Nick got up and hysterically screamed. "Your eyes! Your eyes Eva! What is going on?" asked Nick confused.

"What are you yawning about? My eyes what Nick? What is wrong?" asked Eva looking at Nick who was speechless.

"Are you wearing contact lenses?" asked Nick calming down.

"No, should I?" asked Eva.

"Why your eyes are green they have always been blue? Who are you? Are you Ewalinka? How did you get here? What is going on? Are you playing games with me? It is not funny you know!" exclaimed Nick sitting down on the bed.

"My eyes green why? What are you talking about?" asked Eva

"The other girl at home is called Ewa too she looks just like you and she has green eyes," said Nick getting closer to Eva.

"Stop talking about the other girl. There is only me and no one else," said Eva standing up to look at herself in the mirror on the wall.

"Ah! What happened to my eyes?" screamed Eva in shock.

"Now you believe me?" asserted Nick. Nick and Eva looked confused and did not know what to say. By the time, they got home the other girl Ewa had disappeared, she was gone. Four weeks later Ewalinka met Eva and Nick at school. This was the first time the girls had met. It was like looking yourself in the mirror for both. Since that first encounter both girls had green eyes and same hair color. There was nothing to differentiate the two with apart from the clothes they were wearing. When the two girls met and hold hands they somehow connected. Ewalinka had come to Virginia alone. The fact that they looked identical made sense to Eva. She knew what was required of her. The four weeks Ewalinka was away, she was learning to speak English. Now she could speak in English. For some unknown reason the three became good friends. Since the day, they met Ewalinka and Eva never separated. Ewalinka move into Eva's house, and they lived together switching and taking turns so that Eva's parents will not know. It was weeks after Ewa moved in that Eva's parents started noticing some unusual behavior. Ewa sometimes unaware would speak to her mum in Russian language and then later apologize.

"When did you learn to speak Russian language?" asked Eva's mum.

"Why nowadays you talk to yourself in your room?"

"Is everything ok?" asked Eva's mum concerned about her daughter's welfare.

"Mum I will come back soon wait for me," said Ewalinka getting up and returning to Eva's bedroom. Eva quickly came out to properly address her mum. "What were you saying mum sorry I had to get something from my room first?" explained Eva.

"How did you manage to change your clothes so fast? I was asking you when you learned to speak Russian. I have noticed that nowadays sometimes you speak to me in Russian language," explained Eva's mum.

"I am learning Russian language at school mum," said Eva.

"Why you never mentioned that to me before, Eva my daughter," asked Eva's mum.

"Just wanted to surprise you, mum, I was so sure that I would be able to learn it," said Eva. Since that day, Eva started to learn to speak Russian language both at school and at home. Since the day Ewalinka arrived Eva grew stronger and stronger. She never had sleeping sickness again. Ewalinka and Eva are in the bedroom talking to each other.

"Ewalinka, so if the saying is correct so where are the others. How did you find me if you came all the way from Russia?" asked Eva fascinated by the idea of having a double.

"I fell into a trance, I slept for days. In my dream, I saw Nick not you. It is Nick I came for. It is Nick who directed me in my dream. I saw his face in my dreams. I can feel him. I never knew you existed. I did not sense you because you were in a trance the time I arrived. I felt Nick and came into your house," said Ewalinka.

"So, you came for Nick!? Wait a minute let me get this straight. You came for Nick! That is, it? You didn't know I even existed. But how come you look like me? Would it make sense that you did come for me, maybe your twin sister, just for argument's sake," suggested Eva.

"I know it sounds harsh, but sister that's a fact."

"So why Nick, I don't get it," asked Eva playing the jealous game.

"Not sure yet but he is our link. He is from the bloodline of the Emperor as far as I know," said Ewalinka.

"Don't be absurd, there are no Emperors anymore. Nick bloodline of the Emperor? Do not make me laugh! Nothing royal about that dude. The guy is a jerk if you ask me. He is two years older than us but we are in the same grade as him," uttered Eva feeling a bit jealous and annoyed. We are here to serve him not to judge him," said Ewalinka. One Saturday afternoon Nick was playing outside. When the two girls, Ewa and Eva arrived he had already finished doing his homework. When Nick's father asked about the girls Nick told him that they were twin sisters. Nick welcomed his two friends, introduced them to his father, and they went upstairs to Nick's room. This is the first time both the girls had visited Nick. He was very excited especially when Ewalinka confessed that she came all the way from Russia for him. He felt like some kind of hero. He quickly got some puzzles and games to keep his friends entertained. He went outside his room into the kitchen to fetch some soft drinks. When he returned both Ewalinka and Eva fell asleep into a trance in Nick's room. He remembered the first time he found Eva unconscious and the first day he met Ewalinka. The girls had told him what to do if they both fall into a trance. He kept the room well ventilated and placed a wet cloth on their foreheads. Excitedly he knew someone else had arrived. Excitedly he ran downstairs nearing falling over and straight outside to check. He looked around very enthusiastic. There was no one outside.

"Damn what might have happened," the spoke to himself aloud. He turned around, and he went back in the house. As soon as Nick had opened the door, he heard his father shouting at him. He pinched himself in disbelief. Honestly it was hard for him to believe that this was happening.

"Nick! Nick! One of the twin girls is here looking for you," shouted his dad peeping from the lounge area looking at Nick. He went in the lounge area. He could not believe his eyes.

"I am Nick, and you are?" asked Nick as he stretched his arm.

"Jeva, Jevalina," replied the girl. Nick quickly invited her upstairs. After sometime the two girls woke up and Nick introduced Jevalina.

"Ladies I present to you Jevalina. Jevalina this is Eva and Ewa," said Nick pointing at the two ladies sitting on the bed. Jevalina looked surprised. It was looking at yourself in the mirror. She walked closer to them. They all had gray eyes. The other two girls after looking at Jevalina they looked at each other and both nodded simultaneously.

"Waal, I didn't know I have sisters," yelled Jevalina in shock and disbelief.

"Is it just the two of you or there are others coming?" asked Jevalina wanting to know.

"No one really knows. I am glad you are here with us. Welcome Jevalina."

Answered Nick. Jevalina touched the other girl's hair caressing it slowly.

"What is the color of your eyes? I know mine are gray?" asked Jevalina.

"Blue."

"Green."

The girls answered at the same time. Nick noticed that whoever comes first will have more power to put the others in a deep sleep. The deep sleep was necessary for the other girls to adjust and match the appearance of the new arrival especially eye color. It is hard for the new arrival to match those who have arrived first. Jevalina had come on her own. She had no idea about the other girls until they have met. Nick realized that the only way forward was for all the girls to wear identical clothes. Nick spoke to his dad, who was willing to help. The two girls stayed in the house, Nick, Eva and Nick's dad went to the city for shopping. They bought identical clothes for all the girls. After that the three girls went to Eva's parents' house where they lived together. By the time it was the Christmas festive; there were seven girls altogether all identical staying at Eva's parent's house. Whenever there was a new arrival those who had arrived first would fall in a trance and their eye color would change to match that of the new arrival. When the last girl arrived from South Terras Cornwall England they all gathered together, they spoke for a long time and all of them fell in a trance. After a few hours, they all woke up with one blue and one green eyes. There was no need to choose the leader by casting of stones. It seemed the gods had chosen a leader in Eva and all agreed for Eva to be the leader as she provided accommodation, assistance and other leadership skills. They all wore identical clothes. "Dad. We need your help. We need to raise a lot of money through the internet. The girls have ideas we need a software platform to launch our project," explained Nick to his dad.

"Oh, I see son. There are a lot of social platforms out there just for that. But I guess you want a special one for yourself. Correct?" Asked his father rubbing Nick's head.

"Correct dad. I just thought hey what is the hack? If my dad is the best software engineer in the whole world why use what everyone else use? Why not have our own designed," explained Nick hugging his dad who smiled and replied.

"You are right there. Give me time I will see what I can do."

"Do you have any titles, names in mind?" quizzed Nick's father.

"How about Cool Nick and the Beauty Angels?" suggested Nick with a big smile on his face.

"Sound cool," replied his father.

"Or how about, Nick the Man, here to dominate and rule the world?" bragged Nick sitting next to his dad.

"Sounds like you are looking for trouble. You do not want to invite enemies for yourself son? Do you?" asked Nick's dad.

"No, dad. Maybe I should ask the girls too," suggested Nick.

"Sure Son. Pick their brains. Work together, I think they have your best interests. I have never seen you so determined and happy. I think the girls have been a blessing." Remarked Nick's dad. Nick went to talk to the girls later that day.

"My dad is designing our own website so that we can raise a lot of money."

"That is great, I think that is the way to go about it. Your dad is cool Nick. What is the name of the website have you decided yet?" asked Eva.

"Not really, he thought we should all talk about this," replied Nick looking at Eva.

"But I have decided, Cool Nick and the Beauty Angels," continued Nick.

"Waal, we are the Beauty Angels now?" asked Eva, giggling and laughing. She called the other girls. "Beauty Angels! Beauty Angels! Your presence required here. Come now." shouted Eva calling the other girls with a big smile on her face. The other girls came into the lounge where Nick and Eva were. "From today we are Nick's Beauty Angels!" said Eva walking like a model swinging around and turning back to look at the other girls lifting her arms in the air above her head. The rest of the girls giggled other clapping hands.

"Sounds all right," replied Jevalina jokingly.

"I thought we are the magnificent seven, that way it would be easy to be recognized worldwide. Most people know the magnificent seven as the protectors of the Emperor. The providers of riches, peace and longevity. It would be easy to raise money that way. This is an established brand we just need to make it our own," suggested Eva seriously.

"The legend has it that the magnificent seven are associated with riches and longevity. I think people would subscribe to that idea. Everyone wants to live a bit longer does not you think?" remarked Ewalinka.

"I agree, it is easy to sell an idea the people are already familiar with as in the legend. That way we do not have to sweat a lot. We just tell everyone about the legend on our website," continued Ewalinka.

"We will be implying that we are the magnificent seven, we can post a video, if people see us how we look they will at least believe the legend. What we need is a way to raise enough cash. Without a sweat. Those who know the legend will be happy to subscribe, I think," added Eva.

"So, ladies how about Nick and the magnificent seven?" asked Nick raising his eyebrows anticipating a yes answer.

"Honestly. Who is Nick? No one knows about Nick," explained Devalinja trying to piss off Nick. There was a moment of silence. They all looked at each other and at Nick who remained silent.

"Look Nick, years ago, it was easy for the magnificent seven to protect the Emperor because the Emperor had his bodyguards and army. The Emperor was feared. No one dared attacked the Emperor or said bad things about the Emperor. Emperors are regarded as Sons of the heavens, therefore feared," continued Devalinja.

"I am not trying to be funny. You know why Emperors never lasted a hundred years let alone thirty? It is because more people wanted what the Emperor had. They had gone all the way to make whatever the Emperor owns theirs. Honestly there is a lot of risks involved. To protect you sometimes mean to protect you from yourself. Your publicity will only get you killed." Explains Devalinja. They all knew that Devalinja had a point.

"Surely someone will want the riches and the powers that comes with this. That will mean your head Nick. The world has changed. I do not know what evil will befall you. But it is best we keep your identity a secret," suggested Devalinja.

"The legend has it that whenever the magnificent seven are born, there will be an Emperor to protect. Whenever they come together after the age of seven it means that the Emperor or someone from his blood line will be ready to be served and be protected. What if someone starts to research about the Emperor surely you will be at risk?" explained Devalinja?

"Ok, I think Devalinja is right we should not publicize you, Nick," acknowledged Eva.

"Ok, I get the point. So, what will be the title of the website?" asked Nick feeling put off.

"The magnificent seven!" shouted Jevalina enthusiastically.

"How about Eva and the magnificent six?" suggested Eva.

"Because our names all sound like the name Eva. Is that so?"

"Why not Jevalina and the magnificent six?" quizzed Jevalina

"No girls, I think it will be best as the magnificent seven," remarked Nick.

"Girls!" Shouted Jevalina.

"I have an idea what do we all have in common?"

"We are all identical and we all have blue eyes," suggested Eva jokingly.

"How about now!"

Teased Beverly changing everyone's eyes color to hazel brown.

"Be serious Beverly!"

Requested Eva after noticing that Beverly had turned everyone's eye color to match hers, hazel brown.

"We all have magical powers, so how about; The girls with the magical powers: The magnificent seven?" asked Ewalinka.

"It will be hard to explain what magical powers we have. Why not just call ourselves; The ruthless killers and hand ourselves to the police?" Queried Eva.

"I have an idea!" Screamed Nick getting up.

"How about; The girl with the tattoo and the magnificent six. That way that will resolve the leadership issue. People often follow people who have a leader already. This title will take account of that."

There was a moment of silence and everyone seemed to agree.

"Wait a minute, it should be; The girl with the tiger tattoo and the magnificent six," argued Eva looking at everyone expecting them to oppose the idea. But to her surprise they all saw the title as fitting as she was the leader of the group. They all started clapping hands and nodding their heads in agreement with Eva.

"The girl with the tiger tattoo and the magnificent six. Yes!" shouted Nick. After a few weeks, Nick's father launched the girl's website.

They launched their crowdfunding page entitled; The girl with the tiger tattoo and the magnificent six. They used the legend of the magnificent seven angels who guarded and protected the Emperor. The legend has it that the gods sent the seven angels to help protect and preserve the bloodline of the Emperor. Wars and assassinations had posed a threat to the survival and continuance of the Emperors' reign and survival of his bloodline. The seven angels had powers to protect and defend the Emperor because of these magnificent seven the Emperor lived for more than a hundred years. The Emperor because of these seven angels, was associated with peace as no one dared attack him, riches as well as those in need of protection paid a small fee in exchange for the Emperor's protection. The Emperor was also associated with longevity. The magnificent seven eliminated the Emperor's enemies in a flush, protected him and served him hence the term, long live the Emperor. As the legend, had it every hundred years the magnificent seven are born to protect and preserve the bloodline of the Emperor. As the word spread around about their website the more subscribers they got. It was only a matter of time before they had serious money. As the word spread the more they became popular. They were invited to ceremonies and parties and had a lot of donations in form of money and goods. They all wore identical clothes, shoes, and all used same mobile phones and had the same cars as well. Most big-name brands had signed them to represent them, securing lucrative contracts from the fashion and technology industries. Soon they were a household name associated with fame and riches. Nick gave his father a lot of money from the donations to start and develop his own business. The girls set up rules that they were to keep to maintain a low profile in terms of trouble making. One Friday afternoon Ewalinka was talking to the rest of the girls.

"Ladies I will be going to the city later in the day, to do some shopping anyone wants to come with me?" asked Ewalinka.

"Do not be late coming back home like last time," said Eva. Ewalinka had gone out and did not come back until the next day. She was disoriented and had memory loss. Every time she gets upset she would go into a trance and the others had been there to avoid the worse.

"Learn to control yourself we all have issues but keep your eyes on the ball. We are here to protect Nick and not start a revolution like some of us want," said Eva sarcastically.

"I am not going to do anything stupid, you know," said Ewalinka before continuing.

"I can control my anger. Last time I was just upset you know," explained Ewalinka.

"Every time you go in a trance, who knows what might happen, we cannot be there for you, all the time you know," said Devalinja.

"I know, thanks Dev, so you will come with me, right?" asked Ewalinka.

"All right, if you insist."

"It will be fun, I promise," replied Ewalinka.

"Ok, we will go together," confirmed Devalinja. The girls continued talking preparing for the Friday afternoon shopping. Later that afternoon the girls drove to the city for shopping. They spent the day shopping. It was great fun; they had been to the museum and to the cinema. They returned home later that day and Ewalinka decided to go to sleep early that night. She was exhausted.

"Night girls I am retiring early I had much fun today, thanks to Dev," said Ewalinka getting up and going to her room. Devalinja followed her into her room and they talked to each other. It was a Friday night and everyone was going about their way minding their own business. It was a bit dark outside than most of the nights. The blowing wind was a bit chilly. The rest of the girls and Nick gathered in the lounge room and played games as they normally did. Miles away in the city park a scream was heard. A young man had been attacked in the park. A woman who was passing by had come across the wounded young man as he lay in a pool of blood. She had heard growling noises as if someone was having difficulty breathing. At first, she was afraid to approach the young man. Then she gathered her strength and approached the man who was lying on the ground. She took off her jacket and quickly covered the man. He had a wound on his left side. Some blood was coming out of his mouth. He had problems breathing. He tried to talk but could not as he was choking on his blood. He coughed, and he covered the helper in blood as he spat on her face when he tried to talk to her. She screamed again for help.

"Help! Help! Please help! Anybody help!" She frantically searched for something in her hand bag and retrieved a mobile phone. She dialed the emergency number.

"Operator. I need help!"

"There is an injured man lying in a pool of blood. Please help! I need an ambulance straight away," said the lady in a louder voice. Operator:

"What is your location? I need your address."

"It is central park in the city center, near the museum. Please hurry he is choking on his blood. Hurry!" shouted the woman.

"I will send an ambulance straight away," said the operator before continuing.

"Keep on the line until the ambulance arrives," said the operator.

"Ok, hurry!" replied the lady. Minutes later the ambulance arrived, and the man was taken to the hospital. The woman who found the wounded man did not go to the hospital in the ambulance. She had given her details to the ambulance crew as they suspected that the man was attacked. In case the police needed to question her about the incident.

"What have you got here?" asked one of the nurses who had received the man soon before he died.

"A JD, wounded possibly an animal attack, not sure, but severe blood loss." Replied one of the ambulance crews handing the man to the nurses at the hospital. Soon afterwards the man died. The ambulance crew had indicated that the patient was clinically dead the time they arrived to help him. He had severed blood vessels and a deep wound to his chest. One of the vital organ, namely the heart was damaged. The ambulance crews had written Dead on Arrival on the paperwork they gave to the nurses at the hospital. "No need for cardiopulmonary resuscitation (CPR), heart severely damaged." Said the nurse to another nurse who had just arrived.

"Make arrangements for the body to be taken to the mortuary," requested the nurse. The other nurse completed some forms on a clipboard; JD, DOA, a severe wound, heart damaged, Fão: Police. Quickly the police were notified, and the nurses collected vital information and samples from the body like saliva on the wound and bagged and labeled all these. Later, his body was taken by the staff from the hospital mortuary and then taken to the mortuary before the police were informed of a possible homicide. Detective inspector Simpson and her partner detective McGowns had just received a call from the hospital of a possible homicide. They were told that a man with wounds had been received at the hospital and that they were required to investigate as a normal procedure. In cases where a hospital receives patients with severe wounds be it gunshot wounds or stab wounds they had to inform the police.

"We have a possible homicide case at the hospital. We should head there as soon as possible." Said detective McGowns.

"What is the case number? Another gun crime I suppose?" Inferred detective Simpson.

"H316, possible animal attach," replied detective McGowns.

"Animal attack in Virginia? Are you sure?" asked detective Simpson.

"That is what the report says," replied detective

McGowns.

"Has the animal control and rescue officer been informed? We cannot let a dangerous animal possibly a dog, run free in the city. Can we?" asked the detective.

"Long time since I dealt with an animal attack case," said the detective.

"That is what I like about this job. Every day is different," replied detective Simpson. The two detectives talked about this case and the job in general on their way to the hospital. In all cases, which needed to be reported to the police, the coroner would do a post mortem examination as soon as all the evidence and samples are collected with the permission of the police. The victim had no any form of identification. It took the hospital hours before the victim can be identified through dental records. The victim was one Teddy Millsway. He had been mauled to death by what appeared to be a dog because of the bite wounds. They proceeded to the coroner's office.

"What do you have for us doc?" asked detective Simpson sitting down on the chair in front of the coroner's table.

"Possible animal attack. Severed left side, damaged heart which is the cause of death. I have just received blood and saliva results from the lab," said the coroner.

"So, what can you tell us?" asked detective Simpson.

"At first I thought canine attack but blood results indicate otherwise." Said the coroner looking at the detectives.

"All bloods and saliva test indicates that the attacker was indeed human," explained the coroner. The bite wound indicates a canine attack but results inconclusive." Said the coroner.

"How can the blood and saliva from the wound all be human?" asked detective McGowns.

"The victim's blood type is AO whereas the other type of blood is B, but all human blood."

Confirmed the coroner. The detectives spoke with the coroner for some time before they left for the crime scene in the park. Saturday afternoon the girls and Nick had busy schedules in the morning. They all went about doing their weekend duties and tasks. In the evening, they gathered together and were watching the news while some were preparing food in the kitchen.

"Girls come and watch this!" Shouted Beverly to the other girls who were in the kitchen.

"What is it?" replied Devalinja.

"There has been an animal attack in the park near the museum," said Beverly. In the news, it was reported that a young man was mauled in the park by an animal and the police were urging everyone to be vigilant. On hearing this Eva was upset. She called Ewalinka and dragged her to one side.

"Did you have to do that?" Asked Eva.

"The young man in the news is Teddy. the one who knocked Nick to the ground. Remember? Did you have anything to do with this?" asked Eva looking at Ewalinka straight in the eye.

"I do not know what you are talking about," replied Ewalinka.

"Only you can't seem to forgive and to forget," explained Eva.

"Listen Eva, I did you a favor. That guy knew more than he was supposed to. Eliminate any threats. Remember?" said Ewalinka cunningly.

"You left your footprints all over the place, you are supposed to clean your mess," said Eva

"Don't you worry about that; you want fame? I will give you fame." Said Ewalinka walking away from Eva.

"It's not about fame. I do not want the wrong people snooping on us, you know," shouted Eva.

"Yeah, yeah, you always say that. If you cannot do anything, then I must do something. You are the leader. What leader?" sarcastically asked Ewalinka.

"Listen. That poor lad was not a threat at all. Just a silly bully, you know!" remarked Eva.

"He was snooping on us. So, I did you a favor," said Ewalinka. You, listen right now! I make decisions around here. You are putting everyone at risk. I do not want to start something that will make us get killed so you should not too. That is the last time you are going to do something stupid like that," said Eva upset.

"Or else what?" asked Ewalinka with her eyes wide open.

"If you care about us then you will stop doing that?" said Eva.

"It's not about that, of course I care that's why I did that," replied Ewalinka.

"I don't get you, what's your problem?" asked Eva. "It is not like Nick is the president of this country, where he can cover-up everything. I am saying that your actions put us at risk," added Eva.

"You know what? I do not want to talk about this," said Ewalinka going to her room leaving Eva stood there. Later that night Eva gathered everyone and talked about what had happened. The animal control officer was informed of the animal attack in the park.

He went to the scene of attack to investigate. After gathering the required information, he went back to his office. Later that night a group of animal control officer gathered in the central park with tranquilizers and rifles to flush out the animal. They believed it to be a dog. People were informed to be vigilant as there was a dangerous animal on the loose. All night the animal control officers were in the park searching for this dangerous animal. In the morning, they gave a news briefing to the people who had gathered and the media.

"We searched all night for the dangerous animal but we found none. We urge the public to be vigilant. We will remain vigilant too. Two animal control and rescue officers will patrol the park each day until further notice. Any possible sighting please ring the emergency line as soon as possible. Thank you." Officer Brown finished addressing the crowd and the media who had gathered.

CHAPTER SIX

Years after this Nick and the girls had received a lot
of funding through their website and lucrative
contracts from all over the world. They had millions
of dollars in their bank accounts. Over the years more
people had donated through their crowdfunding
website. It seemed though also that their popularity
rose soon after the animal attack in the central park.
Those who knew the legend believed them. The more
the animal attack news spread the more the people
who subscribed to their website. It was about
believing the legend what mattered the most. Nick
had given his father some money from the donations
to start his own business as a software engineer. Years
later Nick's father received a note demanding money
or that Nick will be in danger.
"Nick my son can we talk," said Nick's father sitting
down on the sofa in the lounge room.
"Yes, dad. Is everything ok?" asked Nick sitting down

next to his father. The two had been busy lately and did not have time for a one-to-one chat, this was the perfect time for them to chat.

"There is something that is bothering me," he paused and looked at his son for a while.

"Since the day, you were born life has been a blessing. I know it has been tough since losing your mother but I am glad that she gave me you," there was a moment of silence. "I wish mom was here, we could all be very happy," said Nick.

"I know where she is in heaven she is very happy," said Nick's father. They all kept quiet for a while. Nick's mum had died soon after birth. Nick was born after 10 months. She had complications during the birth of Nick. They waited for a natural birth. Nick's father had insisted on the C-section but his wife had refused. The doctors had to artificially induce labor, but it took more time to deliver the baby. She had complications soon after birth and died after wards. After that the two had been inseparable. Nick's father opted for a self-employed job since losing his job. This had given him the much-needed time to spend with Nick. Since his birth his father had kept a secret although it is no longer a secret to Nick. Over the years, he had found out that he had a tattoo on his back. He never knew how he ended up with a tattoo. His father over the years had insisted that Nick's tattoo was a birthmark.

"My son over the years I have been worried about you and your future," explained Nick's father. "Everything turns out to be fine dad, so no need to worry too much," replied Nick.

"Since the day, you were born, I didn't know what to do. Your mum left me to take care of you alone. It was difficult especially the first days," he paused and touched Nick's head.

"I remembered one day you slept for days I think. I was so worried I took you to the hospital and the doctors said you had carbon monoxide poisoning. Those days we had a gas stove. After that day, I replaced everything with electrical. I ended up designing my own that used solar energy so that you grow up healthy. That time something unusual happened," he stopped talking and looked at his son. "The day you were born, a marking on your back developed as soon as you took your first breath. I was so scared I did not know what to do. I asked the doctors, but no one seemed to know what it was. The doctors advised that I go to the church and ask the priests and the Bishops there. Even there no one seemed to know what it was. The first months you kept falling into a trance. The more you did that the more the marking on your back developed," he paused and drank water from a glass on the table. Nick looked surprised and frightened at the same time.

"The Chief Bishop advised we get you baptized. So, one Sunday morning I took you to church. Your auntie came to help me with the chores. That day I do not know but something happened. I did not want to tell you this all these past years but I think you are now grown up. You will understand this. I think you already know by now," said his father looking at his son.

"Ok, the day of baptism, something miraculous happened. As the Chief Bishop was pouring water on your head to baptize you, you fall into a trance," he stopped and took a long breath before continuing.

"Something came out from the marking on your back and went into the water at the altar. The water turned red as blood started coming out of the markings. Everyone was shocked some women fainted. Ever since the blood dried, and the markings turned into a tattoo as you see it today," he looked at his son who was very shocked and afraid. "Nothing to be afraid of. I understand now what this is all about. The arrival of the girls and everything. I believe everything is for your good. Since the day of the baptism I had been researching about the tattoo on your back and what it means. I wrote to too many scholars and fortune tellers if they know what the tattoo meant. No one knew what this was. I had forgotten about it when one day an old Chinese man visited me at work. I was surprised because I had never written to anyone abroad let alone China. I asked him who had sent him and how he knew me and where I worked. I had assumed that he had received one of my letters but to my surprise, no, he had not," he paused and looked at Nick.

"So, what did he say?" asked Nick.

"He took off his shirt and showed me a tattoo on his back. He explained that he had a vision during the time he falls into a trance. In his vision, you are the bloodline of the Chinese Emperor because of your mother. I said no way she had no Chinese roots. Then he went on to explain the family tree and how the last bloodline was sent abroad for safety after the assassination of the last Emperor. That is how your mother is related to the Emperor. In his vision the legend has it that seven girls called the magnificent seven would all come to help and protect you for the next hundred years. He left China after seeing the vision and he came here using telepathy sensing. I only believed him when I saw you with the girls. He had foretold me all about this."

"You are the Emperor per the legend only that you don't have an Imperial dynasty and kingdom to rule. He never mentioned anything about that. I believe it by the way you have raised the money with the help of the girls."

He paused and smiled. Nick smiled too knowing that he was probably the richest person his age in the whole world.

"Since the girls arrived it all started to fit in place and make sense. Every hundred years the legend has it that seven bodyguards will be sent to protect the Emperor and when I saw all the girls together I just knew it. You are destined for bigger things; I do not know how and when. This also brings me to the main reason I called you today to have a chat with you. I received a letter some time ago, in fact this is the second letter. The first one was months ago, after I opened my own business, thanks to you," he paused and rubbed the head of his son before continuing. "This letter has some issues I thought you should know about. I do not know who sent the letters but they are saying that I wrote to their friends some years ago, asking for help. Which I did like I said earlier on. But these people they are not friendly. They asked for a lot of money to keep silent about you and the girls. The days I received the first letter I had no money you too you were struggling, so I ignored the letter. They initially asked for $2million we had no money so I ignored them. A few weeks ago, I received another letter this time demanding $5million. They somehow accessed my bank statement. They said they know where the money is coming from, my business is just a cover-up. They said we are robbers we are stealing money in the name of the Emperor and such a crime in the ancient China is punishable by death. They are saying they are the true holy protectors and descendants of the Emperor. They are saying that if we do not pay the money, then they are going to get us killed." He paused and looked at his son. Nick knew that his father was concerned about this, the look on his face said it all. They had the money but was it morally correct to hand over the money to them. How will that end? Bad could be anyone's guess. Giving-in to blackmail would mean death anywhere, what if they ask for even more money in the future how is this going to end? They could not go to the police mainly because of Teddy Millsway death. The legend had it that the magnificent seven would kill anyone who is a threat to the Emperor. They did not want the cops snooping around them.

"So, dad what do you suggest?" asked Nick looking very worried.

"The old Chinese man told me that this was going to happen. The girls would only protect the Emperor unless the Emperor authorized them to protect someone else, how I do not know. Even if we pay the money, what if tomorrow they start asking for billions? My main worry is not the money; it is your safety. Once we give them the money it will be accepting that we also killed that boy, what is his name again?" he asked Nick and paused.

"You mean Teddy," said Nick looking at his father.

"Yes Teddy. What do you suggest we do? Probably it is best you talk to the girls first," said Nick's father.

The two agreed that Nick speak to the girls and hear what they must say about all this. The girls had insisted that Nick's father stayed with them, but he had refused insisting on staying in his house instead of moving in with them. The girls had reassured Nick that they would protect his father. The only problem was that he lived a bit far away from them and it would be problematic to react in such a short notice if there was a problem. Ewalinka had volunteered to move in with Nick's' father for some time until they have found a solution to the problem, but his father had refused playing down the blackmail and threats. In the end, they decided that he kept in contact all the time and they regularly visited him as well. His main worry was that this could go on for months if not years. The girls could not trace the letter or the person who had sent the letter. Nick's dad came back home one day to find that his place had been burgled? It seems nothing was stolen, but the house had a strange smell. He quickly dialed Nick and the girls for help. Eva was the only one at home that day. Quickly she jumped into her car and drove to Nick dad's house. She phoned the other girls to let them know what had happened.

"Eva, hey are you ok? It's Tony I need your help."

"I am on my way there right now," said Eva to Tony. She drove her Mercedes Benz C class as fast as she could to Tony's house. She arrived at Tony's house and quickly switched off the car engine. She got out of the car and left the driver door open. Straight she headed to the front door which was open, pushed it in and entered the house.

"Tony! Tony! Are you okay? Where are you?" she shouted as she rushed inside opening the other doors.

"Tony, it's Eva, where are you?" shouted Eva entering the study room. The study room was the computer room for Tony, Nick's father. That is the room he spent most of his time researching and designing software. As she entered the room she saw software disks, cases and papers lying all over the floor. The computers in this room were all switched on. She walked further into the room and stumbled on something. She stopped and knelt to pick something up. She looked at the disk which was on the floor. She touched the disk with her finger and rubbed something on her clothes.

"Tony, it's Eva. I am here where are you?" Shouted Eva as she got up. She looked around in the room and approached the other door which was slightly closed. She pushed the door open, still no sign of Tony. There were drops of blood on the floor leading to the ground floor rooms. Quickly she rushed downstairs following the blood drops. The drops lead her to the ground floor guest room. Smoke was coming out of the door. She rushed inside to find out what was happening. She stumbled on something on the floor. She felt an excruciating pain on her left side. She opened her eyes as she lay on the floor. The whole room was filled with the magic stones and there were fumes from these stones covering the whole room. She saw a man's boots coming toward her as she lay on the floor. They were shiny black shoes. She tried getting up but soon finds her energies quickly vanishing. The man came to her and knelt beside her. He lifted his right hand and dialed a number before putting the phone to his ear.

"We got the subject boss," said the man getting up and walking away from Eva. Eva felt weak and found herself having difficulties to breath and passes out. Ewalinka was with Nick. They had gone to a different city to complete a business deal. Nick wanted to buy real estate in the neighboring city. Ewalinka had thought it a good idea if they had gone together. It was an hour's drive from their home city. Nick was driving, and they were now coming back. The road they used was a mountainous road. The scenery was beautiful. Nick had thought it a good idea to show Ewalinka the beautiful scenery on their way back. The problem was with phone reception. There was no network.

"I tried to make a phone call to my dad, just to let him know how the meeting has gone but my phone has no signal," said Nick Ewalinka took out her phone too to check if she had any signal.

"I guess mine too," said Ewalinka as they continued with their journey. Nick took out a CD from the groove compartment and rubbed it on his shirt before putting it into the CD player. They drove for a while listening to the music. It was a good day, they had completed the deal, they were heading home. A lot was happening in their lives now.

"How come you never talk about your mum?" asked Ewalinka.

"I don't know much about her, in fact I never saw her." He looked at Ewalinka quickly before looking in the road ahead.

"She passed away the day I was born."

He paused and looked at Ewalinka again.

"Somehow it feels like she died so I can be here. It is so unfair. Why her? Everyone has his or her mum. I feel mine has been taken away so unfairly." He drove for a while before continuing talking to Ewalinka.

"She could be here with us, but hey that's life. I know she will be proud of me," he looked at Ewalinka. "What about you, you don't talk much about your parents?" said Nick looking at Ewalinka briefly. Mine, it's a long story, most just like everyone of us. I left home when I was seven and that is the last time I saw my parents. Where ever they are now I hope, they are okay." She said and looked at Nick who was driving before continuing.

"I don't have that emotional attachment to my parents than most of these kids." said Ewalinka lighting up a cigarette. She puffed for some time and opened the car window. She blew the smoke through the window and looked at Nick.

"It's just the way I am. I do not think about my parents that much. I have responsibilities and my family is with you and the rest of the girls," she paused and looked at Nick who slowly smiled and continued driving.

"I am flattered and privileged to have you in my life," said Nick taking a glance at Ewalinka. They continued talking, and they drove for a while. The music was playing as they drove back home. Twenty minutes passed and Ewalinka took out a second cigarette lit it up and started smoking again.

"Ah! Something is wrong!" screamed Ewalinka in pain. She quickly threw out the cigarette through the window.

"Do you want me to stop the car?" asked Nick swerving in the road as he looked at Ewalinka. She touched her stomach as if in pain and slumped back on the car seat. She looked outside through the passenger window. She looked at Nick.

"What's wrong?" asked Nick.

"I don't know but something is wrong. I cannot breathe. I am going to pass out." Said Ewalinka. Nick quickly applied brakes, swerving in the road before the car came to a halt.

"Ewalinka, Ewalinka! Look at me," said Nick holding Ewalinka. She opened her eyes and looked at Nick. "Your eyes are changing. Why are you shaking? Are you feeling cold? Talk to me?" said Nick quickly attending to Ewalinka.

"Eva is in trouble. I am going to pass out. Take me back quickly. Leave the windows open. Hurry Nick, hurry," said Ewalinka in a small soft voice. Nick quickly started the car engine and took a quick glance in his rear-view mirror before setting off.

"Hang in there I will take you home now. Hang in there Ewa," said Nick as he drove as fast as he can. Ewalinka's eyes had changed color. Normally her eyes are shining green. When they are all together they all have, blue eyes imitating those of the leader of the group which is Eva. When they are apart, they all have their natural eye color. Ewalinka's eyes had changed from a shining green to blue color. This is normally a sign or call for help signal. All seven girls had different eye color. Eye color identified who was in trouble and needed help. Eva was in some sort of trouble. They were too far to assist. Hopefully the others will receive the signal and help. Nick drove for about ten minutes before Ewalinka fell into a trance. If she was home, the others would have taken her into the room with the magic stones. They were too far away from home. As he drove back home, he heard a loud noise and the passenger window was smashed into pieces. He swerved the car, driving on the edges of the road, and tried to control the car by driving into the correct lane. He wondered what was happening. He looked at the passenger seat. Ewalinka lay still and there was broken glass everywhere. Somehow a black bird had smashed its way through the closed passenger window. It laid next to Ewalinka with blood coming out of its mouth. The bird flipped its wings as it breathes its last breath. Ewalinka laid on the passenger seat and Nick drove back home. Nick's father had come back home to find his house broken into. He rang his son and the girls. He then went in the house. Nothing still seemed to have been stolen. He went into the study room. Someone had switched on his computers. The study room was a mess. All his disks and papers were on the floor. Someone was in the study room looking for something. Someone had tried to access his files but with no luck. The first thing that came to his mind was that it was a bunged burglary. That did not make sense as nothing was stolen. Then a cold sweat of fear run down his neck and back. He knelt to pick up some disks on the floor. He picked one up and rubbed it on his shirt. He picked up the disk wallet and placed the disk in the wallet. The next thing he felt was a sharp pain coming from the back of his head. He felt a feeling of warm water dripping down his neck. That is the last thing he remembered. "The boss wants him alive with his brain fully functioning. So why did you hit him in the head?" Asked the man in the dark suit looking at his partner who was standing over Nick's father.

"What if he had struggled and fought back," replied the man.

"I am just following the boss's orders," replied the man in the dark suit.

"Okay, collect all the disks and all the paperwork

hurry up," said the other man. The two started collecting papers and disks and shuffling these into the bag. They carried Nick's dad to their car and bundled him inside. The other one went back in the house. He came out and went to the garage. He opened the garage and went into Nick's dad's car. He drove his car out and followed the other driver in front.

"Boss we got the main subject," said the man in the suit talking over the phone.

"Don't harm him, I need him alive. Park where I told you and do as previously arranged." The line went dead after that. They drove for a while and the car turned into a side road. They stopped and parked the cars.

"The man in the suit took his mobile phone and dialed a number. The phone can be heard ringing. It rung for some time before someone answered. "Hello, we are in position what's your status?" asked the man at the other end.

"We have the main subject move in as planned."

The man in the suit replied before cutting off the line. A car drove at Tony's house and parked behind the house facing the road. Two man quickly got out of the car wearing spaceman suits. They opened the door of their car. Quickly they took out a big jar like the ones they used to store alcohol at the brewery. They were wearing gloves and space masks that their faces could not be recognized. They helped each other carrying the jar inside the house. Quickly one of them came back to close the car door. He quickly went back inside the house holding a small bag. They went straight downstairs.

"Make sure the windows are closed," said the other

man. Slowly they open the jar. The other man made sure that his spaceman mask was fitted properly. Slowly they took what looked like a flask from the jar. Slowly they placed it on the table. The other man opened the small bag he had brought in. He took out what appeared to be bigger forks and placed these on the table. He took out what appeared to be an aluminum roll and laid it down in the basement. They poured out the contents of the big flask onto the aluminum foil. With the big folks, he spreads the contents onto the aluminum foil.

"Be careful, don't get us killed that thing is highly dangerous you know." Remarked one man to another.

"I know what I am doing," replied the other man. After that, the other man opened the small bag again and took out a bottle of some liquid. Slowly he opened the bottle.

"Are you ready?" he asked the other man.

"Let me check the windows first," said the other man walking to the window. He made sure the windows were closed before returning to the table.

"Ready, let's start," said the man. They opened a small bottle with some liquid and sprinkled the contents on top of the rocks from the big flask. A big cloud of smoke is released from the rocks. The smoke rose quickly upwards before descending again. They sprinkled again the rocks. Another big glow and cloud is released from the rocks into the air. The cloud quickly descends. They repeated the same process until they were unable to see each other. The room was filled with smoke so dense that their mask was covered with the smoke. As soon as the smoke meets their suit, it condenses into water droplets. Soon a lot of droplets started trickling down their spaceman suits. They left the basement heading upstairs. They left the house and headed to their car. They sat in the back of their car and waited. When Eva arrived, she had found the door opened. She went straight down in the basement after discovering blood droplets coming down from the ground floor. This was the study room where Nick's dad spent most of his time developing software. Eva had been suffocated by the fumes in the room. The stones had realized enough smoke to choke and tranquilize a big elephant. She had never been near the strongest stones ever. All her life she had been exposed to the green stones only. The heavy duty silver-gray stones were for the other six. As the leader one of her requirements was never to be near the silver-gray stones. These were too powerful and would cause a lot of wear and tear. Obvious she was weak she could not handle these. She had passed out. The last memory she had was that of seeing the big shining black shoes of that man in the room as she lay on the floor. She had never felt weak like this before. The fumes had overcome her. She lay on the floor unconscious. The two man with spaceman suits rushed into the room. They put an oxygen mask on Eva's head before carrying her outside into their car. The other man went back into the house slowly he removed the magic stones and put them back into the flask one by one using the forks. He then put the flask into the jar. He opened the windows in the basement and sprayed some liquid. He then left the basement and took Eva's car keys. He then drove Eva's car following the other man in front. Half an hour later the man driving Eva's car took out a mobile phone and dialed a number. He waited for someone to answer on the other end.

"Yes!" replied the other man on the other end. "Proceeding per plan. We got the second subject. House clear. Over." He put the phone down after talking into the phone before continuing driving. Some miles away two man are talking to each other in the parked car. A phone call interrupted their conversation.

"Copy that over," the other man in the parked car replied into his phone. He started the car engine and drove the car.

"We are good to go. The place is clean now," said the other man to his partner. The screeching of the car tire can be heard as the car left heading for Tony's house. Tony's car had been left parked there. The other man had jumped back into their car leaving Tony's car parked there.

"We just follow the plan," said the driver.

"Sure! How long did the boss say he is going to be?" asked the man. As soon as we arrive, we will give the okay call. He told me he is parked nearby waiting for our call," replied the driver.

"Do you think that he will cooperate," asked the passenger.

"None of our business. I am just doing my job," replied the driver.

"If we make him talk and cooperate, I think the boss can reward us. After all, they stole money from a lot of people," said the passenger. The two drove to Tony's house. They entered the driveway and parked the car. They inspected the area to make sure that no one was looking at them. They then dragged Tony out of the car and into his house. By the time, they arrived the fumes had cleared. They bundled Tony downstairs and waited for their boss. Tony had woken up but disoriented. The boss arrived a few minutes later.

"Transfer money right now into this account." The boss took out a small note from his right-hand pocket and placed it on the table. Tony did not reply at first instead he spat in the face of the boss.

"I want $2 million right now transferred into this account or else," said the boss before being interrupted by Tony.

"Or else what?" asked Tony in an angry voice. The boss could sense some tension in Tony's voice.

"We know you have the money. We want you to transfer the money into this account," said the boss switching- on Tony's computers which were left on standby.

"I am not going to transfer any money to this account. I don't have the money? Even if I did, I would never give you the money," said Tony.

"You are not taking us seriously," said the boss nodding his head to one of the bodyguards. The bodyguard moved forward and started punching Tony. That went on for some time before the boss raised his hand. The bodyguard stopped and moved backward. The boss approached again and asked Tony to transfer the money into his account. I cannot transfer any money," said Tony with blood coming out of his mouth.

"Get up!"

Shouted the bodyguard lifting Tony up. He dragged him to the computer chair.

"Transfer the money now or else we will kill you," said the boss. There was silence in the room. Tony raised his head and tried to log-onto the computer. A password error message appeared on the screen. He shrugged and touched the back of his head. He looked at his hand which was now covered with blood. He rubbed the blood on his shirt and tried to log-on again. Still the password error message appeared on the screen. The other bodyguard came near him and punched him in the face.

"Log-on now and transfer the money or else you die," repeated the boss. A lot of thoughts were rushing through Tony's mind. He had sent a help signal already. It was a waiting game now. He needed only time before help arrived in the form of his son and the girls. What is taking them so long? They should be here at least by now. Where is Nick? Where are the girls? He never thought of the worst that can happen. He had heard stories about how the magnificent seven defended the Emperor with such a swiftness never equaled by any man. Thirty minutes plus gone and still no sign of him or the girls. Tony kept thinking to himself. The boss realized that Tony was playing time games. They had taken Eva and they know Tony was not aware of that. The only threat and as far as the boss knew was Nick who was miles away and being taken care of. Tony was not the kind of man who will run to the police for help. The boss took out his phone and scrolled down a number.

"Hello, it's me," said the boss before pausing for a while.

"Seems he is not cooperating and I don't think we have enough time," he paused and looked at Tony.

"I am afraid that he left us with no choice. Can you initiate Plan B," the boss looked at Tony and then at the bodyguards?

"I ask again please log-on and transfer the money now," said the boss with a soft calm and polite voice. He would be happy to have the money in his hands than to have blood on his hands. Tony knew that something was wrong. He tried to login again. The password error appeared on the screen. It happened so fast that he opened his eyes to see himself kissing the floor with excruciating pain on his chin bone. "Get up and transfer the money now! Or else you die!" said the boss this time with a deep strong voice. Tony tried getting up, but he was kicked in the stomach.

"Get up right now and transfer the money!" shouted the boss. Tony got up on his feet. Wiped the blood from his lips and sat back in his chair. He put his hands over the keyboard with his fingers spread on the keyboard. He started typing on the keyboard. Access denied, read the message on the screen. He shrugged before trying again. The boss raised his hand to the bodyguards.

"You left me with no choice."

The boss stood there for a while looking at Tony. Where are they? What is taking them so long? How long can I play this game? These are the questions that kept running in Tony's mind. The bodyguards approached him and started punching him up. He realized they meant to kill him as they heavily punched him. At one-point, he had thought of transferring the money they had requested but the thought of his son gave him courage. He imagined that happening to his son. Surely Nick would not survive all this. He had expected everyone to be there after half an hour at most. Something must have happened to Nick. He thought to himself. What about the girls? The stories he heard about them were they all fake stories? Surely, they should have come to his rescue. He thought to himself. Tony felt his head very heavy. The pain was unbearable.

"Stop, I will transfer the money," screamed Tony as he tried to get up. They stopped for a while and looked at each other. They waited for him to get up and sit on the chair. After sometime he managed to get up. This time his head was very heavy. He could not think straight. He had suffered too much blows to the head. He sat on the chair and typed in the password. Access denied. The message appeared on the screen.

"What, that can't be right!" Tony typed again this time quickly with his eyes wide open. The same message appeared again on the screen. He typed quickly again. The password was wrong. How is that possible he asked himself? "Don't waste our time. The boss was right. You are never going to cooperate," said one of the bodyguards.

"Transfer the money and the boss might let you go." Continued the bodyguard. This bodyguard would prefer money than blood on his hands. He had hoped that Tony was going to transfer the money. He had thought that money meant nothing to him. He was educated, and he was rich. It was not his money after all. They did not sweat to get this money. After all, rumors have it that they conned people to get this money. They used the legend story to gain the trust of billions around the world. If it was easy to get the money, why would he sacrifice his life. It did not make sense to him. At one-point Tony, had thought the same. He had realized that money was nothing. He nearly gave-in to the blackmail demands. The only thing that stopped him was his son. Surely if he made it easy, next it would be Nick and the girls. This time he was going to log-in and buy more time but he password was wrong. He looked surprised and worried at the same time. What had happened? Surely that is the same password he had used every day for the past month. What is going on? Had he forgotten? He thought to himself.

"Listen, transfer the money now or else we carry out the boss's orders," said one of the bodyguards. Tony tried frantically to log-onto the computer but without any success. He looked at the computer screen. It was when he read the small message on the screen that he noticed the problem. He had entered a wrong password so many times that the system automatically logged him out. He had to wait for another thirty minutes to reset the password. Surely it was more than an hour now since he had called for help. Surely something bad must have happened to Nick. The bodyguards looked at each other. One of them picked up the bag they had brought in. He took something out and placed it on the floor. He looked around the room and knelt. He pulled the wires and took the plug to the nearest electrical socket. He plugged in the plug and hit the switch button. He connected the other ends to a machine he took out from the bag. They both hold Tony's hands and tied him. They connected electrodes to him. One of the bodyguards knelt near the machine. He switched on the power button and moved backward away from Tony. He was holding a switch.

"Ready," asked one of the bodyguards.

"Yes, stand back," replied the other. The sound of a power generator can be heard coming from the machine. They looked at each other before Tony screamed in pain. They kept increasing the voltage. His condition deteriorated and afterwards went into cardiac arrest. They removed the electrodes and the machine and left Tony for dead. Tony laid on the floor, first he felt dizziness then problems breathing. He threw up and slowly went into unconsciousness. One of the bodyguards came to where Tony lay, he knelt and checked his pulse. He had no pulse, and he was not breathing. The other bodyguard connected the electrodes to the computers plug and switched on electricity. A large popping up sound can be heard and smoke is seen coming out of the computers before they all went silent.

"Job done, ready to go," said one of the bodyguard bundling the cables and the machine they had used into the bag.

"He's gone, just a matter of time now." Replied the other bodyguard. They left Tony's house, got into the car, and drove off.

"Boss! Job done! It's going per plan."

"Okay meet me as planned," said the boss before cutting the line off. Eva was taken to one of the house in the nearby suburbs. They put her in the basement and waited for her to wake up. Nick arrived home and parked his car in the driveway. Quickly he ran to the passenger side and opened the door. Quickly he took Ewalinka out and carried her into the house and straight to the room with the magic stones. He ran downstairs to the lounge to make a phone call. There were messages on the answer machine. First, he dialed Eva's phone but her phone kept ringing without answer. He tried the other girls', to let them know, but no one picked up their phones. He tried ringing his dad, but the phone kept ringing with no answer. "Damn where is everyone today? Why everyone not answering the phone?" Nick asked himself loudly. He put the receiver down and paused for a while. While thinking, he noticed the voice message light flashing. He picked up the receiver and dialed voicemail. Beep first message: Left today at 4pm in the afternoon.; Nick my son something has happened. I found that the place has been broken into but it seems nothing has been stolen. This is the main reason I need you right now. Come with the girls. I am afraid it is that ransom money. Please come quickly. Dad. A female voice from the answer machine can be heard saying to call back please press 1. For message details please press 2. For your next message please press 0. A moment of silence passed as Nick pondered what could have happened. Everyone's' seemed not to have answered their phones. He stood there not knowing what to do. A voice can be heard from the answer phone repeating the options again. Nick pressed 0 and waited. For message details press 2 and for your next message please press 0. Nick pressed 0 again and waited. There was a beep, and it was Eva. Guys I have been called I am going to Tony's house there seem to be some problems of some sort at his house. I am going there right now. As soon as you get this message, please come to Tony's house as soon as possible. End of the message. For message details…. Nick quickly pressed 0 for the next message. He waited while the answer phone repeated the options again. The next message was from Nick's dad asking for help. This time he sounded nervous and afraid. Quickly Nick pressed buttons on the receiver and dialed his father's mobile phone. Still there was no answer. Ewalinka needed more attention right now and was not supposed to be left alone. All the other girl's phones were ringing, but no one was answering. Nick ran upstairs in the room with the magic stones where Ewalinka was. She was in a trance and no one knows when she would wake up. It was one of their rules that in such a state she was never to be left alone. He checked on her before going downstairs. He picked up the phone again and dialed Eva's, phone. The person you are dialing cannot take your call right now. Please leave a message after the tone.

"Damn! Where is everyone?" while he was downstairs, he heard a large sound and the sound of glass breaking. He ran upstairs to the room with the magic stones. In all commotion, he had forgotten to open the windows. The upper window was broken into pieces. There was broken glass all over the place. He checked Ewalinka, and she was ok. He walked a few steps toward the door and stopped. He looked down there were watery footprints heading toward the hole in the window. There was chaos in the city center. People were running from different directions. Screaming and shouting. No one seems to know what was going on. There was confusion. Shop windows were broken down. A car left the main road and hit the embankment causing a water pipe to burst. People gathered to make sure that the driver was okay.

"What happened? Are you okay?" asked one onlooker.

"I don't know for sure," replied the car driver.

"Are you hurt? Can we call for help?" asked another onlooker.

"I am all right I guess," replied the car driver touching himself before continuing.

"I thought I saw something," he paused and looked around.

"What do you mean," asked another onlooker who had come to help.

"I am sure I saw something, but," he paused and looked around. He looked worried. There was a moment of silence. The onlookers all gathered to hear what he was going to say next.

"I saw some kind of animal…," he paused and looked around again. All the onlookers all look at each other before looking in the area surrounding them.

"An animal? Are you sure?" asked one onlooker. The car driver did not answer but instead checked his surroundings first.

"Yes, an animal crossing the road. So, I swerved to avoid hitting it and ended up on the embankment," said the car driver. All the onlookers started talking to each other. One took out his phone and called the ambulance.

"I think this guy is hallucinating." Said the onlooker who dialed for an ambulance.

"People can get disoriented after an accident," said another onlooker.

"I am telling you, I saw an animal crossing the road. I was looking ahead and wide awake. I do not need an ambulance I am okay. Do you think I am hallucinating? Jesus!" said the car driver getting back in his car.

CHAPTER SEVEN

Meanwhile in the road ahead there was a car accident pile-up. Car alarm siren can be heard from a distance. People are gathering around. One driver gets out of the car to check the front of his car. The bonnet is slightly open. The hazard lights are flashing. There is steam coming out from the open bonnet. Another driver jumped out of his car and approached the driver in front. He starts screaming at the driver in front.

"Why did you suddenly stopped the car? Are you mad? Are you trying to get me killed? You freak?" shouted the driver of the damaged car as he lowered his head to talk to the driver of the car in front. The driver of the car in front has his head on the steering wheel. Blood is trickling down his head. A continuous horn sound is coming out from the car. The driver is badly hurt. He made a sudden stop that made the following car slump into his car. The other cars swerved on both sides trying to avoid the collision. That caused a pile-up of cars blocking the road. One by one most of the drivers got out of their cars and stood behind the open driver's door to see what was ahead. In the pavement, ahead to the right-side pedestrians are running away as if being chased away. There is commotion no one knows what is happening. The window of the women clothes shop is broken into pieces. A huge opening is left and everyone inside can be seen running in different directions and some running out of the shop. Moments later the other window of the women's clothes shop is smashed into pieces as well. Everyone in that area is running away from that area. People are coming out of the shops ahead and as soon as they see other people running in their direction they run too for their lives. One woman came out of the shop carrying bags of clothes in both hands. She seemed unaware of what was happening. She walks few steps ahead. Suddenly she screamed and threw the clothes bags she was holding into the air. She turned around quickly as if surprised and scared. She stood there before collapsing and falling to the ground.

"What's happening? Why is everyone panicking and running around behind us?" asked one shopper to another who had just come out of the shop.

"Not sure but few minutes ago, I heard that there was an accident of some sort," replied the man. "Whatever it is, it seemed to have sends everyone running," replied the man.

"I can see people running toward us," said the man raising his head to see further behind them. "Shouldn't we be running away too?" asked the other man. He looked behind and saw people coming toward them.

"I am going I can't wait to see what it is I better run now," said the other man crossing the road and disappearing into the nearby buildings. On the other side of the city people have gathered outside a clothes shop.

"Move backward please! Move backward!" shouted one female

"I said move backward!" yelled the lady pushing people backward. A girl is lying on the floor. Few people are kneeling next to her. Others had surrounded them to see what was happening. The lady got out of the clothes shop and collapsed outside the shop. Helpers had run to her aid. Bags of clothes are lying few meters away from them. The shop assistant had run outside as soon as the lady had fallen. She had tried to revive the lady with no luck. Another passer-by had volunteered to help with resuscitation. The shop assistant had run back into the shop to call for help. She had returned to find that a huge crowd of people had gathered around. She had tried to push the crowd backward to give the collapsed lady plenty of fresh air. After pushing the crowd backward, she knelt again.

"Is she breathing now?" asked the shop assistant. "Yes, but she seems still unconscious," replied the passer-by who was giving her first aid.

"I have called for help." Remarked the shop assistant. "That's great. She need a lot of fresh air and the people are not helping at all." Said the passer-by looking at the crowd. People had gathered, and some were still approaching to find out what was happening. The shop assistant rose again and started pushing the crowd backward. That went on for some time. After a while the passer-by shouted to the shop assistant.

"She is up! She has come around!" The collapsed lady had come around. She had slightly opened her eyes. She seemed confused at first. She looked at the passer-by and shouted.

"Eva! Eva!" she quickly got up and sat on the ground. As she tried to get up, she felt hands holding her shoulders and firmly pushing her to the ground.

"No! No! Please sit down! Rest a little," said the passer-by.

"Tell me where is Eva!" shouted the lady who had collapsed.

"It's okay sit down for some time," said the shop assistant.

"You fainted after leaving our store," said the shop assistant before continuing.

"Please get up and wait for a while in the shop. I have called for help," said the shop assistant helping the lady who had collapsed to get up. The collapsed lady got up with the help of the shop assistant. She touched her forehead and closed her eyes slightly before staggering into the shop. She seemed a little disoriented. They walked for a while and entered the small room inside the shop. The door had a first aid label sticker on it.

"Do you want water to drink?" asked the shop assistant.

"No I have to go. My friend is in trouble!" shouted the lady who had collapsed. She got up and walked to the door. The shop assistant followed her quickly and placed her hand on her shoulder.

"Are you sure you are okay? I have already called for help. The ambulance is on its way. Can you not leave?" said the shop assistant.

"I have to go you don't understand. My friend is in trouble. I cannot stay," said the lady who had collapsed opening the first aid room door. She walked across the shop floor and out of the shop. The shop assistant run after her. She stood outside the shop and watched the lady who had collapsed leave. The lady who had collapsed disappeared into the crowd. Nick picked up his phone and tried to ring his father. The phone rung but no one answered. He went back into the room with the magic stones. Ewalinka was laying on the bed. She was lying on the bed as if there is no tomorrow. There was a raised fireplace which looked like an altar with shining green stones. Slight rays of white smoke can be seen emanating from the green stones. They give the whole room a florescent green glow. Nick is pacing from one corner to the other. He is not sure what to do. Can he go and check upon his father leaving Ewalinka alone? Or can he wait for her to come around? Where are the other girls? He asked himself. Surely something bad might have happened. Is my father okay Nicked asked himself? He kept worrying and a lot of questions seemed to trouble him. He tried ringing his dad's phone before going downstairs. While downstairs he rang all the other girl's phones, but no one picked up their phone. He paced left and right and stopped. He thought for a while and then quickly he rushed outside. He jumped into his car and drove the car very close to the house entrance. He left the passenger door open. He jumped out of the car leaving the car idling. He rushed inside the house and upstairs. Straight into the room with the magic stones. He carried Ewalinka downstairs and straight into the car. He laid her on the passenger seat. He went back inside the house and came out with a pillow and a soft blanket. He slowly placed these underneath Ewalinka's head and body. He closed the door and carefully drove out of the driveway and into the main road. He headed to his father's house. The boss arrived followed by the other two bodyguards.

"Ask her what she knows. I want to know everything before moving to plan C." requested the boss.

"She is still unconscious boss," replied the bodyguard.

"Give her the oxygen mask, hurry. You might have choked her to death," said the boss.

The bodyguards rushed and did as what the boss had ordered. An oxygen mask was put back onto Eva's head. They all waited. One hour gone still there was no sign of recovery. She was still unconscious and breathing slowly. Her pulse had stopped. After two hours, still no sign of life. Five hours later the boss realized that they might have killed her. The fumes might have been too much for her. Everyone panicked.

"What shall we do boss with this girl?" asked one of the bodyguards.

"It might be too late now to do anything. She should have been up by now. Any more time without help she might end up with brain injuries. We do not want that." The boss paused as if thinking for a while. "Wait one more hour if she doesn't come around then get rid of her," said the boss. The bodyguards drove off toward the city center. After sometime the car came to a sudden stop. One of the bodyguards came out of the car and looked around before dragging an unconscious girl out of the car. He left her beside the road. Jumped back into the car and the car sped off.

"Hello, we got rid of her," said the bodyguard in the passenger seat.

"Was she dead?" asked the boss.

"Clinically Yes. I do not think she can recover from this. She was not breathing and had no pulse at all," replied the bodyguard.

"We left her beside the road so it looks like a hit and run," said the bodyguard.

"Okay, get rid of that car," ordered the boss with a strong voice.

"Copy that," replied the bodyguard.

"Hello! Help! Operator, I need an ambulance. Please hurry."

"Where are you? What is the problem?" asked the operator.

"I am in Central Highway after Rosemary road. A woman is badly hurt. Please hurry!" replied the woman.

"Is she breathing? Does she have a pulse?" asked the operator There was a moment of silence as the woman checked if the girl was breathing. She holds her hand to check her pulse.

"She is not breathing, and she has no pulse but her body is warm," replied the woman.

"OK, keep on the line until the ambulance arrives".

"Hurry! Please hurry!" pleaded the woman. She removed her jacket and covered the girl. She took out her scarf from her hand bag and gently placed it under her head. The girl had head injuries she might have hit the ground when she fell. It seems she had fallen from the car or a victim of a hit and run. A lot of questions kept popping into this woman's head without answers. She waited for the ambulance. Ten minutes later an ambulance arrived followed by the police car that blocked the road. One ambulance staff jumped out of the ambulance with a trolley bed. Another one jumped from the front seats of the ambulance. They checked the lady while still on the ground. She was unconscious. They lifted her onto the trolley bed and quickly placed her in the ambulance. The door closed living the pedestrian who had found her standing there. The siren could be heard as the ambulance sped off heading toward the nearest hospital. The woman had a drip placed on her hand and an oxygen mask. The ambulance staff at the back of the ambulance with the unconscious lady took the unconscious lady's body temperature. After that he started completing the paperwork. Temperature 34'C JD, Unconscious False, Pulse Faint heartbeat, Possible hit and run, Location Central/corner Rosemary Road, Oxygen and drip. As soon as he had finished writing the notes, the ambulance entered the hospitals' A&E and the back doors opened. Two nurses from the hospital came to take the lady. The ambulance staff handed over the unconscious lady to the hospital staff.

"JD, unconscious, faint heartbeat, no pulse. Treatment: oxygen gas and drip." said the ambulance staff handing the clipboard to the nurse. The unconscious lady was rushed inside. Two other nurses met them and took over. Quickly they rushed to the operating room. The lady was placed on the hospital's oxygen supply machine. The doctor entered the room and started writing something down at the same time examining the unconscious lady.

"CPR followed by defibrillator," shouted the doctor. Quickly the nurses rushed to start CPR. They started chest compression. As soon as the nurse started administering CPR, the other nurse started preparing the defibrillator. Chest compression followed by artificial ventilation was performed and after 5 minutes the defibrillator was used. The process was repeated before the nurse checked the unconscious lady's pulse and breathing. There was no improvement and the unconscious lady was placed on the mechanical oxygen supply and monitored. Two days passed by and the lady was still unconscious. Vital signs did not return and the unconscious lady was verbally declared dead. She was taken to the mortuary. It was hours later when the mortuary staff felt a pulse and she was rushed back to the emergency room where she fully recovered. In South Central France, Bellac Limousin a couple are distraught and are comforting each other. Their windows had been broken several times by burglars. The only strange thing was that nothing was stolen. They had reported this to the local police. Their main concern was with their daughter. They were concerned for their daughters' safety. It seemed on all occasions the room where she slept was the one always with broken windows. They had moved her from room to room. When she was four years old, they had relocated. After a while the windows were broken again. The night before her seventh birthday her parents had spent the night with their daughter. They were very happy and had bought her a lot of presents. They had looked forward to holding her seventh birthday party. They had read her a bedtime story. She was very happy. Her parents had been very strict with her movements since the burglars. They had been very worried about their daughter. She had few friends but on special occasions like her birthdays she could invite a lot of friends. On previous birthdays, she had invited her friends to sleep over. The day of her birthday her parents had woken up to find her room empty. She was gone. The windows were not broken, it seemed she had deliberately left. They could not understand why she had run away from home. They had thought that since it was her birthday, a friend had visited her. They had thought that a friend might have invited her to her house. They had waited for her to come back. Hours passed by without any sign of her. They had made phone calls inquiring about her but no one had seen her. It was after the second day that they filed a missing person report at the police station.

"What seemed to be the problem," asked a woman who was sitting beside them waiting for her turn to be served.

"Life can be so painful, you know," said Bridgette. "Our daughter disappeared a day ago," added Benjamin.

"Our beloved daughter did not come back home yesterday," said Bridgette.

"It was her birthday yesterday. Still, I cannot believe it. Where could she go?" asked Benjamin. Benjamin and Bridgette had spent a good six years with their daughter. She had never left them before. This was her first time, and they did not know what had happened to her.

"Next please," said the woman at the desk. Benjamin and his wife Bridgette stood up and walked to the desk. They pulled the chairs and sat in front of the desk.

"We would like to file a missing person report," said

Benjamin hugging his wife who was crying.

"Our daughter is missing. Our beloved daughter did not come back home," said Bridgette taking out a handkerchief from her bag. She blew her nose and put the handkerchief back in her bag.

"How long has she been missing?" asked the woman at the desk. "She left on her birthday and did not come back" said Benjamin holding his wife's hand. "That was a day before yesterday," added Bridgette. "Has she done this before? Are there friends where she might have gone?" asked the woman at the desk. "This is the first time she had done this. Friends? Not sure really," said Benjamin.

"We woke up to say happy birthday to our little girl and the next thing we know she was gone," added Bridgette.

"Ok I am going to take some details," said the woman at the desk. She opened a drawer and took out a file. She took a blank paper report and started writing down something. She then asked her name and age and her friends details. After a while the woman at the desk got and left them for some time. She later came back and sat down. She picked up the phone and dialed a number. She waited for the person on the other end to answer the phone.

"Hello, it is Rosetta. I have an urgent one. File number 106. Can you look at this straight away?" said Rosetta.

"Straight away. I got it. Thanks," replied the person at the other end of the line.

"Thanks, that's all we can do for now. We have all the information we need. One of us will look at this straight away and contact you as soon as possible." said Rosetta Benjamin and his wife left the police station and headed home. This was the most distressing time in their life. No words could explain how hard and painful they felt. As soon as they arrived home, they heard a knock on the door. Quickly they rushed to open the door.

"Hello. I am here to ask you a few questions regarding the disappearance of your daughter. I am a private investigator," Juditha stretched her arm and looked at Bridgette and Benjamin.

"Do you work for the police also?" asked Benjamin.

"We are linked, I have my own private company but sometimes they ask me for help," said private investigator Juditha.

"Can we talk inside?" asked Benjamin inviting the private investigator inside the house. He leads the way and Juditha followed him. Bridgette too entered the house. They sat in the lounge and started talking.

"I quickly checked your files and records," she paused and looked at the couple before continuing.

"Our records or should I say the records held by the police shows that you had problems of burglary before this." asked Juditha.

"Yes, we have had our share of bad luck. Our house was vandalized several times. Nothing was stolen though," said Benjamin. They spoke for a long time before Juditha left their house. She had collected her photos and other items she thought might be helpful in finding their daughter. She had posted her photos in the missing person photos in newspapers and on the internet. They had searched the whole area of Bellac, Limousin with no luck. There were appeals on the television as well. News of her disappearance had spread all over Bellac and Limousin. Their daughter had few friends, they were worried about her since the burglaries. She had rarely visited her friends in a long time.

CHAPTER EIGHT

One day Judith was in her office. It was a normal day as usual. She was busy in her office. The disappearance of Benjamin and Bridgette's girl had given her sleepless nights. She had not found any leads. She could not understand why their daughter left. There was no break- in. It seemed she had left the room deliberately as the door was opened from the inside. She had looked at this case for the past six months with no clues at all. She had seen Eva's picture on the missing person wall in her office for the past six months. Every day that picture had reminded her of her failure.

"I have never felt so useless before all my life." Said Juditha.

"Why? I think you are the best private investigator around." Remarked Mark standing up from his chair and sitting down on Juditha's desk.

"That girl on the wall," said Juditha pointing at the

picture on the wall of a blonde girl with blue eyes. "That girl oh I see," said Mark.

"We can't win all the time," continued Mark. "I know but with this case for the first time. I am clueless and have no leads at all. No one in whole France had provided any information," added Juditha. In all other cases, at least one or two people had phoned-in with information. Even if the information later turned out to be incorrect," continued Juditha. I have looked at this from all angles still I have no clues. I have looked at the break-in reports. Nothing makes sense," said Juditha. Mark stood up and walked to the wall. He looked at the pictures on the missing person board. There was a blonde girl with shining blue eyes.

"If she was in Bellac surely someone might have seen her by now. It has been six months since she last vanished," said Juditha.

"It must be hard for the parents," said Mark looking at Juditha. Mark and Juditha had worked together for the past five years. They had solved a lot of cases together some with happy conclusions and some with not. They were a reputable team that the local, national and foreign police forces were constantly seeking their services. Juditha was the daughter or a former police officer. Her father had retired early since the accident that nearly costs his life. Juditha had shown much interest as a kid. She had dedicated her life to solving problems and making the community a better place for everyone. This case had made her think twice. There were no leads at all. No sightings or any information. All her friends had seen her in the afternoon the day she vanished. The local police force had searched for her for days everywhere with no luck.

"Maybe we should look at this from a different angle," suggested Juditha.

"What do you have in mind?" asked Mark.

"Put yourself in her shoes. How far will you have to go? If you were running away from home?" asked Juditha.

"Let's see. I am a six, I mean seven years old kid. I am scared at home. Probably because of the break-ins. The night before my birthday I run away from home. Where would I go?" inferred Mark as if asking himself.

"Correct," said Juditha. I would probably go to a friend's," said Mark looking at Juditha.

"We asked all her friends and their parents. We checked all of them. No one was with her or saw her the night of her disappearance." Replied Juditha

"No one at all?" asked Mark.

"Yes, no one," replied Juditha.

"What if she went outside and was abducted?" asked Mark. "That's a possibility, but we checked everyone in the area and surroundings. They are all clean. There has been surveillance," said Juditha.

"What about the parents?" asked Mark. What do you mean? What about the parents?" asked Juditha.

"You know what I mean," replied Mark.

"Don't even think like that. They are clean too. We checked them too," said Juditha.

"So, what is the new angle you were talking about?" asked Mark.

"I think we should expand our search to include foreign nations," said Juditha.

"It would make sense. That could also explain why there is no information at all regarding this case."

"That makes sense," added Mark going back to the

missing board in the room. He looked again at the picture.

"We should contact other private investigators abroad and search abroad as well," said Juditha.

"How are we going to do that?" asked Mark.

"I think I have a better idea," Juditha quickly stood up and entered the file storage room. She looked at the boxes on top of the file cabinets. She brought one of the boxes and put it on top of the desk. She opened the box. She searched inside for a while. "Bingo!" she screamed. She took out a small diary and sat on her chair.

"Imagine this small diary was sat in there for the last five years," said Juditha blowing dust from the diary. She quickly opened the diary and flipped the pages. She stopped and looked closely at one page in the diary. She quickly reached for the telephone number and dialed a number.

"The number you are trying to call is no longer in use," Juditha heard this message as she tried to get hold of someone.

"Damn! The number is no longer in use," said Juditha to Mark.

"Who are you trying to call?" asked Mark I met a friend of mine. We were classmates together but now she works for Interpol," paused Juditha as she started typing on the computer keyboard.

"See if I can find her on the internet," said Judith searching on Google and LinkedIn.

"No results. That means I must go to Lyon as soon as possible," remarked Juditha.

"Interpol. Last time I checked all information was classified," said Mark.

"I know that's why I needed the contact details of a

friend of mine," said Judith. They looked at this case in detail the whole day and without even knowing it soon it was home time. They said goodbyes, and each one left the office heading home. The following day Juditha drove to Lyon. After nearly five hours of driving Juditha finally arrived in Lyon. She headed to the Interpol headquarters. The place was very secured and there was no access for the public. Information here was treated with the strictest confidence. Several times she had phoned this place she had been refused access to any information. Data protection and confidentiality had been cited as reasons for not sharing sensitive information. Years later she had met her friend. She was now working here, and she had profusely insisted to help Juditha with any information that she needed. Juditha arrived at the reception.

"Bonjour!"

"Bonjour Madame!" replied the male receptionist

"I am here to see a relative of mine by the name of Sylvia Louisa." Said Juditha.

"Sylvia Louisa," repeated the receptionist scrolling in the big book on the table. Juditha waited there looking around. The place was a big place well decorated inside. The building had large glasses surrounding it. There were security guards outside. Electrical glass lifts can be seen going up and down the building. People can be seen coming out of the lifts and some going into the lifts.

"Yes, Sylvia Louisa, third floor office 3," said the receptionist.

"Oh thanks. Any chance you can let her know that I am in the reception and I am expecting her," said Juditha. The receptionist picked up the phone and scrolled down and then drew a line with his finger across the book until he reached an extension number.

"451," he murmured.

He dialed the number and waited. The phone rung for some time and no one answered. He scrolled in the book again and dialed another number.

"Bonjour. Madame, Sylvia Louisa please," said the receptionist.

"Hold on I check for you," replied the person on the other end of the phone line. The receptionist looked at Juditha and pointed at the receiver with his right hand while holding the receiver between his collar bone and chin. A few minutes later the person on the other end spoke to the receptionist.

"What is your name?" asked the receptionist. "Juditha Sancrust," replied Juditha

"Juditha Sancrust," repeated the receptionist to the person on the other side of the line. "This is regarding to what? Private or business? What is your contact number?" asked the receptionist.

"It's private visit. I will be staying at the hotel Villa Maria room two ground floor," said Juditha to the receptionist who in turn repeated the same to the person on the other end of the line. She took a pen and wrote down her telephone number on a piece of paper and gave it to the receptionist. Juditha left the Interpol headquarters in Lyon and headed to the city center to her hotel. Sylvia was out of the office. She had gone somewhere for a meeting and she will be later in the office that day. Juditha had driven for nearly five hours from Bellac to Lyon. She was exhausted and wanted to go to her hotel room and rest. She arrived at Villa Maria and headed to the reception.

"How can I help you?" asked the receptionist at the hotel.

"It's Ms. Sancrust. I have a hotel reservation. Room 2," said Judith.

"Do you have any form of ID Ms. Sancrust?" asked the receptionist. Judith moved her hand bag in front of her from the left side and opened the bag. She looked inside and withdrew a passport and handed it to the receptionist.

"Merci Madame." Replied the receptionist at Villa Maria. She waited and looked around as the receptionist entered her passport details in the computer. After a few minutes, the receptionist gave Juditha her passport back and two card keys.

"Enjoy the stay at the hotel, Ms. Sancrust," said the receptionist with a big smile on his face. Juditha headed to her hotel room. She flipped in the key-card and entered her room. The room was a Victorian type room with a king size bed in the middle of the hotel. A big mirror on top of the bed. A desk and a single sofa. She walked towards the red curtains and opened the curtains. She took her hand bag and placed it on top of the dressing table. She walked to the door inside her hotel room. She opened the door and sighed from exhaustion. She removed her shoes and entered this bathroom. There was a big tube and a glass shower next to it. She removed her clothes and opened the tube water after checking its temperature. She waited for the tube water to rise before entering in the tube. She was there for some time thinking about that girl who had disappeared. She snoozed for a while and was woken up by the phone ringing. She quickly got up and the line soon died. There was a message light flashing on the answer phone. She went there and picked up the receiver and listened to the message after pressing one. The message was from Sylvia. She had asked Juditha to ring her back once she had the message. Quickly she dialed Sylvia's number and waited.

"Hallo! It is a long time since I last saw you. How are you? What brings you to this side?" asked Sylvia.

"I am fine. Just thought I could visit my old friend," explained Juditha.

"That's fine. It is really nice of you visiting me," commented Sylvia.

"Can we meet after work? You can come to my hotel room later?" proposed Juditha.

"Yes sure. 7pm is that okay with you?" asked Sylvia.

"7pm it is. See you soon," replied Juditha. The line soon died and Juditha finished taking a bath and ordered room service. She looked forward meeting her friend. 7pm at night there was a knock on the door.

"Wait, I am coming," said Juditha. She rushed to the door and opened the door.

"Hallo!" Said Sylvia hugging her friend. These two had not seen each other for a very long time. It was such an emotional reunion. They talked and ordered dinner. After dinner, they spent some time together. They both had agreed that Sylvia slept at the hotel as well. It was late at night that Juditha asked her friend for a favor.

"My friend I need a favor from you," said Juditha getting up from the hotel bed and taking a file from her hand bag. He walked to the bed and gave Sylvia the file. She opened the file and started reading it. A picture of a girl fell from the file followed by a paperclip. The picture had become loose as the paperclip slipped. She picked up the picture. She looked at the picture and in disbelief shook her head. "Missing? The world has gone mad. We have cases of missing children every day?" explained Sylvia.

"I need help in searching for this girl abroad. I just thought it will be easy to ask for any sightings and any information. I will appreciate any help you can offer." said Juditha.

"I will continue searching as well. I have planned a trip to some countries abroad," continued Juditha. "At the time of her disappearance there lived some foreigners in the neighborhood. There were Spanish, Russian and Canadian people living in the neighborhood. There was a couple also from Germany," said Juditha. "We will ask for help all over the world. If I get any information, then I will contact you," said Sylvia. They spoke about other things for the rest of the night and slept. In the morning, they both left each heading in a different direction. They said goodbyes and left. The next weeks were very busy for Juditha. She had been to Spain. One of the person who lived in the street as Benjamin and Bridgette was from Spain, Madrid. She had printed a lot of posters with the girl and distributed these. She spent some days asking people for any information. After that she had returned to Bellac, Limousin France. Mark had volunteered to travel to Germany. He had gone to Munich. The other person who was staying in the same street as Benjamin and Bridgette at the time she disappeared was Voight. He was not married but had a partner. He was from Munich and had left months after the girl disappeared. After finding out where he came from Mark had volunteered to go there. Mark asked a lot of the people who knew Voight. No one seemed to know anything. No one had seen the girl anywhere. After a week in Germany Mark returned home with disappointing news. After more weeks of traveling the pair could not afford to travel anymore. This case had put a financial burden on the pair. They spent the past weeks searching for this girl. They had not looked at other cases. That means there was no more money coming into their business. The next trip to Russia was canceled due to insufficient money. After her researching and investigations Juditha had found out that there was another neighbor who had left few days before the girl disappeared. He was from Russia, Moscow. Juditha had his contact details in Russia. She looked for private investigators in Moscow and posted the file to them. It took days to arrive. Once the file arrived in Moscow's private investigators' office, they had phoned her to let her know about their investigations. Weeks passed by without any information. Sylvia had suggested that Juditha offer a reward if she wanted any information regarding the girl. She accepted the idea. Traveling meant not concentrating and dealing with any new cases. This had put a financial burden on her company. Mark had concentrated on new cases after the Germany visit but that did not help. Juditha had promised to offer a reward for any information as soon as she had secured the funds. It took another two weeks for things to go back to normal. Juditha had secured the reward money. Posters, newspaper article and appeals on television were all made and circulated. One Friday afternoon Juditha was in her office completing reports for that week. She had been busy for the past weeks. This coming weekend she had planned to spend time at home away from work. She had promised herself that she will not take work to her home. She just wanted to enjoy her life. She could not remember the last time she had cooked food at home and socialized with friends. She had spent all the past weeks eating in restaurants and looking at this girl's case. She was about to finish work when she received an international call from Moscow. This was the breakthrough she wanted. The girl had been seen. The caller knew where she was and had further proof that it was her in the form of the pictures. The caller wanted money upfront and to meet first face to face before he realized any information. Juditha had offered to send the money with western union. The caller insisted that he had no ID and it will be hard to collect the money. He wanted cash in hand. He got some details of him and bought a plane ticket from Bellac, Limousin France to Russia, Moscow. The following morning, she was on her way to Moscow. This could be the breakthrough she wanted. She landed in Moscow. She phoned Mark to update him about her travels. After talking to Mark, she checked-in the hotel. After an hour, she headed to the meeting place in Moscow. She rang the person with the information.

"Hallo! We talked over the phone yesterday. I am Juditha," said Juditha. The man talked to her in Russian and later continued.

"My English no good! But money first then I show you," said the man.

"I have the money can we still meet in the park as planned," asked Juditha.

"Of course, Money first then I tell you," said the man

mixing both Russian and English in a sentence. It was late in the afternoon. She arrived in the central park. She approached a statue of a warrior on a chariot. She looked around before she sat on the bench. She looked at her watch and looked around. People were sitting in the park enjoying their day. Some were going their way in all directions. She was very nervous and excited at the same time. She had heard of many money frauds. She was hesitating about going to Moscow but somehow, she found the guts and traveled all the way to Russia. She looked at her watch again.

"Only five minutes has passed," she whispered to herself. It felt like she was seated there for a very long time. Suddenly the phone rung and sends her on the edge.

"Hello," she answered the phone hoping that it was that man with the information.

"Judy take care, if it's a hoax don't worry about the money. Just come back I want you back here safely," This was Mark reassuring Juditha.

"Thanks Mark. I will find out soon," said Juditha. Before she has even finished talking to Mark, she heard a voice coming from behind her.

"Do you have the money," asked a small man covered in dirty. He looked at her and a strange feeling crippled her. Surely this was a hoax. This was a fraud. The man was filthy he looked like a beggar. It seemed he had skipped the shower for a good week. His face was covered in dirty. He had one tooth missing. He was wearing a winter wool hat with the long tails covering his ears. He wore gloves with fingers missing. He wore two different kinds of shoes. She looked at him and panicked. Although it was in broad daylight. She remembered Mark's words and looked at the other people nearby. No one seemed to care. The small man stretched his hand as if asking for change.

"Juditha. The money!" said the man with a strong voice. When she heard, him call her by her name she felt a little relaxed.

"It's' you," shouted Juditha surprised and a little shocked.

"Yes. It is me," the small man looked at himself and noticed why Juditha looked surprised.

"Oh, sorry about this but it's for your protection. You do not want to get in trouble, here do you?" asked the man before continuing.

"Any problems you say I am begging for coins. See no problem at all," said the small man shrugging and raising his shoulders.

"The money first," repeated the man.

"Oh sorry," said Juditha taking out an envelope from the purse.

"What about the girl where is she," asked Juditha.

"Don't worry I show you the girl," said the small man taking out a large A4 envelope from his jacket. The envelope had grease on it. He took the envelope and gave it to Juditha. She opened the envelope quickly and looked at the photos. She slumped back on the park chair in disbelief. She felt like crying. It was her. There was no doubt. She had seen this face for the past months and it was all over her mind. She saw this girl even in her dreams. She flipped through the photos once again. She wanted to cry with joy. She wanted to call Mark. She wanted to see the look on the face of her parents as she brought her back to them. All the hard work has paid off, she thought to herself.

"Now you believe me?" asked the man Juditha did not answer but instead just looked at the man and nodded.

"So where is she? Is she okay?" asked Juditha.

"Don't worry I show you. You give me more money?" asked the man.

"Yes! Yes! I give you more money. Show me where she is."

"Okay, we go tomorrow. I take you there. I must talk to my friends' tomorrow morning. We meet her again 8am in the morning," said the man before he walked off. He walked for a few minutes and looked back. "Bring the money tomorrow. Okay," said the man before he vanished in the bushes. Juditha got up quickly and headed to the hotel. On her way, she phoned Mark and told him everything. They all were very happy. They all wished that everything goes well the next day. She scanned the photos and sent them to Mark to do a similarity test. She could not sleep that night. That night was the longest night in her life. She kept waking up to check the time.

CHAPTER NINE

The next day arrived and Juditha was very happy. This is the day everything will start making sense she thought to herself. She woke up early and left the hotel heading for the central park. She arrived half an hour early. She sat there for a while. She thought of phoning Mark but then again thought that it would be wise to call him after getting Eva. That morning Mark had rung her but she couldn't take his call. He had left a message about the photos. Later on the short man arrived to take Juditha to Eva. "Morning Juditha," said the short man. "I am Carlos. If you have the money. Give me then we will be on our way," continued Carlos. Juditha opened her purse and took out her wallet. She took out $300. Carlos did not waste time. He quickly took the money and folded it before putting it in his socks. They were on their way. They got in a taxi and left the central park. Juditha was nervous, but this is the moment she was waiting for. After a few minutes the taxi arrived. They parked near the house and waited for a while. There was no one at the house. After twenty minutes Juditha got out of the taxi and walked toward the house. She has never been this nervous before. Anything can go wrong. She might put Eva in danger. If the abductor knew she was with the police, he might relocate or kill he altogether. Did she have to inform the police first? There were so many questions that kept popping into her head. She went to the neighbor's house first. "Hello. How are you?" said Juditha as she entered the neighbor's yard.

"Hallo. I am okay. Thank you," said the neighbor, the lady in her mid-thirties.

"I am a relative of the neighbors. It seems there is no one home," said Juditha stretching her hand to greet the lady. The lady instead opened her arms and hugged Juditha at the same time kissing her on the cheeks. How long have you known the neighbors?" asked Juditha taking out a photo of Eva. She gave the photo to the lady.

"I am Juditha by the way," added Juditha. The lady did not reply she looked at the photo for a while. She inspected the photo and then invited her in the house. "I am Ursula, people call me Urla." She said leading Juditha to the lounge room.

"Eva, oh she is a wonderful girl," said Urla. "Did you say Eva," asked Juditha very surprised. She still uses her original name she thought to herself.

"Yes. She is called Eva. That little sweet girl. Always by herself, with no parents around and that fool Luke leaving her alone all the time locked up in that house," said Urla sounding upset and annoyed getting up and going to the kitchen.

"Tea or coffee?" she asked.

"Coffee two sugars," said Juditha following Urla to the kitchen.

"So, this girl is always by herself? Where are her parents?" asked Juditha.

"Who knows they don't say much? He does not want anyone to talk to her. You rarely see him. You see him at weekends only," said Urla. She gave Juditha a cup of coffee. They both went back in the lounge area.

"So, when is the last time you saw them?" asked Juditha.

"Honestly Luke, two, three days ago, and the girl Yesterday. She stood outside as if waiting for someone for the whole morning and afternoon. She looked worried. She kept going inside and after a few minutes comes out and stands at the gate," said Urla sipping her coffee and pausing for a while.

"Who else lives at the house?" asked Juditha. She has a baby minder who comes there two or three days a week to do the chores. Probably she is there. I do not know which days she comes," said Urla looking at Juditha.

"Is Luke married? Does he have a girlfriend?" asked Juditha standing up and looking at the teapot collection in the display cabinet.

"I got those from Ukraine. There are very rare. Here in Moscow you cannot afford them," said Urla pointing at the display cabinet. There was a moment of silence as Juditha drank her coffee.

"It's a nice collection. My grandmother used to collect teapot and chinaware before she died," said Juditha.

"Luke married! I never saw him with anyone. I only

see him with Eva. Maybe the baby minder is his girlfriend. No one knows what happens behind those closed doors," said Urla. The two talked for a while. Juditha's phone started ringing. She put her coffee cup down and reached for her handbag. She took out her phone and answered it.

"Bonjour," said Juditha.

"Bonjour Juditha. Its Mark. Are you free to talk it is about the girl?" asked Mark.

"Yes sure," Juditha pointed at her phone looking at Urla and walked outside.

"The test results are out. Perfect match! One issue though, eye color did not match. I guess there are hundred possibly explanations. Just be aware of that," said Mark before hanging up.

"Ok thanks Mark," Juditha stood there pondering what all this means. She was about to go inside when the front door of Luke's house opened. She stood there hoping to see Eva coming out of the house. A lady in her late twenties came out of the house and started smoking outside. She quickly went there and introduced herself.

"Hallo. I am a distance relative of the family. My name is Juditha," said Juditha extending her hand to greet the lady.

"I am Magda. I am the housekeeper," said the lady putting out the cigarette.

"I need to talk to you I just need to get my handbag from the next door. I will be in a second?" said Juditha walking next door. She returned after a while. She took out the photo of Eva she had and gave it to Magda. She looked at it, there was no doubt it was Eva.

"Come in," said Magda. They both went inside the

house. Juditha was excited. She wanted to meet Eva and ask her a lot of questions.

"Are you related to Luke?" asked Juditha. No I am just a babysitter," replied Magda.

"Is Luke, Eva's dad?" asked Juditha

"Sit down please any refreshments?" asked Magda handing back Eva's photo.

"No thanks. I just had a cup of coffee," said Juditha taking back the photo from Magda and putting it on the table.

"How old is Eva now?" asked Juditha getting up to look at the photos on the wall. There was no doubt. This was the missing Eva. Magda went to a room in the house and brought a piece of paper which she handed to Juditha. This was Eva's birth certificate. It shows that she was born in Moscow.

"So, per this birth certificate Eva is seven years old, born on. wait a minute." Said Juditha quickly putting her hand in her handbag. She took out a small diary and quickly flipped the pages. She looked bewildered.

"So where are Eva's parents?" asked Juditha.

"As far as I know they are dead. Luke is Eva's uncle," said Magda looking suspicious. Juditha looked at the birth certificate and wrote Eva's parents' names down.

"So, this Luke, is he still at work and where is Eva?" asked Juditha putting back the diary and the photo into her hand bag. Magda did not reply, instead looked at Juditha.

"Luke and Eva, when are they coming home?" asked Juditha this time getting up. She had sensed that Magda had realized that she was not relative.

"Who are you? What do you want?" asked Magda angry.

"Where is Luke? Where is Luke? You do not know?" asked Magda.

"Know what?" asked Juditha surprised.

"Luke was killed yesterday and Eva is in intensive care," said Magda holding tears.

"I didn't know that. Luke is dead!? Which hospital is Eva in? Do you know?" asked Juditha leaving the house.

"EMC," replied Magda. Juditha left the house and quickly got into the taxi and shouted EMC. The taxi driver started driving.

"Hello Ms. Is everything okay?" asked Carlos.

"Mr. Carlos. You are still here?" asked Juditha opening her purse and taking out $100 and giving it to Carlos. I think you have to get off here. Thank you very much. If I need your services, I will call you," said Juditha looking at the back seat where Carlos was seating. The driver stopped the taxi and Carlos got out and waved goodbye. The taxi headed to Moscow EMC. Juditha took out her phone and dialed a number. The phone can be heard ringing but without anyone answering it.

"Come on Mark answer the phone," said Juditha talking to herself. She tried again and this time Mark answered the call.

"How are you Judy? Is everything ok?" asked Mark

"I think I have found her. To cut the long story short. Luke the abductor is dead. The poor guy was killed yesterday. The bad news is that the girl is intensive care. I do not know what happened. That is where I am going now," said Juditha taking out her small diary.

"Listen, Mark, I need a favor. Have a background check on one Pavel and Sasha Orlov? I want to know where they are? If they are dead how they died? If they have ever been to France especially Bellac, Limousin. Check also date and place of birth of Eva, Benjamin and Bridgette's daughter," asked Juditha. She paused for a while before continuing.

"I will call you after the hospital visit."

"Ok, I will check straight away," answered Mark. The taxi arrived at the hospital and Juditha went inside.

"I want to see Ewalinka Orlov I am a relative," said Juditha asking the receptionist.

"She is in intensive care ask for the doctor on the fourth floor," replied the receptionist. Juditha looked at the time and walked toward the lifts. After a few minutes a bell is heard and the lift door opened. She quickly got inside, and she pressed the fourth floor button. "Doors closing and lift going up," a voice of a female can be heard coming from the lifts' speakers. On the level floor the doors opened and Juditha quickly left the lift and headed for the reception.

"I want to see Ewa in intensive care I am a relative," asked Juditha looking around to see if there was a doctor nearby.

"Left corridor and turn left again you won't miss it. The doctor is there," said the receptionist pointing to the direction for Juditha to take. Juditha quickly left and headed to the intensive care unit. She entered inside and the machines can be heard beeping. Ewa is lying on the bed with tubes attached to her. An oxygen machine is attached to her. She lay there peacefully.

"How can I help you, it's doctor Antoni?" asked the doctor

"I am a relative. How is she?" asked Juditha looking at her.

"She is a fighter. She was in a kind of shock but she is stable now. It is a pity the way she lost her uncle?" said the doctor writing something down on the clipboard he was holding. Juditha for some time looked confused.

"Sorry doc. Did you say uncle?" she asked looking surprised. "Yes, uncle Luke was robbed and killed today. I understand the poor girl witnessed it all. She was found unconscious next to him," paused the doctor looking first at Ewa and then at Juditha.

"Luke is Ewa's uncle?" whispered Juditha not expecting any answer from the doctor.

"Are you okay?" asked the doctor after noticing that Juditha was surprised by all this.

"I thought you said you are a relative?" asked the doctor.

"Yes, doctor I didn't know about Luke," remarked Juditha.

"I think it's had enough to lose both parents the same day and then lose your uncle like this. Poor girl," said the doctor.

"Both parents dead?" repeated Juditha trying to piece the puzzle together.

"Benjamin and Bridgette all dead?" asked Juditha. "No, it's Pavel and Sasha all killed in a car accident the same day. Luke Sasha's blood brother then raised Ewa," said the doctor putting his writing pen in his pocket. Juditha did not say anything she stood there for a while and took the photo from the hand bag. She handed the photo to the doctor. He took it and looked at the photo.

"Is this the girl lying there?" asked Juditha. The doctor took the photo and looked at it. He looked at it for some time before squinting his eyes to check

Ewa's eye color.

"Not sure why, but 100% this is the girl lying there. Eye color is slightly different, but eye color changes all the time," said the doctor.

"Do you have medical records for this Ewa from this hospital?" asked Juditha holding her chest. The doctor understood and asked Juditha to follow him. They went to an office down the corridor.

"Take a seat, please," said the doctor before seating in front of the computer.

"Ewalinka Orlov," said the doctor before heating the enter key.

"Yes, Ewalinka Orlov born at this hospital, mother Sasha, father Pavel, Eye color at birth green. Date of birth 25 November current age seven years," said the doctor seating back in his chair.

"One more question, do you have Luke's medical file here at the hospital?" Asked Juditha. The doctor for a while kept silent and then asked Juditha.

"What is this about? This side is for children only. Why so much interested in Luke? No one will give you that kind of information. What is this about?" asked the doctor.

"It's a long story. I am a private investigator from France," she paused and looked at the doctor.

"I am searching for a girl called Eva, and this is her picture. She was born on 25 November as well and she is seven years as well. Her parents are Benjamin and Bridgette and they live in France. As far as I know they have never been to Russia. Their daughter Eva was born in Bellac, Limousin France. Day before her seventh birthday she was abducted that is what I believe and hence my presence here," said Juditha producing her ID.

"I think Luke abducted this girl from France or somehow ended up with her. The birth certificate might be fake or something. I just can't explain it," said Juditha.

"Any chance they might be twins? That is the only plausible explanation?" said the doctor.

"I have Eva's original birth certificate from the hospital in France. Any chance someone might have tempered with your system?" asked Juditha.

"Highly unlikely. Medical records cannot be erased or tempered with." Said the doctor.

"Okay, I will check Luke's file for you but this stays here," said the doctor. Thanks doctor that would mean a lot to me," said Juditha.

"Luke, blood brother of a one Sasha Chenkov also Sasha Orlov. When Ewa's parents died, Luke adopted Ewa as his own daughter," said the doctor. On hearing this Juditha did not know what to do. She went to Ewa's room and spend some time with her. At doctors' advice, she left the hospital, with many questions than before. She headed to her hotel room. Juditha arrived at her hotel and as she was passing the reception, the receptionist stopped her.

"Ms. Juditha. Ms. Juditha. I have a message for you. Your friend Mark called but left no message. Juditha went to her room, and she slumped on the bed and slept for some time. Half an hour later she woke up and rang Mark.

"Hello Mark."

"Hey Judy how did it go?"

"It's not our girl but you won't believe the resemblance. She is seven as well by the name of Ewa which is Russian but same as the English Eva," paused Juditha.

"Woo! What a coincidence. What are the chances of that happening?" Asked Mark.

"I would say one in a trillion. I still cannot explain the whole thing. What do you have for me?" asked Juditha.

"Pavel and Sasha Orlov died in a car accident. They had one daughter Ewalinka later adopted by a one Luke Chenkov," said Mark.

"Ok so what about Eva?" asked Juditha.

"Evalina Petit, born 25 November Limousin France, current age seven years old. Born to Benjamin and Bridgette Petit. Everything checked out I phoned the hospital too they have her birth records," explained Mark. There was a moment of silence before Juditha spoke.

"I guess it's another dead end see you tomorrow and thanks Mark".

"Ok see you soon, bye," replied Mark ending the call. Seven o'clock in the morning the next day Juditha woke up. She took a shower and eight o'clock in the morning she ordered breakfast. She had a cup of coffee, a toast with bacon and egg, a bowl of cereals and an apple and she was ready to check out and go back home. After breakfast, she started going through her notes. This was another dead end. Check out time arrived and Juditha checked out of the hotel. The taxi was waiting for her outside.

"Airport please," said Juditha as she got into the taxi. "Ok. Madame," replied the taxi driver. One day I must come and visit Moscow when I have enough time to see the city thought Juditha as the taxi left the hotel. Moscow was different from Limousin France where Juditha worked. Moscow looked more alive, different, although very cold. Juditha looked outside the window. Moscow seemed to have a variety and plenty of shops. The taxi headed for the airport after leaving the city. After some minutes the taxi arrived at Domodedovo airport. Juditha got out of the taxi and headed for terminal two. She looked at her watch it was 12:25 afternoon. Her flight was after 2 hours. She headed straight to the check-in desk and began check-in. 13:05 afternoon she received a call.

"Hallo. It is Juditha speaking. How can I help you," asked Juditha seating in the waiting area?

"You have an incoming international call please stay on the line," said an automated voice.

"Juditha it's Sylvia. I have some good news for you. I have been trying to get hold of you. I have information regarding the issue we discussed the other day. I have a contact by the name of Milaki Kovich in Kurgan." Said Sylvia before being interrupted by Juditha.

"Kurgan, you said," asked. Juditha

"Yes," answered Sylvia.

"I am in Moscow right now I had a lead, but it's a dead end. My plane fly out in less than two hours," said Juditha a bit skeptical.

"I think this person is reliable. He is not after any money. I just thought you could check it out while you are still there. Kurgan city is two hours away from Moscow by flight," said Sylvia. There was a moment of silence as Juditha thought this over.

"Cancel the flight I will book another flight in a day or two. I have a gut feeling it is worth checking out," said Sylvia trying to convince her friend.

"Ok. I guess I should fly there. Do you have a physical address?" asked Juditha.

"Yes. Just hold on," Juditha hold the line while Sylvia

got the address.

"Kurgan city, Abrahams Cathedral," said Sylvia.

"Ok thanks I will keep you updated," said Judith writing down in her small diary. Juditha picked up her phone and dialed Mark's mobile but the line was busy so she left a message. She took out her phone and bought a ticket online to Kurgan city from Moscow. The flight was a two-hour journey to Kurgan airport. She checked-in online and after another two hours wait she left Moscow for Kurgan city. She checked-in a hotel and contacted Milaki Kovich. Hello. I understand you have some information for me," said Juditha.

"Who is this?" asked the man on the other line. Juditha replied.

"It's Juditha, I got your details from Sylvia from France." Ok. Come to the church tomorrow. Then we can talk," said the man. The phone line died after that. Juditha did not have the chance to ask some questions. Abrahams Cathedral is located near the city gardens. The Cathedral can be seen from a distance. The Cathedral seems robust yet beautifully made. The golden domes can be seen from afar. This is the center of the community in Kurgan. Religion plays an important role in people's lives. This is a Russian Orthodox church. The big service is normally on Sundays. Most of the people here know each other. Kurgan has a small population. The church is the center of focus. Juditha arrived at the church and entered inside. She went in and sat on a church bench. Inside the Cathedral was huge and beautifully decorated. There was no church service. People were coming inside and making personal prayers as they wish. She sat there observing the worshipers. People would come in, make a cross sign, and proceeded to the front of the church. There they would kiss the altars and pillars in front. After that they would stand in front of the altar and sing with lower voices. When they have finished, they would go to the benches and kneel. They will start praying after that. She sat down there observing the worshipers for twenty minutes. While observing the worshipers, a man came and sat behind her.

"Madame Juditha my name is Milaki we spoke on the phone earlier on." Said the man as he put a big brown envelope next to Juditha.

"Yes. It is me," she replied looking at the envelope besides her. She took the envelope and opened it. She took out the photographs and a small note fell on the floor.

"Careful not to lose that," said the man as Juditha knelt to pick up the small paper. She quickly placed it inside and looked at the pictures. Déjà vu and déjà vecu are the appropriate words to describe what Juditha was feeling as she looked at the pictures. Surely there must be a mistake, Juditha thought to herself. "Has this girl been to Moscow? Was she born in Moscow? Is she staying with a lone parent? How old is she," Juditha didn't finish asking before the man interrupted.

"Too many questions. Do not worry Madame we have plenty of time," said the man trying to make Juditha relax. The man continued. Yes. The girl has been to Moscow. Everyone has been to Moscow Madame. Yes, she was born in Moscow," the man paused as a worshiper came by and asked to pass to the other side. After the worshiper, has passed they continued their conversation.

"Where was I?" asked Milaki before continuing.

"The girl stays with her father I guess. As far as I know the girl is seven years old." The man stopped talking and waited for Juditha to look at the pictures. She looked at all five pictures. Surely this was Ewalinka. She came to the last photo and stopped. She looked at the lightening in the church. She took the last photo and brought it close to her face. She quickly searched in her bag and took out her phone. She scrolled through apps and pressed one button. The searchlight on the phone came on. She pointed the light on the picture. The girl in the picture had gray eyes. She was a splitting image of Ewalinka. There would pass for twins with Ewalinka.

"What age did you say she was?" asked Juditha.

"Seven years Madame," replied Milaki. When is the last time you saw her?" asked Juditha.

"Sunday church service," replied the man.

"Do they attend the church frequently?" asked Juditha.

"Every Sunday as far as I know." Replied Milaki.

"The small paper is the address where she lives," said Milaki. Judith dipped her hand inside the envelope and took out the small paper. She looked at it and put it back in the envelope.

"I would like to meet this girl or her father if possible," said Juditha looking backward at Milaki. He looked at the worshipers coming their way before he replied.

"If you know what to say, that's their address in the envelope. If you say you are from the church, you will be more accepted. I understand the girl was baptized here," Dimitri and his daughter lived in walking distance of the church. Since his wife, Enya died he had looked after his daughter with the help of his sister. Jevalinka was the name of Dimitri's daughter. She was now seven years old. She had grown to be a strong girl. Dimitri was sitting in the lounge with his daughter and sister when they heard a knock on the door.

"Jevalinka stood up and ran to open the door,"

"Who is it?" shouted her father. A woman from the church father!" replied Jevalinka.

"Ok let her in," shouted Dimitri. The door can be heard being forcefully closed. Jevalinka ran ahead in the lounge area where her father was watching the news on the television. Jevalinka stood in the lounge and shouted to the woman from the church to come in the lounge. Hesitantly Juditha walked into the lounge. She looked at Jevalinka for a while. She looked like Ewalinka.

"Sit down please any refreshments?" asked Nancy Dimitri's sister.

"Yes. Thank you. Coffee please two sugars," said Juditha as she was sitting down. Dimitri took the television remote control and reduced the volume and sat up straight in his chair.

"What brings you here sister?" asked Dimitri. Juditha looked at Jevalinka for some time before replying.

"I have been to the church. We are going from house to house today to offer support and prayers to all church members," said Juditha.

"Your girl has grown up fast. I have one of the Bishops telling me she was baptized at the church," said Juditha looking at Dimitri. When Dimitri heard. Juditha talk about baptism he looked a bit upset. Juditha noticed this and quickly changed the subject. "Kids nowadays grow up very fast. Soon you will be looking for a place for her at the school," said Juditha peeping in the kitchen.

"Nancy how far with the coffee?" shouted Dimitri before answering Juditha.

"Beginning of next year, she will be starting school," said Dimitri. Nancy came back with a tray. She gave Juditha a cup of coffee, orange juice for Jevalinka and a cup of coffee for Dimitri and a glass of milk for herself. They spoke sometime about the church and life in general.

"So, you are Jevalinka's biological father?" asked Juditha. There was a moment of silence before Jevalinka asked Nancy.

"What is a biological father Nancy?" They all laughed before Dimitri answered.

"Yes, I am the luckiest dad in the whole world." He stopped and looked at Jevalinka.

"She has grown up strong. When she was a baby she was in and out of the hospital. When Enya died, I never thought I can manage own my own. A big thanks to auntie Nancy," said Dimitri looking at Nancy who smiled and drank her milk.

"So, I assume Enya is Jevalinka's mother?" said Juditha.

"My wife Enya left us," he stopped for a while and breathed heavily before continuing.

"She gave me the most beautiful and intelligent baby. It could have been more than perfect if she was here," Dimitri touched the head of his daughter and rubbed her hair.

"So, what happened to her, your wife?" asked Juditha.

"We were just unlucky. On 9 December seven years ago, Enya died minutes after giving birth to Jevalinka," he stopped talking and touched his forehead. Juditha was about to take out her small diary before she realized that that would raise suspicion. She memorized the date. Ok there is a difference between Ewalinka, Eva and Jevalinka. The striking thing was that all their names were different forms of the name Eva. All the names were the equivalent of the English name Eve. It seems Jevalinka had a different birthday to the other two. All three would pass for identical triplets.

"Initially the due date was 25 November," paused Dimitri. Juditha looked surprised on hearing this. "Did you say 25th of November?" repeated Juditha. They all looked at her.

"Yes, 25th of November," replied Dimitri before continuing with his story.

"We checked-in the maternity ward at the hospital in Moscow. Enya could not go into labor naturally. The doctors said that it was common, so they said we can wait for up to two weeks before thinking about other emergency delivery procedures," said Dimitri. He paused and drunk his coffee. They all looked at him and waited to hear what he was going to say next. "We came back home and after two weeks we went back to the hospital. The doctors insisted that we have a C- section. Myself I was scared, but she was enduring to the end. After five minutes, only Jevalinka was born. I was very happy. Baby and mother were all fine until after a few minutes everything went wrong. She had internal bleeding, and she lost a lot of blood," Dimitri wiped the tears from his eyes.

"Which hospital was Jevalinka born?" asked Juditha. "PMC in Moscow. We were referred from the EMC," said Dimitri. Another hour Juditha was still talking to

Dimitri and Nancy about other things. She left and headed back to the church. She phoned Milaki and arranged to meet in the church again.

"What do you know about Jevalinka's baptism?" asked Juditha.

"Not much why?" asked Milaki.

"Nothing just curious. Who can provide this kind of information?" asked Juditha.

"I have to ask someone to check which Bishop performed the service." I can get the information after a day or so. I will be in touch," said Milaki. Judith left and headed to the EMC hospital. He went straight to doctor Antoni, but he was busy so she waited for him. Half an hour later the doctor passed the message to the receptionist that he can see her. She went to his office. It's you again! How can I be of further help?" asked the doctor.

"You won't believe this." Said Juditha taking out an envelope from her handbag. She took out the photos and gave them to the doctor. He took the photos and looked at them.

"Yes. Ewalinka or the missing girl, eh Eva. Correct?" asked the doctor putting the photos on the table and looking at Juditha.

"You won't believe this," said Juditha sitting down on the chair in the doctor's office. She took out her diary and wrote something down before tearing a page and giving it to the doctor. The note read; Jevalinka Alexandrov Date of Birth: 9 December Father: Dimitri Alexandrov Mother: Enya Alexandrov Hospital of birth: PMC The doctor looked at the note and for some time starred at Juditha. Quickly he typed something on the keyboard. He scrolled down the mouse for a good ten minutes reading notes from the hospital files.

"So, these girls could all have been born on 25th of November. They are strikingly identical. Are you superstitious in any way?" asked the doctor. The doctor sat back in his chair looking at Juditha.

"What are the chances of something like this happening?"

"I don't know what to believe anymore," said Juditha looking at the doctor.

"I am a doctor I believe in science," said the doctor getting up. He walked to the door and made sure that it was closed. He came back to his seat and sat down. "What I am going to tell you is highly confidential and should not leave this room otherwise I am finished," said the doctor putting his arms together. He leaned forward and placed his arms on the desk. "In all medical files these girls were born with strange markings on their backs. Engraves were noticed on birth. They all have childhood health problems. They fall unconscious for days. The scary part is that NE of the most qualified doctors at the PMC in Moscow advised them to go and see the Chief priest regarding the tattoo's," said the doctor.

"What kind of tattoos are they?" asked Juditha. "Come, follow me," said the doctor getting up and opening the door. He headed toward the intensive care unit. Juditha quickly grabbed the photos that were on the table and followed the doctor. They entered Ewalinka's room. She was still sleeping, but she had stabilized. She was breathing normally. "Close the door," said the doctor leaning on Ewalinka's hospital bed. He let her sleep on her left side and opened the back of the hospital gown she was wearing.

"Look, I have never seen a tattoo like this before. It is so perfect to have been done by a human hand. Look, the tattoo has blood vessels feeding it. In the notes, it is written that the tattoo was of same color as the skin but the blood vessels made it look darker. Blood acts like the black ink," said the doctor before looking at Juditha.

"Is there any medical explanation for this?" asked Judith.

"Honestly, no!" said the doctor looking at Ewalinka who was sleeping like an infant. Judith moved close to Ewalinka and sat on her bed looking at the tattoo. She was very curious about all this. She slowly put her hand over the tattoo and touched it.

"What are you doing, don't touch her, don't touch the tattoo? We do not know what it is. You do not want to get involved in this. It could be a demon," said the doctor looking at Juditha.

"It is okay I touched the other girl today. I think it will be fine," said Juditha placing her hand over the tattoo again. Suddenly the girl giggled, laughed, and shouted, Jevalinka, before opening her eyes. They both looked shocked. Juditha removed her hand quickly. They both looked at the girl. She had her eyes wide open. They all saw her green eyes shining as she looked at them.

"I told you not to touch her!" shouted the doctor looking at Ewalinka. As they all were looking at her, her eyes changed from green to gray. They looked at each other in shock. Ewalinka fell asleep again. The doctor moved quickly to her side and brought an oxygen mask from the oxygen machine and placed it on her. He pressed a button on the machine. Two nurses came running in and Juditha was dragged outside by one of the nurses. The door to the intensive care was closed and Juditha was asked to wait outside. After half an hour, the doctor came outside of the intensive care unit and spoke to Juditha. She is going to be alright. She has stabilized. She is on oxygen treatment," said the doctor.

"Follow me let's talk in my office," said the doctor. They entered the doctors' office and Juditha stood next to the window looking outside. The doctor sat down on his desk and quickly started typing on the computer. He brought up Jevalinka's medical file. He read the file and after some minutes spoke to Juditha. What happened in there?" asked the doctor shaking his head.

"I have never seen anything like that before," added the doctor. Juditha was quiet for some time before she replied. I can't explain it. It is beyond human circles." Said Juditha sitting down in front of the desk. "She shouted a name, honestly I thought I heard her saying, Jevalinka," said Juditha.

"Me too. I am sure she said Jevalinka," said the doctor.

"Did you see her eyes changing color, or it's just me?" asked Juditha I saw that too at one-point I thought I was hallucinating as well. That is why I came to check her medical file. Her eye color at birth is green, but they changed to gray. Looking at Jevalinka's medical file she is the one with gray eyes," said the doctor.

"I felt the tattoo when I touched her. I felt like it was also tattooed on my back. As I touched her my eyes felt warm, then watery," said Juditha. The doctor paused and looked at Juditha in surprise.

"What color are your eyes?" asked the doctor. Juditha walked away from the window and sat in front of the doctor.

"Hazel brown," replied Juditha looking at the doctor. He stood up and asked Juditha to come and stand near the window. He looked at her. Her eyes were gray too. Juditha quickly opened her handbag and took out a make-up mirror. She looked in the mirror before screaming.

"Holy Mother of Jesus! What is going on!" she shouted. Juditha left the hospital and headed back to Dimitri's house. She was curious, she wanted to find out what had happened to Jevalinka if anything at all. Dimitri, Jevalinka and Nancy were sat in the lounge area watching the television as usual. Jevalinka started dosing off. Dimitri tapped Nancy pointing at Jevalinka who was dozing off while seated on the couch. They both laughed and Nancy said.

"Someone wants to sleep already without even eating auntie Nancy's best dish". Slightly Jevalinka opened her eyes.

"Ewalinka is coming she is putting me to sleep."
They both looked at each other. They both did not know anyone called Ewalinka. They thought that she was talking in her dreams.

"Who is Ewalinka?" asked Dimitri surprised by this.
"My sister," replied Jevalinka. They both laughed at her. Dimitri replied sarcastically.

"I did not know that you have a sister," they both laughed and Nancy got up to take her to bed before she replied.

"I didn't know too, I only found out today," said Jevalinka. They both looked at each other they realized that Jevalinka was not dreaming. She was wide awake.

"Don't touch me when my sister arrives," said

Jevalinka. Dimitri replied sarcastically.

"Ok when your sister comes we won't touch you. Auntie Nancy have you heard that?"

"Don't worry my niece we won't touch you," said Nancy. Before Nancy finished talking there was a knock on the door. They both froze for a while they did not know what to do. They looked at each other in shock. Jevalinka smiled and opened her eyes. She looked at her dad and spoke to him,

"Now you believe me?"

Her eyes changed from gray then green and she fell on the couch. She fell asleep. Quickly Dimitri got up and went to open the door. He was expecting to find a young girl standing at the door. He opened the door quickly and saw Juditha standing there.

"Is everything Ok Dimitri? You look like you have seen a ghost," said Juditha. Dimitri stood there speechless with his eyes open wide. Seconds passed without him saying anything.

"Dimitri, are you going to let our visitor in or what?" shouted Nancy. Dimitri seemed to have awaken from a trance.

"Oh, come in Juditha, everything is ok," said Dimitri standing aside letting Juditha pass the door way. He followed her and sat down on the couch.

"The princess is already sleeping? She must be very tired," said Juditha sitting next to where she was sleeping. Both looked at each other without saying anything.

"What brings you back here sister?" asked Dimitri looking at Nancy. There was a moment of silence as if Juditha was thinking of what to say. Still church business," said Juditha.

"I just wanted to see how princess has been," added

Juditha covering Jevalinka with a sleeping cloth. "Very strange, I thought that you told me that your name was Juditha?" said Dimitri looking at Nancy who nodded her head in agreement. Juditha looked surprised for some time before replying.

"Yes. My name is Juditha," said Juditha sitting up straight in her sofa. They both looked at each other and looked at Jevalinka who was fast asleep. Juditha started worrying and feeling very uncomfortable. She realized that Dimitri and Nancy had found out that she was not from the church.

"Ok. I can explain. I can tell you the truth," said Juditha sitting up straight to confess. They all looked at her waiting to hear what she was going to say.

"I am not who you think I am," said Juditha. She felt ashamed and tried to explain the whole thing.

"I am not…," said Juditha before being interrupted by Dimitri.

"We know your name is not Juditha, you are Ewalinka," said Dimitri sitting back in his chair.

"Who?" asked Juditha.

"Ewalinka!" said Nancy smiling and pointing at Jevalinka who was fast asleep.

"Jevalinka told us your name," continued Nancy. Juditha looked confused and shocked. Surely, she would have remembered telling Jevalinka that her name was Ewalinka. What was going on? Did Jevalinka felt Ewalinka? What was going on? Juditha asked herself.

"I am a bit confused here," said Juditha looking puzzled.

"Explain to me what happened?" politely asked Juditha. Auntie Nancy sat up straight and started talking.

"Jevalinka said that her sister Ewalinka was coming just before you arrived. We laughed it off then we heard the knock on the door. It was a shock to see you. We both guessed that you two talked before, the first time you came here," said Nancy. Juditha was trying to remember whether she mentioned Ewalinka to any of them. She knew when never mentioned Ewalinka to Jevalinka. So how come she knew Ewalinka? Telepathically did she feel Ewalinka.? She kept asking herself these kinds of questions. Ok she realized that one thing was for sure, Jevalinka felt Ewalinka just like at the hospital.

"What exactly did Jevalinka say." asked Juditha looking at Dimitri.

"She said my sister Ewalinka is coming and asked us not to touch her when she arrives. We thought that was a joke. But soon after that you arrived, and she fell asleep," said Dimitri.

"Did anything happen to her?" asked Juditha

"What do you mean?" asked Dimitri looking at Nancy.

"Any changes, at all." asked Juditha.

"I don't understand what you mean," explained Nancy looking at Dimitri. Juditha could not find an easy way of saying this. She looked at both Dimitri and Nancy and for a while there was a moment of silence.

"Did her eyes change color?" asked Juditha. They both looked at each other without saying anything. "Her eyes did they change color from gray to green?" asked Juditha waiting patiently trying to anticipate the answer. She looked earnestly at their faces trying to gage what they were going to say. They looked at each other for a while before both replying at the same time.

"Yes! How did you know that?" Juditha sat back on the sofa mesmerized. Minutes elapsed before she started talking again.

"I met Ewalinka at the hospital few days ago," she paused and looked at Jevalinka. She pulled her handbag close to her and took out Ewalinka's photos. She looked at these before giving them to Dimitri. "Oh, my God! I cannot believe this!"

He looked very surprised and handed the photos to Nancy. As soon as she looked at the photos Nancy screamed in pure shock.

"How is that possible? How can they be sisters?" asked Nancy. "I was there when my daughter was born. How is this possible," said Dimitri? Judith just sat in her sofa as they both looked at the photos. "Surely what are the chances of that happening and how come they know each other. Is this some kind of joke?" asked Dimitri. Juditha explained what had happened, and they looked at each other mesmerized.

CHAPTER TEN

Sean is driving his family to their new home in Charleston a small village town in St Austell, Cornwall England. The weather was very hot with temperatures high above 25'C. The sun roof of their car had been left open. The blowing wind brought some much-needed fresh air to cool them down. Sean and his wife Sarah had been driving for some hours. They were in South Terras which is rich in minerals. There were a lot of mines most of them abandoned or disused. This area was once a very rich town with plenty of people earning a living in the mines. Ever since the minerals had been depleted and most mines were abandoned. As they approached this area Mevelyn fell asleep suddenly.

"She must have been tired," said Sean to his wife who was covering Mevelyn with a rug.

"I think it's the heat. It is that hot even myself I feel like sleeping too," replied Sarah. They had been driving for few hours and it seemed the journey was never ending. They had at least an hour left on the road. A strong gale wind came from nowhere; the car was shaken as the wind caressed the sides of their car. A storm of wind and debris rises to the sky. A huge shadow is seen in front of the car as the wind is lifted into the sky. The car swerved in the road before Sean brings it to a halt. Mevelyn did not wake up. She slept on the car seat like a baby.

"We are close to the sea now. We will be in Charlestown after an hour," said Sean to Sarah. "Some gustily winds blow from the sea at high speeds and suddenly circle the surround area before they disappear. The area because of its proximity to the sea a lot of the unknown phenomenon were common in this area. An hour later the family was in Charlestown. They arrived and unpacked their belongings into the new house close to the seaside. Sean took Mevelyn from the car and took her inside the house. She was still sleeping. It was a long journey, and they all knew that their daughter was very exhausted. Ever since she was a child, she wanted to be very close to water. At night, she would leave her room and open water into the tube and sleep there for some time. To their surprise, she does not drown.

"Darling put her on our bed until her room is ready," said Sarah carrying boxes into the house.

"I think this is the perfect home for Mevelyn. She loves water and there is a swinging pool too at the back. I just need to spend some time cleaning it before we can start using it," said Sean carrying Mevelyn into the house.

"Daddy I want to go to the water outside," said

Mevelyn as Sean laid her on the bed.

"Honey! Mevelyn is awake, and she wants to go outside and play!" shouted Sean to his wife.

"Not now we are all busy who will keep an eye on her?" asked Sarah.

"Mummy said not now later when we have finished unpacking. Ok?" said Sean. Mevelyn looked at her dad and nodded in agreement. She slept for a while whilst they unloaded the car.

"So, Darling do you think things will be okay this side," asked Sean.

"Hopefully yes this is a small town and hopefully everyone will understand," said Sarah.

"I would prefer my daughter to live a normal life. We cannot keep on moving from city to city," said Sean.

"I know babe, I want what's best for her too," said Sarah putting the boxes on the table and taking a breath. By 8pm they had finished unpacking and cleaning up. Mevelyn woke up and went downstairs. Her mum was in the kitchen.

"My daughter you are up already? I was not expecting you," said Sarah tidying up in the kitchen.

"I want to go outside mummy just for a while for fresh air," said Mevelyn peeping through the door. "It's too late now, you can go in the morning. Ok?" said Sarah walking toward her daughter. Sarah opened the door and stood on the door way with her daughter. It was dark outside despite having a full moon. You could hear the huge waves colliding with the walls that holds the sea water. Crickets can be heard from a distance. It has been a long journey, and all Sarah wanted to do was to go to bed and sleep as if there is no tomorrow. Mevelyn was always attracted to water. Several times her mum had woken up in the morning to find her daughter not in her bed. Only to find her in the tube sleeping in the water.

"Don't worry you will make other friends here. You will go to a new school and make new friends," said Sarah touching Mevelyn's hair.

"What if they start calling me names and laughing at me?" asked Mevelyn holding her mum's legs with both hands.

"You do not worry about that everything is going to be okay," said Sarah comforting her daughter. Mevelyn was born with two different eye colors. She had one very bright blue eye and the other one was green. They had left their previous house because Mevelyn was being taunted all the time. People called her names at school. She never felt different from the others yet she found it difficult to adjust and to be accepted. Peter was a local fisherman; he had lived all his life in Charlestown. He used to go fishing with his friends. One night they were all about to go fishing when Peter's girlfriend had a row with him. She wanted to leave him. Peter had tried to negotiate with her but she had insisted on leaving. Instead of going fishing with his friends that night Peter drove Janice to Truro city where her parents lived. Peter had insisted that his friends wait for him but they had proceeded without him. On return he found out that his friends had gone. They normally went fishing for a week or more. Janice was gone and his friends had gone fishing. Peter went to the local shop and bought some beers. He returned and sat on the edge of the walls holding the sea water. He drank his beer. He had been dozing off but the noise of something jumping into the sea-water woke him up. He looked disoriented and confused. He looked around and noticed that he was on the wall that holds the sea water. Surely, he heard something jumping into the water. He stood up but staggered a little and nearly lost his balance. He walked backward few steps from the edge of the wall and looked around. There was no one. He walked a few steps toward the edge of the wall to look at the sea water. There was nothing. He climbed down the wall which hold the sea water and started walking toward the sea. He walked on the beach sand and only stopped walking when he felt the cold sea water touching his ankles. He lifted his legs and walked backward. He walked back to where he was sat before on the sea wall and sat there. He took another beer and started drinking.

"What!"

Shouted Peter getting up to see what was going on in the sea. The water in the sea ahead of him suddenly shone as if there was a light beaming underneath. A bright fluorescent green color is seen emanating from underneath. Peter dropped the beer bottle and as it landed on the ground it shattered into pieces making noise. Some shining creature popped out of the water blinded Peter who covered his eyes with his hands. By the time he had the chance to look again the creature had gone. At one-point, he wanted to run away but somehow he did not feel afraid. He walked toward the sea again and stood in the water with water level right to his knee level. He neither felt cold nor afraid. He stayed there until the sun came out and after that he went to his house to sleep.

"Darling, did you find out about that issue we talked about?" asked Sarah looking at Sean.

"Not really I think we are in the right place though. This is where our daughter will find peace and comfort. Close to the sea waters," said Sean siting on the bed next to his wife Sarah.

"It has been a tough road for her hopefully she will start living a normal life," remarked Sarah. They looked at each other for a while and Sean hugged his wife. Mevelyn had been in and out of the hospital as a child. She had difficulty sleeping. She slept well near water. Sean and his wife Sarah had been to the hospital and local fortune tellers. Mevelyn was a special girl. She was born with two different eye colors. This had never been witnessed before although it was common among domestic cats. She also had a strange marking on her back. No one could explain what this was. One night Sarah woke up, she could not sleep. She sat in her bed and looked at her husband. He was sleeping peacefully. She got up and decided to go downstairs to have something to drink from the refrigerator in the kitchen downstairs. She had just passed Mevelyn's room when she noticed something. The door to her room was open slightly. She pushed the door wide open and looked inside. Mevelyn was not in her bed. She quickly looked at the window in her room, the window was closed. She was about to go downstairs when she saw a florescent green light coming from the bathroom. She stood there for some time in shock. Not knowing what to do. She slowly walked toward the bathroom door. The green light was beaming out through underneath the door. She stood there for a while outside the bathroom door. Then she slowly pushed the bathroom door open. As soon as the door opened, she saw a blinding green fluorescent light coming from the tube. She shielded her eyes quickly and looked away. Soon the light faded, and she rushed inside when she saw her daughter floating on top of the water. The tattoo on her back was emitting the green light. It was still shining whenever she was in the water. Her head was outside the water but her body was all immersed into the water. She picked up her daughter from the water and called her name. The green light disappeared as soon as she took her out of the water. Mevelyn opened her eyes and looked at her mum.

"Mummy I want to sleep," she said to her mum pushing her lips out.

"Okay let's go to bed," replied Sarah taking Mevelyn into their bedroom.

"Sean push to that other side, let Mevelyn sleep here for a while," asked Sarah.

"Why, she has her own bed," said Sean before he paused for a few seconds.

"Alright. Bring her here," said Sean before moving to the edge of the bed creating enough space for Mevelyn.

"What's wrong Darling?" asked Sean.

"Nothing Darling she is wandering again. In here better because I can keep an eye on her," said Sarah covering Mevelyn. Sarah sat on the bed, one thought wanted to tell her husband what she had seen. She remembered Sean saying the same thing some weeks ago. One night Sean woke up to find a green light coming from his daughter's room. He opened the door to check but as he opened the door. The green light disappeared. Mevelyn was sleeping in her bed. He went in to check if there was someone else. But it was Mevelyn only. He closed the door and went to tell his wife who thought he might have been dreaming. She did not want to start worrying about her daughter so she intentionally dismissed the idea. But deep down she knew this was true. A lot of strange things were happening. Her daughter had an unexplained tattoo on her back. She was born with two different eye colors and she wanted to sleep in the water. All these were strange enough for her. They had left their house, their friends and their jobs just for the sake of their daughter. She had insisted that she wanted to stay near the sea. Charlestown was the perfect choice. It was close to the sea. It was a small city with few people. They hoped that their daughter would make friends here and go to the local school in St Barnabas. Early morning the beach was covered by a group of people who had gathered. There was an ambulance and a coast guard police van. People had gathered as news of a man washed to the shores had been circulating. A woman jogging early in the morning had discovered the body. The coast guard had been informed, and they were quick to attend. Night before there were gustily winds with huge waves colliding with the wall that holds the sea water. It seemed this man had been overcome by the strong winds and the waves. The divers had been summoned to search the whole area. Peter heard a knock on his door.

"Who is it?" asked Peter but there was no reply. He lifted his heavy head and stood up. He walked to the door and opened the door.

"Oh, Peter is here," said one of the man looking at the other man. Four man stood outside Peter's house. "Why you look like you have seen a ghost," asked Peter giving shade to his eyes.

"I am afraid you have to come with us," said one of the man walking away from Peter. The others followed and Peter spoke before going inside the house. He came out holding his t-shirt and putting on his sandals.

"What happened is everything ok?" asked Peter following the four man. "I am afraid there has been an accident," said one of the man stopping to wait for Peter giving him a chance to catch up.

"What kind of accident you are talking about?" asked Peter holding the man's shoulder.

"It's regarding your friends we thought you were with…," the man did not finish talking before Peter interrupted.

"Are they ok, all of them," asked Peter, but the man did not answer he looked toward the sea. Peter stopped as he saw a group of people at the edge of the sea.

"Oh, my God! What happened?"

He rushed toward the sea. The body of a man was about to be put in the van that had just arrived.

"Wait! Wait!" shouted Peter running to the trolley bed that was being loaded into the van. He rushed to the trolley bed and opened the sheet that was covering the man.

"Oh! No! Where are the others?"

He rushed to the coast guards who were in their patrol boat.

"There were four of them. What happened? Is someone out there already searching for the rest?" asked Peter quickly.

"Don't just waste time here go out there and search for the rest. I will go with you".

Peter jumped into the coast guard patrol boat.

"Let's go what are you waiting for?" shouted Peter. The boat drove off toward the sea. They searched for the rest of the man with no luck. For days, the search for the remainder of the fisherman went on with no luck. Peter sat next to the sea waiting for the return of his friends but no one turned up. One night he was sitting on the wall that holds the sea water. He was not drinking that night. He was thinking about the past weeks. Janice had somehow saved his life. He could have been out there no one knows in what state. He could be dead by now. He took out his phone and dialed Janice's number. But the phone kept ringing without anyone answering. He sat there for a long time. He was about to get up to go home when he saw what he thought was a small girl getting into the water.

"Hey where do you think you are going its dangerous in there? Stop there!" shouted Peter. He stood up and run down the wall onto the beach and straight to the place he had seen the young girl. She had disappeared. He did not see what had happened. He stood there for some time hoping to see her but she had already gone. He thought of calling for help but thought of waiting for some time. He looked around but there was no sign of the girl. He stood there for some time before heading back to the wall. He heard some noise coming from behind him. He looked and saw the sea shone. There was a green light beaming from underneath the water. Looked so beautiful that he did not panic. He walked slowly toward it, bubbles were being released and as they emerged on top they burst creating waves that radiated from the central area to the edges. The green light started radiating outward toward Peter. He looked surprised not knowing what to do. He stood there for a while. He looked inside the water and the water was all fluorescent green. The light moved toward him under water. He looked down into the sea water and saw the green light under water very close to him. He lifted his left and right legs walking backward as the light approached him nearly touching his legs. Quickly he tried walking backward but facing in front but soon all his legs were under this green light. He felt a sting first then after that he felt like he was being tickled. He remembered as a little boy playing with his dad. His father would tickle him under his arms and under his ribs and he would laugh until his ribs aches. He felt the same feeling as the green light surrounded him. He started laughing and giggling. As the light covered a large area behind him he continued laughing until his ribs were aching. He knelt on the sea shore waters giggling and laughing uncontrollably. The sea waters slowly drugged him deep into the sea and soon he found himself in the sea away from the shores. Life had been good for Sean and Sarah since they moved to Charlestown. Charlestown was a small town with few people as compared to the big city they were staying before. Their daughter had been the main reason they had relocated. Here she had found peace close to the sea. The only thing that worried them was the deaths of the fishermen days after they moved in to their new house. Rumors had it that the fifth fisherman named Peter committed suicide days after his friends died. The bodies of all the man were later discovered days following the discovery of the first man. Peter's body was found on the shore line too. He had died with a big grin on his face and his eyes wide open. Weeks after the incident Sean had taken time off work. They had spent time together as a family. Mevelyn had been going to school. She had shown real interest at her new school. There were swimming classes as part of her studies. Swimming class was her favorite. There were two big swimming pools at the school unlike her previous school which had one that was not in use after a student drowned there. The only problem was from a bully at the school called Thomas. Since they met, he had been calling her names and inciting others to call her names too. The school had been great for her. There were few pupils as compared to her previous school. Mevelyn had eyes with different colors. Her right eye was a bright blue color were as her left eye was a green color. To her she never felt different. She was just like the other girls. She did not see a big issue about this yet pupils at her last school had driven her to change the school. Pupils called her names, but she felt gorgeous. Several times she had looked herself in the mirror and all she saw was a beautiful girl with beautiful eyes. Although she had never seen anyone like her before that was not an issue to her. She felt normal and beautiful. She had refused a request by her friend to wear contact lenses. She just wanted to live a normal life just like everyone else. Posiah was in the same class as Mevelyn. They had met on the first day when Mevelyn started school. They had clicked from the first day. Posiah was the only pupil who did not bother or dared ask why Mevelyn's eyes were of a different color. They became real friends from the first day and ever since they were inseparable.

"Why you look sad today Mevelyn?"

Asked Posiah sitting down next to her friend on lunch break. Mevelyn put her sandwich back into her lunch box and looked at her friend.

"That boy Thomas came to me today and asked me

why I am a freak." Said Mevelyn closing her lunchbox.

"Thomas!!? Who listens to that jack I do not even look at him. He is just a bully." Said Posiah looking at her friend. Most pupils when they look at Mevelyn they look surprised but Posiah never treated her differently. The other pupils when talking to her they look surprised as if they had seen a ghost.

"I never thought myself different," said Mevelyn pushing her hair back that had covered her face.

"I look in the mirror and see a beautiful girl," she paused for a while as she opened her satchel and took a hair clip. She holds her hair with the hair clip before continuing.

"This boy today he came and looked at me and said, awe freak! And he left," explained Mevelyn. Posiah looked at Mevelyn for a while before answering her friend.

"Honestly, I would not let that bully bother you and I wouldn't waste my time worrying about that," said Posiah comforting her friend. They sat down for a while before the siren went off. They strolled back to their class. After class, they always had a swimming class. They went to the swimming pool. There were other pupils as well. They started swimming. Most of the pupils would come out of the water and rest then go back into the water. Mevelyn once she is in the water she stays there surfacing to take breath. She was very good at swimming. She would go under the water right at the bottom and surfaces again in seconds. They swam for nearly half an hour taking breaks in between before the other boys joined in. Among them was Thomas. They rushed into the swimming pool splashing the water as they jumped into the swimming pool. Others cheering and whistling. The other girls quickly swam to the edges of the swimming pool and out of the water. Mevelyn was still at the bottom of the water when the boys jumped in. She heard noises and resurfaced. All the other girls came out of the swimming pool and started drying themselves with towels. Mevelyn swam to the other end of the pool avoiding Thomas. Thomas started splashing water at Mevelyn.

"Get out of the water you freak!" shouted Thomas splashing water toward Mevelyn. The other boys followed suit. Mevelyn looked around looking for Posiah but she was out of the pool already drying up herself.

"Let's go Mevelyn!" shouted Posiah.

The other girls started walking away from the pool toward the big glass doors out of the swimming pool.

"Ok wait for me Posiah!" shouted Mevelyn swimming toward the steps which were used to get out of the pool. As she was about to get out of the pool Thomas pushed her away from the steps back into the waters.

"You freak you can't even swim!" shouted Thomas. The other boys started laughing and splashing water at her and at each other. A water fight broke out everyone splashing water at each other.

"Thomas pushed Mevelyn down the water. She went under the water and swam toward the other steps about to get out of the swimming pool. As she was swimming, she felt her leg being touched. She looked around and saw Thomas.

"Let go off me," shouted Mevelyn.

"Freak! You cannot even swim," grinned Thomas as his friends jeered her as well.

"Call me freak again and see," said Mevelyn upset with a trembling voice. Thomas laughed and looked at his friends who were splashing water at each other. "Freak! Freak! Freak!" shouted Thomas splashing water at Mevelyn.

"Ah!"

Growled Thomas holding his noise. The other boys swam to the exit and onto the steps and out of the water. Thomas opened his eyes and saw that the water was red with his blood. He felt very angry, and he swam toward Mevelyn and dragged her back into the water. She was on the steps about to go out of the pool. Thomas pushed her under the water. She fell right down at the bottom of the swimming pool. She lay there for a few seconds before swimming back to the top. She took a long breath and swam under the water. Thomas followed her underneath. The other boys were quiet now looking in the pool. Soon after some pupils left running as the water in the pool started turning green. Thomas looked down underneath and saw a shining green light under the water. The green waves rose fast and soon this green light covered him. He felt a sharp stinging sensation followed by a tickling sensation. Then he started giggling and laughing uncontrollably. As soon as Posiah heard Thomas laughing, fear gripped her, and she ran to the swimming pool attendant's office. Thomas could not stop laughing even as he drowned under the water. Mevelyn emerged from underneath and swam out of the pool. No one was there, everyone had run away. Soon afterwards Posiah returned with the swimming pool attendant. She was surprised to see standing there.

"Where is the girl?" shouted the swimming pool

attended looking inside the water. She saw a boy in the pool and jumped inside quickly.

"I thought you had drowned," shouted Posiah running toward her friend. She hugged Mevelyn before they started walking out of the indoor swimming pool building. The swimming pool attended dragged Thomas out of the water and did first aid on him. His nose was broken. After a few compressions to his chest he threw up water and started coughing, followed by uncontrolled laughing. "What happened did you see anything?" asked the swimming pool attended. Mevelyn looked at her friend for a while before answering.

"I was swimming, and we collided. He then sunk into the pool," paused Mevelyn as she wiped water from her face before continuing.

"I tried to help him but he was too heavy I couldn't carry him out of the pool. So, I came out of the pool to ask for help," she stopped talking and looked at her friend who looked down. The ambulance was called and Thomas was taken to the hospital. Mevelyn had learned her lessons. The last time something like this happened at her previous school she was honest and that put her into trouble. She had been banned from the swimming pool. The pool was later closed and that had forced them to relocate. Some time ago at her old school Mevelyn was swimming in the pool at school. Everyone had gone home and as usual she had stayed behind. There was a swimming attended who used to patrol the indoor swimming pool. Her office had a large glass window, and it was next to the swimming pool. The day in question she had gone to town but had let Mevelyn's teacher know. Mrs. Cubinska was the junior grade teacher. Mevelyn had gone into the pool and had swum for some time. Then she started dosing off and miraculously she stayed afloat. Mrs. Cubinska came to check if there was still anyone in the indoor swimming pool before she left the school.

"Is there anyone here?" She shouted as she walked inside the indoor swimming pool. Her voice echoed the closed building. No one answered, Mevelyn was fast asleep. She looked around and did not see anyone. She was about to go through the heavy glass doors when she saw a green reflection coming from the swimming pool. She stopped and turned around and quickly walked toward the swimming pool. As she approached the pool she saw a girl floating on top of the water surrounded by a florescent green light that quickly disappeared as soon as she had woken up.

"Mevelyn what are you still doing here?" she asked Mevelyn. She knelt to pick her up but somehow, she slipped and fell into the swimming pool. Somehow the ring she was wearing on her finger got caught up on the drainage lid on the side of the pool. She panicked and screamed for help. The way she screamed frightened Mevelyn who fell unconscious but somehow still managed to float on top of the water. Mrs. Cubinska saw a beaming green light coming from Mevelyn's back. She stopped screaming and shouting. somehow she felt like she was being tickled and she started laughing as the green light covered the whole swimming pool. As she relaxed the ring that was stuck got unstuck and she dragged Mevelyn out of the pool to safety. It was months after this incident that another girl drowned in the swimming pool after arguing with Mevelyn. She was heard laughing uncontrollably moments before she drowned. Thomas was taken to the hospital after the near drowning experience. He could not stop laughing. After they had explained that he nearly drowned the doctors suggested that he was in shock. The laughing was because of the severe trauma that he experienced. His body had experienced such trauma that itself induced the uncontrolled laughing as a defense mechanism to counteract the severe trauma.

"Doctor what is happening with this boy?" asked one of the nurse. Thomas had been brought to the A&E in Truro Cornwall. He had not stopped laughing since the accident at school.

"The boy has experienced severe trauma often common in severe cases where he witnesses sudden death," said the doctor flipping Thomas' chart that was on the clipboard.

"The only time I witnessed something like that was many years ago, when I was a junior doctor." The doctor stopped and looked at Thomas. He walked toward the nurse and continued.

"This boy had witnessed the death of his father."

He paused and looked at the nurse who at first seemed confused.

"Oh, I mean years ago," he paused for a while.

"His father had fallen off a combined harvester on a farm and the harvester tipped and crushed him into two pieces. The boy had witnessed all this," said the doctor.

"It must have been hard for that boy to witness such an incident," said the nurse.

"You know the body is the most amazing thing in the whole world," said the doctor taking off his reading glasses. He looked at the nurse with wide-opened eyes and his face showing great enthusiasm.

"The body anticipates pain caused by witnessing such an event and automatically as a defense mechanism activates that part of the brain that counteract that pain,"

He paused and looked at the nurse who was listening attentively.

"Any severe trauma can trigger the body into shock to minimize the damage. But," he paused for a while and moved closer to the nurse.

"In severe cases the body triggers the laughing mechanism as a way of minimizing the trauma and induce healing without shutting down. This kind of laughter that is continuous is part of a defense mechanism," said the doctor.

"So, this will stop on its own or what doctor?" asked the nurse.

"The nerve endings send a signal to the brain as a form of a defense mechanism to try to avoid the impact caused by witnessing a traumatic event. And if the body thinks that there is still a danger that mechanism will not be stopped. So, to answer your question. We will let the body stop triggering the laughs. We can help to calm his nerves. In that case, he will be kept for observation until we think he is okay," said the doctor. After the incident at the school the pool was cordoned off for a few weeks while inspection was underway. Mevelyn started going to the sea at night. One afternoon after school Posiah insisted that Mevelyn come with her after school to meet her parents. The night before Mevelyn had told her parents that Posiah wanted her to meet her parents. They had agreed after a long discussion.

After work Sean was to pick her up from Posiah parents' house. After school, they went together to Posiah's home. Posiah had never judged or said anything regarding Mevelyn's eyes. They arrived at Posiah parents' house. They were greeted by Posiah's parents as they entered the house. Posiah's mum had cooked a lot of food and had bought chocolates and sweets. They had something to eat. It was after playing outside that Posiah invited Mevelyn to her room. They both rushed upstairs, and it was only after a few seconds that Mevelyn was heard screaming. Posiah's mum rushed upstairs to find out what was going on.

"What is wrong Posiah? Why Mevelyn screamed like that?" asked Anete as she entered her daughter's room. The girls had entered Posiah's bedroom and threw themselves onto the bed. Excitedly Kitty, Posiah's cat had jumped onto Mevelyn and stretched her arms. Mevelyn got up and sat on the bed before screaming.

"Posiah! What is wrong?" asked Anete in a high voice breathing heavily as she had come upstairs running. Neither Posiah nor Mevelyn answered her. Both just stood there. Mevelyn looked like she had seen a ghost. Her face was pale. She did not look at Anete or Posiah. She looked at the cat for a while. Anete stood there speechless. Posiah moved toward her friend and tried to hug her.

"Don't touch me!" shouted Mevelyn.

"What's wrong?" asked Posiah shocked and surprised at her friend's reaction.

"Please tell me what's wrong! What did I do wrong?" begged Posiah. Anete realized what was wrong. She had anticipated that this might happen. Her husband had not listened to her and instead he had supported her daughter Posiah. Mevelyn stood there with her eyes wide open looking at the cat. The cat jumped from the bed and started rubbing against Mevelyn's feet.

"Now I know why you never said anything. You like me because I remind you of that," said Mevelyn with her eyes wide open pointing at the cat and then looking at Posiah at proximity. She stormed out of the bedroom and ran outside.

"No! Mevelyn. Stop. It is not like that let me explain," shouted Posiah following her friend outside. Anete knelt picking up Kitty who was on the floor.

"Ah, you poor thing see what happens if you don't listen. Do not worry it is not your fault," she put the cat down on the carpet and started walking out of the room. Kitty followed her and as he was about to leave the room Anete quickly clapped her hands. Kitty stopped following and went back inside as she closed the door behind her. Mevelyn went outside first and then came back and entered the lounge room where she collected her satchel and left going out of her friend's family property. Posiah followed her.

"Please give me a chance to explain!" earnestly asked Posiah.

"Explain what?"

Mevelyn stopped and turned around facing Posiah who was following her. She opened her eyes breathing heavily. Posiah had never seen her friend like this before. What did I do wrong? Everything seemed okay until when Kitty jumped on you. Are you afraid of cats?" Posiah asked sincerely. What are you trying to do? All along you like me because I reminded you of your cat. I thought you care about me. You are just like everyone else," Mevelyn turned around and started walking away.

"Wait Mevelyn. I do not know what you are talking about," said Posiah holding Mevelyn's shoulder. Mevelyn realized that she had over reacted, her friend genuinely did not do this intentionally.

"Your cat has eyes like mine," there was a moment of silence.

"I know but it's not a big deal," said Posiah. I thought you are close to me because I remind you of your cat," said Mevelyn looking down. Honestly I had the cat even before we met. My mum bought the cat for me when I was a little kid and ever since he was my best friend until I met you," said Posiah holding Mevelyn's shoulder.

"That's one scary cat you got there Posiah I must admit," said Mevelyn laughing holding her friend too. They both sat down and started laughing.

"Tell me I am not like that cat," said Mevelyn jokingly.

"You are not like Kitty cross my heart," said Posiah. Anete came outside and found the girls rolling on the lawn outside laughing. She went back inside leaving the girls talking outside. Kitty was a different cat. Kitty had two different eye colors and above that he looked like two cats joined together. His head was split into two colors at the center of his head. The left side was black with a shining green colored eye whereas the right-hand side was white with a shining blue eye. The first time you looked at him somehow you would think that you are looking at two different cats joined together. That was the illusion that confused even Mevelyn.

"Have you thought of getting contact lenses?" asked

Posiah sincerely.

"If this is important to you then why not wear contact lenses?" continued Posiah.

"Honestly, my parents had asked me about that but I refused. I want to be me. I do not feel different. This is the way I am and I do not want to live a lie for the rest of my life. I want to be natural and be myself," she sat down and looked at Posiah as she talked. "At my last school, they started calling me a freak. It hurts. I just told my mum that I did not want to go back to that school again," said Mevelyn. Posiah stood up astonished

"Really?" she asked Mevelyn.

"Yes!" said Mevelyn. Posiah smiled and pointed at Mevelyn with her eyes squinted.

"I know why. You loved a boy at that school. Right? That is the only reason that can make you quit," said Posiah interrogating her friend. Mevelyn smiled and started writing down on the lawn with her index finger.

"Yes. I liked a boy called David. He liked me at first I guess. Then they started calling me names. Then in turn he started avoiding me and it hurts," she paused and looked at Posiah. The girls continued talking until Sean and Sarah arrived. After sometime Mevelyn jumped into the car and Sean and Sarah drove off heading home.

"Posiah's mum told me that you were scared by Kitty?" asked Sarah. Mevelyn did not answer straight away she looked outside the window. She could see part of the sea as Sean and Sarah drove her home. There her destiny awaits. It was only a matter of time. She knew deep down she was born to serve someone else. Maybe the way she looked had meanings in another life. For once she understood what it meant to be different. She had reacted to Kitty yet Kitty was like herself. She was not ugly. She was beautiful than most of the girls. She would pass easily for a super model. This had never been an issue until now. She realized no matter what she does she will not be accepted as normal. Her destiny lies somewhere else. Probably somewhere else all this would make sense.

"Why are you not answering your mum?" asked Sean as he quickly took his eyes off the road driving his car home.

"Sorry. What was the question?" asked Mevelyn. "Anete told me that Kitty, Posiah's cat scared you. Is that correct?" asked Sarah looking at Mevelyn who was sat at the back seat as they headed home. "Honestly, I don't know what happened I just panicked," said Mevelyn looking embarrassed. On sensing this Sean tried to change the subject.

"They seemed to be a good family and Posiah is a good person," said Sean as he drove home. Sean don't start see, you are changing the subject again," said Sarah in an irritated voice. This was their source of arguments. Sarah was brought up in a family where they tackled the bull by its horns. Whereas Sean was brought up in a family that was very protective. Sean never wanted to discuss personal problems much whereas Sarah wanted every detail and was quick to propose solutions.

"Darling Mevelyn reacted to the cat because of the way it looked not just because she was frightened. I would like Mevelyn to wear contact lenses. We cannot keep on moving from city to city. There is a simple solution. You are his dad why cannot you convince her that this is the best way?" shouted Sarah looking at her husband who seemed unconcerned.

"She is my beautiful daughter and I would not change her," said Sean looking in the rear-view mirror. His eyes met with Mevelyn's and Mevelyn smiled and looked toward the sea.

"So, can we go to the osteopathic doctor sometime this week and get contact lenses?" Sarah asked her daughter. Mevelyn looked outside through the window before answering her mum.

"Yes, mum can will go," the car drove for some time and they were nearly home. It was already getting dark. There was silence for some time and Sean switched on the CD player and played Mevelyn's favorite song by Celine Dion, my heart will go on. The car drove on for some time and soon they found themselves near their home. They arrived home, and they got in the house and sat in the living room. Sarah went to prepare dinner. Mevelyn stayed a little while and asked if she can be excused and went upstairs to her room. She had had a great day apart from the initial incident. After dinner Sarah entered her daughter's bedroom, and they had a girl to girl chat before retiring to bed.

"Sean!! Sean!! Our daughter is gone! Wake Up!" said Sarah frantically waking up her husband Sean who was still asleep.

"Sean! Wake up! Find my daughter!!" said Sarah weeping uncontrollably. That morning Sarah had woken up early. She had gone to the bathroom. On her way, back to their bedroom she had found Mevelyn's door open. She had entered her room only to find her missing. She ran downstairs hysterically shouting her name. But Mevelyn was nowhere to be seen. She opened the front door and went around the house desperately searching for her daughter. She shouted her name and went back to her room. She lifted her duvets and for a few seconds sat on her bed wondering what had happened. She looked on her bed and saw the corner piece of paper protruding from underneath the pillow. She quickly lifted the pillow and the static electricity from the silk pillow cover made the note flew into the air following the same path taken by the pillow as Sarah lifted it from the bed. It seems like everything was happening in slow motion to Sarah. She could clearly see the paper flying into the air turning and flipping from side to side as gravity beats it. She remembered the time when Mevelyn was young. She used to take her to the park and let her play with a kite. She remembered the time she made her a paper airplane. She remembered how she threw the plane in the air and how smoothly it landed on the green lawn next to her. As she was thinking all about this, the paper flipped and turned as it headed its way onto the floor. It all happened in a few seconds but it seemed long enough for her to remember some wonderful memories with her daughter. She suddenly knelt on the floor and stretched both her hands. The note landed in her hands just like the paper airplane she once made for her daughter. She stood up and sat on her daughter's bed. She flipped the note and it read; Dear Mommy Please don't be sad or angry at me. It's time now for me to go to my family. I love you so much you and daddy. I must go maybe see you again one day. I will miss you Your beloved daughter Mevelyn. Sarah had never been this confused in her entire life. She is my daughter how can she write that she is going to her family? These are the questions that came popping into Sarah's head. She felt empty. Mevelyn was the source of her existence. Since giving birth to her no day had passed without her daughter. It felt wrong. She bursts into tears and cried uncontrollably. She got up and rushed to her husband holding the note in her hand. Sean was still in bed when Sarah bursts into their bedroom crying uncontrollably. Sean quickly woke up and hugged his wife.

"What's the matter Darling?" Asked Sean taking the note with one hand that was in Sarah's hand. He read the note. He put the note on the bed and hugged his wife for a long time. Over the past years, Sean knew that this day would eventually come. Their daughter was special. They had seen so many miracles over the years to know and understand this. They knew it was a divine calling. The tattoo on her back and all the things they had witnessed made it easy for him to understand all this. That was her destiny. She was never going to escape her calling. This was her divine calling. They hugged for a long time and they cried together. Sean slowly laid Sarah on their bed.

"Darling don't cry. Everything is going to be fine. This is her destiny. Let's celebrate her life and cherish the memories we had," said Sean walking to the bedroom stereo.

"I want my daughter back with me!! I am her mother. Do you know how painful it is to give birth and look after her all these years? Why me? Please find my daughter," shouted Sarah crying uncontrollably. Sean looked at his wife who was wriggling on the bed like a snake sliding on the grass heading for cover in the bushes. Sean opened the CD compartment of the Sony stereo and loaded the Celine Dion CD. The song my heart will go on started playing. Sean walked to the bed and lay next to his wife. They hugged and Sarah even cried more profusely as the song started playing. They hugged in each other's arms listening to the song.

CHAPTER ELEVEN

Yunnan Province southwest of the Republic of China in a small village of Gaojuin in the mountains is born a young daughter to Li and Liang. They had lived in the mountains for some time cultivating rice. It rained most of the time in the Yunnan Province. Li and Liang had been childless for a long time. Eight years after losing their first child through miscarriage Liang finally gave birth to a beautiful healthy daughter. The priest at the temple in the mountains had foretold them about this birth. They had stayed in the mountains with the temple priest for nearly two years before their daughter was born. It was such a happy time for the couple. They had eagerly waited for the birth of their daughter. The night of birth it was raining very heavily. There was lightning and thunderstorms the night of birth. It was windy as well. The tree branches were being swerved from one side to another. The skies were dark, but the lightning was lighting up the skies. Echoes of thunder had been heard from the nearby mountains. The local midwives had been invited to assist with the birth by the temple priest. Liang had been in labor for hours. Everything was ok although Li was very worried which was understandably after having lost a baby eight years ago when Liang had a miscarriage. Sometime early in the morning on 25 November Evangelina was born. The priest noticed that she had a dragon tattoo on her back. As it was raining, he lifted the baby upwards and lightning struck in the skies. A light moved in the dark clouds shining the dark skies from left to right like a snake. A huge loud thundering sound followed the lightning and echoes were heard from the surrounding mountains which frightened the baby causing her to cry. A second lightning is seen beaming in the skies lightning the whole area where they were. This made the baby cry even more. The third lightning struck in the ground nearby and is beamed back into the skies causing the nearby bushes to start burning. The tattoo at the back of the baby shined as light is beamed from it. The baby cried in agony as a burning mark is left imprinting the dragon tattoo. The priest rushed and took a blanket and covered the baby after touching the tattoo at the back with a soft wet cloth. The priest named the baby Evangelina meaning the first angel to bring good news. After her birth, they went back to their village in the opposite mountains. They stayed in the mountains for most of the time. Whenever Evangelina left the mountains, she would fall sick and had to be carried to the temple where she would sleep for days before recovering. Since her birth all the first years she kept talking about going to see her sisters. This not only shocked her parents this also brought much fear and discomfort to Li and Liang. What do you mean you will go and see your sister? Asked Li talking to his daughter.

"Yes, daddy. I will go and see my sister soon from far away," said Evangelina pointing to the skies. Li looked in the skies for a while. Surely how did Evangelina knew that she had a sister? Since his wife had a miscarriage Li had not told her daughter about this incident. She was too young to understand this. Li had insisted that Evangelina never knew about the miscarriage.

"Eva, so why you want to leave us? Me and your mother are your family. Are you not happy having us as your family," asked Li looking at her daughter? Evangelina had been sick for some time in her life.

"I was born to be with my sister." She paused and looked in the sky.

"Here if I stay I will be sick all the time," said Evangelina. Fear run down Li's spine leaving him feeling cold and frightened.

"Once I am with my sister, I will never be sick again I will be strong all the time," said Evangelina. The fear of losing his daughter struck Li.

"Liang! Come here and listen to what your daughter is saying."

"I'm coming I have nearly finished preparing the meal," Liang came out quickly and sat on her husbands' lap. She hugged him and kissed him. She stood up and sat next to Evangelina. Eh, so, what is the story?" asked Liang.

"I want you to hear it from herself. Eva tell your mum what you just told me." Said Li sitting up and leaning forward. Evangelina looked at her parents and waited for a few seconds clearing her throat.

"Yes, mummy I want to go and stay with my sister and family far away," said Evangelina pointing into the skies.

"You don't have a sister Eva and we are your only family," said Liang.

"I know I have a sister. If I stay here, I will be sick. With my sister, I will be okay all the time," said Evangelina. Liang looked sad and turned away looking at her husband.

"Why did you tell her about the miscarriage?" asked Liang upset. There was a served Buddha. They were like soldiers too. They were taught to fight and to defend themselves. It was after spending time with the priests that he finally revealed the purpose of Evangelina. There were other kids six of them all identical born on the same day and roughly at the same time. These were to protect the Emperors' family line. After the persecution of the true Emperor many years ago, all his relatives were in diaspora hiding there. After a hundred years, the future Emperor was to be born. With him seven soldiers to guard and protect and serve him will also be born with special powers that they will not be defeated in any way. Evangelina was one of the seven. When they heard this Li and Liang were very happy. They celebrated the news to the surprise of the priest.

"You should be grieving for your daughter," said the priest looking at Li and Liang who were smiling hugging each other. He was expecting them to cry for their daughter because they were never going to see her again or at least for the next hundred years.

"We will rejoice instead. For our daughter, has been chosen. It is better for her to leave us and be alive than for her to be taken away like our first baby," said Li shaking the priest's hand. For them it was better for her to be living somewhere else. Full of life and happiness.

"When all the magnificent seven are not together they will keep on falling sick and spending more time in a trance communicating and healing each other. When they are, together there is no such thing as sickness. They cannot afford to be sick. They cannot afford to go in a trance. After the age of seven they will stay together for ever protecting the future Emperor who will be born at the same time or few years before them." The priest paused to take a breath. He lifted his cup of ice tea and drunk for a while.

"At the age of seven she will cease to be your daughter. Any emotional attachment to you will cease. She will start talking to you about her real family." He paused as they started talking to each other. He waited for them to finish talking. After a while Li looked at the priest and spoke.

"That what she started telling us a few weeks ago," said Li looking at his wife.

"She said she will go to stay with her sister," added Ling. They paused for a while and there was a moment of silence.

"Honestly we thought she wanted to die. Ever since she was a baby she had been sick all the time. We thought she knew about our dead child. And going to stay with her sister meant dying. Now you understand why we are rejoicing?" said Li smiling at his wife.

"We can't lose another child, that will kill us. We have been through a lot and I do not mind spending the rest of my life with my wife Liang," Li paused and hugged his wife who in turn kissed him.

"Knowing that our daughter is alive," said Li looking at Liang who nodded in agreement.

"When it's time they will keep on falling sick and sleeping for days. This is the way they call each other and tell each other and you that it is time for them to go," said the priest before drinking his tea. He stood up and poured water in the kettle and started boiling water. He sat down and continued.

"When it's time to go, they became sick. This helps stops the emotional attachment to you. When they are around you they fall sick. As soon as they are away from you they are strong again. That is a signal to start the long journey. Whenever the other one's need help, your daughter will fall sick and go into a trance where she will sleep for days. As she is sleeping the other one will use her energy to fight disease or the enemy or to communicate with each other," said the priest. They all looked astonished and worried for a while.

"So, when that time comes will she still see us as her parents, her family?" asked Li.

"On the day, she leaves she will be completely unattached to you emotionally otherwise she won't go. This emotional attachment will make her weak and make her be afraid, so it is not good. For some they will still feel love for you but the love for her other six sisters will be greater, much greater to drive her to initiate the journey," said the priest.

"What happens if I try to stop her leaving us and lock her inside the house?" asked Liang.

"In all cases, on the day of departure she will put you in a trance so that you won't stop her. This is true in most cases. There is only one incident I heard over the years," said the priest putting some wood on the burning fire. There was a moment of silence. Li and Liang looked at each other.

"The only incident I know of is when the unthinkable happened," said the priest before he paused to have a sip of the hot tea he had just made.

"Yes. The legend had it that on the night of departure, the mother of this Emperor warrior locked him in the house and gave him the root of the magic tree. This made him go in a trance and sleep the whole night. In the morning, he was still in a trance but his father found his mother eaten to death by an animal. The door to his bedroom was broken down." The priest stopped and looked at the couple before putting a stick into the fire spreading the burning hot ashes.

"The terrifying part is that, the tattoo he had at the back was for a mountain lion. When the father came back, he found the tattoo literally bleeding and blooded footsteps heading to the son's bed which disappeared close to the tattoo. In a panic, he ran to his friends' house and asked him to go to town and ask for help before heading back home. It was his friend who found him mauled to death," said the priest.

"So, did his friend find his son?" asked Li.

"His son was gone. The legend has it that the father tried to stop him too hence the consequences," said the priest.

"I have a question for you there is something that have been bothering me for quite a long time," said Li hugging his wife.

"Yes, what is it?" asked the priest.

"What really happened with that child? I mean Winglee's son?" asked Li. T injecting its venom into his bloodstream. The poison then blocked and attacked all his nerves. The poison groups on all major nerve points blocking the body's defense system. In responds the body induces a defense mechanism that blocks pain and makes the body relax buying time. This in turn makes the person feel like being tickled which in turn makes him laugh uncontrollably. At this moment, the only thing the body can do is to buy time until external help in the form of an antidote can be introduced in the blood stream to eat away the poison. But if not treated then the person will laugh to death." There was a moment of silence.

"So why Winglee accused my daughter if it was a fish that can cause this?" asked Li.

"Honestly I don't know. I think because she did not go and call for help quickly enough. That could explain Winglee anger. His argument is that his son could have been saved," explained the priest.

"As I recall Winglee said there were not anywhere near the water. They were playing in the house. His son touched Evangelina who in turn poisoned him. I asked my daughter several times, but she said she was asleep. She does not remember anything," said Li. The priest looked at Li and his wife.

"The legend has it that the tattoo is a defense mechanism. Whenever she is asleep, the tattoo activates itself ready to attack. If it happened, it was in self-defense. She probably was asleep. Touching the tattoo can make one prone to attack. These men and women, boys and girls are often greater than thousands of soldiers. Before these magnificent seven Emperors were protected by thousands of Imperial guards. Men up to 1500 would protect the Emperor at any one time. Disloyal, coups and hunger all led to the development and introduction of these magnificent seven. These were in responds to the problems with the Imperial guards. Most Emperors were dying at the hands of their bodyguards who organized coups. This was because of hunger. Emperors would not spend all their fortune on their guards alone. They were so many up to 1500 men. Feeding them, providing shelter, and giving them allowances would in the end only mean that the Emperor would become corrupt, stealing from the poor to sustain the guards. This would mean the Emperor becoming unpopular too." Li and Liang listened attentively as the priest explained life during the Emperor's days.

"When the last Emperor was being attacked, he sent his last son to the temple priest to help him hide his son to preserve and maintain his blood line for future generations. The priest sent his best seven warriors to help the Emperor. They fought like wild animals killing thousands of enemy soldiers. They entered the Imperial dynasty and vowed to die first before any single drop of blood was lost by the Emperor." The priest paused and poured more tea before drinking this tea for a while. Li and his wife waited eagerly to hear what happened next. The priest opened a small bottle of incense. He poured a small amount into the fire for a few seconds the fire burned ferociously before sweet smelling smoke is released into the air. The extra fire quickly died down.

"The Emperor was running out of money. The daily amount to feed the guards was enormous. Most guards were never given allowances that they think they deserved. This caused mistrust and when the rival barbarian leader offered all his guards, a genuine salary some of his own guards turned against the Emperor resulting in the invasion. The Emperor had refused stealing from the poor. The poor people were often levied heavily, and they were over paying taxes to fund the Imperial dynasty. The leader of the barbarians had been stealing for years from the poor. The magnificent seven warriors surrounded the Emperor, and it was hard for the enemy to attack him at close range. They were very skilled that they killed hundreds of men who advanced trying to kill the Emperor. The leader of the barbarians had made an oath to reward anyone who beheaded the Emperor. The magnificent seven had also made an oath to die first before any drop of blood was spilled from his body. They vowed to protect the Emperor until their last breath. This meant protecting the Emperor to a level unseen before. The magnificent seven surrounded the Emperor and blocked all attempts to pierce his body with arrows and spears. They in turn took arrows meant for the Emperor in an act of loyalty. This gave a new meaning to the word to serve, to protect and to honor. In an act of defiance, they were shot several times all over the body taking turns. The soldiers had surrounded them with bows and arrows. The barbarian soldiers sent twenty arrows a time. Which meant breaking some and being struck by some. They fearlessly took the arrows meant for the Emperor. They were pierced a hundredth times each yet they still stood their ground. The leader of the barbarians was running out of patients that he ordered all his men with bows and arrows to draw and strike. That meant a thousand arrows directed at seven men and surely that would mean the death of the Emperor before they died. They stood and looked at each other. They hold their swords in their hands and surrounded the Emperor. They heard a lot whistling as the arrows approached them. They blocked what they can with their swords. Another wave was released, and they fought again making sure that the Emperor was safe. When they knew that the end was near there was no other choice, they raised their swords and as soon as they were pierced and after they noticed that the Emperor had been hit too they pierced their hearts with their swords at an angel of forty-five degrees at an incline. On their last breath, they all moved backward surrounding and protecting the Emperor and stabbing him too in the process with their swords. They knew the Emperor was dying anywhere. All seven swords entered the Emperors body at the same time and slowly all their blood was poured into the Emperors' body through the grove on their swords. Their blood and the Emperors blood was mixed together. This was very symbolic as this represented the link, the platform and the idea of serving, to protect and to honor for eternity. This brought the circle of trust. This linked the Emperor to the seven warriors through blood. This gave rise to the magnificent seven with special powers. Although it was treason to kill the Emperor and never heard of that the temple priest would stab the Emperor. This ritual was for the future preservation of the Emperor's bloodline. He had for the first time asked for help from the temple priest and this is the only help they could give him, help for eternity. Death also by their swords enabling the mixing of their blood and the Emperors before their last breath. This would mean the linking of all the future protectors of the Emperor himself. The mixing of the blood enabled the synchronizing of everything and everyone." Said the priest. After a few more stories from the temple priest Li and Liang went home with their daughter.

"Hurry!! Hurry!! Come with me!" Shouted Chang holding Evangelina's hand.

"What is it?" Asked Evangelina following Chang. "Just follow me you will see for yourself," said Chang running as fast as he can. They ran for a few minutes before Chang stopped and waited for Evangelina who was still behind him. Evangelina was breathing heavily after running for a few minutes.

"Shh, don't make any noise," said Chang putting his index finger across his lips. He knelt and edged forward slowly and quietly. He waved for Evangelina to follow him. She knelt and edged forward too following Chang. Chang waited behind a big tree and waved to Evangelina asking her to come forward next to him. She arrived, and both hid behind the big tree.

"Don't make any noise look ahead behind the bushes," whispered Chang. Evangelina looked ahead and saw a large animal. It raised its head as if it had seen Evangelina. Quickly she hides behind the large tree and asked Chang.

"What is that animal called, I have never seen one like that before?" asked Evangelina. Chang looked at the animal and said.

"It's a Komodo dragon," he looked excited with his eyes wide opened he continued talking to Evangelina. "Today is my first day to see one. I have just heard stories about the Komodo dragon from the temple priest." They looked again at the Komodo dragon and decided to edge forward. They slowly approached the animal. Evangelina looked at the animal again at close range and asked Chang a question.

"Is this the real dragon the priest was talking about the other day?" Chang took time to answer and looked at Evangelina.

"This is not the one the temple priest was talking about. That one can fly this one is similar but can only walk on land," replied Chang.

"Have you ever seen the one that can fly?" asked Evangelina looking at Chang who sat down next to her.

"Not really but it would be great to see one. I heard it can breathe out fire as well. Wow that is just bliss," said Chang. They sat for a long time watching the animal and after a while the animal started walking away. They watched the animal disappear into the bushes before going back home.

"Mummy today I have seen a dragon," said Evangelina running to her mum and standing in front of her. She looked excited.

"A dragon? Where? Are you sure?" asked Evangelina's mum Liang.

"Yes, mummy a real dragon. You can ask Chang he saw it too," said Evangelina looking really excited.

"Ah, I see you mean a Komodo dragon," said Liang.

"Yes. That is what Chang said it is called," said Evangelina drawing the Komodo dragon on the ground.

"Ah that must have been quite an experience for you. Was it the first time you have seen one?" asked Liang.

"Yes, mummy I was scared at first but after some time I realized the dragon was not bothered about us," said Evangelina.

"The real one the priest was talking about the other

day can fly. It can breathe out real fire," said Liang opening her mouth wide and pretending to breathe out a fire with her eyes wide open. Liang knew something was up. Evangelina had a dragon tattoo on her back. Weeks after Chang came to Evangelina's home. He asked if they can go and see if they can find the Komodo dragon again. Evangelina told her mum, and they left. They looked in the area they had seen it before but it was not there. They walked for a while and arrived at a water spot, there was that Komodo dragon drinking water. They sat nearby and watched it. It noticed there were there but continued drinking water. After drinking water, it entered the shallow water. Chang and Evangelina waited for it to come out but it did not. Chang stood up and started walking toward the shallow water.

"Hey where are you going? You cannot leave me here alone?" screamed Evangelina.

"Follow me be quiet though. Ok?" whispered Chang as he slowly headed to the shallow waters. Few bubbles can be seen on top of the water making waves that quickly dispersed outwards. Evangelina stood up and followed Chang. They reached the shallow waters and looked around to see if they can spot the Komodo dragon. Chang slowly entered the shallow waters.

"Hey.! What are you doing you are not supposed to enter the waters!"

Whispered Evangelina holding Chang's hand.

"It's ok. The Komodo dragon does not bite. I just want to make sure that it is okay," said Chang putting his hands underneath the water. Evangelina stood there for a while on the edge of the shallow waters.

"Come and see!"

"I have seen it. It is inside the water?"
"Really?"
Excitedly asked Evangelina getting into the water too. As soon as she had entered the water. Chang screamed jumping up and down.
"What's going on? What happened? Are you okay?" Hysterically asked Evangelina. Chang stood in the waters and started laughing pointing at Evangelina. "It's not funny you know," said Evangelina. The Komodo dragon heard Chang's screams and it run under water further away from Chang splashing water as it escapes in fear. Somehow Evangelina lost balance and fell in the shallow waters. She was submerged into the shallow waters.
"Eva, are you okay?" asked Chang as he quickly jumped into the water swimming toward Evangelina. A green light started illuminating into the water coming from Evangelina's back. He touched her shoulder to see what it was before letting out a loud scream as if stung by something. A few minutes later he started laughing uncontrollable. Evangelina remembered the last time that happened. Winglee's son ended up dead. Quickly she submerged herself into the water. She looked for a fish nearby. She heard a loud sound and a splashing of water. A huge dragon flew out of the water flipping its wet wings. Evangelina was splashed with water from the dragon's wings. The dragon tried to fly but fell back into the water. There was a huge thundering sound as the dragon fell back into the water. The green light disappeared. Chang saw the dragon and kept laughing pointing at the dragon. Evangelina realized what had just happened. She quickly swam to where Chang was and dragged his hand into the water toward the

dragon. The dragon sat underneath the shallow waters. Chang and Evangelina jumped on its back and waited. The dragon stood up and flipped its wings splashing the water. Soon they were up in the air. Chang needed help. His body was shutting down. He had been stung by a fish. If not quickly treated, he might die. The dragon flew to the mountains. It arrived near the temple and landed. Quickly Evangelina ran for help. The Chief priest was there with the other monks.

"Come quickly my friend need help. I think he has been stung by the fish," said Evangelina holding the priest's arm and dragging him outside.

"Where is he?" asked the priest. Evangelina pointed to the place where they had landed. Chang was there rolling on the ground laughing uncontrollably. The priest carried Chang back to the temple as fast as he can. Evangelina stood there looking around. "Dragon! Dragon. Where are you?" whispered Evangelina. She looked around and the dragon was nowhere to be seen. She waited for some time and slowly walked toward the temple occasionally looking back just in case she sees the dragon again. When she was sure that the dragon had gone she quickly ran toward the temple and entered the temple. Chang was lying on the floor next to the fire place. The priest quickly brought something like a cloth wallet and knelt beside Chang. He took off Chang's shirt and opened his cloth wallet. He took out a small bottle and poured the contents in a small hand washing dish. He took out a clean cloth and dunked it in. Quickly he squeezed the cloth and dosed Chang's body. Chang was still laughing and Evangelina entered the temple and sat next to Chang.

"Is he going to be okay?" asked Evangelina.

"I hope so it does look very bad.", said the temple priest as he took out a small bottle from the cloth wallet. He shook the small bottle and smelled it a little. He quickly then put it under Chang's nostrils. He let Chang sniff the contents of the small bottle several times. Soon Chang was fast asleep. The priest stood up and took hot water from the kettle and walked back to where Chang was. He knelt and poured the hot water in the small hand washing dish. He took a towel and started cleaning Chang's body with the hot water. After he had finished, he took some needles and slowly and carefully started piercing Chang's body leaving the needles there. After he had finished Chang had needles all over his body protruding and standing upright. The priest opened another small bottle and poured the contents into the fire. A nice smelling aroma filled the whole room.

"Is he going to be ok." asked Evangelina.

"Yes. He just need more sleep and rest. Let him sleep for now," said the priest putting back his items. Evangelina sat next to Chang.

CHAPTER TWELVE

"Hey. Are you okay? Who are you with?" asked the security guard at the mall in the city. Evangelina looked puzzled. This was the first time she had seen such a big building with plenty of people in it.

"I'm with my sister. Yes, I am okay," replied Evangelina looking around at the people sitting in the park outside the mall. A lady got up and started walking toward them. Evangelina entered the shop in the mall and straight to the elevators that takes people up the shop top floor. She stepped hesitantly on the lifts. As soon as the lift started going upwards she tried to get off by going down the lifts but soon, she found herself on the first floor. She walked inside looking at the clothes and the dolls wearing clothes inside. They all looked alike. She stopped for a while and looked at one of the dolls. She started imagining what her sister looked like. She had never met her sister. She just knew she had to start staying with her.

She left the shop and went to the eating area in the mall. She decided to sit there and rest for a while. There were so many people there. There were kids with their families too. For a while she started thinking about Li and Liang her parents. She had left them in Yunnan Province. She was far away from home. As she was thinking about the life she had left there in her home village a woman approached her and stood next to her. She stood there for a while without saying anything.

"Are you my sister," asked Evangelina looking at the smartly dressed lady in front of her. She smiled and looked at Evangelina without answering her question. "What do you want to order?" asked the lady.

"Are you my sister," questioned Evangelina getting up and looking at the lady straight in her eyes. She looked at her for a while.

"No. I am not your sister but I can be your friend. Why? Do not you have money?" asked the lady. Evangelina walked around the lady looking at her clothes and shoes and her hair.

"You know what! I can be your sister today. Tell me what you want to order," said the lady but Evangelina seemed far away. She looked at her attentively.

"Ok. I will bring you this, see if you like it," said the lady writing something down before leaving. Evangelina sat there for a while looking around as if searching for someone. After ten or so minutes that lady came back with a goody bag and handed it to Evangelina. She opened inside and looked inside. "Oh, thank you but I'm not hungry. I am waiting for my sister," said Evangelina.

"Ok you can take the food and eat later," said the lady going to the next table. Evangelina sat there for some time before taking the bag and leaving the food mall. Mevelyn arrived at the shopping mall and stood exactly where Evangelina was standing. The security guard who had talked to Evangelina was still there. "So, did you find your sister?" asked the security guard. Mevelyn looked confused and looked at the security guard. What was he talking about she asked herself?

"I don't know what you are talking about, I just arrived," said Mevelyn.

"I spoke to you earlier own you were looking for your sister," said the security guard. She looked puzzled for a while. Immediately, she went into the shop and exactly did what Evangelina did on the conveyor lifts. She went up the mall and looked at the clothes. She left the shop and entered the food mall. She walked straight to where Evangelina had sat and sat there. The lady in the mall came and spoke to her.

"You came back did you find your sister?" asked the lady in the food mall. Mevelyn looked surprised, but she realized that one of the girls might be looking for her.

"No but if she comes back tell her to wait for me," said Mevelyn leaving the food mall. She walked into one of the clothes shops and admired the clothes in there. There were very big mirrors everywhere. She passed one of the mirrors and then came back to see her image. She looked in the mirror and looked at herself. She checked her face and eyes then walked out of the shop. After leaving the shop she felt like she wanted to sit down. She fell asleep for a few minutes. When she woke up, she saw another girl standing in front of her. She stood up quickly.

"Who are you? Why are you imitating me? How long

have you been standing there?" Asked Mevelyn circling the other girl.

"I am you. You can be me if you like," said Evangelina. Mevelyn looked surprised. She stood very close to Evangelina and looked her in the eyes. She could see herself. It was like looking in the mirror. "You have eyes like mine too? Really?" asked Mevelyn.

"Come in the shop come please."

Said Mevelyn dragging Evangelina into the shop. They walked very fast toward the big mirrors. They stood in front of the mirror. They both could not believe it. They were spitting images of each other. They both felt strong.

"So, are your eyes naturally like mine?" asked Mevelyn.

"Why you don't like my eyes?" Asked Evangelina teasing Mevelyn.

"I thought I was the only one with eye color like that," said Mevelyn. Evangelina walked close to the mirror and looked in the mirror.

"Wow!! What happened? How come I have one blue and the other green?" asked Evangelina looking at Mevelyn.

"My eyes are brown, naturally brown." Said Evangelina.

"Wait, a minute. You are naturally brown?" asked Mevelyn a bit surprised.

"Yes, as brown as it gets," said Evangelina.

"You cover for me does that mean you are stronger than me," asked Mevelyn.

"Honestly I don't know. Stronger me? I do not think so. I fainted in one of the clothes shops downstairs. So, I guess you are the strong one," remarked

Evangelina.

"I fainted too just before you came I was very weak," said Mevelyn.

"I arrived here first so technically I am the strong one. You came after me so you need the protection hence I look like you. There are two of you," said Evangelina smiling at Mevelyn.

"I am glad we are finally together. I waited for this for a long time," said Evangelina. The girls hugged for a very long time before setting off home.

"So, do you stay with your parents? Your mum and your dad?" asked Evangelina. Mevelyn looked puzzled and looked at Evangelina.

"Do you?" asked Mevelyn.

"No really. I was until I came here," said Evangelina. "Me too I left home and arrived today as well," said Mevelyn. She realized that for a while Evangelina looked worried and scared. Don't worry I know there is someone too to help us find our home?" said Mevelyn.

"How can you tell? I could not feel you nor see you in my dreams. The priest said I will be able to know exactly where you are," said Evangelina admiring the big beautiful buildings and shops.

"How do you think we ended up together? I went into the mall and the security guard came and asked me if I have seen my sister. Did you tell him you were looking for your sister?" asked Mevelyn. Evangelina stopped and looked at Mevelyn.

"Yes, I spoke to the security guard," said Evangelina. "I then went to the food mall, and a lady came to me and spoke to me as if I was there before. That was my first time there. See there is something that links us I just do not know what it is," said Mevelyn.

"How did you know I was sitting on that bench outside the shop?" asked Mevelyn.

"I felt like a heavy burden was put on top of me. I felt weak and wanted to sit down. I think this is the first time we got linked together. Then after that I had a smooth feeling in my eyes. I went to look in the mirror and my eyes color had changed. After that I just knew where to go. It is like following your footsteps," said Evangelina. They arrived at one big house in one of the suburbs in the city.

"Listen we cannot go inside the house at the same time. Always avoid people we need to be in the room on top, the one with the light on with the window opened," said Mevelyn.

"When you go inside go normally pretend you are their daughter. Do not talk too much just say you are going to sleep. Go inside that room. That is the room of one of the girls. She looks exactly like us but she has a different eye color. Come close to me look in my eyes and tell me my eye color. I will check yours too," said Mevelyn looking at Evangelina.

"Yours have turned all blue," hysterically replied Evangelina.

"Yours are now all blue as well. So, it means that another girl in the house has already fainted. We act like her now to gain access into the house. Go straight into her room and touch her on her tattoo and hide. Wait for me in there. Do not come out before I come in. Ok?" said Mevelyn.

"Ok. I understand," replied Evangelina.

They hugged each other and Evangelina stood up and walked toward the big gate to the house. The door opened, and she went inside. Mevelyn waited for a signal outside. She stood in the cold looking at the room upstairs. Five minutes passed by still there was no signal. What could have gone wrong thought Mevelyn. Evangelina was supposed to go straight away upstairs. Even if the door was locked all she had to do was to knock and go straight to the room upstairs. She looked like the daughter who lived there anywhere. Ten minutes later still there was no signal. What had happened? Why she did not return if there was a problem. Ok five more minutes then I will go and check inside myself thought Mevelyn. She was about to go inside when the light of the top room went off. That was the signal she was waiting for. She went straight to the gate and opened the gate. She went to the front door which was open. As soon as she entered the house a large dog came running to her wriggling its tail. The dog was very playful every time she tried to go upstairs the dog would go in front there to get the nuggets. The dog just picked up the nuggets and came back straight to her. She started walking going upwards.

"Who is it?"

A voice came out of one of the rooms with the door open. Mevelyn stopped, and the dog made a noise. "Eva is that you?" Asked the voice again. Mevelyn stood there for a while. The girl staying here is called Eva too? She looked puzzled. As she stood there she heard the door opening behind her. The dog quickly ran downstairs and started barking waiting for the door to open. Eva is that you? Why are you not answering me?" asked a trembling female voice.

"The front door suddenly opened up, and a man walked inside closing the door behind him. Mevelyn quickly walked upstairs. The other door opened as well where the female voice was coming from. An old lady stood at the door.

"Why are you not answering your grandma?" asked the old lady.

"Sorry grandma I am going to my room now," said Mevelyn going upstairs. Quickly she ran to Eva's room. She opened the door and switched on the light whispering calling Evangelina. She saw the other Eva sleeping on the bed.

"Evangelina where are you?" whispered Mevelyn. The closet door opened. They both jumped on the bed and looked at the other girl who was sleeping. Mevelyn touched her on the tattoo. She looked like them. Evangelina screamed after looking at the sleeping girl.

"Ah she looks like you!" said Evangelina holding her mouth.

"Shh don't make a noise," said Mevelyn. It was not long enough before there was a knock on the door.

"Quickly, quickly hide," said Mevelyn.

"Eva, its daddy how was your day?" said a man's voice. There was a moment of silence before Mevelyn replied.

"It was all right. I am sleeping now," shouted Mevelyn.

"Ok I will see you tomorrow. Good night." Said the man going downstairs. The dog can be heard making noise and following the man downstairs.

"So, when does the other girl wake up?" asked Evangelina looking at the other girl who was sleeping peacefully on the bed.

"Did you give her your antidote? Did you touch her tattoo?" asked Mevelyn.

"Yes, I did first thing when I entered the room," replied Evangelina. They both stood up and walked to the closet. They opened the clothes closet and looked inside. She had a lot of clothes. Quickly the girls went inside and started taking and trying the clothes. They laughed and giggled as they posed as the fashion models. Minutes later a knock is heard on the door.

"Who are you with Eva? Who are you talking to?" asked grandma. The two girls giggled and Evangelina shouted.

"No one grandma. I am now sleeping," they both giggled and the door of the other room is heard being shut. The girls wore Eva's clothes before sleeping on the bed. They spoke about their separate journeys and talked about their lives before this day. Ewalinka opened the door and walked into the house. She felt a little dizzy. Her plan was to go straight to her bedroom, but she also wanted something to drink. She walked slowly into the kitchen trying to avoid waking up the dog. She opened the door fridge and started drinking milk.

"I thought you said you were sleeping," said Timothy Eva's step dad.

"Ewalinka quickly looked at Timothy and spit some milk in Timothy's face."

"Very sorry, it's only that you scared me," said Ewalinka wiping her mouth. Timothy quickly took the kitchen towel and cleaned his face. Quickly Ewalinka went upstairs and into her room. She stood there speechless. What! The four of us in one place! Thought Ewalinka. She quickly jumped on the bed and touched the other two ladies on their tattoos. She already had been staying with Eva. It was the other two girls that needed her antidote. In the morning, there was too much laughter, uncontrolled laughing and giggling as all the girls finally came together. They all had green eyes. It was such a good experience especially for Mevelyn. The idea of additional three identical girls to join them made the experience worthy living. Now she did not have to worry about her eyes. She can have perfect eyes of same color without contact lenses, the most thing she wished for. Now what was left was to meet Nick the future Emperor. Years Later Nick arrived at his father's house leaving Ewalinka in the car. He went inside calling his father. "Daddy! Daddy! Where are you?" He went upstairs to his bedroom, but he was not there. He went downstairs in the study area. The place had been ransacked. He knelt in the study room. There was blood on the floor and on top of the papers. He touched the blood, this was still wet. He got up and went outside through the study's back door. He looked in the garage. He went back in the house and downstairs. His father had been brutally murdered. He was beaten up and then electrocuted. He had gone into cardiac arrest moments before he died. He had waited for his son and the girls to save him. It was too late his plan had failed. He wanted to stall, but this had been perceived as noncooperation that in the end they did not even bother about his money. They were quick to kill him. Nick ran and knelt lifting his father from the floor. He was dead. He was now cold. Nick sobbed uncontrollable. He had brushed aside his father's fears. He sobbed and sobbed until he had no more tears to shed. Ewalinka woke up and entered the house. She went straight in the basement. She stood there and just could not believe what she was seeing, she cried with Nick. Surely how could this have happened? They were supposed to protect Nick and all his friends. If they cannot protect his father how on earth are they going to protect Nick, let alone themselves? This was a wake up call for them. Ewalinka stayed with Nick and Tony his father. Eva left the hospital heading home. Her head felt very heavy. She could not remember exactly what had happened. She remembered bits and pieces. The last time she remembers was when she was at Tony's house. She had received a phone call from Tony asking for help. She remembers not seeing Tony but being attacked. She was hit on the back of the head by something heavy. She fell unconscious. Where was her car? Maybe the car was still at Tony's. These are the questions that kept popping to her head. She was sad. Something must have happened. She arrived at Tony's house. There were a lot of people gathered outside. She knew something bad had happened. She threw herself to the ground. Tony had asked for help. They could not protect him. If they cannot protect Nick's father how can they protect Nick and themselves. She felt low. She felt sad. How was she going to meet Nick? What was she going to say to Nick? All this was their idea. If they had not got involved Tony could still be alive today. What is Nick going to say about all this? Eva asked herself a lot of questions regarding this. It had been three days since the death of Tony. Eva got up and walked toward the house. All the other girls were inside with Nick. When they saw Eva, they were all happy for they thought that she was dead too. They hugged each other for minutes. They sat down and consoled Nick. Weeks after his father's death Nick received a ransom letter demanding $5million dollars. The letter looked like the one Tony had shown him.

He regretted not acting quickly. They should have attacked them first instead of waiting for them to attack.

"I told you the last time that this is the only way to stop this. When are, you going to listen to me?" Asked Ewalinka circling the table. The other girls were sat there too all six of them.

"We have to take caution there are a lot of things that can go wrong," said Eva trying to calm down Ewalinka.

"Listen to yourself. You nearly got killed that day. You want to wait again until someone is dead? Is that so?" shouted Ewalinka looking in Eva's face.

"I personally think that Ewalinka is right. Let's attack first." Said Mevelyn. Eva stood up and shouted sending papers flying in the air.

"Have you heard what I said? I said let's be cautious about this. I know they used something against me. They knocked me out," said Eva standing in front of everyone.

"What if they have used the magical stones against us?" quipped Eva. Everyone realized that Eva had a point. That could indeed explain why they were all weak.

"We don't want to end up dead. Let's find out their strength and their weakness before we embark on the attack. The only way forward is not to wait but to attack. Nick's father is dead because we waited." Said Ewalinka. They all kept quiet for a while. They knew they had failed. It could have been Nick. They stayed and talked for a very long time. Later Ewalinka retired to bed. She was exhausted and needed to sleep early. The others stayed talking in the lounge area. Ewalinka could not sleep. She got up from the bed and went into the room with the magic stones. She felt upset. She perceived herself as the strong one. The day of the tragedy she was weak and was in a trance the whole day. Mevelyn followed her into the room with the magic stones.

"I know it has been a tough time for you and everyone else." Said Mevelyn. I can't stop thinking about it," replied Ewalinka.

"We can't just sit and wait you know," continued Ewalinka.

"I think we have to do something fast," said Ewalinka. There was a moment of silence.

"What do you have in mind? I can help. You can always count on me." Said Mevelyn in a soft low voice. They talked for a long time and after talking they all went to bed.

CHAPTER THIRTEEN

"When do you think, we should pay our friend a visit?" asked Dino. Marek hesitated to answer instead looked outside the window.

"I think it's too soon boss," quipped Marek looking at his boss Dino.

"How can you say it's too soon when we have nothing to show for it?" asked Dino.

"This time no casualties I want him alive. I want that money. All of it. You hear what I am saying?" asked Dino who touched the table with both his hands spread apart looking at Marek. Trying to make Tony transfer money to their accounts was unsuccessful. Tony ended up dead. He had refused to cooperate. Dino did not want any problems with the police he had to take Tony out. Tony had preferred money to life. They had only asked for $2million but he had vehemently refused to cooperate. Dino was a man of his word having been in the Russian KGB he knew a lot about trust, honor and betrayal.

"Did he reply to the ransom note?" asked Dino siting down.

"Not that I am aware of," replied Marek.

"Maybe you ought to send him a reminder," said Dino. Marek paused for a while and asked his boss Dino.

"What do you have in mind?"

There was a moment of silence as Dino thought to himself.

"At the mean time send another ransom note give them a deadline," said Dino.

"What is your plan? The girl we took died?" asked Marek.

"The idea is to let them think that the girl still exists. No need to worry now. He got our message. Cooperate or he ends up like his father. Now it will be easy. He knows we mean business," said Dino. "Get all the other guys let them know that a date has been set," Marek and Dino go back a long way. They were both part of the KGB protecting leadership of the Central Committee of the Communist Party of the Soviet Union. After the collapse of the KGB they had feared for their lives seeking protection in USA. Over the years, they had been collecting ransom money and getting away with murder. They had one motto; cooperate or die. The days of the KGB had taught them a hard-life's lesson. They knew that it is a thin line between trust and betrayal and a thin line between life and death too. Dino never remarried again. All his family was murdered during the days he was in the KGB. Ever since losing his wife and kids he had vowed somehow to revenge. He had a girlfriend and several mistresses. Ransom business was an easy business for Dino. They had collected ransom money even when they were in the KGB. Marek was asleep when he was woken up by a knock on the door. He got up and walked toward the door. He opened the door and his wife who was still in bed shouted from the bedroom.

"Darling who is it?"

"It's the sales person I will be with you in a moment," said Marek shutting the door.

"Yes. How can I help you?" asked Marek.

"I am detective Silks and I am investigating the murder of a one Tony Layton. I have some few questions to ask," said detective Silk taking out a small note book from his pocket and a pen.

"What does that have to do with me?" asked Marek looking very uncomfortable about this.

"Your car was seen near the crime scene at the same time we think the crime was committed," said detective Silks. Marek stood there looking if anyone was watching. Dino would not be pleased if he heard this. "It could have been another car like mine. I was not in that area at all. Do you have proof that it was my car?" asked Marek.

"No I don't have," replied detective Silks.

"I am afraid that in that case I don't have anything to say to you. Have a nice day detective?" Marek went inside his house and left the detective snooping outside.

"Who was it?" asked Irina, Marek's wife.

"No one Darling. Nothing to worry about," said Marek reaching for the phone. He dialed a number and waited for the answer.

"Yes. What seems to be the problem?" asked the man on the other end.

"I have a rotten KGB outside my door asking too many questions," Samarkand going into the kitchen. "Don't worry about that we meet tonight as planned," said the man on the other end of the line. After that the line soon went dead. Marek put the phone back and went to sit on his bed with his wife. "What is wrong you look like you have seen a ghost?" asked Irina. Marek tried to pretend that everything was ok.

"Nothing to worry about everything is going to be fine," said Marek getting in bed. They laid down for some time. That morning after talking to Marek detective Silk went to meet Nick.

"I am very sorry about your father," said detective Silks trying to break the ice.

"He will be greatly missed."

"I am missing him already," replied Nick.

"Is there anything you can tell me about the whole issue leading to the death of your father?" asked detective Silks.

"What can I say. Where should I start," Nick asked himself not expecting the detective to reply?

"Few weeks before his murder," said Nick pausing for a while touching his forehead.

"He received a blackmail note or a ransom note if you want to call it that way, asking him for $2million. They threatened to kill me," said Nick looking at detective Silks.

"My dad brushed the whole thing aside. He said he does not give in to blackmail and all that stuff," said Nick. The detective wrote something in his book before asking Nick more questions.

"Did your father ever thought of seeking help from the police?" questioned detective Silks.

"Not that I am aware of," replied Nick.

"How long has this been going on? How many ransom notes he received?" asked detective Silks.

"Honestly I think this has been going on for a while. I saw two ransom notes, but he always burned these?" said Nick.

"Did they manage to get his money?" asked the detective.

"Not really I checked all his accounts. It seems they did not?" replied Nick.

"So, you must also agree that this is likely to happen to you as well. These people were after your father's money and they did not get any. Would that not be true also to say that these people may strike again?" asked the detective.

"Yes. It is true but I object to what you are inferring to," said Nick shaking his head.

"I know it sound bad but it's for your own protection. We just keep an eye on you. Just to make sure that you are safe," said detective Silks.

"Thank you but no thanks," said Nick getting up. There was a moment of silence. The detective looked at Nick and asked a question.

"Are you okay? Have they already contacted you? Are you being blackmailed? If so we are here to help," said the detective getting up too. Nick refused to say anything and led the detective to the door. The detective took out his card with a telephone number and left these with Nic.

"If you still want to talk, here is my number."

The detective stood there for some time before leaving.

"Hi it's Silks, detective Silks. Is there a chance you can put a tail on a one Marek Konska?" said the detective before pausing for a while.

"Yes. Of 24 Beverly street," said the detective. He thanked the person he was talking to and got in his car. There was something strange about Marek. He had done a background check on him and he looked more like the likely culprit. A former ruthless corrupt KGB. He lived in the suburbs of Beverly Hills yet he worked as a bouncer for another former KGB Dino. Dino wanted his hands to remain clean. Marek was the likely man to do Dino's dirty jobs. Blackmail was big business during the Soviet-era. After its collapse these former KGB's ended up without work and facing criminal charges against them that they ended up in America. They say old habits die hard. Dino had a chain of hotels and night clubs in the city. Over the year's people had been murdered or disappeared without any trace. Tony Nick's father was one of the recently murdered victims. In broad day light in his own home he had met his demise. They seemed unstoppable. They were fearless. It seemed they covered their trails perfectly. After one hour, an unmarked police car parked few meters from Marek's house. Detective Silks' phone rung.

"The bird has just landed. The first letters of the reg. Victor, Charlie, Six. Over," Detective Silks understood the message, and he drove off leaving the unmarked police car to tail Marek. Marek left his house on foot. He did not even bother taking his car. His years in the KGB had taught him all the tactics used in cases like this. That is why he liked America. He knew he would be tailed. His aim now was to lose the tail. He had done this before and he welcomed the challenge with much great appreciation. KGB was no joke. It is unlike modern training and all that stuff.

He was in the middle of executing his plan to lose the tail when his phone rung.

"Just check there might be a tail on you. We meet tonight. If you cannot lose the tail let me know we can reschedule or change the venue," Marek did not even have a chance to answer before the line soon died. Marek went to work as usual after losing the tail. It was business as usual. After work on his way to the meeting Marek received a telephone call from Dino asking him to abort the planned venue and instead was told about the new venue. The police car that had a tail on Marek arrived at the meeting place and was parked outside. There were two officers in the car in plain clothes. They sat in the car away from the house where the meeting was supposedly going to take place. One hour passed by and there was no any activity. Lights in the house were on. Another hour passed still there was no sign of Marek. The officers sat in the car. They both started dosing off. It was the large noise that woke them up. The noise was coming from the roof of their car. It sounded like some heavy animal had just jumped on top of their car. They heard growling and saw watery prints left on their front window screen. It was not a long when someone tried to open the door on the driver's side. They looked in that direction but saw nothing. One of the officers switched on the headlights. Still nothing could be seen. The roof of the car parked in front of them collapsed inside. The alarm of that car went off. Hazard warning lights were activated. As soon as the alarm went off the wooden gate to the house they were watching was smashed down. No one said anything they just looked at each other. A few minutes later. A man came out of the house running very fast and he tried to open his car that was parked in the street. The two officers watched in horror as they saw the man being dragged away into the bushes. "What was that?" asked one officer.

"I was about to ask you the same question."

"Why you didn't get out of the car and used your gun?" quipped one officer to another.

"And shoot what?" asked the other officer. The other officer did not reply, he looked at his partner in disbelief. Surely there is nothing they could have done. There were up against an unknown entity. What was that? Was the main question that needed an answer but no one was prepared or equipped to answer that question. Both men just sat in the car and watched. They had never been this scared before. It took a long time before they literally got out of the car. They looked on top of their car. The other officer touched the top of their car with his hand before he jibbed.

"Awe what is that?" Shaking his hand. He had touched some salivary mucus stuff.

"What was that?" Asked the other officer.

"Who knows just make sure you don't catch anything? Ok partner?" said the other officer taking the first aid kit from the bonnet. He took out an antiseptic bottle and a clean cloth and gave this to his partner. The other officer quickly wiped his hands. The other officer returned to his seat and tried to radio the headquarters.

"Hold on. What are you going to say? What did you see?" asked the other officer. Officer Brown waited for a while thinking.

"We can say that there has been an animal attack," replied officer Brown.

"Look this will look bad on us. I do not want to spend even a minute on any psychological valuations. Whatever it is it left the two of us. Look who they went for? The bad guy. Whatever it is I would give it time to clean all this mess. These former KGB's think they can come to our country and just kill at will." Shouted officer Riley.

"Look at it this way. If it had been that crook Marek or Dino. Would you have stopped this from happening if you had the chance? Or you would have been rejoicing that it is less blood off your hands," asked officer Riley. Officer Brown realized that officer Riley had a point. No matter what no one would feel sorry for a man like Marek or Dino. These were the scums of society. They might have money and houses everywhere but society would be a better place without them.

"You see, Brown," said officer Riley getting into the car with his partner.

"People like Marek and Dino are too clever for us. Let's admit it. You will never beat them. All those years in the KGB has made them invincible. To be honest, we will never get a conviction," officer Riley spoke passionately holding officer Brown's shoulder. "Just look tonight. Those two were supposed to be here. Holding the meeting just there in front of us. Is that not the reason why we are here?" questioned officer Riley looking at officer Brown. Officer Brown knew Riley had a point but all his life he had done what he thought was right.

"Yes, intelligence directed us here. Marek and Dino as far as I know they were supposed to be here," said officer Brown.

"You see that's my point. I believe whatever it is it

was after them too. You tell me now how we can stop them? I want these crook's dead. Why waste tax payer's money taking them to court? If it was that two-faced KGB crook Marek who was dragged in the woods I would be rejoicing right now," Officer Riley paused for a while taking his cigarette out of his pocket and lighting one.

"I want them to face justice too. I want to do it the right way, you know?" said officer Brown lighting up a cigarette too.

"I'm with you all the way Brown. I am just saying tonight I did not see anything. If it was Marek or Dino. I would radio the headquarters right now myself. These crooks are still out there. Just tonight partner turn a blind eye. You are not doing anything wrong. You did not see anything so am I. Ok partner?" said officer Riley blowing the cigarette smoke through the open window. Minutes later the two officer's drove off their car heading home.

"Bad news boss," said Marek talking to Dino on the phone.

"Alexandra didn't make it yesterday. I heard this morning that his body was found in the woods mauled to death. His limbs were missing,"

Marek paused for a while giving Dino time to absorb all this.

"Where did this happen?" asked Dino much concerned.

"Our meeting point. Where we were supposed to be yesterday," said Marek.

"Are we still to go ahead with tonight's meeting?" asked Marek nervously. There was a moment of silence. Dino for the first time realized that soon he might be out smarted. Something more powerful that

KGB was after him. All his life he had always made good calls. No wonder he was very successful in the KGB. He trusted his instincts. Once Marek told him about the rotten ex KGB meaning detective he had rescheduled all his plans. But what was it now, really? Mauled to death in the suburbs of Beverly Hills was never heard of. What was he up to this time he wondered?

"Cancel tonight appointment as well. Spend time with Irina until further notice," said Dino before putting the handset down.

"Marek kept holding the phone even after the line had gone dead. So many thoughts were running in his head. Who was responsible for this? Was he safe? Why Dino mentioned Irina. Was Ira in danger? He quickly lifted the phone and dialed Ira. The phone rung for some time without any answer. He became a little nervous. He waited another ten minutes and dialed again. Pick up the phone woman," he spoke to himself.

"Hello Ira speaking," a woman voice can be heard on the other end.

"Darling how are you and the kids?" asked Marek. Okay Darling. I was in the bathroom I did not hear the phone ringing," said Ira with a high voice.

"What time are you coming home?" continued Ira. "Tonight, same time or even earlier I will let you know once I finish work. I love you," Marek put the phone down soon after talking to his wife. Marek was once hardcore. Brutal and unrepentant. It was the death of Dino's wife and kids that changed him. Dino was the strongest man you could ever meet. He was good at his job and always one step ahead of everyone else. He was brutal and had no feelings. No one knew he had a family. People like him were thought of not capable of loving. It was the murder of his wife and kids that changed him to become even a worse monster. Agatha had thought of escaping the country days after her husband left the KGB. She was harassed and threatened with death. She was escaping with the kids. She got into her car and drove. Hours in the roads coupled by fatigue and tiredness she soon found herself in trouble with the rebels near the border. They ordered her out of the car. She complied with their request and her kids followed too. They stood there for a while as the rebels spoke to each other. She realized that they were not to let her go. So, she ran for it crossing the road. She crossed the first side of the road. Her children followed too. The rebels tried to stop her by holding her woolen sweater which she quickly removed running off. A Mercedes Benz car was coming from the other side at full speed. The driver failed to stop hitting her sending her flying only to find herself between the wheels of another car. On seeing this her children, a boy and a girl followed too only to be crushed by a bus. Marek for the first time felt fear crippling him. Dino rarely canceled appointments especially the ones involving money. Marek finished work and went straight home without taking a shower at work. He arrived home and went to take a shower. His wife and two kids were sitting in the lounge area watching a movie. It was ten minutes into taking the shower when he heard a large growling sound coming from the living room. He quickly took the towel and wrapped himself with it. He wiped his face and opened the bathroom door. Slowly he advanced into the lounge area. He heard a large growling sound and looked in the lounge area. A large watery animal like a lion was on top of his wife. He could see that there was blood coming out of her mouth. Her heart and all her left side had been severed. His son and daughter were all dead. As he stood there another watery animal with shining green eyes came out of the spare room and stood in the corridor looking at him. Fear crippled him and he ran back into the bathroom and tried to close the door behind him. The door was broken down. The last thing he saw were two large shining pairs of eyes fixed at him. Detective Silks heard about the death of Marek and his family and he attended the crime scene. He looked around the whole house looking for clues. The police at the scene had attributed this to a wild animal or a large dog. Surely whatever it is this was unnatural. Marek's heart was badly severed that he lost a lot of blood and died. "So, what do we have here?" asked detective Silks.

"I have never seen anything like this before. It is beyond human belief." Answered the crime scene investigator. Detective Silks walked around trying to piece together what had happened. There was no doubt some savage attack went on here. Kids too were mauled to death. Detective Silks drove his Audi Quattro from the crime scene heading toward the city. A lot of questions were running in his head. What kind of animal would do that? Was it a wild animal and shouldn't the public be alerted? He reached down in his pocket to check the message he had just received on his pager. The report from the lab was ready to collect. He stepped on gas and headed to the crime scene laboratory just outside the city. As soon as he entered the building he met the lab technician who was on his way out.

"Eh detective! Your report is ready to collect!" said Lucas going out of the building.

"Is it home time already for you?" asked detective Silks.

"Not really. I am going to our sister lab in the city and will be back soon," Lucas waved to the detective and rushed outside. Detective Silks went inside and collected the lab reports and headed to Nick's house. Half an hour later he was at Nick's.

"Do you have time I need to talk to you about something that's really important? I think you will want to hear this," said detective Silks.

"I am kind of busy make it fast," replied Nick.

"One of the suspects, actually two of the suspects to have murdered your father had been found dead this morning," paused the detective looking at Nick's reaction. Nick looked unbothered just this morning he had received another ransom note or if you want to call it a blackmail letter. Surely these people had nothing to do with the blackmail he thought to himself.

"Is that all?" asked Nick going back inside the house. Nick was about to close the door when the detective placed his hand on the door and stopped the door from closing.

"It's not their deaths that I am concerned about. It is the way they died that is my main concern. You see, they were all mauled to death by some kind of animal." The detective said this looking both sides to make sure that no one was listening. Nick stood there for a while thinking.

"We have never come across such brutal savage. His wife and kids were not spared too," said the detective moving backward as if he was about to go. On hearing this Nick looked away for a while pondering what to do next. Why his wife and kids? That was disturbing for a while.

"I don't know anything about this," Murmured Nick before he closed the door. Surely it sounded like Ewalinka and Mevelyn but they had never killed women and children before thought Nick. Nick was about to go upstairs when there was a knock on the door. Hoping it to be one of the ladies Nick rushed downstairs and opened the door.

"Detective what can I do for you," said Nick looking at detective Silks who was flipping pages from his small book.

"Do you own a big dog by any chance or do you know anyone who does?" asked the detective.

"No. I do not own one and I do not know anyone who does. If that is all, goodbye detective." Nick quickly closed the door and rushed upstairs leaving the detective standing outside.

CHAPTER FOURTEEN

Chang is at Tsinghua University which is one of the most beautiful universities in China. He is walking in the Imperial gardens of the Qing dynasty. The gardens are magnificent, glorious, and mysterious. He is wondering what life would have been like during the Emperor's days. He walks in the gardens of the university formerly the Emperor's in the Qing dynasty. The tour guide comes to Chang, and they started a conversation.

"Dear Mr. Chang. How are you finding the tour so far? These gardens are glorious, magnificent, and mysterious. That is what I like about Beijing. It is full of surprises," said the tour guide Mr. Wang Lan. Chang looked around, no doubt the Imperial gardens were beautiful and full of mysterious stuff. I was looking forward to seeing these Imperial gardens," said Chang mesmerized by these beautiful Qing dynasty gardens.

"Wait until you have been to the Forbidden city, the Imperial palace the home of all the Emperors. It will take your breath away," said the tour guide.

"It's my next stop. Right?" asked Chang looking at the tour guide manual.

"Yes. Mr. Chang that's our next destination," Chang spent the few hours at the university before heading to the Forbidden city the home of the Emperors. For over 500 years the Forbidden city has been the palace for Emperors. In ancient China, Imperial bodyguards lived their entire lives in the Forbidden city. All protectors and servants of the Emperor spent their lives in the Forbidden city. To serve, to protect to honor meant more than life itself. Imperial bodyguards sacrificed a lot to honor and serve and protect the Emperor. Allegiances to the Emperor was for the rest of ones' life and in the aftermath, as well. The Imperial bodyguards will be on guard serving the Emperor for eternity. Chang had visited the Forbidden city for himself to be able to understand life as an Imperial guard. He was going to stay overnight before heading back to Yunnan Province. He was going to come back to Tsinghua University where he was to study a master's degree in Chinese history and culture. Chang had grown up with the temple priest being taught ancient Chinese history and culture. Listening to all the legends and myth. Ever since the day he last saw Evangelina a lot of questions had bothered him. He had more questions than he had answers. In a month's time Chang, would be enrolling at the university to further his studies. All his life he had been fascinated by Imperial dynasties, Emperors and their bodyguards. After the disappearance of Evangelina many questions remained unanswered. The past month he had been in Linton district Shaanxi Province to see the terracotta army. This brought a new meaning to serve and to protect. The Emperors' bodyguards were for all eternity. This made him understand why people would leave their biological parents and spend the rest of their lives protecting and serving the Emperor. It was interesting to him and everyone who witnessed the buried life sized Imperial guards. Once one is chosen to serve, to honor and to protect that will continue until afterlife. As far as Chang was concerned the legend was true or at least that is what the people at that time believed. Chang having grown up surrounded by the temple priest all he knew as a child was that the stories were legends. Stories not real entirely but which to some extent were true. These were told to guide us, to make us strong and to give us the belief that help to shape our society. Did he believe in the stories he heard from the temple priest? This is one of the questions that led him to study Chinese culture and history at the university. He had seen miraculous things and heard stories which science could not dispute as real. Having spent nearly four years at the university what did he make of all this, the legends he heard, the disappearance of Evangelina. That day he nearly laughed to death what happened? What carried him from the water to the temple? That day was he hallucinating because of the poison? Was he stung by the fish or by Evangelina? What is meant by the tattoo on Evangelina's back? Are there still Emperors and are there still modern day Imperial bodyguards with super powers? Four years on and he cannot still answer all these questions. Would another degree provide answers to all these questions? Chang had been awarded the research grant to study Chinese history and culture. This would fund all his living expenses and the research costs including traveling. After visiting Tsinghua University, a month ago, on a tour, Chang arrived at the university to start his research degree fully funded by the university and the national heritage council and history of China.

"Hello. My name is Chang. I have just arrived and I will be doing a research degree," said Chang extending his hand to greet the lady he met at the foyer.

"Hallo. I am Lin. I am a master's degree student as well studying sciences," said Lin with a big smile on her face. The two spoke for some time before they said goodbyes and Chang went to his flat. The coming weeks Chang was very busy preparing his research proposal. On a Friday, he handed in his research proposal and went out to the Friday Night Disco at the university where he met Lin again. They spoke for some time and Lin invited Chang to her flat.

"So how are your studies so far?" asked Chang to break the ice.

"Yes. Awesome, I guess. I have been busy with the research proposal you know." Said Lin getting drinks from the small fridge that was in her flat.

"Me too I guess. But mine was straight forward from the start. I know what I want to know so it has been easy for me. I know what I want my research to be about," quipped Chang.

"You can tell me what is your research about?" asked Lin jokingly. There was a moment of silence.

"Mine is about legends, myths and folk stories. I think

this is an interesting topic," said Chang getting drinks put on the table by Lin. Lin laughed for a while before talking to Chang.

"You can't be serious. Legends? What can you get from a legend? A legend is just a made-up story. Just like a bed-time story you tell to kids for helping them to sleep," she paused for a while. Okay partly this pierced Chang's heart that he failed to breathe properly for a good two minutes. This cheeky and arrogant lady cannot stop showing off, thought Chang to himself. He sipped his drink calming his nerves. Lin realized that she had been straight forward and to the point and that this man cannot stand her arrogance. She tried to justify` her stance.

"I am a scientist. Full stop. I do not believe in legends, myths or any wishful thinking." Said Lin tossing a drink. They both drunk their drinks for a while before continuing their conversation. I had the belief that some legends are true whereas some are not. I grew up surrounded by legends and myths. My research will be to uncover the truth behind these legends," said Chang excitedly. Lin replied sarcastically.

"Awe lucky you," said Lin.

"What is your favorite pet or animal and why?" asked Lin trying to change the subject.

"I think a dragon and because I ride one," said Chang seriously. Lin looked at him thinking that he was joking. She could not stop laughing.

"This guy makes me laugh. Be serious!" Said Lin. Chang noticed that this girl will never take him seriously.

"Do you mean a Komodo dragon?" asked Lin. Chang paused for a while thinking.

"A real dragon, one that can fly," replied Chang. Lin burst into laughter. She laughed uncontrollably rolling on her bed. Chang stood there wondering what to say for Lin to take her seriously.

"What about you what is your favorite animal or pet and why?" asked Chang a bit embarrassed. She laughed for a while and she stood up wiping tears of joy from her eyes.

"I would say a cat because cats don't depend on humans. You do not worry about a cat than you do for say a dog," said Lin. They spoke for a while about cats and dogs before Lin asked Chang about dragons.

"On a serious note, do you believe about dragons and all that stuff?" asked Lin.

"Honestly I do. One gave me a ride when I was a kid?" said Chang. This freaked Lin, this time she did not laugh but instead tried to understand Chang. They spoke for a very long time. Weeks that followed saw Chang and Lin getting to know each other better and better that they ended up dating.

"So, what is your research about?" asked Lin looking at Chang's laptop.

"It is about flying dragons and Imperial bodyguards," replied Chang jokingly. They both laughed before Chang spoke again.

"Have you ever heard about the legends of the magnificent seven?" asked Chang. Lin paused for a while and took off her reading glasses. She wiped them using the corner of her blouse.

"Yes, I grew up hearing that story. It is said that seven Imperial bodyguards from the temple bloodline will be born every one hundred years to protect the bloodline of the future Emperor. Is that the one," asked Lin. Over the few weeks they were together she started understanding Chang. This was a very sensitive topic for him. He had some emotion attachment to this issue. They spoke at great length about the legend of the magnificent seven.

"Just like you I want to find scientific explanations to everything regarding the legend. When I was growing up, I deeply believed in the legend. After studying at the university, I started doubting all things about the legend. I was passionate about this legend that the awarding body chose me out of nearly 2000 students to be awarded this research grant," said Chang. They spoke together and spend most of the time together. Over the next weeks, Chang had research a lot of information about the legend of the magnificent seven. He researched about any missing girls at the same time when Evangelina disappeared. His focus was mainly in China it never occurred to him that this could be global. Evangelina per common beliefs at home was somewhere in China waiting to serve an Emperor. Even Evangelina's disappearance was never mentioned anywhere. He went by what he knew best. His first research point was his home village where he grew up Yunnan Province. He traveled back home with a lot more questions in the form of questionnaires and research prints. He collected all the information he can regard Evangelina's birth and life as a kid in Yunnan. Evangelina as a kid suffered from the sleeping sickness disease. She normally fell into trances and slept for days. Was this because of the magic powers or something sinister? He measured car Chang. Chang looked excited by some findings. "We start with the good news first. I have found out that Yunnan Province has an abandoned uranium mine. It constantly produces carbon monoxide gas.

Depending on the wind pattern, this carbon monoxide is large enough to cause the sleeping sickness disease. This could scientifically explain why kids in that area fall into trances and slept for days. There are a lot varieties of fish no one in particular can cause the uncontrollable laughter symptoms." Said Chang flipping pages of the file.

"What about the distance from the river where you saw the Komodo dragon to the temple? Is it feasible that maybe Evangelina carried you to the temple?" Asked Lin.

"The distance from the river to the temple and the terrain made it impossible for Evangelina to have carried me to the temple. The Komodo dragon is no way in a state to carry human beings over a long distance. So, in that case there is still an unanswered question," said Chang putting the papers down. "There are still more unanswered questions. The legend says that seven magnificent warriors will be born with special powers to protect the Emperor, right? If that is the case it means all born at the same time. No human being can have seven babies at the same time. Especially considering that they are all to be identical. How do you resolve that?" Asked Chang standing up and walking to the book shelf. He took one book and opened it. He read it for a while.

"It could be that there are born from different parents with same genes?" said Lin. Chang came back and sat next to Lin and typed something on his laptop.

"Even if that is the case they all must be born at the same time?" said Chang looking at the laptop screen. "I checked hospital records in Yunnan before I came here. No girls or boys born there at the same time or with same date of birth. I checked with the maternity hospital here in Beijing. There are no more than four babies born at the same time the very same day. The legend has it that every hundred years it is either all boys or all girls. If my instincts are correct, I think if it is true they will be girls." Chang paused and looked at Lin.

"It could be in all China not just here in Beijing. I know Beijing, Forbidden city was the home of the Emperors but look at it this way. The Emperor asked for help from the temple priest many years ago because he was under attack. He was killed together with all the seven temple warriors. His son or daughter surely could not have remained in the Forbidden city. As I know he went into hiding to preserve the blood line. So, it could be in any other city in China," said Lin holding Chang's shoulder. Chang stood up and took all the research papers that were lying everywhere and put all in his drawer. "Listen I think we deserve a break from all this can we go and have something to eat?" Said Chang getting his jacket from the coat hanger.

"I thought you were not going to ask," said Lin kissing Chang. They left Chang's flat and strolled in the park on their way to the restaurant. Weeks went by without any clues of finding more information about this legend.

"My research seems to be going nowhere," said Chang talking to his friend Zhang.

"Mine seems okay I have been all over at first, now I am targeting areas where I can collect enough data for my research," said Zhang before continuing.

"What seems to be the problem?" asked Zhang.

"I am kind of stuck. I have been to the Forbidden city

to get any kind of information relating to my research topic with no luck," said Chang.

"The only thing with research degrees is for you to know your subject and research about them. If you put yourself in their shoes, you will understand a lot." Quipped Zhang. Chang sat there for a while.

"The closest clue to all this is the disappearance of Evangelina. Maybe I should put myself in her shoes." Said Chang quickly getting up and searching for the legend story on his laptop.

"Assuming she didn't die. If she is the chosen one inverted comas where would she go to serve this Emperor. Are there still Emperors today? And where?" asked Chang quickly researching on his laptop.

"Japan! Highly unlikely Emperor ought to be of Chinese bloodline I think," said Chang.

"Ok. Let's look at it this way. Take that girl's, date of birth and departure date and use these as your guideline. They are born on the same day and they leave at the same time to initiate their services," said Zhang.

"Ok. It makes sense, let's see Evangelina went missing on eh," said Chang flipping the pages of his diary. Chang typed Evangelina's date of birth and her missing date. Only one article popped up, but it was in Bellac Limousine, France. He did not even read about it. He dismissed it quickly. Surely this should be in China only he thought to himself. Lin visited Chang that evening, and they spoke about the research.

"I will be back soon. I will go and get something to eat. What do you want to eat?" asked Chang wearing his jacket.

"The usual Dear," replied Lin. Chang left Lin in his flat. Lin took Chang's laptop and started browsing search history. He checked through all previously opened files. There was only one file outstanding from the rest, France. When Lin saw this file, she got curious. Quickly she opened the file. This was a missing report of a young girl called Eva from Bellac Limousin, France. She read the whole report. She could not see the relevance. She scrolled down and clicked at the picture that was there for the presumed missing girl. Her phone rung and she quickly took it out from her hand bag and answered the call. It was one of her friends calling. They spoke until Chang came back. He just looked at the picture on the laptop screen and dropped all the food on the floor. "Oh, my God! Evangelina!" said Chang quickly picking up the laptop. Lin got up and rushed to Chang.
"What's wrong Darling?"
She asked looking at Chang who looked like he had seen a person woke up from death.
"It's Evangelina!" said Chang sitting down.
"Are you sure? This one is missing too somewhere in France?" said Lin holding Chang's shoulder. Chang read through the article before taking a long breath. "This girl is also called Eva? What a coincidence. What are the odds of that happening? Born on same day, disappeared on the same day, have the same name and look alike too but are from two countries miles apart?" asked Chang. Lin looked speechless. All along she was just going with the floor because she fell for Chang but now even her she started believing in the legend. That night Chang did not sleep. He collected all the information can possibly can. The

next flight was to Bellac Limousin France. After twenty and half hours of traveling, he was in Toulouse. The hire car was ready, and he drove to Bellac. Three hours later he was in Bellac, Limousin. He headed straight to 30 Bellissimo Road.

"Hello. Can I speak to Benjamin or Bridgette Petit." Asked Chang talking in the telephone system at the gate?

"What is this regarding to?" asked the woman.

"I need some information regarding Eva," said Chang.

"Ok. Wait," replied the woman. Few seconds later the electrical gate opened slowly. Chang went in and as he walked to the front door a woman stood at the door.

"Hello! My name is Chang," said Chang stretching his hand.

"Come in Mr. Chang," said Bridgette walking to the kitchen.

"Any refreshments?" asked Bridgette.

"Water please," replied Chang. Bridgette went into the kitchen and brought water for Mr. Chang. She walked to the stairs and stood on the side holding the rails and called her husband.

"Benny, come down stairs we have a visitor."

"Ok I will be down in a sec," replied Benjamin. Chang looked around looking for any pictures of Eva. He stood up and walked toward the fire place. There was a family photo hung beside. He looked at the picture. He could see the young Evangelina. He recalled that day he went with her searching for the Komodo dragon. He stood there for some minutes. Bridgette walked into the kitchen making coffee for Benjamin.

"Coffee or tea Mr. Chang?" asked Bridgette peeping

from the kitchen.

"Coffee, two sugars," shouted Chang without even looking at Bridgette. He looked at the other portrait photo of Eva. He looked closely. She had shining blue eyes.

"What brings you here Mr..?" asked Benjamin siting down on the couch.

"Mr. Chang. It is a long story," said Chang siting down.

"She is a beautiful girl," said Chang looking at the family photo album.

"Oh. Yes. She is a big girl now where ever she is," said Benjamin. Chang waited for Bridgette to finish making the coffees. A few minutes later she joined Chang and Benjamin in the lounge area.

"I don't know where to beginning and how to say this," said Chang siting forward on the edge of the couch.

"I am trying to find out what happened to Evangelina, who I can say was more like my sister," he paused and looked at the couple. Benjamin and Bridgette seemed confused on hearing this.

"Do you mean our Eva?" asked Bridgette.

"No. Yes. I mean. I knew another girl called Evangelina. She looked like your daughter Eva. She went missing same day as your Eva," he paused after noticing that he was confusing them.

"I came here because I saw the missing report you posted with the police in Bellac. Your daughter is identical to the other missing girl called Eva too. She was born on 25 November. On her seventh birthday, she disappeared," paused Chang. Benjamin got up angrily.

"What is this? What are you trying to do? You think

this is funny? Why come here to insult us? Get out of my house," shouted Benjamin upset.

"I apologize for any misunderstandings. That is the reason why I am here. Listen to my story first please," pleaded Chang.

"Let him talk first Benny," said Bridgette nodding her head.

"Days before she left she started talking about her sister. She told her mum that she was going to stay with her sister. Her parents had a miscarriage many years before she was born. So, her parents got scared they thought she knew that she was going to die." He paused and sipped his coffee.

"This Evangelina all her childhood she was very sick. She would go into a trance and wake up after days," said Chang who stopped talking as he was interrupted by Benjamin.

"Just like our Eva. She was in and out of the hospital. She fell in trances too," said Benjamin holding Bridgette's hand.

"On the eve of her birthday she left her parents for good," said Chang drinking his coffee.

"Did her parents report her missing?" asked Bridgette.

"No," replied Chang before continuing.

"This is the main reason I came here. In China, there is a legend about the Emperor and the magnificent seven." He looked at them raising his eyebrows. Benjamin understood the meaning.

"No, we never heard of it."

He replied looking at Bridgette who agreed with him. "The legend has it that seven identical girls or boys will be born every 100 years to protect the Emperor. At the age of seven they will leave their biological parents to serve the Emperor." He looked at them as they looked at each other puzzled.

"So, after serving this Emperor will my daughter come back to me?" asked Bridgette.

"I am afraid not the service is for eternity even afterlife."

"Ah, I miss my daughter,"

Bridgette started crying. It has been years since the disappearance of their beloved daughter. Hearing all this brought painful memories back. But is there truth in all this or it just wishful thinking? Asked Benjamin. There was a moment of silence. Chang was carefully thinking about what to say without sounding silly. Let me put it this way. I do not know what to believe. Is the legend true or not? I do not know. But there are a lot of things that is giving that hope. That somewhere there our Evangelina is alive. Said Chang.

"So, do you still have Emperors in China? Is my daughter in China?" asked Bridgette.

"This is the tricky part. There are no Emperors in China now. I do not know where this new Emperor is. I have no leads so far," said Chang.

"There are a lot of things that makes the legend real," said Chang pausing to drink his coffee.

"Such as?" Asked Benjamin. Chang looked at the photo of Eva again. The first and foremost proof is the tattoo," he paused and wiped his lips with his hand.

"Yes, the tattoo. The legend has it that they all will be born with markings depicting the powers and their roles in the Imperial dynasty," said Chang.

"Do you mean tattoos?" asked Bridgette.

"Yes. Tattoos. Evangelina was born with a dragon tattoo," he paused giving the couple chance to say something. They looked at each other and Benjamin hold his wife's hand.

"Our Eva was born with a lion tattoo on her back," said Benjamin. Chang quickly took out his diary and wrote this down.

"So, our daughter is alive," said Bridgette. The couple hugged each other for a very long time.

"So, did you have any leads of her whereabouts the days she disappeared?" asked Chang.

"They were all dead ends. I remember one day receiving a phone call from the police saying that they had leads in Moscow, Russia but later admitted that it was not her," said Benjamin.

"Moscow, Russia?" asked Chang writing this down in his diary. He asked a lot of questions about any strange behavior and about Bellac. He noticed that there was an abandoned uranium mine as well in Bellac. The next day he headed to Bellac police station. There he was told that the reports were archived and was asked to return the following day. The next day he was at Bellac police station.

"Hello, I am Chang. I came yesterday. I need information regarding a missing girl some years ago, by the name of Eva Petit," said Chang.

"We outsourced the investigation to a private investigator let me see if I can get the details," said the assistant officer. She opened a file and looked inside it.

"Oh yes! It is Juditha and Co Private Investigators," she wrote the address. I am not sure if there are still there we no longer use them. Ok thank you very much," said Chang taking the address. He headed to the address which was not far from there. It was a ten minutes' drive. He parked his car and took a long breath before he got out of the car. He walked toward the office. He was excited it seems he was covering ground. Somehow, he looked forward to meeting this Juditha.

"Good afternoon how can I help you?" asked a man sitting at one of the desks.

"Good afternoon. I am looking for Juditha," said Chang.

"What is this regarding to, if I may ask?" asked Mark.

"Can I sit?" asked Chang dragging the chair and siting down.

"My name is Chang. I am looking for a missing girl called Eva. I understand Juditha investigated her disappearance," Chang looked at Mark. Mark sat back in his chair. He looked at Chang and stood up.

"One minute," he said going into the other office. Chang looked at the other desk. He saw a portrait of a girl and a boy. He stood up and took the picture and looked at it. Mark drew his head backward and looked at Chang from the other room.

"Oh, that's Juditha's kids. She is on holiday in Moscow," said Mark.

"Moscow!" Chang shouted.

"Yes. Moscow Mr. Chang. She has been going there since the days of Eva's case." Said Mark. After a few minutes, he came back with a file.

"We charge a fee for information we provide Mr. Chang," said Mark putting the file on the table and dragging the chair behind him. He sat down and flipped the pages.

"No problem," replied Chang.

"So, when does she come back? Juditha I mean," said Chang.

"Oh after 2 weeks she jetted out last week," quipped

Mark.

"Ever since she met Eva she has been going there looking for her. She said she experienced a miracle. She does not seem to age. She still looks the same way, and it is more than 15years since she met them," said Mark flipping through the file. Mark waited for a while looking at Mr. Chang.

"So, you said Juditha met Eva? Who? Which Eva?" asked Chang surprised and excited at the same time.

"How do you want to pay?" asked Mark.

"Oh sorry. Card please," Chang took out his wallet and gave his bank card to Mark. Mark opened the drawer and took out the pay point handset and inserted the card. He entered the amount on the machine and gave this to Chang.

"Pin Mr. Chang," said Mark. Mr. Chang entered his pin number without even checking the amount.

"Are you not going to check the amount Mr. Chang?" asked Mark smiling.

"It's okay," replied Chang.

"Yes, she went to Moscow following a lead searching for Eva. There she met another Eva identical to the one she was looking for. In fact, there were two other Eva's identical to the missing Eva. Honestly myself I did not buy it. It sounded weird," Mark paused as Chang was writing in his diary.

"Do you have photos of these girls?" asked Chang.

"Yes sure." Replied Mark remaining seated. They looked at each for a while.

"Oh yes! How much if I want copies of everything you hold in this office?" asked Chang.

"Look Mr. Chang there has been a lot of traveling involved." Said Mark before being interrupted by Chang.

"I understand it's okay," said Chang.

"$500 American dollars and I will also give you Juditha's address and telephone number," said Mark.

"No problem, card," Chang gave Mark the bank card. Mark went in the office again and brought a portfolio. There were a lot of files. Quickly he took out the envelope with the photos and handed these to Chang. Like a hungry dog, Chang quickly opened the envelope and took out the photos. He looked at the pictures. He wanted to pinch himself. This is more than just a coincidence. What are the odds of this happening? Chang thought to himself. He looked at Ewalinka's photos closely. He then took the other photos of Jevalinka and looked closely. Jevalinka had gray eyes and Ewalinka had green eyes. He quickly picked up his diary which he had put on the table and wrote this down.

"So, you are telling me that Juditha physically met these girls?" asked Chang in disbelief.

"Yes, before they all disappeared," said Mark standing up to make copies of all the files.

"What do you mean they disappeared," asked Chang. Days after she met them, they both vanished without a trace," said Mark. Chang flipped through the reports and looked at Mark.

"Do you have copies of their birth certificates?" asked Chang,

"Yes Mr. Chang they are somewhere in one of the files," said Mark photocopying the files. Chang went through the files and took two reports from two separate files. He looked at them and sat back on the chair. They were two separate date of births 25 of November and 9 of December. Chang looked a bit frustrated.

"The legend has it that all were born on the same day. So, there is something wrong," said Chang in a low voice talking to himself but loud enough for Mark to have heard him.

"Sorry. What legend Mr. Chang," asked Mark. "Ignore me I am just thinking aloud," said Chang "Did Juditha say anything about the differences in the Dates of birth?" asked Chang going through the remainder files.

"Not that I am aware of. Honestly at the time I was very skeptical about all this," replied Mark.

"And now?" asked Chang. Mark stopped what he was doing and came back in the main office. He sat down and looked at Chang.

"Now! I believe miracles can happen. Do not get me wrong Mr. Chang I was a scientist before. There is just a lot of stuff humans have not explored fully if you know what I mean," said Mark leaning forward. "Juditha somehow can communicate with the girls telepathically. When she came back her eye color had changed. She vehemently argued that it occurred after encountering the girls. Initially I thought she had been to the optometrists until one day," Mark paused and looked outside before exhaling out.

"What happened," asked Chang stopping what he was doing and paying a lot of attention. Mark cleared his throat.

"One afternoon we were talking about a different case. Everything was fine until she called me from the other office. She said one of the girls was in trouble and needed assistance. I asked her which one but she did not reply. She just started dosing off. Then she stretched her hand as if to shake my hand but pulled me close to her face and opened her eyes wide. I thought she was playing games. Maybe she wanted some time off I thought to myself. True she was working harder than me. It was when I was about to stand up that I saw what even now I cannot believe actually happened," Mark looked at the files on the table and took both photos of Ewalinka and Jevalinka. He placed them on the table.

"Yes. Yes, continue," said Chang.

"I asked what she was talking about. She pointed at her eyes and said this girl. At that moment, her eyes changed color from hazel to green. I looked at her speechless. As I knelt looking at her, she said and this one too. She closed and opened her eyes. The eyes changed from green to gray in a flash. After that she fell in a deep sleep. I called the ambulance, and they said she was exhausted. After two days, she woke up. Doctors advised that our offices be checked for carbon monoxide gasses and who knows what else. It is a long story. For the past 15 years, she just got obsessed with these girls. Every year she visits Moscow for two to three weeks." Said Mark getting up and going to check progress of his photocopying job in the other office. Chang after meeting Mark went to his hotel. He had been very busy since arriving in Bellac Limousin, France. He had no regrets at all that he had traveled. It was such an intriguing experience. He took a shower and ordered room service. He sat on his bed going through the files. He took a note with Juditha's telephone number. He dialed her number, but he was directed to voicemail. "Its Juditha I am on holiday please leave your name and number I will get back to you as soon as possible." This was the voicemail message. Chang flipped through Jevalinka's files then Ewalinka's. He came across a medical report that stated that she was born on the 9th of December after a C section. It is stated that the expected due date was on the same day as the others which was 25th of November. Enya had complication and died soon after birth. He took his diary and flipped through the pages. This is just unbelievable he thought to himself. After all everything per the legend seems to be true. All four girls technically could have had their birthday as the 25th of November. Chang did not remember the time he went to bed he was woken up by a phone call from Juditha.

"Hello. Its Juditha. How can I help you?" she asked.

"Yes. My name is Chang I met Mark I have been to your office. I am researching on the disappearance of Evangelina. I was wondering if we can meet," said Chang. I am afraid I am in Moscow for the next two weeks. Can we meet after two weeks Mr. Chang?" requested Juditha.

"I cannot wait are you not free tomorrow?" asked Chang typing something on the laptop keyboard.

"If anytime soon, it must be in Moscow," said Juditha.

"OK I will be in touch tomorrow," replied Chang before the line went dead. Chang booked the first flight that morning to Moscow, Russia. The journey seemed like forever. He could not wait to meet Juditha. He had so many questions to ask. Juditha could be the key to this research. Five and a half hours later he was at Domodedovo airport Moscow. He booked a hotel and rented a car.

"I am in Moscow what time will be feasible for you to meet?" asked Chang.

"Three o'clock will be fine if you can come to my

hotel," said Juditha giving Chang the address. Chang drove to the hotel dropping off his language. He left and headed to Juditha's hotel. 2:30 noon he was already there. He went to the restaurant at the hotel and sat there and for the next half an hour he had been looking for Juditha. Finally, she came to the restaurant..

"Mrs. Juditha. It is Mr. Chang." Said Chang extending his hand. They shook hands and Juditha will not let go of Chang's hand. She kept holding his hand and slowly started feeling like dosing off. She closed her eyes and then opened them again looking at Chang. Chang saw her eyes changing from blue to brown. Chang understood what that meant. They sat in the restaurant and Chang asked for water. The waitress brought water and gave it to Juditha. She drank the water, and they sat there for some time before they started talking. Chang could not wait. He had waited long enough. The waiting was killing him.

"Mrs. Juditha how are you feeling now?" asked Chang.

"I guess I am ok now. It happens a lot since I met these girls. My life has never been the same," said Juditha.

"So, you met the girls? It must have been something. Some people wait all their life just to witness that miracle. What happened?" asked Chang.

"I was looking for Eva. Then I got a lead. They said we found the girl, but she was in Moscow. I came here to Moscow. The next day her uncle was killed in the city and she was hospitalized. I went to the hospital looking for her. I just could not believe it. She was not the Eva I was looking for but I got freaked out. She was identical to the Eva I was looking for. They were both born on the same day." Paused Juditha to sip more water.

"Then came the surprise. I had another lead. Out of curiosity I went to check it out. To my sheer surprise this was another Eva identical to the other Eva. The only difference was her date of birth. She was born on the 9th of December. When I went to see the other Eva at the hospital somehow, she knew I had met the other Eva. Honestly, they never met before. I spoke to the doctors at the hospital. He had never witnessed something like this before. He went through their medical records. They had been in and out of the hospital. Going through what I am going through now. I discovered that it is a kind of call for help or communication between these girls. Can you believe it I am 38 years now? I still look the same way I did 15years ago," paused Judith's drinking more water. Chang sat there listening curiously.

"So, what happened after that?" asked Chang.

"I went back to see the other Eva out of curiosity. To my shock, I discovering the strangest thing ever. Just before I arrived she told her dad that her sister was coming to see her referring to me. Her dad told me that her eyes changed color from gray to blue. You know what, the other Eva who was in the hospital at that time had blue eyes too," explained Juditha.

"Did you find out what happened to their parents?" asked Chang.

"For the Eva who was in the hospital, her parents died when she was a little girl. The other Eva's parents, one of them was dead she had her dad only. Her mum died giving birth to her," said Judith's taking out the big envelope from her bag.

"Enya died giving birth to Eva. There were

complications. When she did not go in labor, they had to do a cesarean section. After losing a lot of blood she died. The strange thing is that her due date was the 25th of November," Juditha did not finish talking before Chang interrupted.

"Did you say 25th of November?" asked Chang excitedly.

"Yes Mr. Chang," replied Juditha.

"So, the legend is true," said Chang getting out his diary. He told Juditha about the legend. They spoke for a long time. Chang asked her a lot of questions.

"So, what happened to them?" quizzed Chang.

"The night before they both disappeared I fell in a trance. I was with Mark. I had a strange dream. The next day the doctor at the hospital phoned me to say that Eva had disappeared. I went straight to the other Eva's parent's house hoping to see the two together. She had disappeared as well. That is the last time I last saw them."

"Did they have any tattoos?" asked Chang.

"Yes! They both had tattoos on their back. One of a lion the other one of a leopard. The strange thing is that they were born with these tattoos," added Juditha.

"Do you know where they are? Are they still alive?" asked Chang.

"I cannot answer that but they are alive. Somehow Mr. Chang, you have connections to the other one I can feel her," said Juditha.

"We grew up together. One day she just disappeared. Ever since, I have wondered what happened to her," they spoke and Chang insisted in meeting Eva's dad, Dimitri. Chang and Juditha visited Dimitri and the other Eva' s parent's graves too. He also visited

Enya's grave. The months that followed Juditha and Chang became more close together. They communicated every day about the girls.

CHAPTER FIFTEEN

Months later an article on the internet took them to Cornwall United Kingdom. Another girl called Mevelyn was reported missing on the same day as the others. Per the legend this was the corner stone. 'Through the windows of her soul she will complete the circle. She will unite and bond them together for eternity. For she represents the two worlds. Through her everything is possible. And only through her are the predictions manifested, for no one is like her. She can see both the world's. She shall guide them for no man can see in this world and the world of the gods. Only her has the gift. When Juditha had given Sean and Sarah a hand shake, Chang understood the meaning of the legend for her eyes changed one become a green colored one while the other changed to a blue one. They spent days visiting all the places she had been. They met Posiah her friend as well. Chang researched the area for any abandoned uranium mines in the area. Like all the other areas he had been, there was an abandoned uranium mine. After meeting Sean and Sarah Chang headed back to Beijing, China. Over the past seven months Chang had visited France, Russia and the UK researching about the magnificent girls. He had visited the original places of the girls and had met their families or friends and relatives. So far in his life he had links to five of the seven girls. He knew Evangelina as they grew up together. He had met Benjamin and Bridgette Petit Eva's parents. He met Dimitri, Ewalinka's father, and he had been to Enya's grave Ewalinka's mum. He had been to the graves of Jevalinka's parents. In UK, he met Sean and Sarah Mevelyn's parents.

"What did you find so far about your research?" Asked Lin looking at Chang who had his head sunk into the laptop busy typing something. Chang raised his head and removed his reading glasses. He looked at Lin his girlfriend

"We still don't know where they are. Whatever they do, they do it simultaneously. I think they communicate telepathically somehow. I cannot explain it though," replied Chang before continuing. "I think finding one means finding all seven. They all left on the same day from their original homes and more than nearly sixteen years they haven't contacted anyone back, friends or family members," Lin took one of the research papers and started reading it. "The only way you can find out if this is true is to find the girls now and see all of them with your own eyes," said Lin. Chang stopped typing for some time and answered his girlfriend Lin.

"That's exactly what I have been thinking about lately.

The only person who can help me with this is Juditha. For nearly 16 years she has been looking for them, trying to find them with no luck," said Chang before Lin cut-in.

"There must be a clue somehow in the legend on how to find them or know where they all went," said Lin looking at Chang who gazed at her for a long time.

"I have read the legend and listened to it more than a thousand times surely if there was a clue I might have come across it," said Chang going through the legend again. After reading it he passed the book to Lin. "Darling maybe you might find some clues," said Chang handing the written legend to Lin. Chang picked up his phone and phoned Juditha.

"Yes. Chang. How have you been? How is Lin?" asked Juditha on the other end of the phone line. "Pretty good I guess. Been busy as usual trying to put the pieces together."

"I have traveled to Moscow for the past 15 years looking for clues but with no luck too. First years I used to get real vibes from one of them. Over the years, the telepathy communications have just faded away," said Juditha.

"I searched everywhere in China looking for any rumors about a private secretive Emperor but came up with nothing. We must have missed something," said Chang. There was a moment of silence before Juditha replied.

"All these years I looked for clues in Moscow but now I am starting to think that we are looking in the wrong direction. China could be but I think it could be a new country with freedom where an Emperor can live freely," said Juditha.

"I thought China at first but I am not sure anymore. I

thought Japan but anyone serving the Japanese Emperor must have Japanese blood. So, Japan too highly unlikely." Remarked Chang. Chang spoke with Juditha for a very long time. They said goodbyes and Chang put his phone on the table.

"Chang, can you read the part I have highlighted?" asked Lin giving the legend notes to Chang. Chang took the notes and looked at the highlighted part and it read; 'Through the windows of her soul she will complete the circle.' She will unite and bond them together for eternity. For she represents the two worlds. Through her everything is possible. And only through her are the predictions manifested, for no one is like her. She can see both the world's. She shall guide them for no man can see in this world and the world of the gods. Only her has the gift. Looking at this paragraph I think the person this is referring to is Mevelyn that girl from Cornwall England. She is the one technically who can see both worlds. This might be because of the two different eye colors she has." Said Chang. "What are the both worlds referred to in this paragraph?" asked Lin flipping the pages of the legend notes. "I think it's the world of the living and the world of the dead," replied Chang who continued to speak to his girlfriend. "Unless this could be referring to their past life and the life with the Emperor. If Mevelyn is the link that will unite all of them does that mean that she is the one with all the answers?" asked Chang not expecting a reply from Lin. He quickly took out the file he had complied about Mevelyn and started going through it. There was nothing that can give him a hint about them whereabouts. He had just written down the name of her first school but not actually visited it. "If she has the answers surely, I must go back to Cornwall UK." Said Chang. Two weeks later he was in Cornwall UK. He went to all the places Mevelyn had been to before she escaped. He went to her first school to try to find any answers. A lot of things had changed. The former school was demolished and a new shopping center was built in its place. In Charleston, her second former school was still there. A few things had changed since the days she left. The school had been repainted and renovated but it still was like before. Chang went with Sarah, Mevelyn's mum to the school. She showed him her former class room. They both asked for permission and went into the classroom. She pointed where her daughter would normally sit. He sat down and looked around. He took out his camera and took pictures from all angles and the outside view of the classroom from inside. He visited the uranium mines and with the help of the local fisherman he collected a small sample of the stones and deposits at the mine. After a few days, he flew back to Beijing, China. He uploaded all the pictures and information he had collected onto his laptop. He looked at all the pictures one by one. He came across an article about Cornwall miniature attractions. There was a miniature representation of the statue of liberty and the Jurassic adventure trail. This was in Truro and he remembers Sean and Sarah mentioning that Mevelyn loved going there. What if the land of the gods in the legend represented New York? The statue of liberty can represent the gods. As the gods in Greek mythology were often symbols as giant statutes. Chang thought to himself. Quickly he took out his mobile phone and dialed Juditha's number. The phone rang for some time before

Juditha answered the phone.

"Hello Chang. How are you? Any leads regarding the girls?" asked Juditha.

"I think I know where they might be? The legend reckons that Mevelyn is the link and the guide of all of them as she can see both worlds. She is the only one who can give us the answers. I recently returned from Cornwall. I now know that she might be in New York America." He paused for a while before continuing." There are statues in the miniature garden in Cornwall which she once visited. There is a statue of liberty. I have strong feelings now that this is the city in which they might be," said Chang before being interrupted by Juditha? "America!? I never thought they could be in America. My instincts pointed me to Russia." Remarked Juditha. "I need your help. I think that if they are alive and then you might be able to talk to them telepathy. In that case, can we go together I will pay for all the travel and accommodation expenses. What do you say?" asked Chang. "My pleasure. When do we go?" Asked Juditha. "End of this week but just the two of us. Lin is not coming," said Chang. "Ok that's fine email me the tickets as well," requested Juditha. "Ok. Juditha. I will be in touch". For the past 16 years, the girls have lived with Nick without thinking or caring about their biological parents and friends. Serving the Emperor meant to serve him, to honor him and to protect him for eternity. Pure faithful obedience comes from emotional disassociation with their former life. Nothing must remind them of their past life. Over the years, Nick and the girls had relocated to Beverly Hills. They had bought a huge mansion. With the help of Juditha Chang finally located the girls. For days, he stalked them to see what they do. He did not want the others to see him. He knew that might cause anger and jealous feelings among them. Evangelina woke up to find a man standing in her room going through her things. She screamed very loud, but no one heard her. She got up and started hitting that men with a baseball bat. "Intruder. Intruder. There is a thief in the mansion!" shouted Evangelina. The man covered his head with his hands. "No, no, no I am not a thief," shouted the man. "Nick! Ewa! Anybody home?" shouted Evangelina. He kept hitting the intruder with the baseball bat. "Stop heating me it's me. Chang," said Chang still protecting his head but this time kneeling on the floor. Evangelina stopped and looked at Chang. She fell to the ground and went into a trance. Chang lifted her and put her unto the bed. Chang was about to live the mansion when he heard a car screeching its tires entering the driveway. A huge man quickly got out of the car and entered the house. He went upstairs and straight to one of the rooms. He opened the safe in the room and took out some documents. When he was about to close the safe he noticed that the call for help button from Evangelina's bedroom had been activated. He took his gun and went to her room. He opened the door and saw a baseball bat on the ground. He saw her lying on the bed. "Evangelina are you okay?" Shouted Nick rushing to Evangelina's bed and quickly lifting her up. He checked her breathing and pulse. She was in a trance. Something or someone must have frightened her. He pulled his gun and checked her room. He opened the closets but there was no one. He walked toward the door that leads to the room with the magic stones. The door was open slightly.

This door was always kept closed. He was never allowed in the room with the magic stones. He had never entered the room before. He stood there for some time his heart beating very fast. He looked backward and started walking away from the door to the room with the magic stones. He walked past Evangelina who was sleeping on the bed. He remembered his father. How they had not taken the threats seriously only for him to end up dead. He stopped and looked at Evangelina who lay there so peacefully and yet so helplessly. What if someone is in that room? Who opened that door? The door was always closed? He stood there for some time before he started walking toward the door to the room with the magic stones. He opened the door and entered inside. There were seven beds radiating from the center. There seemed to be an altar at the middle with stones inside. On the other side the green stones glowed slowly giving the room the green effect. He walked to the altar in the middle and he felt a sharp burning sensation on his back shoulder and he fell to the ground breaking his tooth in the process. He bled and blood slowly came out of his mouth as he lay on the floor. A few minutes later he started growling like a wild animal caught in a leg trap. Chang quickly crawled from under Evangelina's bed. He looked at Evangelina on his way out and quickly left the mansion. Ewalinka came back home and found Evangelina sleeping in a trance. She quickly went upstairs and knocked Nick's bedroom. The door was not shut, so she slid it opened. Nick was sleeping on the floor. She removed him and carried him onto his bed. She put him on his bed and wiped the blood from his lips. Both Nick and Evangelina did not wake up for a day. Nick woke up first with pain coming from a broken tooth. He thought he had a bad dream. He could not remember what had happened. Evangelina woke up the second day confused and crying for the first time. "Where is Chang? Where did he go to?" she asked Ewalinka. "Who is Chang? If I may ask?" asked Ewalinka. "Where is my mum? Where am I," asked Evangelina. Ewalinka looked at Evangelina and laughed before sitting next to her. "You must have had a bad dream, Eva. It happens sometimes don't worry about that." Ewalinka tried to comfort Evangelina. She knew that even herself the first days she used to dream about her parents. Evangelina stood up and searched the whole house. The baseball bate was still on the floor. Ewalinka picked it up and put it on top of the shoes' cabinet. That day Evangelina kept asking about Chang and her parents. Ewalinka let her sleep for a while. The rest of the girls came back, and they spoke about what had happened.

CHAPTER SIXTEEN

"Hello can I speak to Mr. Nick?" asked the person on
the phone.
"Yes. Speaking. How can I help you?" replied Nick.
"We were expecting the documents the other day, but
you didn't turn up. We could have processed the title
deeds. When can you bring the documents to us?"
asked the person on the other phone. Nick stood
there confused. He walked to the safe and entered the
safe combinations. The safe door opened, and he
looked inside. Everything else was there, his money,
passports and all other documents apart from the
receipts for the castle he had bought. He stood there
for some time trying to put the pieces together. He
had flash backs of seeing the alarm button from
Evangelina's room activated. He quickly walked out
of his bedroom and walked toward Evangelina's
bedroom. He slides the door open and entered the
room. He had flashbacks of seeing Evangelina

sleeping on her bed. He looked around and out of curiosity he walked toward the room with the magic stones. A feeling of fear crippled him and he stopped. He walked toward the door and stood just outside. He stood there for a while. He pepped inside but could not see anything. It was when he was about to go when he thought he saw something. It seemed something was inside the room. Quickly he walked away from the door of the room with the magic stones, the Forbidden room. He turned around and walked toward Evangelina's bed. He stood there and saw the corner of his document file coming from underneath her bed. He knelt and as he was about to pick the files he screamed and jumped backward. He knelt again from a distance to look what was underneath the bed. This time he did not see anyone. First, he thought he had seen a Chinese guy under the bed and thought to himself what is the hack? He picked up the file and left the room. "Who are you and why are you following me? I am not stupid you know. I have seen you on several occasions this week. What do you want from me?" asked Evangelina as she cornered Juditha.

"I am just walking minding my business I was not following you," replied Juditha fearing that Evangelina might attack her.

"Don't be a smart ass. Do not play games with me. Did Chang put you up to this?" asked Evangelina. She opened her eyes and looked at Juditha with the face that says lie to me one more time and see. She understood the look and quickly extended her arm to greet Evangelina.

"I don't want to touch you. Do I know you?" asked Evangelina with an annoyed voice.

"I apologize I was just scared," explained Juditha. "So, you thought I was going to eat you. Is, that, right?" asked Evangelina.

"No. It is not like that. I just did not know where to start," replied Juditha. Evangelina looked at Juditha like a hungry animal ready to pounce. There was a moment of silence. Juditha looked in Evangelina's eyes and saw evil. She quickly looked away because of fear.

"I came with Chang. He told me that you grew up together," said Juditha pausing for a while.

"Chang wants to see you. He said he has a message from your mother."

"I don't have a mother I don't know Chang. Tell him to stay away from me okay?" asked Evangelina making sure that Juditha understood. She did not reply she just stood there and watched her leave. Later that day Evangelina broke down and started to cry. She had emotional confusion. She kept getting flash backs about Chang, her mum and her dad. Emotional attachment to the past life was discouraged if she had to serve the Emperor for all eternity faithfully. That was the main reason they left home at a tender age of seven. The appearance of Chang had caused much confusion and stress. She started sleeping a look and avoiding others.

"How are you Evangelina? You seem distracted lately. Is everything ok with you?" asked Nick looking at Evangelina.

"I am okay I guess I am a little exhausted," replied Evangelina.

"I had been not myself for the past week or so. But I promise things are going to be fine soon," said Evangelina. Nick stretched his arms hugging

Evangelina and touching her on her back on the tattoo. As he touched her, he felt a sharp burning sensation on his own back and he saw a large watery lion growling standing on the door. He quickly looked at Evangelina and the time he looked again to see if the lion was still there, the lion disappeared. He quickly left Evangelina and went to his bedroom. He looked himself in the mirror. He dressed up to go outside before he heard a knock on the door. As he was looking in the mirror, his eyes changed from very light blue to brown like Evangelina's. He quickly wore glasses and walked to open the door. He opened the door and saw Evangelina.

"There is someone at the door asking for you Nick," said Evangelina.

"Okay thanks I will be down in a moment," said Nick quickly closing the door. After that he left the mansion together with the lady who had visited. Ewalinka returned home and as soon as she had entered the mansion Evangelina started preparing to leave.

"How was your day?" asked Ewalinka.

"Pretty ok I guess I am just going outside for a walk. I need some fresh air. I had been in the mansion for the whole day," replied Evangelina.

"Ok come back soon," said Ewalinka. After she had finished preparing, Evangelina left the mansion, jumped into her car, and drove off. She looked behind to make sure that no one was following her. She drove for some time before parking her car outside a hotel. She switched off the car engine and the lights and waited in the car.

"What is wrong Juditha?" asked Chang as Juditha shock very hard.

"I don't feel good. I feel weak and tired," replied Juditha. She started feeling sleepy and Chang knew that something was wrong. She opened her eyes and looked at Chang.

"This girl is here. I want to sleep for some time. I do not feel very good," remarked Juditha. Chang looked at Juditha's eyes and saw her eyes change color to brown. Chang knew that Evangelina was in the neighborhood. He quickly went outside and shouted her name.

"Evangelina! Evangelina! Where are you? It is Chang! Come out!" He shouted as loud as he can. He looked in the hotel foyer before going outside. Even Evangelina was surprised as to how Chang knew she was outside. She got out of the car and stood at her car with the front door opened. She raised her hand. Chang came running to her as fast as he can. He hugged her and they sat in the car.

"Remember that day I was stung by a fish and I couldn't stop laughing?" asked Chang. She smiled and replied.

"Yes! How can I forget. I had to carry you to the temple," replied Evangelina.

"You carried me? How?" asked Chang surprised. "How come you said a dragon carried us to the temple?" asked Chang. Calmly replied Evangelina. "You believed that? Where can you find a dragon?" she asked sarcastically. Chang looked confused as ever. He looked outside the car in disbelief. All these years he had thought and believed that the dragon carried him to the temple. He had never thought that Evangelina could have carried him to the temple. "Thank you for saving my life Evangelina," said Chang.

"You are welcome," replied Evangelina.

"Why you come to American?" asked Evangelina. Chang looked outside the car for a while before he replied. Your parents sent me. Your mum is very sick," said Chang.

"You came all the way from China just to tell me that my mum is sick?" asked Evangelina. There was a moment of silence.

"I severed any emotional attachment to them. I have a family here now. I was born to serve, honor and protect the Emperor," said Evangelina.

"What Emperor?" asked Chang.

"The Emperor himself!" said Evangelina opening her eyes wide.

"Ok I understand but can you go home with me to see your mother and come back later," asked Chang.

"You are not listening. I left so that I do not go back home again. I will serve, honor and protect the Emperor in this life and in the afterlife." Remarked Evangelina.

"I saw him entering the Forbidden room," said Chang.

"What are you talking about," asked Evangelina.

"I saw your Emperor entering the room with the magic stones. I do not think you are safe now. The legend has it that no Emperor shall enter the room with the magic stones," said Chang looking at Evangelina with worry and stress.

"Don't be stupid. He will never enter that room," remarked Evangelina.

"I was shocked myself to see him going into that room," replied Chang.

"He has never been before. He knew that would jeopardize his protection," said Evangelina.

"It's not his protection I am worried about. It is your safety too," said Chang. Evangelina started the car engine and switched on the head lights.

"Don't be such a wimp," said Evangelina.

"Come and meet my friend," asked Chang.

"No. I must go home now the other girls will be worried about me," said Evangelina asking for Chang to leave.

"You are now at risk the only way now is for you to leave and go home," said Chang.

"Leave this Emperor he had broken the rules of trust and honor," Chang got out of the car and waved goodbye. This was such a strange experience for Evangelina. She had never felt this way before. She drove home and only realized that she had arrived when she saw Ewalinka outside waiting for her. "Where have you been? You make us worry about you all the time. Why? You know the rules. Come home early like everyone else," shouted Ewalinka.

"I am here now that is what matters," said Evangelina parking her car and walking inside the mansion. Few days later Evangelina and everyone else was watching the news when she learns of the death of Chang and Juditha. The two were violently attacked by an animal. Their hearts were all mauled, and they bled to death and then died. This was on the news. Evangelina cried like a baby. Nick and everyone else tried to console her but with no luck. Evangelina knew that some- how Ewalinka was involved. The only person who could have done this was Ewalinka. She was the ruthless one with no fear or emotions. It felt bad. She was about to send him back to China. She became very upset and entered the room with the magic stones. She growled like an animal with anger and rage. Ewalinka came inside the room with the magic stones trying to comfort her. She violently pushed her away and cried for days. Evangelina marks Ewalinka and secretly blames her for Chang's death. One day Nick came back home to find Evangelina and Ewalinka fighting. Ewalinka ran to Nick as she did not want to hurt Evangelina who had lost Chang. Nick intentionally touched her back on the shoulder touching her tattoo. He felt a sharp burning sensation and soon after wards went to his bedroom. He growled in pain. He looked in the mirror and saw his eyes changing to green. After touching all their tattoos Nick discovered that he had more power than all of them put together. He only had to look in the mirror to know who was in the house. Nick embarks on a killing spree leaving a trail of murder and destruction. Mark in France was found mauled to death. Bridgette and Benjamin mauled to death with limps missing. The more Nick killed the friends and relatives of the girls the more he found himself strong and powerful. One evening they were having dinner all sat around the table. They had dinner and half way through dinner Nick fell unconscious for a while. When he woke up his eyes were red. He looked at Ewalinka and saw a lion seated there. He looked at Eva and saw a tiger. He looked at Jevalinka and saw a hairy lion. He looked at Evangelina and saw a dragon. He looked at Beverly and saw a cougar. He looked at Devalinja and saw a cheetah. Viktor had just replaced Marek after his death. Dino and Viktor were in their limousine. They had been to one of Dino's night clubs in the city. Viktor works there for Dino as the bouncer. These two had been together for a very long time.

"Boss when do you think we should take care of that last deal?" asked Viktor. Dino was puffing his cigar. He pressed the automatic button and slowly the window of the limousine opened. The gustily wind of fresh air blew inside the limousine sending Dino's papers flying. Quickly he closed the window after puffing cigarette smoke outside. A sense of fear struck Dino. He tried not to show how he felt. He knew something greater than evil itself was after them. If it was not for money and fame, this was the time he would have quit. Since moving to the US from Russia he had accumulated a large fortune through night clubs and restaurants. He had been in trouble with the police officers several times.

"Yes, sure I haven't forgotten I was waiting for the perfect time," said Dino looking at the time on his watch.

"So, can I tell the boys? I would rather do it earlier than wait." Remarked Viktor. The limousine drove for some time traveling away from the city. It was just after 2am when they came off the motorway and into a secondary road. They noticed a lady lying in the middle of the road. The limousine came to a halt. "What are you doing boss? It could be an ambush boss," said Viktor. Dino ordered the bodyguard who was in the limousine to check the girl who was in the middle of the road. The bodyguard looked everywhere first before getting out of the limousine. He walked toward the girl and knelt to check if she was breathing. As soon as he touched the girl's hand. He heard the largest growling of a pack of wild animals he had never heard before. He looked ahead and saw a pack of wild animals altogether waiting to pounce on him. He froze to death for a few seconds.

Slowly the animals started advancing toward him. He got up and ran as fast as he can toward the car. One of the animals was standing near the car door. As soon as he tried to open the door, the animal devoured his hand and dragged him to the ground. The rest of the animals ran toward him. He screamed and shouted calling for help. Viktor was about to get out of the limousine when he saw the bodyguard being mauled savagely. All six animals attacked him with such ferocious that after a few minutes he was dead. "Drive! Drive!" Shouted Dino as soon as he saw that his bodyguard was dead. The limousine sped off nearly running over the girl in the road. The car went for some minutes without any sign of the animals. They heard the animal jumping on top of the limousine. The other animals jumped on the windscreen and some chased the limousine. The limousine swerved from side to side. The driver tried to swerve the car to get rid of the lion that had jumped on the bonnet. He lost control of the car and the limousine hit the tree nearby. The driver's head was on the crush airbag. He was bleeding from the ears and from the nose. The front bonnet of the limousine was damage and steam was coming out of the bonnet. The yellow hazard warning lights went off on impact with the tree. After a few minutes the driver was dragged outside by the lions and torn to pieces. The leopard entered the limousine through the driver's door but could not access the back seats. A gun shot was fired, and the leopard jumped outside swiftly. The white lion smashed the side window and put its head briefly to see inside the back of the limousine. Another gun shot is fired but missed. The car engine caught fire and more smoke started coming out from the front bonnet. The animals ran for safety away from the burning car. The animals stood meters away watching if anyone was going to get out alive. Viktor and Dino started coughing inside the car. Smoke started coming out of the back seat of the limousine. The back door opened. The white lion came running at Viktor. He fired a shot hitting the animal on its shoulder but that did not stop the animal. It jumped on him embedding its paws in his flesh before holding him by his head. The other lion put his hand in its mouth. This is the hand that was holding the gun. The two animals violently shocked Viktor drugging him away from the car. The other animals waited for Dino's move. The limousine was up in flames. Dino crawled from the limousine as far as he can. When he was a safe distance from the limousine. The animals came for him. They fought each other to have a piece of him. His limbs were torn away when he was still alive. He screamed in agony. He had hoped that the animals would kill him first, within minutes Dino was the food of the crows. After the attack the animals went to Viktor's house for a thorough clean up. They savaged the whole family women and kids included. The following nights after that mauling all their close acquaintances were savaged as well. Dino's night clubs and restaurants were all shut down. Over the next weeks, Nick ordered the mauling of many people he thought and saw as threats.

"My father was unfairly killed. I will not let that happened to anyone of you," said Nick talking to Ewalinka.

"I know but I think you have gone one step too much. We eliminated the immediate risk that should do for now," said Ewalinka sitting next to Nick. "That's what we said before my dad got killed. No one took those crooks seriously until they ambushed us. Do you want that to happen again?" asked Nick staring at Ewalinka. There was a moment of silence Ewalinka knew that Nick had a point. She also believed that Nick had gone too far. This was becoming a personal vendetta. Nick started targeting those who owned things he wanted. He started buying properties after the deal has been signed the seller is later found mauled to death. He started killing all his business partners. Soon he had accumulated enough fortune to be a powerful force to mess up with. Banks and business were robbed continuously as the vehicles transporting money were attacked and everyone inside mauled to death or recently eaten altogether. Evangelina since meeting Chang had been having mixed emotions. Chang had left China looking for her because her mother was not feeling well. It was such an emotional encounter. Years had gone by without her thinking about her parents. She had been sleeping for most of the days. She cried sometimes. The whole thing had started to make no sense as Nick was killing as he wished. They all had accepted to kill only as to self-preserve. Evangelina was confused. Seeing Chang had surfaced emotions which were buried deep underneath. Emotional attachment for her parents grew with each day. She knew Chang had confessed that Nick had been in the room with the magic stones. But Nick had vehemently denied this. One evening Evangelina packed her clothes and walked out of the big tall gates of their mansion. She stood outside for some time and got into her car. She drove off leaving the mansion. She drove for a while before she realized that someone was following her. She looked in the rear-view mirror and saw Ewalinka's car. She sped off trying to lose the tail. She took a right turn and after driving for some time the tarmac disappeared. She had entered a T road with a dead end.

"Jesus!".

She screamed as soon as she has realized that she turned into a dead road. She reversed and turned around going back. She drove for some time and saw Ewalinka going the other way. She stepped on emergency brakes and the car came to scathing halt. She got angry. She got out of the car and waited for Ewalinka to come back after realizing that she was going the wrong way. She turned back and came and stopped behind Evangelina's car. She got out of the car too.

"What do you think you are doing? Why are you following me? You nearly got me killed," screamed Evangelina pushing Ewalina.

"Maybe I am just going my own way too. After all, what do you have to be mad about. I am giving you back-up. Looking after my little sis," said Ewalinka calmly trying to comfort Evangelina.

"I don't like it when you snoop on me, okay? That must stop!" shouted Evangelina.

"Yes, look who is talking I was going to say the same thing too," sarcastically replied Ewalinka.

"What has to stop? I do not know what you are talking about?" asked Evangelina.

"Who is doing it? If it is not you who else?" asked Ewalinka sitting on the bonnet of her car.

"I don't know we should be asking you. You are the wild one. I have nothing to do with all those people," said Evangelina sounding sincerely. Only you have secrets. Look right now where are you going? Who did you tell? If I did not follow you who were you going to tell?" shouted Ewalinka standing up and walking toward Evangelina's car.

"None of your business. I have nothing to hide. Do not push me. It is you with a guilty conscience," said Evangelina walking to her car.

"Why? What did I do wrong? I am not the one who killed all those people," said Ewalinka peeping inside Evangelina's car.

"Oh, look who is running away now," added Ewalinka.

"You killed Chang and Juditha. All those people being found mauled to death I bet you are responsible for their deaths too," said Evangelina pushing Ewalinka from her car.

"Who is Chang? Who is Juditha? You mean that person you were dreaming about the other day. Please! Just your hallucinations. I never met any of them. So how come you accuse me of all those things?" asked Ewalinka.

"You two-faced prick. You upset me by lying. Everyone know you killed those people," said Evangelina pushing Ewalinka. Ewalinka started laughing.

"Everyone thinks it's you," explained Ewalinka.

"Me, why me?" asked Evangelina looking surprised.

"You have secrets. You runaway. You cry all the time. Guilty conscience. Yes?" asked Ewalinka.

"Do you think I would kill my own friend, Chang was like a brother to me. We grew up together. The last time I saw him he was mauled to death. You are a pathetic liar now you want to upset me even more.

Maybe I kill you myself." said Evangelina attacking Ewalinka. The two fell to the ground and rolled over on the edge of the road. Ewalinka hit her rib on the rock that was on the edge of the road. She growled in pain. Evangelina stood up and kicked Ewalinka in the ribs.

"This is for Chang. He did not deserve to die," screamed Evangelina going to her car. She jumped into her car and drove off leaving Ewalinka lying there on the edge of the road. Ewalinka got up. She staggered to her car with blood on her hands. She lifted her blouse and found out that she had been injured on her ribs. She was bleeding badly. She drove her car home. Ewalinka opened the front door only to be greeted by Nick.

"What happened to you?" asked Nick carrying Ewalinka by the shoulder.

"Just a minor accident," Nick took Ewalinka to her bedroom and laid her on the bed.

"Evangelina! Eva! Devalinja! Mevelyn! Anyone home?" shouted Nick. The house was empty. It was just the two of them. Nick touched Ewalinka on her tattoo and he felt Evangelina, his eyes changed color to brown. He also felt the pain she felt the moment when she was injured. Ewalinka after sometime woke up and entered the room with the magic stones. Nick had gone upstairs. He was in his bedroom when he felt a strange feeling. He looked in the mirror and saw his eyes change to green. He felt a strange feeling and enormous pain. He started changing wriggling in pain on the floor. That went on for some time. What happened next, he did not remember. He remembered waking up in the room with the magic stones. He was covered in blood. There was too much blood on the floor. He looked next to him. Ewalinka lay there mauled to death. Her heart had been severed. The other girls came back when he had just left the room with the magic stones. Everyone was screaming uncontrollably. The only thing Nick said was the name Evangelina. Surely Evangelina had insisted on leaving. She had vehemently insisted that her mum was not feeling well, and she wanted to go home for some time. After the death of Chang Evangelina had never been the same again. She would lock herself in her room at times. Everyone thought she was the one responsible for the deaths of all those people found mauled to death. They thought that she was avenging the death of Chang. She strongly thought that out of jealous Ewalinka had killed Chang so that she would not go back to China. When they have, all gathered together, they spoke together and consoled each other. Evangelina had escaped. Nick had suggested that out of revenge Evangelina had killed Ewalinka to revenge Chang's death. Mevelyn went in the room with the magic stones. She fell unconscious. They all gathered around her. She started hallucinating. She started shouting Evangelina's name. She called her name and touched her ribs. Eva lifted her blouse and there was a bruising. Mevelyn started bleeding at the same area on the ribs as had happened to Ewalinka. That went on for some time followed by the period where she slept quietly. The other girls left leaving her alone in the room with the magic stones. Nick was in his bedroom. Suddenly he looked up on the ceiling as if in pain. He felt an excruciating pain going down his spine. He looked upwards and blinked tensing his throat muscles. He looked in the mirror and saw his eyes changed to two different colors. One a green one and the other a blue. He felt his muscles spasms. He growled in pain as he changed. That was the last thing he remembered.

"Good morning Nick," shouted Beverly going downstairs. There was no answer from Nick's bedroom. "Good morning Nick? Are you awake?" shouted Beverly. There was a moment of silence before Nick replied.

"Good morning Beverly," shouted Nick. Beverly stood there for some time wondering how Nick knew that it was her. Most of the time he had thought that she was Devalina. Nick had a flash back. He saw himself on the floor. He felt wet parts on the carpet. He wiped the area with his hand. He looked at his hands. His hand had blood. He quickly got up and changed his clothes. The mansion had a red carpet. That is why he could not see at first that there was blood on the carpet. Beverly went in the room with the magic stones to check on Mevelyn. She felt some sticky stuff on the carpet. She wiped her feet against the carpet and pushed open the door to the room with the magic stones. Slowly the door opened. The smell of blood caught her noise. She quickly entered the room. Mevelyn was not there. She sat on the bed were Mevelyn was. She flipped the bed sheets and she just could not believe what she saw.

"OMG!"

She screamed so loud that it sends panic shock waves in the whole mansion. Nick ran downstairs as fast as he can.

"What happened? What is the matter?" asked Nick as he stood outside the room with the magic stones. "Something bad has happened to Mevelyn. There is too much blood on the bed where she was yesterday. Please find her," she shouted getting out of the room. Nick tried to console her, but she left running. She went outside and started shouting Mevelyn's name. "Mevelyn!! Mevelyn!" she continued shouting as she looked outside the mansion. The other girls came out-side of the mansion. They looked for Mevelyn in the nearby park. Devalina and Nick went in one direction while Beverly and Eva went in another direction looking for Mevelyn. Jevalinka took the other footpath, and they all went out looking for Mevelyn after searching the whole mansion. They searched in the nearby woods with no luck. They shouted and screamed her name as they searched in the woods. Nick and Devalina took the path that was heading to the water fountain. They had a statue made of Nick and the seven girls. This was placed in the garden they had named the Emperors garden of life. This was a beautiful garden with a variety of flowers and fruit trees. There was a thorny bush on the roadside as well. Nick remembered the first time they had spent the day in the Emperors garden of life. It was such an experience. That was one of the days they all bonded together and felt like a real family. They were happy and close to each other. Somehow over the past months Nick just lost it. Greediness had overcome Nick. He did not even know what he was doing. The experience he had had recently brought new meanings to the notion of, to serve, to honor and to protect. As they were walking toward the water fountain Nick stopped and acted strangely. He stopped and covered something on the thorny bush. Devalina was following him.

"Listen Dev can you go over there and check I

thought I saw something moving in the bushes." Said Nick with his eyes wide open. Devalina quickly went to check on the other side. Nick quickly removed a bloodied piece of cloth from Mevelyn's night dress. He quickly advanced forward looking everywhere. As he edged forward, he saw the statue of him and the magnificent seven girls. He stopped and remembered the good times he had. What had gone into him? He asked himself. He stood there for some time. It was the coughing he heard from behind the waterfall that put him into action. He slowly and secretly limped forward. He saw a piece of Mevelyn's night dress with blood all over it. He slowly approached her. She lay there shivering, slowly and carefully he placed one of his hand over her mouth and with the other hand pressed her from the back touching her tattoo. He closed his eyes as he felt a sharp burning sensation on his back where his tattoo was. As he was holding her mouth, she opened her eyes and saw Nick. She tried to scream, but he had his hand over her mouth. She tried to cough, but he squeezed very hard. She was choking and at last she coughed and blood spurts came out through the severed heart covering Nick's face and clothes. Suddenly Nick's eyes changed to match hers. Fear crippled her she wriggled her body and legs. Soon Devalina started running toward the water fountain shouting Mevelyn's name. Nick stood up and quickly cleaned the blood from his face. Devalina arrived to find Mevelyn going in and out of unconsciousness. She quickly knelt and hold her on her lap. She slowly opened her eyes. Nick knelt as to give her a hand. She was very scared of him. She jumped backward away from Nick. That shocked Devalina. She opened her eyes looking at Devalina shaking with fear. She refused Nick to touch her. She looked at Devalina and smiled. She lifted her hand and touched her on her chin before her hand slumped to the ground. Devalina started to cry holding Mevelyn in her arms. Nick stood over Devalina and looked at both the girls. He looked everywhere in the park if someone was coming. He felt that pain again piercing his back. He shrugged in pain. He was about to strangle Devalina when Mevelyn opened her eyes. He moved backward quickly. The other girls came running. They all knelt looking at Mevelyn. Nick stood there not knowing what to do. Mevelyn closed her eyes and opened them again. As they all looked at her, her eyes changed to green.

"Ewalinka," whispered Jevalinka. Then they changed to one green and the other blue.

"Mevelyn."

Whispered Eva and then the eyes changed to brown, they all looked at each other and all at once said.

"Evangelina!" quickly Nick shouted.

"Carry her inside the mansion quickly." The girls all helped each other and carried Mevelyn into the mansion and put her on her bed before taking her to the room with the magic stones where she would recover quickly. The girls thought that she had pointed Evangelina as the person who had inflicted her wounds. Somehow Nick knew how to control her. If he had not intervened Mevelyn's eyes were going to match his. That was re- porting to the girls that he was the man behind all the murders. That night all of them slept in the room with the magic stones guarding her. Nick slept in his room. Several times he had fought the pain from his spine. His eyes kept changing all night. He woke up in the middle of the night to find a lion and leopard laying down in his room guarding him. He thought he was hallucinating. He got up and touched both the animals. They acted like a little cat rubbing themselves on him. He realized that the lion was Ewalinka's, and the leopard belonged to Mevelyn. He had slaughtered both and their weapons in the form of animals were all his. "Stand up!" He shouted and quickly the animals got up simultaneously. He said sit, and they sat at once. He pinched himself for he could not believe that this was happening. Mevelyn fought all night the bleeding on her left side. The girls all tried to help by touching her on her tattoo but that did not help. Early in the morning Mevelyn screamed in pain and died. The girls cried inconsolable, and all slept with her in the room with the magic stones. For two days, they slept with Mevelyn and on the third day Eva opened Mevelyn's eyes. Her eyes had changed and for the first time her eyes had matched Nick's. That morning they all fled the mansion leaving Nick alone.

CHAPTER SEVENTEEN

Evangelina arrived in Yunnan Province, China. It was nearly 16 years since she left her parents' home. A lot of things had changed she could not recognize much of the new buildings. The arrival home of their lost daughter brought tears of joy and cries of happiness too. Her mum and dad could not stop crying and laughing at the same time. It was such an experience. They had never lost hope of seeing their daughter again. Every day for the past 16 years they had looked forward to seeing their daughter come back home. The gods had answered their prayers. Their lost daughter had returned home a beautiful grown-up lady. They hold a party in the village celebrating their daughter's return. Of all the people who came there she only recognized one person, the temple priest. He was now very old, partly deaf, and partly blind. They spoke about the old days.

"Remember me Chief priest when I was a little girl?

Myself and Chang coming to the temple, to listen to some of your interesting stories and legends." Said Evangelina looking at the temple priest. He lifted his head and opened his eyes to see clearly who it was. "Oh, I remember you. You with that crazy kid swimming in that river where he nearly died." Laughed the priest coughing as well. She looked at him and took out a cloth from her satchel and gave it to him. He wiped his face and spat on it and tried to hand it over to her. She giggled and refused to take the cloth back from the priest. They both laughed, and the priest continued with their conversation.

"So where is he now that crazy boyfriend of yours?" asked the priest.

"You didn't know?" Asked Evangelina. There was a moment of silence.

"He died sometime this year," said Evangelina wiping tears down her cheeks.

"How did it happen?" Asked the temple priest. "It was an accident," she replied.

"Ah why the young ones die leaving us the old and the weak. Why the gods takeaway the future generations? So, young, and innocent? The talented all die young. I heard that he was at university too. Is it where it happened?" asked the temple priest.

"Not really. He was in America when it happened," replied Evangelina. They spoke for a long time. Evangelina asked a lot of questions about the legend. The temple priest explained everything.

"Surely something had gone wrong. Someone had broken the oath and trust. Otherwise Evangelina would not feel any emotional attachment to her biological parents."

"Maybe it is because of meeting Chang that has

caused this emotional confusion. It is meant that once you have left home, then you cannot be reminded of your past life. That way you will be loyal until the end of time," said the priest.

"How can we correct this and move forward?" asked Evangelina.

"My daughter, it depends with your heart. Now it is a matter of your heart. You decide what you want," said the priest.

"I do not know what I want. Seeing my parents has brought suppressed feelings in the open. Half of me want to go back sometime in the future. This is what I was born to do. To serve, to honor and to protect," said Evangelina looking at the priest who listened attentively.

"If I were you, I would take it easy. Think about it before you make that important choice. You have time to choose. You can either give up if you do not go back again or continue. It is all up to you," said the priest. They spoke a lot before Evangelina retired to bed. That night she could not sleep. She kept dreaming about Ewalinka and Mevelyn. But honestly after sixteen years away from home. She saw no need to run back to American. There was a lot of time. She thought to herself. The following days she visited the place where a poisonous fish stung Chang. She tried to recall what had happened that day. Chang somehow had been beaten by a fish before he started laughing uncontrollably. She started thinking aloud. But wait a minute. Winglee's son died after laughing continuously for days. He had no contact with any fish. There were not in the water or near any water for that matter. They had been just him and her. She remembered feeling a stinging sensation on her tattoo after coming in contact with him. Could touching her had caused the tattoo somehow to release the poison? Evangelina asked herself, thinking louder.

"Let's stick together. If we do not, we all die. Ok?" said Eva telling Beverly, Devalina and Jevalinka.

"But how is this happening? We are supposed to be protecting Nick. We are the magnificent seven, the holy ones and true bodyguards of the Emperor." screamed Devalina.

"Look I don't know what is going on. Nick somehow broke the rules or discovered something. Whatever it is we are not safe around him," said Eva.

"How come Evangelina runaway? I think she is the one killing people. She is capable," remarked Beverly.

"Don't forget Nick has a tattoo too like ours. There are chances he behaves just like us. He feels just like us. Did you see Mevelyn's eyes after she died? She matched Nick's? So, he is somehow connected and responsible. I just do not know how," explained Eva.

"He changed for the past weeks. I feared him too," added Devalina.

"But Ewalinka confessed that Evangelina attacked her," said Beverly.

"Evangelina thought that Ewalinka killed Chang her childhood friend," said Eva.

"They just had a girl fight but nothing serious. Nick could have taken an opportunity. I think all along he was blaming Evangelina when it is actually him," said Jevalinka.

"If it's Nick, then why is he doing this. We made him rich. He is the richest person and most powerful man in this country because of us. He never showed interest personally in any of us. He is always with Sylvia. What would be his motive then? Even if he is robbing other people we do not care, he need our help so that we can serve him, honor him, and protect him," said Jevalinka.

"Where should we go? Where he cannot find us," asked Devalina.

"Let's stick together we will survive. We need stones to fight back. So, let's start looking for some," said Eva. The girls have been everywhere looking for the stones. They had been exhausted. They decided to go back and take some from the mansion. For days, they traveled back to the mansion hoping that Nick will not be home the time they arrive.

"Listen you girls wait here. I will go inside and check if anyone is home. I will get the stones and we will all go together," she entered the house. She had never felt so afraid in her life. She slowly and secretly limped into the house. The house was quiet. She remembered the first time the other girls arrived. It was such an emotional time for her and all the other girls. She walked inside and went upstairs. She opened the room with the magic stones. She saw a lion and a leopard on the carpet sleeping. The lion woke up as she entered the room. The animal roared waking up the leopard.

"Ewalinka, Mevelyn, it's me Eva," she said with a small voice. The animal stood up and looked at Eva. They growled and snarled showing Eva their teeth. She slowly walked backward and as soon as she was out of the room with the magic stones she ran as fast as she can toward the door. She opened the heavy door and saw Nick standing on the veranda. They came face to face and Nick growled in pain and looked at Eva. She looked in his eyes and saw his eyes changing color. They changed to green as he twisted his head from one side to another. They then changed to one green and one blue. Then Nick placed his hands on Eva's shoulders and looked at her. Nick's eyes changed to blue matching Eva's. As soon as she has seen this, she fought very hard. Nick released her, and she ran out of the mansion yard. The other girls were watching this. She ran in the opposite direction to where the other girls were. Nick ran inside the house first. The other girls froze and remained hiding there for some time before the door opened. A lion and a leopard came out and sniffed around the yard. The lion sniffed the ground going toward the other girls who were hiding. They froze to death with a fear in their hiding place. The leopard followed Eva's scent sniffing in the direction she had gone. The lion stopped just a few meters from the girls' hiding place. They stood their ground but shivering uncontrollably in fear. The lion roared exposing its sharp teeth. Nick then opened the door and stood just outside the door and shouted at the lion.

"Ewalinka come on. Come on boy," said Nick to the lion. The lion stood there for some time looking at the place the girls were hiding. The girls on hearing Nick calling the lion by the name of Ewalinka were shocked and mystified. All they could do was staring at each other covering their mouths with their hands. "Come on boy let's go!" shouted Nick. The animal then ran toward him and went after Eva followed by the leopard and Nick. The girls rose from their hiding place and ran for their life in the opposite direction. Eva ran as fast as she could. She fell and hurt her leg. As she lay on the ground, she could hear the lion and the leopard's footsteps thumping the ground. She remembered those days they used to go to eliminate

Nick's enemies. It was more like that except that those days they were all a team. Now she is the hunted. Somehow Nick seemed to control the animals. She felt a sharp burning sensation coming from her tattoo. She lifted her head and saw Nick with the lion and the leopard on his sides. She lay there and quickly got up. Nick shouted something and in a flash, she fell into a sleep that lasted few minutes. She woke up to find a tiger seating just above her head. She felt weak and scared but somehow, she felt secure as she looked the animal in the eyes. She recognized this tiger. She saw herself. The animal had blue eyes just like hers. She stretched her hand and touched the animal. The animal licked her face and nose wriggling its tail. The animal then sits in front of her facing the other two animals and Nick. The animals charged at each other.

"Go! Go!" shouted Nick. The lion and the leopard ran as fast as they can be charging at the tiger. The tiger ran forward too. The animals met and fought viciously. The tiger overpowered the two animals. They stood there for some time. Nick walked toward Eva who was sitting on the ground. The tiger tried charging at him. The lion and the leopard came running and started the fight again with the tiger. Nick arrived at Eva. He knelt and looked at her. She felt frightened. He had shining blue eyes.

"Everything is going to be okay," said Nick stretching his hand. Eva refused to touch him but got up herself. Quickly Nick touched her chest and with the other arm touched her at the back on the tattoo. She felt a burning sensation from the back on her tattoo. Nick screamed and growled in pain. His eyes changed color to green and then to one green and one blue and then back to all blue. Nick then slumped on the floor wriggling in pain. The animals stopped fighting, and all walked toward Eva. The animals gnashed their teeth and growled slowly circling Eva including her own tiger. She realized that now somehow Nick controlled the animals. She got up and ran away from the scene as fast as she can. The three animals chased her. She was knocked to the ground, and the animals tore her to pieces. She remembered those days what it was like to protect Nick. They had killed and mauled people to protect their future Emperor Nick. Now somehow the Emperor was killing all of them. Was this the true meaning of; to protect, to honor and to serve? She felt betrayed. This is not the meaning of to protect that she had in mind. They had vowed to die protecting the Emperor not to die by his hand. somehow she felt cheated and hopeless. As she lay there dying bleeding to death Nick came and looked at her with no emotions at all. He knelt and looked at her in the face opening wide his eyes. She slowly closed her eyes. She remembered Evangelina telling them about the legend of the magnificent seven who served the Emperor who protected the Emperor and honored the Emperor until the day they died. She remembered the day she left her parents at the age of seven. She smiled and opened her eyes. Nick following the animals' lead. They followed and tailed the other girls. It was not long until they caught up with them. The lion, the leopard and the tiger all surrounded them. The girls screamed for help.

"Eva, Ewalinka, Mevelyn, it's us." Shouted the girls. The animals stood there growling and showing their teeth. Nick stood there looking at the girls. The girls picked whatever they can to defend themselves. Nick started growling in pain his eyes changing from gray, to hazel and then to amber and back again. As soon as Nick slumped on the floor, the animals went for the girls. It was an ugly scene. There was blood everywhere. The girls cried until they cannot cry. Nick woke up and stood and looked around. Three bodies of the girls lay on the ground mauled to death. He looked around and saw six animals. There was a tiger with blue eyes staring at him, a lion with green eyes, a white lion with gray eyes, a cougar with amber eyes, a leopard with one green and one blue eye and a cheetah with hazel eyes. After a few weeks in China Evangelina said goodbyes to her parents and the temple priest. She had decided to go back to America She felt she was born to serve and to honor Nick. She had spent years protecting the Emperor and stopping now would only make her life worthless. She had seen her parents. She was very happy but she could not sleep night after night as the other girls called her for help.

"Hello. Nick. It is Evangelina. I will be coming back tomorrow can you pick me up at the airport," asked Evangelina without giving Nick any chance to reply. There was a moment of silence.

"Yes sure. Nice to hear from you. What time are you arriving tomorrow?" asked Nick.

"7pm at night," replied Evangelina.

"How are the girls and Ewalinka? Tell her I will apologize to her tomorrow. It's a long story we will talk tomorrow," said Evangelina. Nick thought for a while before saying anything.

"I will tell her when I get home. Where are you?" asked Nick.

"I am home in China," replied Evangelina.

"Ok. See you tomorrow," said Nick putting the phone down. Nick drove to the airport the next day. He left early, precisely, an hour before arrival time. He had looked everywhere for Evangelina for the past weeks with no luck. It was a shock surprise to hear her asking him to pick her up. The first days the girls knew everyone's moves. Nothing went on without them knowing. Evangelina seemed clueless as to what was happening. Nick had realized that somehow, he could simply depose the girls of their powers. All the powers can be his if he wanted. He had a lot of blood on his hands that a few more droplets would not make any difference. What would be the difference now? He had shed blood already. Evangelina was to complete the link and make him the most powerful man in the whole country if not the whole universe. He walked out of his car at the airport and walked toward the arrivals area of the airport. The doors opened as soon as he was near them. A female voice can be heard announcing arrivals. He went inside the airport and stopped. He looked at the big screens in front of him. He noticed that the flight was arriving one hour late than the planned time. He quickly took out his phone and dialed the hotel in town.

"I need hotel rooms for two; separate rooms for the night," said Nick on the phone.

"Any preferences Mr..?" asked the receptionist.

"It is Mr. Nick. Double beds, quiet area extra bed linen," replied Nick.

"What time do you expect to check-in?" asked the receptionist.

"Any time after 8pm," replied Nick before putting the phone back in his pocket. He went back to his car after buying some drinks. He sat in his car and fell asleep for some time. He woke up when he started feeling pain coming from his spine and when his muscles started to spasm. He woke up quickly and got out of the car. He went to stand in the smoking area and lit a cigar. He started smoking waiting for the plane to arrive. Before she left for China, Evangelina had mixed feelings. Emotional attachment to Chang and her own parents had meant divided attention. Coming back to the USA meant that she had never felt so sure about anything in her life. She had been with her parents. Now her aim and main goal was to serve, to honor and to protect the Emperor. She looked forward to meeting the other girls especially Ewalinka. The time she left she was confused. She regretted fighting with Ewalinka over silly things. She looked forward to making up to her. The first thing she wanted to do was to apologize and make things right with everyone. The plane landed, and she joined the arrivals queue. Her heart was thumping with excitement. The exit queue felt like taking ages. At last she was the one in front. She took a long breath and waited for the automatic gates to open. As soon as the gates opened she walked forward quickly, excitedly, and happy. She eagerly looked forward to meeting Nick. Nick stood there in the arrivals lounge. He had his shades on. He was wearing one of his expensive suits. His hair was shining from afar. He was always more of a gentleman, smartly dressed all the time. As soon as he saw Evangelina he opened his arms. She dropped the bags on the floor and ran toward him. She felt like a little girl. Nick and the girls are the only family she had been with for the past 16 years. Nick removed the shades he was wearing and threw them to one side. She ran and threw herself at Nick. He lifted her up before hugging her. They stood there in each other's arms. Everyone looked at them. It felt like two people who had not seen each other in years yet it was only a few weeks since Evangelina had left. After a while Nick took Evangelina's bags and placed them into his car. They drove to the hotel. "Hey really good to see you again. It felt like a long time since you left. How has life been treating you?" asked Nick. He quickly took a glance at Evangelina before looking forward in the road ahead of him as he drove to the hotel. She smiled at Nick.

"It has been great but I miss you and all the ladies," replied Evangelina lowering the mirror in the car to see herself. She looked in the small mirror in front of the passenger seat before licking her lips to smudge the lipstick.

"I am glad you came back so early. I was afraid that you were going to spend months away from me and the ladies," said Nick concentrating on the road.

"Just couldn't stay away for so long. I just miss everyone. How are the ladies especially Ewalinka?" asked Evangelina going through her purse.

"They are all good. We were talking about you the other day," said Nick looking in the rear-view mirror.

"Really? What did you talk about?" asked Evangelina in an excited voice.

"You know. Everything about you," said Nick looking at Evangelina.

"I am looking forward to meeting everyone," said Evangelina.

"Yes. Sure! But, tonight, we stay in the hotel in the city. I just thought that after all those hours flying we can stop by at the hotel for the night, then tomorrow we drive home," said Nick looking at Evangelina. The car swerved for a short time before Nick gained back the car control.

"That's okay. Thanks. I am tired it is true. I can do with an early nap. Good thinking Nick," replied Evangelina. Nick smiled and continued driving until they reached the hotel. They checked-in and Nick went to Evangelina's room. They sat down and spoke for a very long time before they said good night to each other. Nick left Evangelina's hotel room and went across the doorway to his own hotel room. He sat on the bed and took his phone. He dialed and spoke to a female voice. Half an hour later he heard a knock on the door. Room service he thought to himself. He got up in his boxer shorts and a vest. He walked toward the door and opened it. He looked surprised and for a while did not know what to say.

"Hey, I thought you were sleeping," said Nick.

"I just couldn't see. Are you going to invite me in?" asked Evangelina.

"Ah,"

Nick hesitated for a while.

"Yes sure! Come on in," replied Nick.

For the first time, he saw Evangelina differently. It is just strange how she has grown-up from a young girl to this lovely beautiful lady. She was wearing her red night dress and a big white gown with the red heart-shapes on it. All these years Nick had looked at her more like a sister.

"I just spoke to Sylvia on the phone she will visit us tomorrow," said Nick trying to dilute the atmosphere.

"Oh! Sylvia. How is she? I cannot wait to meet everyone tomorrow," replied Evangelina trying to hide the embarrassment.

"If you want me to go, I can go and sleep. I was just bored on my own," said Evangelina covering up her legs with the big gown.

"No. It is okay. Keep me company we have a lot to catch up on," replied Nick. They spoke for some time before Evangelina looked at Nick. She stood up and walked toward Nick. She put her arms around his neck and tried to kiss him.

"Eva! What are you doing?" asked Nick holding Evangelina's arms. She did not reply she put her head on his right shoulder. He hugged her and kissed her head. They stood there for a while. She took his hand and drugged him toward the bed. She sat on the bed looking at Nick.

"We can't do this. I have Sylvia. If she finds out," said Nick.

"Shh you talk too much. How is she going to find out? I need you too you know Nick," whispered Evangelina in a small soft voice.

CHAPTER EIGHTEEN

The following morning, they got in the car and Nick drove home. No one said anything to anyone. The only thing they could hear on their way home was the sound of the engine of a high-powered Lamborghini. They arrived at the mansion and Nick opened the doors.

"Eva, Ewalinka, Deva, Mevelyn, Jevalinka, Bev!" shouted Evangelina with excitement. Evangelina left her bags in the doorway and ran upstairs.

"Nick. Where is everyone? You said the girls are all home. Where are they?"

Hysterically asked Evangelina. Nick took some time before replying.

"They went on holiday a week ago. They insisted on going all together. I had refused but then Eva came to me and insisted that they were all identical sisters and therefore they must go together, so I let them go. I was supposed to go too, but I had business deals to complete," said Nick holding Evangelina's hand. She felt lost for some time.

"Look, Eva, you yourself you left without even saying goodbye. Listen, in a weeks' time or two, they will all come back. We will be together again in no time. So, relax make yourself at home and welcome back," said Nick kissing Evangelina on the forehead. She knew Nick had a point, but she did not understand why he did not tell her that in the first place.

"Where did they go on holiday?" asked Evangelina. Nick froze for sometime. He looked lost.

"Eh…," he murmured something.

"Honestly, they didn't tell me they said it was a secret. So, they asked me not to worry too much about them as they were going to come back in no time." Replied Nick taking Evangelina's luggage upstairs. Evangelina entered the room with the magic stones and started crying. She discovered that Nick was not telling her the truth. Something was wrong she felt it. She sobbed in there and fell asleep. Sylvia came and spent some time with Nick in his bedroom. Evangelina woke up hearing a woman giggling and laughing and the voice was coming from Nick's bedroom. Strong feelings of jealous gripped her, and she walked toward Nick's bedroom. She arrived at the door. The door was not locked. She did slide it, opening it slightly to see what was going on inside. As the door opened, she saw a half-naked Sylvia cuddling Nick. She pushed the door wide open very hard and stood still in the doorway.

"Evangelina are you ok?" asked Nick pushing Sylvia to one side and walking toward Evangelina who was standing at the door. Evangelina stood there without saying anything. She felt betrayed and cheated on.

Why was this happening to her she asked herself? It seemed the world was falling apart in front of her. She ran to her room crying. She had missed the other girls.

"I am taking Sylvia home I will be back for dinner. Prepare dinner when it is time. See you soon," Nick and Sylvia left the mansion. Evangelina went into the kitchen and started making dinner. She looked at her watch, it was nearly two hours after Nick and Sylvia had left and it was getting dark outside. Dinner was ready but Nick was nowhere to be seen. Evangelina sat on the dinner table, she remembered all the past years she sat with the other magnificent girls. She remembered how everyone looked forward to the dinner. Dinner time was probably the best time of the day for everyone. Everyone had a chance to say something. This was the only time they all could gather and be together as a family. They shared stories, jokes and together they were a real family. For an hour, she sat there wishing that things went back to what it was like those old days. Not long after that, Nick entered the mansion. Evangelina heard the sound made by the big door as Nick opens it. Nick walked inside and entered the dining room. She was happy to see Nick. At one-point, she thought Nick was not going to come back. She had imagined Sylvia as the type of woman who would not let a man like Nick go home alone. So, seeing him come back was a relief. It was now just the two of them. She warmed up the food and served Nick. She remembered that Nick used to like the way she cooked.

"What about you? Did you eat already? Where is your dinner?" asked Nick.

"I ate already I was tired and hungry to wait any

longer, you took ages. Why?" asked Evangelina. "Business as usual my Dear Evangelina," replied Nick.

"You never change Nick; money will never be enough. Start thinking about your future, about us," said Evangelina sitting down joining Nick. Nick just nodded and kept enjoying his meal. Evangelina looked at Nick and there was a moment of silence. After gathering her nerves, she took a strong breath and spoke.

"I want you to know something," said Evangelina. "Yes! What is it?" asked Nick. She paused for some time looking at Nick.

"We had an argument the day I left. We fought for some time before I knew that she was just wasting my time. So, I left. I left her there lying on the floor. I am so sorry," said Evangelina breaking down to tears. Nick stopped eating and took the table cloth and wiped his mouth.

"Who are you talking about?" asked Nick. Evangelina did not reply but kept sobbing for some time. Nick stood up and hugged Evangelina putting his arms around her shoulders as he stood behind her kissing her in the head.

"I love the girls you know. It was just my stupidity. Just a misunderstanding. I should have comeback with Ewalinka," she paused and kissed Nick's hands. "So, you fought with Ewalinka?" asked Nick.

"I thought she had killed my childhood friends," replied Evangelina. There was a moment of silence. "So, now," asked Nick.

"To be honest, I don't know now," replied Evangelina. Nick on hearing this he stood straight removing his arms from Evangelina's shoulders.

"Did she say anything about me or the fight?" asked Evangelina feeling guilty.

"Not really, I remembered her coming home with a broken rib the other day, but she just locked herself in her room," replied Nick. Nick realized that something was wrong. Evangelina on the other hand realized that Nick was hiding something from her.

"Scratch my back," asked Evangelina pointing at the tattoo. Nick took his hand and touched Evangelina on the tattoo. He immediately screamed in pain. "What is it?" asked Evangelina.

"Nothing," replied Nick putting his index finger in his mouth. He took a dinner cloth and wiped his finger. They sat on the dinner table and continued talking. Nick started feeling hot and dizzy. He looked at Evangelina and saw a dragon sat on the dinner table. He started hallucinating and laughing uncontrollable. He could not stop laughing. He interchangeably kept seeing Evangelina and sometimes the dragon sat on the dinner table and that made him laugh even more until his ribs hurts.

"Take the wine and wash down as well," said Nick looking at Evangelina. Nick had seen the dragon eating meat on the dinner table and that was exceptionally funny to him that he offered the dragon some wine to wash down the food with. Nick laughed uncontrollably and died laughing. The poison had finally stopped all his vital organs from functioning. Evangelina fell in a trance and saw Nick murdering Ewalinka, Mevelyn and the rest of the girls. They had left their parents to serve and to protect Nick the Emperor for eternity only to die at his hand. How was that to be? They had sacrificed their lives leaving their parents behind. Severing any ties with their biological parents. Leaving all their past behind them only to die at the hands of the Emperor the person they vowed to protect, to serve and to honor. How can this be, how life can be so cruel? What does it mean to protect, to serve and to honor? Is this the real meaning of to serve, to honor and to protect for eternity? Is this the mark of the magnificent seven bodyguards? Is not it an irony that the one you are to protect is the one who will end your life. They say it is a thin line between trust and betrayal. This whole episode brought a new meaning to, to serve, to protect and to honor. This was so unfair she cried uncontrollable. Later that night she heard some noises coming from the room with the magic stones. As Nick lay his head on the table, dead, Evangelina stood up and walked toward the room with the magic stones. She opened the door and screamed. There was a brown lion, a white lion, a leopard, a tiger, a cougar, a cheetah, and a strong white flying unicorn. She stood there at the doorway and realized that all the other girls were dead for real. She felt weak and afraid. What was happening? Her world was falling apart. She wished she did not come back. She wished she had stayed in China. The animals all gathered around and growled with saliva flowing from their mouths. The animals charged at her but as soon as she touched her stomach the animals all stopped and sat down. Evangelina is sat in a water tube at home. She has been in there for some time. She has been screaming loud. At last cries of a little baby boy can be heard coming from the room with the magic stones.

"This mansion is for sale for $500million it has been abandoned for a few years now. Just need some renovations." Said Zoe talking to David.

"It is a great mansion and I think my wife Elina, would love it," replied David. They walked inside the mansion. They viewed most of the mansion before David heard some noises coming from one of the rooms.

"I thought you said no one lived here," said David looking at the sales agent Zoe.

"Yes, as far as I know the mansion had been empty for some time now," replied Zoe. They saw a light shining from underneath the door of one of the rooms. David walked toward the room and slowly pushed the door open. They could not believe what they saw. Smoke was coming out from the green stones on the altar. The stones gave the room a green color. There was a small boy sat on the back of the white shining unicorn surrounded by a tiger, a dragon, a white lion, a brown lion, a cheetah, a cougar and a leopard. Zoe on seeing all this screamed throwing all the papers she had in the air and ran for it. The animals charged at them. They ran as fast as they can out of the mansion, jumped into the car and drove as fast as they can from that mansion.

SOME YEARS BACK.

Somewhere far east in the mountains of China. In Hunan Province, it has been raining for the past three days. People have been trapped indoors. No one has been in the rice fields for the past three days. Normally the locals spend their time in the fields harvesting rice. After all the chores were done, this was the happiest time of the day for the children in the village. This meant that it was time to go to Gongzhou, the eldest man in the village. The best story telling master of all times. Excitedly the children would go and gather around a fire waiting for Gongzhou to come and tell them his best stories, legends, fairytales and mysteries.

"Boys and girls today I am going to tell you a story I have never told anyone before," paused Gongzhou puffing his pipe full of herbal essences. He continued talking.

"This is about the seven magnificent bodyguards of the Emperor. The last master who told me this story died the day he first told anyone this story," remarked Gongzhou before being interrupted by Yenyang. "Master does that mean that you are going to die after telling us too?" asked Yenyang curiously and intuitively with a wide face with eyebrows raised looking at the other kids.

"Wow! The master is going to die!" said the other kids in one voice looking at each other. Gongzhou was not expecting a question like that from his audience. He smiled and marveled at Yenyang's intelligence and line of reasoning.

"Why you ask clever Yenyang? Don't you want to hear the story?" the kids whispered among themselves.

"It must be a great story. Do not let him change his mind. We want to hear the story," said the other kids. "I don't care if you die master just don't die before telling us the story," quipped Alina. All the other kids saw the funny side of Alina's remarks and burst into laughter. Even the master himself laughed too.

"I don't know what to say master but I would be

happy, tantalized and intrigued if you would kindly tell us the story," replied Yenyang.
"I am not afraid to die. This is a great story even if I die after telling you this story. I will be a happy man in afterlife clever Yenyang."
"We want to hear the story master. Please tell us," shouted the kids in one voice.
"Ok. I will tell you the story," said Gongzhou before puffing his pipe.
"Once upon a time in Imperial China, when everything was sacred and special. There was a powerful Emperor called Zhou. The Emperor was also known as the Son of the heaven as most believed that he was chosen and represented the gods. He had a son who was the leader of the Imperial army, and a young daughter called Beautiful Sun aged six years old. His kingdom and the ruling family was called the Zhou dynasty. The Zhou dynasty had a stronghold of more than ten thousand bodyguards who protected the Emperor and at least one hundred honor bodyguards who were based at the Imperial palace. One night the Emperor received news that his dynasty was under attack from a stronghold from the north ten times bigger than his army. For years, no one had dared invade his dynasty. His son commanded the respect of all man and he had been loyal to his father, the Emperor. On the night of the attack, the Emperor woke up his daughter, Beautiful Sun. 'My daughter, ran to the holy man, tell him that I sent you, tell him that we are under attack and the Emperor requests a miracle. Tell him that we are being attacked by a much bigger stronghold of the north army. Say to the holy man that the Emperor asks you the holy man to give my daughter the

miracle he promised me years ago. Say to him, the Emperor now need that miracle you offered me many years ago, in peace time, but one which I refused. Now is the time, we need the miracle as soon as possible. The Emperor put his arm on his daughter's shoulder and said.

"Don't come back unless you have seen the miracle," requested the Emperor to his daughter Beautiful Sun. As soon as her father had finished instructing her, Beautiful Sun was off to the mountains. She ran as fast as she can to the magician, the holy man. The magician lived in the mountains. No one would dare go to the mountains without the Emperor's permission or an invitation from the magician. Most who had gone there had been knocked down by the magician. His powers were so strong that he worked for the Emperor directly. For many years, he had lived in the mountains alone translating messages from the gods. He was also called the holy man. He was the link between the Emperor and the gods. He would go into trances for days and when he wakes up, he would deliver the message from the gods to the Emperor. Even the Emperor had never been to the mountains. Only his young daughter had been, only the little holy ones were regarded as pure and therefore worth of visiting the holy mountains. The day of the invasion the Emperor was convinced that there was enough time for his daughter to go to the mountains and to return before the Imperial dynasty was under attack. The invasion was so fast that he lost his son that same night. The Imperial dynasty was invaded and all the Imperial guards and bodyguards were slaughtered. The Imperial dynasty was attacked and captured by the foreigners of the far north, called

the Mondols. They invaded at night and by dawn the dynasty was captured and all slaughtered by a stronghold from the far north ten times their stronghold. The Emperor was captured alive with his wife. The leader of the Mondols removed the heart of the Emperor while he was still alive and ate it. This was per their custom. The Emperor's wife was killed too the same way. The Emperor had waited eagerly for the return of his daughter but that was in vain."
"Holy man, his highness the Emperor has sent me with urgency. His beloved dynasty has been invaded by the beasts from the north, the man eaters, the barbarians the unholy Mondols. He sent his pure beloved daughter, to the holy mountains of the gods, so that you, the holy man, give me a miracle which I will take to him and save the Emperor's dynasty from being withered by the beasts from the north. The Emperor has requested that, you the holy man, fulfill the promise you made to the Emperor many years ago, in peace time. The Emperor now need the miracle. Ask the gods to save the Emperor and give us the magic present so that we can defeat the beasts from the north. Our dynasty and our blood line shall continue as it has for so many years now. Give us the magic present as soon as possible before we all perish," said the Emperor's daughter Beautiful Sun kneeling on the ground. The holy man when he heard this he knelt too and looked to the skies and chanted a holy prayer to the heavens.
"Behold, the day has come, the holy man has been relieved of his duties. Now the young holy ones are now the guardians of the Emperor and the Imperial dynasty. The holy man has served you honestly and faithfully so now it is time the holy ones serve you."

He finished chanting his prayer and to the Emperor's daughter he said.

"You the holy ones, you shall be the new protectors of the Emperor, you must serve him and guard him for eternity. He shall not need tens of thousands of armies nor bodyguards but just the magnificent seven, the holy little soldiers. The gods shall give you six more of you and together you shall be seven. You shall all look alike that no one on earth shall separate one from the other. You will be identical and you shall protect the Emperor. You will have tattoo markings at your back with your accompanying protection weapon. You will have a different weapon and shall all serve the Emperor as one but many. The Emperor shall distinguish you by the color of your eyes. To ordinary people you all shall look alike and have the same hair. But the Emperor and his son or daughter shall use the weak green magic stones to see the true colors of your hearts. The one with the blue color eyes representing the blue skies and the white clouds shall be your leader unless another one is chosen differently by the casting of stones." Said the holy man. The holy man prayed to the gods. As the holy man touched the silvery-gray stones, he fell in a trance after breathing gasses from these stones. "The Emperor's daughter looked on in shock and despair. She stood there not knowing what to do. As the holy man fell into a trance laying there on the ground, a big shiny dragon popped out of nowhere. The legend has it that the girl was astonished and very pleased when she saw the dragon. Surely this is the sign my father the Emperor had requested she thought to herself. She quickly jumped on the dragon and flew to the Imperial dynasty. When they arrived, the Imperial dynasty had already been captured and invaded. Tragically the Emperor was already slaughtered. Surely there was no use of the holy man as he there to serve the Emperor. Since this day, the holy man never woke up. The dragon from that day stayed with the young princess, her father the Emperor was dead. Many years before this anointment of the magnificent seven, the Emperors were easily killed. They never lasted enough to establish and rule until old age. There were invasions, coups from the Imperial bodyguards and poisonings of the Emperors. All these reduces their life span and the time they are in power as rulers of their kingdoms. The question was that if the gods are holy and the Emperor is his son often called the Son of the heaven why then did he die before old age? Hence the magnificent seven were there to ensure the survival of the Emperor. After their establishment and anointment, the Emperor needed not have hundreds or thousands of bodyguards in the Imperial dynasty but just the magnificent seven. Since their anointment, the legend has it that the Emperors had lived up to one hundred years hence the slogan: Magnificent seven make you one hundred folds, implying that the magnificent seven protected the Emperors making them reach one hundred years. They also made the Emperor rich and powerful because anyone the Emperor protects was also protected by the magnificent seven. People paid a small fee in the form of gold and silver for protection. This meant that everyone wanted to be under the Emperor's protection. Hence everyone loyal to the Emperor would safeguard his or her own safety as well as no one wanted to be an enemy of the Emperor. Everyone was therefore loyal to the

Emperor. In years to come, because of the magnificent seven the Emperor had no enemies, anyone against him would be eliminated by the beasts within the magnificent seven. The Emperor was associated with the magnificent seven, with riches and wealth, with peace and the most sought out of all which is longevity. 'Long live the Emperor'. The legend has it that for every one hundred years there will be seven magnificent protectors of the Emperor, the holy ones who will protect the Emperor all his life until the day he dies of old age. Every one hundred years the seven new bodyguards of the Emperor are born, and the legend has it that, at the age of seven they will leave their parents and travel on their on to the Imperial dynasty to start initiation and training. At the age of seven they will denounce their emotional attachment to their biological parents. At the age of seven they will no longer be the daughters or sons of their biological parents but they will be the sons or daughters of the Emperor. For every one hundred years if the previous magnificent seven were boys then the next lot will be girls. Everyone hundred years the magnificent seven are of the same sex either all boys or all girls. They will all be identical in appearance even though they have different parents. Their blood and DNA will be the same, fingerprints and voices will all be the same. The only difference will be in eye color depending on what kind of protection they give to the Emperor. Only the Emperor and his biological son or daughter will be able to differential who from who. The holy man was responsible for the passing on of information to the Emperor. This was top secret. Only the Emperor and the holy man knew who was who of the magnificent seven. No one else could be in contact with the Emperor. The secret was in their eyes. All seven had special unique strengths and characteristics. The legend has it that the Emperor is divine and regarded as the Son of the heaven therefore a divine entity must protect him. The Emperor since he is holy shall not be killed or die until old age. The magnificent seven protectors all had different roles and jobs to ensure the survival of the Emperor. At the Imperial dynasty, there was a special room for the magnificent seven only, where the stones were kept. Even the Emperor himself was forbidden to enter this room. The room was for the seven bodyguards of the Emperor. The legend has it that these stones during enemy invasion would give the magnificent seven special powers. Whenever the Emperor needed help depending on what kind of help he was after, one or more of the seven would go into this special chamber where the stones were kept. The stones were of different colors; the silvery gray ones were the most powerful ones, quick response and on-the-spot response. When it was an emergency and protection was needed very fast, they would use these stones. The black-green-yellow stones were for a longer response where there was no emergency. If something was needed say tomorrow one of the magnificent seven would touch or lie down on these stones. When there was no emergency most of the magnificent seven would touch the green-only stones. Which stones to use depended on the age of the magnificent seven and which one of the magnificent seven. The legend has it that of all the magnificent seven one of them would survive to see one hundred years. This member of the magnificent seven would be chosen by all through casting of stones on the first day they come together. Their names interpreted per the tattoo they have on their backs which will be written on the stones. These stones will be put in a jar and the jar shaken and then one person of the magnificent seven will pick a name on the stone from the jar. The name of the person picked will be the anointed one who will never sleep on or touch the silver-gray ones. The legend has it that, the magnificent seven members whom the gods will chose to represent them was the one with same eye color as their place of residents, the heaven. The gods were believed to live above in the sky which is mostly blue and white. This chosen person would be the one to live longer than the rest of the magnificent seven. This is because the silvery-gray stones were the most powerful ones and would release a lot of magic gasses that in the end these gasses and their strength would end up killing the members of the magnificent seven in their late nineties. The chosen one was forbidden to touch the silver-gray stones therefore the chosen one will live up to one hundred years as he or she has less exposure to these powerful gasses. Per the legend this is how the Emperor was protected. The magnificent seven when there was danger would go into the chamber and touch or lie on the stones depending on the fastness and speed of action needed. The stones would release a gas. The gas puts the member of the magnificent seven into a trance. He or she remains in a deep sleep in the locked chamber also protecting her or him but the animal or protection entity which could be identified on the tattoo marking would wake up and kill the enemy instantly by severing the heart. Then comes back into the chamber through an opening at the top or bottom back into the chamber and back "into the tattoo". Then the magnificent seven members will wake up as normal. Job done, enemy eliminated, and the Emperor protected.

THE END